Praise for Chris Kuzneski's debut novel, THE PLANTATION

From James Patterson, bestselling author of *Kiss The Girls* —
"*The Plantation* is a rip-roaring page-turner with an ingenious idea. Chris Kuzneski's writing has the same kind of raw power as the early Stephen King. No reader will easily forget it."

From Nelson DeMille, bestselling author of *The Lion's Game* —
"Wear your running shoes when you read *The Plantation.* This is the most action-packed, swiftly paced, and tightly plotted novel I've read in a long time."

From *Word of Mouth Magazine* —
"There's no such thing as the perfect book, but this comes darn close. . . . Thrilling, simply thrilling!"

From Douglas Preston, bestselling author of *Relic* —
"*The Plantation* is a powerful read with a great plot twist. Right from the opening scenes the book takes off, and all I can say is hang on for the ride."

From Lee Child, bestselling author of *Echo Burning* —
"Excellent! High stakes, fast action, vibrant characters, and a very, very original plot concept. Not to be missed!"

From Pam Stone, M.S.C. Book Review —
"I absolutely loved *The Plantation.* I was breathless, reading every last word slowly so I wouldn't miss a single thing. When I reached the end, it was phenomenal, everything was all tied up into a nice tight bow. . . . Thank goodness that he's working on another."

From Thom Racina, bestselling author of *Snow Angel*—
"*The Plantation* is powerful stuff. A gripping novel that smells of gunpowder and reeks of heroism. Wow! Chris Kuzneski has written a sensational yarn. I can't wait for the next one!"

From Amazon.com—
"Mr. Kuzneski is a great storyteller. Sometimes humorous, sometimes shocking, but always riveting. His characters are full of life, and his fast-paced plot takes many unexpected twists and turns. . . . I can honestly say this is one of the most exciting books I've ever read."

From Phillip Tomasso III, author of *Tenth House*—
"Gripping and frightening. Chris Kuzneski's first novel, *The Plantation*, is thrilling from beginning until the end. His smooth and easy writing style, his crisp and witty dialogue, and his genuine talent for setting and pace blend together to create one of the most unnerving books I've read in a long time."

From Martin J. Smith, author of *Straw Men*—
"*The Plantation* is scary good, and Chris Kuzneski is a writer to watch. The chase starts on page one and doesn't stop until Kuzneski has wrung you dry."

From Barnes & Noble.com—
"*The Plantation* has everything you could possibly want in a book: action, suspense, humor, romance, and many memorable characters. . . . Of course, all of this begs me to ask the author one question: Where have you been all my life?"

From James Tucker, author of *Tragic Wand*—
"A graphic tale of revenge and torture that becomes more sinister with each turn of the page."

From Lee Meadows, author of *Silent Suspicion*—
"A mile-a-minute page-turner. . . . Chris Kuzneski clearly joins the ranks of Nelson DeMille, James Patterson and Tom Clancy as authors who define the 'thrill' in thriller!"

From E.I. Book Review—
"*The Plantation* has everything I look for in a novel: thrilling action, great plot twists, and lots of humor. . . . I don't want to give away too much, but I assure you that it's well-worth your time and money."

From BookBrowser—
"Full of suspense, with an explosive and unexpected ending that is hard to forget—even long after you have finished reading it. I enjoyed Kuzneski's hard-hitting style and, in anticipation, will be scanning bookshelves for his next novel."

From Sarah Lovett, author of *Dantes' Inferno*—
"Kuzneski is a talented new writer. *The Plantation* hits the mark!"

From Ivy Quills Reviews—
"With dark suspense and intriguing plot twists, *The Plantation* is not to be missed. . . . Pick it up for an adventure, and you won't be disappointed!"

From Robyn Glazer, reviewer for *Mystery News*—
"*The Plantation* is the kind of book that can skyrocket an author's career. The writing is crisp and never falters. . . . I absolutely loved this book!"

From Borders.com—
"This action-packed thriller will send shivers up and down your spine. With all its plot twists and turns, you might want to put on your seat belt. . . . I loved *The Plantation.*"

For the latest reviews and information,
please visit the author's website:
www.chriskuzneski.com

Coming soon from
Chris Kuzneski:

SIGN OF
THE CROSS

THE PLANTATION

CHRIS KUZNESKI

PARADOX
Pittsburgh New York

This is a work of fiction. The events described here are imaginary. The setting and characters are fictitious and not intended to represent specific events, locales, or persons, living or dead. Any resemblance is purely coincidental.

The Plantation

"Thriller of the Year" is from Amazon.com

For additional information, please visit:
www.chriskuzneski.com

Author photo by Joyce Kuzneski
Cover design by Robert Crabtree
Website design by Randy Raskin
Special thanks to Ian Harper

Publisher's Cataloging-in-Publication Data
(Provided by Quality Books, Inc.)

Kuzneski, Chris.
The plantation / Chris Kuzneski. -- 1st ed.
p. cm.
ISBN 0-9715743-0-8
1. Mystery fiction. I. Title
PS3611.U9647P53 2002 813'.6
QBI33-167

Library of Congress Control Number: 2001119664

Printed in the United States of America

To mom and dad:

You've made all of my
dreams possible.
Thank you from the
bottom of my heart.

THE PLANTATION

Chapter One

Thursday, July 1st
Icy River, Colorado
(122 miles southwest of Denver, CO)

Robert Edwards hurdled the fallen spruce but refused to break his frantic stride. He couldn't afford to. They were still giving chase.

After rounding a bend in the path, he decided to gamble, leaping from the well-lined trail and opting for the dense underbrush of the forest. He dodged the first few branches, trying to shield his face from their thorny vegetation, but his efforts were futile. His speed, coupled with the early-morning gloom, hindered his reaction time, and within seconds he felt his flesh being torn from his cheeks and forehead. The coppery taste of blood soon flooded his lips.

Ignoring the pain, the 32-year-old struggled forward, increasing his pace until the only sounds he heard were the pounding of his heart and the wheezing of his breath. Eventually, when he could move no more, he turned and scanned the timberland for any sign of his pursuers. He searched the ground, the trees, and finally the dark sky above, looking for something out of the ordinary. He had no idea where they'd come from—it was like they'd just materialized out of the night—so he wasn't about to overlook anything. Hell, he wouldn't have been surprised if they'd emerged from the underworld itself.

Their appearance was *that* mystifying.

When his search revealed nothing, he leaned against a nearby boulder and desperately fought for air, but the high altitude of the Rockies and the blanket of fear that shrouded him made it difficult to breathe, nearly impossible. In time, though, the pungent aroma of the pine-scented air reached his starving lungs, and they instantly quivered with delight.

"Oh my god," he whispered in between breaths. "I made it."

Unfortunately, his joy was short-lived.

A snapping twig announced the horde's deliberate approach, and without hesitation Edwards burst from his resting spot and continued his journey up the sloped terrain. After an ascent of a few hundred feet, the Colorado-native reached level ground for the first time in several minutes and used the opportunity to regain his bearings. He studied the acreage that surrounded him, looking for landmarks of any kind, but a grove of bright green aspens blocked his every view.

"Come on!" he growled. "Where am I?"

With nothing to rely on but instinct, Edwards turned to his right and sprinted across the uneven ground, searching for something to guide him. A trail, a rock, a bush. It didn't matter as long as he recognized it. Thankfully, his effort was quickly rewarded. The unmistakable sound of water overpowered the patter of his own footsteps, and he knew that could mean only one thing: Chinook Falls was nearby.

Edwards increased his speed and headed for the source of the thunderous sound, using the rumble as a beacon. As he got closer, the dense forest that had concealed the dawn abruptly tapered into a grass-filled clearing, allowing the crystal-clear water of the river to come into view. It wasn't much, but to Edwards it was a sign of hope. It meant that things were going to be all right, that he'd gotten away from the evil presence in the woods.

While fighting back tears of joy, he scurried across the open field, hoping that the campground near the base of the falls would be bustling with early-morning activity, praying that someone had the firepower to stop the advancing mob.

Regrettably, Edwards never got a chance to find out.

Before he reached the edge of the meadow, two hooded figures dressed in black robes emerged from a thicket near the water's edge, effectively cutting off his escape route. Their sudden appearance forced him to react instantly, and he did, planting his foot in the soft soil and banking hard to the left. Within seconds he'd abandoned the uncovered space of the pasture and had returned to the wooded cover of the nearly impenetrable forest. It took a moment to readjust to the darkness, but once he did, he decided to mount the rocky bluff that sat before him.

After reaching the top of the gradient, Edwards veered to his right, thinking he could make it to the crest of the falls before anyone had a chance to spot him. At least that was his plan. He dashed as quickly as he could, focusing solely on the branches that endangered his face, and that prevented him from seeing the stump that sat before him. In a moment of carelessness, he caught his foot on its moss-covered roots and instantly heard a blood-curdling snap. He felt it, too, crashing to the ground like a truck with a missing axle.

But he wasn't done yet.

In a final act of desperation, Edwards struggled to his feet, tried to pretend like nothing had happened, but the lightning bolt of pain that exploded in his tattered limb was so intense, so agonizing, he collapsed to the ground like a marionette without strings.

"Shit!" he screamed, realizing the hopelessness of his situation. "Who the hell are you? What do you want from me?"

Unfortunately, he was about to find out.

Chapter Two

Mars, Pennsylvania
(13 miles north of Pittsburgh, PA)

It was after 10:00 a.m., but Jonathon Payne didn't feel like waking up. Begrudgingly, after hitting the snooze button on his alarm clock several times, he finally forced himself out of bed and struggled into the bathroom.

"God, I hate mornings," he moaned.

After getting undressed, the brown-haired bachelor twisted the brass fixtures in his elaborate shower room, then eased his chiseled, 6' 4", 230-pound frame under the surging liquid. When he was done, he hustled through the rest of his morning routine, threw on a pair of jeans and a golf shirt, and headed to his distant kitchen for a Pop Tart.

The 34-year-old lived in a 13,000 square-foot mansion that he'd inherited from his grandfather, the man who raised him after his parents' death. And even though it was built in 1977, it still had the feel of a brand-new home due to Payne's passion for neatness and organization, two traits that he'd developed in the military.

Payne had entered the U.S. Naval Academy as a member of the basketball team, but it was his expertise in hand-to-hand combat, not dunking, that eventually got him recognized. Two years after graduation, he was selected to join the MANIACs, a highly classified Special Operations unit that was comprised of the ten best soldiers that the **M**arines, **A**rmy, **N**avy, **A**ir Force and **C**oast Guard could find. Started in 1989 at the request of the Pentagon, the MANIACs' goal was to complete missions that the U.S. Government couldn't afford to publicize: political assassinations, anti-terrorist acts, etc. The squad was the best of the best, and their motto was fitting: If the military can't do the job, send in the MANIACs.

Of course, all of that was a part of Payne's distant past.

He was a working man now. Or at least he pretended to be.

When he reached his bustling complex, complete with a breathtaking view of the Pittsburgh skyline and office space for 550 employees, Payne noticed one of his executives already heading to lunch.

"Mornin'," Payne groaned.

"Barely," the vice-president laughed.

Payne smiled at the wisecrack, then made a mental note to dock the bastard's wages. Well, not really. But as CEO of his family's company, Payne didn't have much else to do, other than show up for an occasional board meeting and cash his immense paycheck.

Everything else, he let his underlings handle.

Most people in his position would try to do more than they could handle, but Payne understood his limitations. He realized he wasn't blessed with his grandfather's business acumen or his passion for the corporate world, and even though his grandfather's dying wish was for him to run the company, he didn't want to screw it up. So while people with MBAs made the critical decisions, Payne stayed in the background, trying to stay awake.

The moment Payne walked into his penthouse office his elderly secretary greeted him with a stack of messages. "You're here early today," she exclaimed. If anyone knew about Payne's lackadaisical mornings, it was her. "Ariane just called. She wants to discuss your plans for the long weekend."

"What?" Payne laughed. "She must be mistaken. I'd never take a long weekend. I swear! Work is *way* too important to me!"

The secretary rolled her eyes. Payne had once taken off six days for Yom Kippur, and he wasn't even Jewish. "D.J. called, too. In fact, he'd like you to go down as soon as you can."

"Is it about a case?" he asked excitedly.

"I have no idea, but he stressed it was very important."

"Great! Give him a call and tell him I'm on my way."

With a burst of energy, Payne rushed down the stairs, stopping only to admire the raised lettering on D.J.'s smoked-glass door.

David Joseph Jones
Investigative Services

Boy, he liked the sound of that, especially since he'd helped his best friend achieve it.

When Payne inherited the large office complex from his grandfather, he gave D.J., a former lieutenant in the MANIACs, a chance to live out his dream. Payne arranged the necessary financing and credit, gave him an entire floor of prime Pittsburgh real estate, and provided him with a well-paid office staff. And all Payne wanted in return was to be a part of his friend's happiness.

Oh, and he wanted to be D.J.'s assistant on the glamorous cases.

And business cards that said Jonathon Payne, Private Eye.

One more thing: If D.J. ever took surveillance photos of naked women, he wanted to see them, too—unless the subject was fat. Or really old and wrinkly.

But other than that, he just wanted his friend to be happy.

Payne waived to D.J.'s receptionist as he strolled across the gray carpet, then turned the knob to the investigator's door.

Jones was sitting behind his antique desk with a scowl etched on his thin face.

"What's up?" Payne wondered. "Trouble in Detectiveland?"

"It's about time you got here," Jones barked. His mocha skin possessed a reddish hue that normally wasn't there, and his finely drawn features practically danced with anger. "I've been waiting for your ass all morning."

"Whoa, big fella," Payne joked with a lisp. "I'm not that kind of girl."

Jones grimaced. "Not today, Jon. Something's up."

Payne smirked at the verbal irony. "I bet it is, but I told you I'm not that kind of girl."

"Jon," Jones growled. "This is important."

"OK, OK." Payne plopped into the chair across from Jones, then propped his feet upon the desk. "I came down as soon as I got your message. So, what's the deal?"

Jones exhaled as he eased back into his leather chair. "Before I say anything, I need to stress something to you. What I'm about to tell you is confidential. It's for your ears only. No one, and I mean *no one*, is allowed to know anything about this but you. All right?"

Wow, Payne thought to himself. This sounded like something big. He couldn't wait to hear what it was. Maybe a robbery, or even a murder. Jones' agency had never handled a crime like that. "Of course, my man, of course. You can count on me. I promise."

Relief quickly flooded Jones' face. "Thank god."

"So, what is it? A big case?"

Jones shook his head, then slowly explained the situation. "You know how you have all those boxes of gadgets near my filing cabinets in the storage area."

"Yeah," Payne replied. He'd been collecting magic tricks and assorted gizmos ever since he was a little boy. His grandfather had started the collection for him, buying him a deck of magic cards when Jon was only five, and the gift turned out to be habit-forming. Ever since then, Payne was hooked on the art of prestidigitation. "What about 'em?"

"Well," Jones muttered, "I know I'm not supposed to mess with your stuff. I know that. But I went in there to get some paperwork this morning, and . . ."

"And what? What did you do?"

"I saw a pair of handcuffs in there, and, um, they looked pretty damn real."

"Go on," Payne grumbled, not liking where this was going.

"I brought 'em back here and tried to analyze 'em. You know, figure them out? And after a while, I did. I figured out their trick."

"You did?"

"Yeah, so I slipped them on to test my theory, and . . ."

Payne stared at D.J. and smiled. For the first time, he realized his friend's hands had been hidden from view during their entire conversation. "You're handcuffed to the desk, aren't you?"

Jones took another deep breath, then nodded sheepishly. "I've been like this for three freakin' hours, and I have to take a leak. You know how my morning coffee goes right through me."

Laughing, Payne jumped to his feet and peered behind the desk to take a look. "Whoa! That doesn't look very comfortable at all. Looks like the masturbation chapter of the *Kama Sutra.* You're all twisted and . . ."

"It's not comfortable," Jones interrupted. "That's why I need you to give me a hand."

"Hey, I told you I'm not that—"

"Help," he quickly corrected. "I need you to give me some help."

"Gladly," Payne chuckled. "But . . ."

"But what?" Jones demanded, his face getting more flushed by the second. "Just tell me the secret to your stupid trick so I can get free. I'm not in the mood to joke around here."

"I know. That's why I don't know how to tell you this. I've

got some bad news for you."

"What do you mean by bad news? What kind of bad news could you possibly have for me?"

Payne patted his friend on his arm, then whispered. "I don't own any fake handcuffs."

"What? You've got to be kidding me." Jones tried pulling free from the desk, but the cuffs wouldn't budge. "You mean I locked myself to my desk with a real set of cuffs. Jesus, I can't believe this!"

"Not exactly something you'll put on your private eye résumé, huh?"

Jones was tempted to curse him out but realized that Payne was the only person who could currently help him. "Jon? Buddy? Could you please go get some bolt cutters for me?"

"I could, but I'm actually kind of enjoying . . ."

"Now," Jones screamed. "This isn't a time for jokes. If my bladder gets any fuller, I'll be forced to piss all over your office building. I swear to god I will!"

"OK, OK. I'm going." Payne bit his lip to keep from laughing. "But before I leave . . ." He placed his hand on the cuffs, and with a flick of his wrist, he popped off the stainless steel device—a trick he'd learned from a professional escape artist. "I better take my handcuffs so I know what type of bolt cutters to get."

Jones stared in amazement as his best friend walked across the room. "You son of a . . . I thought you said they weren't your cuffs."

Payne shrugged. "And I thought you promised not to mess with my stuff?"

* * *

Since Payne had already been at work for ten grueling minutes, he figured he'd earned a much needed break. So instead of returning his girlfriend's message by phone, he decided to escape the boring hell of his corporate life and visit Walker in person.

Ariane Walker had recently been named the youngest vice president in the history of the First National Bank of Pittsburgh (FNBP), an amazing accomplishment for a 28-year-old female in the boys' club world of banking. She was born and raised in nearby Moon Township, a fact that she and Payne were often kidded about since he grew up in Mars. Both of them took it in stride, though. Normally, they just replied that their relationship was out of this world, and they meant it. They'd been dating for over a year and had *never* had a fight—at least none without pillows.

As Payne strolled to Ariane's office, a journey he tried to make a few times a week, he peered down at Pittsburgh's gleaming skyline and smiled. Even though he grew up hating the place—a city that used to be littered with steel mills, industrial parks, and the worst air this side of Chernobyl—his opinion had slowly changed. In recent years Pittsburgh had undergone an amazing metamorphosis, one that had transformed it from an urban nightmare to one of the most scenic cities in America.

First, the steel industry shifted elsewhere, leaving plenty of land for new businesses, luscious green parks, and two state-of-the-art sports stadiums. Then, the water of Pittsburgh's three rivers—the Allegheny, the Monongahela, and the Ohio—was thoroughly dredged, making it suitable for recreational use and riverfront enterprises. Next, buildings received facelifts. Bridges received paint jobs. The air received oxygen. This mutt of a city was given a thorough bath, and a pure pedigree had somehow emerged.

"Hey," Walker said the moment Payne knocked on her office door. "I called you earlier. You get my message?"

"Yep, and since I had nothing else to do, I figured I'd pay my favorite girl a visit."

"Well, I don't know where she is right now, so I guess I'll have to do until she gets back."

Payne sighed as he moved closer. "Oh well, I guess you're better than nothing."

The chestnut-haired executive grinned and gave him a peck on the cheek. "We've got to make this quick, Jonathon. With a long weekend coming up, I've got a lot of work to do."

"But you still have tomorrow off, right? Or am I going to have to buy the bank and fire you?"

"Oh, how romantic," she teased. "No, that won't be necessary. Once I leave here at 5:00, I'm officially free until 8:00 a.m. on Tuesday. The next 111 hours are all yours."

"And I'm going to use every one of 'em. I swear, woman, I don't get to see you enough."

"I feel the same way, man. But one of us has to work, and I know it's not going to be you."

Payne grimaced. "It certainly doesn't look like you're working too hard. I mean, here you are, a highly paid bank official, and instead of doing something productive for this financial institution, you're sitting at your desk, undressing me with your eyes."

Walker blushed slightly. "Please."

"And now you're begging for me. Damn, girl, get ahold of your passion. You're embarrassing me."

Walker smacked him on the arm and ordered him to calm down. "So, what is it that you want anyway?"

"Hey, you called me. Remember?"

"Please don't remind me of my bold and desperate act."

Payne shrugged. "I can't help it that you're easy."

"That's true," she teased. "I think I get that from my grandmother. She used to run a brothel, you know. But enough about Nana. What are we going to do tonight?"

Payne shrugged again. "Some of the new holiday movies come out today. I guess we could grab some dinner and catch a late flick."

"Your treat?"

"I don't know," he scoffed. "You claim I don't even have a job. Why should I pay?"

Walker faked a growl. "That wasn't a question, Jonathon. That was an order. Your treat!"

He loved it when she called him Jonathon. He really did. But she was the first one he'd ever met that could make it sound sexy. With anyone else, the name gave him flashbacks to the days when his parents were still alive. *Jonathon* was the name his mother used when he was in trouble. Big trouble. Like the time he accidentally ran over the neighbor's cat with a lawn mower.

Meow—with a stress on the owwww!

"Of course it's my treat," he finally laughed. "I pay for all the women I'm currently dating."

"Well, we can talk about your hookers later. In the meantime, do you have the time to take me out to lunch? If you wait outside, I think I could probably sneak out of here in a couple of minutes."

Unfortunately, it took her nearly half an hour to get away, but once she did, they strolled hand-in-hand above the scenic city, enjoying the warm summer sun and each other's company. In fact, they were so lost in their own little world that neither of them noticed the black van that started following them the moment they'd left the bank.

Chapter Three

Longview Regional Hospital
Longview, Colorado

Tonya Edwards sat in the OB-GYN office, nervously waiting for the results of her tests.

Normally, she was an optimistic person, someone who always looked at the bright side of life, but a first-time pregnancy has a way of changing that. Anxiety and fear often replace calm and joy in the grand scheme of things, and as she waited for her doctor, the tension gnawed away at her very large stomach.

When the door to the examination room finally opened, Tonya wanted to jump to her feet to greet the doctor, but it was physically impossible. She just wasn't in the condition to make any quick movements.

"How are you feeling?" asked the middle-aged man. "Any better?"

"Not really, Dr. Williamson. I'm still nauseous, and I have a slight headache."

"And how's the little fellow doing today?"

She grinned and patted her belly. "Robert Jr. is doing fine. He's been kicking up a storm while I've been waiting for the results, though."

"Well, I've got good news for both of you. Everything looked perfect on the tests. No problems at all."

Relief flooded Tonya's 33-year-old face. After taking a deep breath, her lips curled into a bright smile. "That is such good news, doc. You wouldn't believe how worried I've been."

"Actually," he chuckled, "I probably would. I've been doing this for many years, and I've seen this happen many times before. Tension tends to bring on the flu-like symptoms. First-time mothers have it pretty rough, Tonya. Especially someone like you. Since you no longer have your own mother to talk to, you really don't have anyone to help you through this. Sure, Robert is there, but this is all new to him, too. And he certainly has no idea about the physical changes that you're going through, now does he?"

Tonya smiled as she wiped the moisture from her eyes. "No, he's kinda clueless on the physical stuff. In fact, I had to tell him how he got me in this condition to begin with."

Dr. Williamson burst into laughter. "Well, I must admit I expected him to know at least that much."

"Oh, don't get me wrong. Robert is a wonderful husband, and he's going to make a wonderful father, but you're so right about him. He's clueless when it comes to my body and this baby."

"I'm sure he's doing the best he can, so take it easy on him."

"Don't worry, I will."

When her appointment was over, Tonya headed down the corridor towards the elevators. After pushing the button, she felt a little lightheaded so she leaned against a nearby wall and rested.

"Are you all right?" asked a male in a blue nurse's outfit.

The voice startled her, and she instantly opened her eyes. "What? Ah, yeah, I'm fine. Just very tired."

"How many months are you?"

She laughed as she touched her belly. "Eight down, one to go."

"I bet you're excited, huh?"

Tonya nodded her head enthusiastically. "But I don't know what I'm looking forward to the most: having a baby or getting my body back to the way it used to be."

The black man grinned. "Well, I admire you women. You go through so much in order to bring something so precious into the world. I've got to hand it to you."

"Well, somebody's got to do it, and it certainly isn't going to be a man."

He nodded. He couldn't agree with her more. "So, what were you doing here?"

"I just had an appointment with Dr. Williamson. He wanted to run a few tests to make sure I'm fine."

"And everything went well, I hope?"

"Perfect."

"Good," the man said. "I'm glad to hear it."

As he finished his statement, the elevator door slid open, revealing an empty car. Tonya took a few steps forward but appeared to be a little unsteady on her feet.

"Wow," she muttered. "I suddenly don't feel very good."

The man grimaced, then patted her reassuringly on the arm. "I'll tell you what. If you hold the door for me for just one second, I'll get something that will help you feel better. OK?" She stared at him with a look of confusion. "Just trust me, all right?"

Tonya nodded, then pushed the *door open* button and held it. The man jogged halfway down the hall and grabbed a wheel chair that had been abandoned in the corridor. Pushing it as quickly as he could, the man returned to the elevator slightly out of breath.

"Your chariot, madam."

She smiled, then settled her wide frame into the olive-green seat. "Normally you wouldn't catch me in one of these for a million bucks, but to be honest with you, I think the rest will do me good."

"Well, I was heading outside anyway, so it would be my

pleasure to assist you all the way to the parking lot."

"Thanks," Tonya said as she pushed the button for the lobby. "I appreciate that."

As the elevator door slid shut, the smile that had dominated the man's face quickly faded. He reached into his pocket and grabbed the hypodermic needle that he'd prepared an hour earlier. After removing the leak-proof cap, the man inched the syringe towards the exposed flesh of the unsuspecting woman.

"Don't worry, Tonya," he whispered softly. "The baby won't feel a thing."

Then, before she had a chance to question his comment or the use of her name, he jabbed the needle into her neck and watched her succumb to the potent chemical. The elevator door opened a minute later and he wasted no time pushing the sleeping woman through the lobby, right past the security staff at the front desk.

"She looks tired," said one of the guards.

"Dead tired," he answered as he rolled her towards the black vehicle that waited outside.

* * *

Later that night, Payne and Walker went to the movies as planned. The theater was so packed, though, they were actually relieved when the film ended.

"So, what do you think?" he asked. "Did you like it?

"Like what?"

"Um, the movie we just saw?"

Walker smiled, then giggled at her atypical behavior. "I'm sorry, Jonathon. I've got a slight headache from that darn crowd. I guess I'm kind of out of it right now."

"No problem, as long as you aren't trying to back out of tomorrow."

"No chance there, mister. In fact, I think I have our entire weekend planned."

"Oh, you do, do you? Well, what do I have to look forward to?"

Walker glanced at him and smiled warmly. "I figured we'd start off tomorrow morning with breakfast and a round of golf. Then, when I'm done kicking your butt like I normally do, we can grab some lunch before heading back to your pool for some skinny-dipping and a variety of water sports that will never be a part of the Olympics."

"I don't know," Payne laughed. "The TV ratings would go through the roof if the Olympics used some of the events that I have in mind."

"Well, I'll make sure I thoroughly stretch before we begin. I don't want to pop my groin."

"Good, 'cause that's *my* job."

She blushed slightly. "Then on Saturday, if you're not too tired, I figured we can practice some more water sports."

Payne threw his arm around her shoulder and squeezed. "That sounds pretty good to me. But one question still remains: What's on the itinerary for tonight?"

Walker faced Payne and frowned. "Actually, nothing but sleep. As I mentioned, I've got a headache, and I think it has something to do with a lack of rest. I just want to go home and crash. I hope that's OK with you."

"Sure, that's fine." He was disappointed but didn't want to make her feel guilty about it. "I guess I'll just go home and do some paperwork. You know me: My job always comes first."

Chapter Four

Friday, July 2nd
Plantation Isle, Louisiana
(42 miles southeast of New Orleans, LA)

The cross was ten feet high and had been built with this sole purpose in mind. The carpenter had used the right kind of wood, soaked it in the perfect kind of fuel, and planted it into the ground at the appropriate angle. The Plantation had one shot to do this right, and they wanted it to go smoothly. It would be the ultimate mood setter for their new guests.

"Torch it," Octavian Holmes snarled through the constraints of his black hood. The wooden beams were swiftly set aflame, and before long the cross' fiery sparks shot high into the nighttime sky, outlining the row of cabins that encircled the grass field with their bright effulgence.

Ironically, the image brought a smile to Holmes' face. As a child, he had witnessed a similar scene, a cross being burned in his family's front yard, and it had evoked a far different reaction. It had terrified him. The bright glow of the smoldering wood, the sharp stench of smoke, the dancing specters in white hoods and sheets, the racial taunts, the threats of violence, the fear in psyche, a scar that had remained for years. But things were his father's eyes. All of it had left an indelible mark on his young different now. He was no longer a scared boy, cowering behind his family for strength and protection. No, now the roles were reversed. He built the cross. He controlled the guest list. He was the aggressor. He was the keeper of the flame.

Finally, a chance to exorcise some of his personal demons.

Over the roar of the blaze, he continued his commands. "Bring them into formation."

A small battalion of men, dressed in long black cloaks and armed with semi-automatic handguns, burst into the cramped huts and dragged the hooded captives toward the heat of the flames. One by one, the confused prisoners were placed into a prearranged pattern, three lines of six people, and ordered to stand at attention while facing the cross. When the leader of the guards was finally happy with the setup, he let his superior know. "We're ready, sir."

"Good," he replied as he settled into his raven-colored saddle. "Drop your hoods."

In unison, the entire team of guards covered their faces with the thick black cloth that hung loosely from the top of their cloaks. When they were done, the only thing that remained uncovered were their eyes, and they burned like glowing embers in the dark Louisiana night.

"It's time to show them our power."

With sharp stilettos in hand, the guards charged towards the prisoners and swiftly cut holes in the white cotton bags that had been draped over the heads of the captives.

"Ladies and gentlemen," Holmes growled as he trotted his stallion to the front of the group. "Welcome to the Plantation."

He paused dramatically for several seconds before continuing. "I'm sure that each of you would like to see your new home, but there is currently something preventing you from doing that. It is called duct tape, and it will be very painful when you pull it off." He laughed quietly. "Don't worry, your eyebrows will grow back."

Slowly and painfully, the prisoners removed the strips from

their faces, tearing flesh and hair as they did. Then, once their eyes had adjusted to the light of the intense fire, they glanced from side to side, trying to observe as much as they could. The sudden realization that they were a part of a large group gave some captives comfort and others anxiety.

"Impressive," Holmes mocked. "I'm very pleased with the guts of this group. Normally my prisoners are weeping and praying for mercy, but not you guys. No, all of you are too strong for that."

He clapped sarcastically, slamming the palms of his black leather gloves together.

"Now that you've dazzled me with your inner strength, it's time for me to show you how weak you really are. While you are a guest on my island, there are strict rules that you must follow. Failure to do so will result in severe and immediate punishment. Do I make myself clear?"

No one in the group dared to speak.

"My god, I must be going deaf! Why? Because I didn't hear a goddamned word from any of you." He rode his horse slowly between the lines of prisoners. "Let's try this again, but this time I want you to scream, *Yes, Master Holmes!*" He trotted his mount back to the front of the assembly, then glared at the captives with his eyes of flame. "Are you ready? Failure to follow my rules will result in severe and immediate punishment. Do I make myself clear?"

Unfortunately for the prisoners, less than half of them had the courage to answer, and that infuriated Holmes.

"Listen up, you dumb bastards, I think we have a problem here. A lot of you are used to the freedom that you were blessed with in society. You had the right to do what you wanted, and to say what you wanted, and to think what you wanted. But all of that has changed. That freedom has evaporated into thin air, like smoke from this burning cross."

The eyes of the prisoners glanced at the clouds of ash that

slowly rose into the fiery night.

"You are no longer members of a free society. You are now possessions. You got that? Possessions. And as my possession, you are governed by the rules that I'm about to share with you. Failure to comply with *anything* that I say will result in swift and decisive action. Do you understand?"

"Yes, Master Holmes," mumbled most of the crowd.

But that wasn't good enough for Holmes. He shook his head in disgust, pissed that he'd have to hurt one of his captives in order to make a point. "Bring out the block," he ordered.

Swiftly, two guards ran to the side of the field and lifted a four-foot wooden cube onto a small cart. Then, as the prisoners stared in confusion, the guards dragged the large chunk of wood to the front of the crowd.

"Thank you," Holmes sneered as he climbed off his horse. "But before you hustle off, I'd like you to do me a favor."

"Yes, sir!" the guards said in unison.

"Do you see the tall man at the end of the front row?" Holmes pointed at Paul Metz, a father of two from Missouri. "Bring him to me."

"Me?" Paul shrieked as he was pulled from the line. The eyes of everyone in attendance followed his path to the front of the group. His family, who'd been standing next to him, trembled with obvious fear. "What did I do?"

"So you *can* talk. See, I wasn't sure you had the ability to speak until now. Why? Because a moment ago I asked the group to answer a question, and no sound came from your lips."

"I answered, I swear."

Holmes slammed his gloved hand onto the wooden block, and the sound echoed above the roar of the fire. "Are you calling me a liar?"

"No," Paul sobbed. "But I swear, I answered you. I yelled my response."

"Oh, you yelled your response, did you? I was staring right at you, focusing only on you, and from my vantage point, nothing! No sound, no head movement, not a goddamned thing."

"I screamed, I swear."

Holmes shrugged his shoulders at the claim. He had no desire to argue with a prisoner. It would set a very bad precedent.

"Put your hands on the block," he said calmly.

"What?"

Holmes responded by slapping Paul in the face. "Don't make me tell you again. Put your hands on the fuckin' block.

The 45-year-old closed his eyes and eased his bound hands onto the wood. His entire body quivered as he did.

"Now, choose a finger."

Paul opened his eyes in fear, staring into the hooded face of his captor. "Please, not that," he begged.

In a second flash of rage, Holmes threw a savage punch into the prisoners' stomach, knocking the breath from him with the warlike strike. Paul instantly collapsed to the ground in front of the wooden block.

"Give me a finger, you stupid fuck, or lose them all."

From his knees, Paul reluctantly placed his hands on the wood and extended the pinkie of his left hand. As he wiggled it, he sobbed at the impending horror. "This one, Master Holmes."

Holmes smiled under his hood of black, enjoying the moment of omnipotence. This was the type of respect he would demand from all of his prisoners, and if they failed to comply, he'd make sure that they had a very unpleasant stay.

"Now," he shouted to the transfixed crowd, "I'd like each of you to observe the following." With the vise-like grip of his left hand, Holmes grabbed Paul's wrist and pinned it to the wood. "This man ignored a direct order from me, and because of that he will be severely punished."

With his right hand, Holmes grabbed his stiletto, then paused to enjoy the surreal nature of the moment. In the presence of the cross' dancing flames, the length of the 5-inch steel shaft gleamed like Excalibur in the regal hands of King Arthur. The crowd, covered in hoods of white, gaped in awe at the spectacle that they were witnessing. And Paul, kneeling on his knees, wailed as he waited for his punishment to be executed.

"Let this be a lesson to you all."

With a quick downward stroke, Holmes rammed the razor-sharp blade into Paul's knuckle just below his fingernail, immediately severing the tip. A flood of crimson gushed from it, glistening in the fire light as it slowly engulfed the wood's flat surface. Paul screamed in agony while trying to pull his damaged hand off the block, but Holmes was simply too strong for him. After lifting the knife again, he plunged the blade into Paul's finger a second time, severing it just below the middle knuckle.

"Stop!" Alicia Metz shrieked as she listened to her husband's primal wails, but a guard instantly silenced her with a malicious backhand.

"Not yet," Holmes answered. He pulled the imbedded blade from the block of wood again, and this time buried it into the edge of Paul's palm, dislodging the last section of his little finger with a sickening snap.

"Why?" she sobbed as she slumped to the ground. "Why are you doing this? What have we done to deserve this?"

Holmes glanced at the three chunks of finger that sat on the chopping block and smiled, admiring his own handiwork. "I'm sick of her babbling. Gag her."

Two guards rushed to the fallen woman and quickly wrapped her mouth and face in several layers of duct tape.

"Anything else, sir."

"Yes," he laughed. "Get this man some first aid. It seems he's had an accident."

Chapter Five

The Kotto Family Estate
(near the Gulf of Guinea coast)
Lagos, Nigeria

Hannibal Kotto stared into his bathroom mirror and frowned at the flecks of gray that had recently emerged. Even though he was 51, he didn't look it. In fact, people always assumed that he was ten years younger than he actually was.

"You can't be young forever," he sighed while splashing water on his dark face. "Thank god wealth is more permanent."

After opening his plush purple curtains, Kotto gazed across the manmade moat that encircled his majestic grounds and observed a team of workers as they pulled weeds from his impeccably maintained gardens. All of them were new employees, and he wanted to make sure that they were following his specific orders. Unfortunately, before he had an opportunity to evaluate their performance, his phone rang.

"Damn," he muttered. "There's always something."

Kotto reached into the pocket of his robe and pulled out his cellular phone. "Kotto here."

"Hannibal, my dear friend, how are things in Nigeria?"

For the first time that day, Kotto smiled. It had been a while since he'd spoken with his business partner, Edwin Drake, and that was unusual. They normally spoke a few times a week.

"Things are just fine. And what of things in South Africa? Is Johannesburg still in one piece?"

"Yes, and I still own most of it," laughed Drake, an Englishman who made the majority of his money in African diamond mines. "But with the civil unrest in this bloody city, my extensive holdings are not nearly as impressive as they used to be."

"That is a shame, but it is a common drawback to life in Africa. Governments come and governments go. The only thing that's constant is conflict."

"A more accurate statement has never been spoken."

Kotto smiled. "So, Edwin, where have you been hiding? I thought maybe you were getting cold feet about our recent operation."

"Not at all," Drake chuckled. "I couldn't be happier with our partnership. The truth is I had some last-minute family business to attend to in London, and I honestly didn't want to call you from there. I never trust those bloody hotel phones. You can never tell who's listening."

After a few more minutes of small talk, Kotto finally steered the conversation to business. "Edwin? I was wondering what you thought of the last shipment of snow you received. Was it to your liking?"

"Snow? Is that what we're calling the product now? I like the sound of that."

"I'm glad. I felt we needed a code name for the merchandise, and I hated the term they use in South America."

"You're right. Snow is so much simpler to say than *cargo blanco*."

"Exactly. And since both of us speak English, I figured an English word was appropriate."

"Why not something Nigerian? Couldn't you come up with something colorful from your native tongue?"

Kotto laughed loudly. He always got a kick out of the white man's unfamiliarity with Africa. "Edwin, I *did* come up with a word from my native tongue. English is the official language of Nigeria."

"Really? I didn't bloody know that. I'm so sorry if I offended you."

"It's all right. I'm used to your ignorance by now," Kotto teased. "But I hope you realize I don't walk the streets of Lagos in a loin cloth while carrying my favorite spear."

Drake couldn't tell if his friend was lecturing or joking until he heard Kotto snicker. "Hannibal, I must admit you had me going for a while. I thought I might've hit a nerve."

"Not at all. I just thought a moment of levity was in order before we continued our business."

"Yes, it was rather pleasant. Thank you."

"So, what did you think of your last shipment of snow? Did the quality meet the expectations of your buyers?"

"In some ways yes, and in some ways no."

Kotto frowned. It wasn't the answer he was hoping for. "And what do you think needs to be improved?"

"Honestly, I'd say the overall quality. I think my buyers were hoping for something better than the street product that I sold them. They wanted something purer. You know, upper-class snow."

"Well," he replied, "the last batch was just a trial run. From what I understand, the next shipment we receive will be the best snow yet."

*   *   *

Since there was such a diverse mix of young and old, male and female, there appeared to be no correlation between the prisoners of the Plantation. But Harris Jackson knew that wasn't the case. He knew the reason that these people had been pulled from their lives and brought to this secluded island. He understood why they were being humiliated, abused, and tortured. He relished the fact that they were stripped of their homes, their possessions, and their pride. All of it made sense to him, and he was going to enjoy his authority over them for as long as it lasted.

In the flickering firelight, Jackson stared at the 17 people in front of him and savored how each of them were shaking, literally trembling with fear. God, how he loved that. It made him feel indestructible.

"Ladies and gentlemen of the Plantation, my name is Master Jackson, and my job on this island is leader of the guards. When you address me, you shall use the name Master Jackson or sir. Nothing else is acceptable. Nothing less will be tolerated."

Under his black hood, he smiled. When he'd worked as a lawyer during his short-lived legal career, he loved addressing the jury—trying to get them to listen, hoping to catch their eye, convincing them to believe—and for some reason, his orientation speech made him think back to his days in the courtroom. The days before his disbarment.

"As I'm sure you know, none of you were given a chance to change your clothes since your arrival on the Plantation. Some of you are covered in filth, and some of you are clean. A few of you are dressed warmly, and others are not."

He stared at Susan Ross, a 16-year-old who'd been abducted from a community pool in Florida, and appreciated the way her teenage body looked in her bikini. He made a mental note to pay her a visit later. "In order to make everybody equal, I'd like each of you to disrobe."

Despite his command, nobody moved. They just stared straight ahead in absolute shock.

Like Holmes before him, Jackson shook his head in disappointment. "What a shame. I assumed that each of you had a pretty good understanding of your situation by now. I figured the Ginsu display from earlier was going to keep you in line for the rest of your visit." Jackson shrugged his broad shoulders as he walked toward the prisoners. "I guess I was wrong."

Jackson stopped in front of Susan, his six-foot frame towering above her shoeless five-foot-five. "I'm looking for a volunteer," he roared in the voice of a Parris Island drill sergeant. "And personally, I think *you* will do nicely."

Despite her panicked cries of protest, he lifted her half-naked, 110-pound body over his shoulder and carried her towards the chopping block. Two guards offered assistance, but he quickly ordered them away. He was enjoying himself far too much to let them share in the fun.

When he reached the wooden cube, he set her gently on the ground, then grabbed her tightly around her neck so she couldn't run away.

"What do you want from me?" she cried through the cloth of her white hood. "What are you going to do to me?"

"You'll find out soon enough," he whispered into her left ear. "And I must admit I'm looking forward to it." He pushed his crotch against the small of her lower back, and she immediately felt his excitement start to grow. "Can you feel how hard I am? That's because of you, you know. All because of you."

Susan tried squirming free from his grip, but Jackson was simply too strong for her. As she repeatedly tried to pull away, he simply laughed at her attempts to regain freedom.

"Are you quite done?" he asked in a civil tone.

After one more try, she reluctantly nodded her head.

"Good, because I'm dying to begin."

Like a tarantula, Jackson's black fingers crawled down her nubile flesh, gradually creeping across her firm stomach, then sliding under her bathing suit and into the thick, blonde patch that protected her groin. As he raked his fingernails through her coarse hair, he instantly noticed how the texture sharply contrasted with the softness of her delicate white skin.

"Do you like my magic fingers?" he whispered into her ear. "Do you like it when I touch you?"

Before she could respond, he lifted her off the ground and forced her to stand on top of the bloody chopping block. She tried to avoid the crimson liquid that covered the wood but to no avail. Within seconds, her bare feet were coated with the red fluid that had gushed from Paul Metz's severed finger.

"As I told you a moment ago, I would like each of you to take off your clothes. But apparently, you're not as threatened by me as you were by Master Holmes. Now, because of your ignorance, this young girl has to suffer."

"Please don't hurt me," she sobbed. "I was being good, Master Jackson. I didn't do anything wrong. I was being good."

With a mischievous smile, he placed his dark hand on the back of her leg and slowly, sexually, stroked her inner thigh. "I know, my dear, but it's not my doing. You should fault your fellow inmates for ignoring my instructions. They're more to blame than I." His hand crept higher and higher on her smoothly-shaved leg until it stopped on her firm buttocks. "Remember, I'm not to blame for this. Please, bear me no ill-will."

Taking his stiletto from the folds of his cloak, Jackson slowly raised the blade behind the unsuspecting female, inching it towards his ultimate target. The sharp steel shaft glistened in the light of the raging fire, filling the trembling crowd with thoughts of the supernatural.

"I want you to kneel for me," he purred. "And I want you to take your time."

Without complaint, the girl slowly dropped to her knees while his unblinking eyes followed the curvature of her cheeks on their downward path. When she reached the chopping board, he heard her groan as she sank into the slick, cherry liquid that coated the surface, and the sound brought a smile to his lips.

"Now raise your hands above your head and hold them there."

She did as she was told, and her movement electrified him—her unquestioning compliance literally made his heart race faster.

"Remember," he breathed, "no ill-will."

Jackson placed his hand on the girl's uncovered back and searched for the perfect spot to make his incision. Once he found it, he lifted the knife to her flesh, tracing the ridges of her spine with the broad-side of his cold, metal blade. As he did, he noticed the sudden emergence of goose bumps, not only on her skin but on his as well.

Gathering his emotions, Jackson inched the stiletto to the mid-section of her back, the spot directly between her shoulder blades, then paused.

This was where the cut would be made.

Turning the blade to the appropriate angle, Jackson gazed at the crowd to make sure that they were watching. They were. The entire throng was focused on the hypnotic movements of his knife like he was an ancient Mayan priest preparing for a ritual sacrifice. Pleased by the attention, he redirected his gaze to his trembling target.

"It's time," he whispered.

With a quick slash, Jackson sliced the strap of her bikini top. Then, before she had an opportunity to flinch, he carved her swimsuit bottom as well, exposing her breasts and groin to the audience and the humid Louisiana night.

A wave of humiliation flooded over the girl. She tried to cover her body by crouching into a tiny ball on the wooden cube, but Jackson wouldn't allow it. He yanked her from her bloody perch and forced her to retake her position with the rest of the prisoners.

He would've preferred to wrap her in his arms but knew this was no time to be playing favorites. He had to treat everyone the same in order to set the rules, in order to get their respect.

Besides, he'd have a chance to make things up to her later—when they were alone.

Chapter Six

Wexford, Pennsylvania
(11 miles north of Pittsburgh, PA)

Despite the early hour, Jonathon Payne managed to smile as he drove to Walker's apartment. Normally a grin wouldn't make an appearance on his lips until much closer to noon, but since he was spending the entire day with her, he woke at the crack of dawn in an atypically good mood.

"So this is what 7:30 looks like?" he laughed to himself. "Wow, the sun is up and everything."

Dressed in khaki shorts and a white golf shirt, Payne pulled his Lincoln Navigator into the crowded lot outside of her building. After finding a parking spot, he walked under the maroon awning that sat above the complex's entrance and buzzed her unit to be let in. When she didn't reply, he tried the system a few more times before he walked back to the parking lot to make sure that her Honda Accord was in her assigned space. It was, and in his mind, that meant she was definitely home.

"Come on, girl. I know you're scared to face me on the golf course, but this is ridiculous."

Slightly frustrated, Payne strolled back to the intercom system and tried the buzzer several more times, yet nothing changed. He was still unable to get Walker's attention. "I wake up early for the first time this decade, and this is how my girlfriend punishes me. Man, I'm going to beat her by twenty strokes instead of my usual ten."

As Payne stood in the entryway, pondering what to do next, he noticed a thin strip of gray electrical tape sticking to the frame near the automatic lock of the security door. Moving closer, he realized that the tape started outside the frame and ran inside the building, purposely jamming the door open.

"Oh," Payne mumbled, figuring the intercom system must be broken.

Thankful to be inside, Payne jogged up the carpeted stairs to the second floor and was surprised to see the thick fire door at the top of the steps propped open with a large stick.

"Great security," he mumbled in passing.

Without giving it much thought, Payne continued his journey down the hallway towards Walker's apartment when he finally noticed something he couldn't dismiss. A piece of gray tape had been placed over the peephole of his girlfriend's door—tape that wasn't there when he dropped her off the night before.

Suddenly, a wave of nausea swept through Payne's stomach. He wasn't sure why, but he knew—he just knew!—that something had happened to Ariane.

Something bad. Something tragic.

Payne pounded on her door as loud as he could and prayed that she'd tell him that she had overslept or had been in the bathroom when he was buzzing her apartment. But he knew that wasn't the case. He knew, without a doubt, that something was wrong, seriously wrong.

"Ariane!" he yelled. "It's Jon. Open the door! Come on, honey! Open up!"

When his loud pleas went unnoticed, Payne ran down the lengthy corridor at top speed and leaped down the steps three at a time. Bursting through the front door like a tiger from its cage, Payne sprinted to his Navigator, where he quickly dialed Walker's number on his portable phone. "Come on, baby! Answer the phone. Please answer the damn phone!"

After four rings, Payne heard a click on the line. It was her answering machine.

Payne cursed loudly as he waited to leave his message. "Ariane, if you're screening your calls or you're still in bed, pick up the phone. . . ." There was no response. "I'm really worried about you so *please* call me as soon as you hear this message. Try me on my cellular immediately, OK? I'll carry it with me until I talk to you."

He hung up the phone in disgust, then sank back into his front seat. "Think, goddammit, think. Where could she be at this time of day?"

Payne racked his brain for possibilities, but couldn't think of any logical explanations. Most stores weren't open at that hour, but even if they were, she would've taken her car to get there. Most of her friends would still be sleeping or getting ready for work, so they wouldn't have picked her up. Her family lived out of state, so she couldn't be with them.

No, something had happened to Ariane, and he knew it.

Picking up his phone again, Payne dialed his best friend and waited for him to answer.

"Yeah?" David Jones croaked. "What is it?"

"D.J., it's Jon. Something's happened, and I need your help."

That's all that he needed to hear. Less than a half-hour later, he was pulling next to Payne. "Have you heard from her?"

Payne replied by shaking his head.

"OK, but that doesn't guarantee that something bad has happened. I'm sure there are a thousand possibilities that could explain where she is, so just tell me everything that you possibly can. I'm sure we can figure out some sort of rational explanation for this."

Payne smiled slightly, then extended his hand to his friend. "I appreciate you coming over so early in the morning. I feel better just having you here."

"Would you please stop flirting with me in public?" Jones joked, trying to ease his friend's tension. "I only like your sweet talk behind closed doors, big fella."

After a brief moment of laughter, Payne leaned against the back of his vehicle and closed his eyes. "D.J., I'm scared." He took a deep breath as the color slowly drained from his face. "You know how I used to get bad feelings back when we were in the MANIACs?"

Jones nodded. "Your gut's saved more asses so than Preparation H."

"I don't know why, but I'm getting the same bad feeling right now. I know that something's happened to Ariane. I don't know what, but something."

"Jon, listen. We've been out of the military for a few years now, so the tuning fork in your stomach is bound to be rusty. Right? Besides, you're not used to being awake at this time of day. Hell, I'm sure your entire system is out of whack."

Reluctantly, Payne agreed.

"Why don't you fill me in on everything, and hopefully we can come up with some kind of solution together."

Payne nodded. "I walked Ariane to her door last night. She had a headache and said she needed to get some sleep. We made plans for this morning, then I went home."

"You didn't stay the night?"

"If I had," he snapped, "do you think I'd be out here?"

"Sorry, I just—"

"No," he apologized. "I'm the one who should be sorry. I didn't mean to yell at you. It's just, I don't know. . . ." He paused for a minute, trying to gather his thoughts. "I would've stayed the night, but she had a headache and thought it would be best if she got some rest."

"So, you didn't have a fight or anything?"

"Not at all!" The look on Payne's face suggested that he was offended by the insinuation. "She just needed some rest, OK? Simple as that."

"Jon, I believe you. I just had to ask to be sure. What were your plans for today?"

Payne nodded. "I was supposed to pick her up at 7:30. We were going to grab a light breakfast, then head straight for the golf course. She told me that she'd made an 8:30 tee time."

"Fine. Now walk me through this morning."

"Surprisingly, I woke up early and actually showed up on time. I tried buzzing the intercom, but there was no reply. Next, I checked the lot for her car, and it's here." Payne pointed towards her Accord. "I went back to the front door, and that's when I noticed the electrical tape."

"Electrical tape? What electrical tape?" The two of them hustled to the building's entryway, and Jones studied the way the adhesive had been placed over the lock. "Well, if something has happened to her—and I'm not saying that anything has—then I doubt we're dealing with professionals."

"Why do you say that?"

"Look at the placement of the tape. Instead of running the strip over the lock in a vertical fashion, they placed it horizontally."

"And that's wrong?"

"Definitely. When you're breaking into a secured building, you want to conceal your point of access the best you can. That way, if someone comes across your entryway, they won't know the building has been breached. That's why a professional will never break a window or bust down a door. It's not something that you can easily cover up."

Normally, Payne would've teased Jones about the encyclopedia he carried around in his head, but because of the situation, he let the moment pass. "And in your opinion, is this lack of professionalism good or bad news for Ariane?"

Jones shrugged. "To be honest with you, it could be good,

could be bad. If something has happened to Ariane—and it's still a very big *if* in my mind—then there's a good chance that other mistakes have been made as well. And that'll increase our opportunity to find her."

"That sounds good to me. So, what's the bad news?"

"If this isn't a professional job, there's a better chance that someone will panic, and if that happens . . ." Jones didn't have the heart to finish the sentence.

"Understood," Payne grunted. "Let me show you upstairs."

The two men climbed to the second floor, and Jones shook his head at the use of a stick as a door prop. "Definitely not professionals," he muttered as they continued their journey toward Walker's front door. "And you tried calling her, right? Maybe she's just sleeping and can't hear the door from her bedroom."

"I tried more than once, but the answering machine keeps picking up."

"How about the hospital? You mentioned she had a headache last evening. Maybe she called for an ambulance in the middle of the night."

Payne shook his head. "I thought the same thing so I called all the local hospitals while I was waiting for you. They assured me that she wasn't there."

Jones nodded, trying to think of any other possibilities that could have escaped his mind, but he could think of none.

"I realize everything I've shown you is suspect at best, but this is the thing that really got me going." He pointed to the tape that covered Walker's peephole—the same type of tape that covered the lock on the front door. "There's nothing innocent about this. And I guarantee you this tape wasn't here last night. No way in hell."

Jones grimaced. "Did you knock on the door?"

"For several minutes, but I got no response. I even tried yelling, but she just didn't answer."

Jones patted his friend on the shoulder and tried to reassure him, but it was difficult to do with all the mounting evidence. "What kind of security system does her apartment have?"

"I had them install alarms on all the windows and the two doors. I also had a camera mounted inside the peephole, but obviously, they must've known about that."

"Not necessarily. Just because they put tape on the door doesn't guarantee that they knew about the camera. They could've been trying to prevent her from seeing into the corridor for some reason. Hell, for all we know, maybe her neighbor across the hall was doing something illegal, and he wanted to guarantee his privacy."

"But how does that explain the fact that she's missing?"

"I have no idea," Jones grunted. "But I'm trying to keep as many options open as possible. Have you tried talking to her neighbors? Maybe they saw something."

"I was reluctant to do it without a second opinion, but now that it's after 8:00 and you're beginning to see my point of view, I'm willing to try anything."

Jones nodded his approval. "Why don't you handle this floor while I head downstairs?"

"Fine, but if you find anything, please let me know immediately."

"Will do," he assured his friend. "And Jon, keep the faith. We'll find her."

Knocking on each door, Payne started with Walker's neighbor from across the hall, then slowly made his way down the corridor. Everyone that he talked to was friendly and immediately knew who Ariane was—females of her beauty tend to stand out. Unfortunately, no one saw or heard anything out of the ordinary, and no one could account for the electrical tape over the front lock.

After speaking to the last of her neighbors on the second floor, Payne was tempted to call Ariane one more time, but before he had a chance, he heard D.J. running up the stairs in an obvious state of excitement.

"I think I've got a witness," Jones exclaimed. "He's waiting downstairs in the hall." Within seconds, the two men were standing in the doorway of Apartment 101. "Sir, this is Jonathon Payne, Ariane's boyfriend. Jon, this is Mr. McNally."

Payne shook the hand of the elderly man while trying to ascertain as much as he could about him. McNally appeared to be in his mid-80s, walked with the aid of a metal cane, and closely resembled Yoda from Star Wars—minus the green color. His apartment was cluttered with heirlooms and antiques, yet for some reason a framed *Baywatch* poster of Pamela Anderson hung near the entrance to his kitchen.

"Mr. McNally, D.J. tells me that you might've seen something that could help me with Ariane?"

"Who the hell is D.J.?" the old man snapped. "I didn't talk to any bastard named D.J."

Jones looked at Payne and grimaced. "Sir? Remember me? I talked to you about two minutes ago. My name's David Jones, but my friend's call me D.J."

"What the hell kind of person has friends that would refuse to use his real name? You kids today. I just don't understand your damn generation."

"Sir, I don't mind. D.J. is just a nickname."

"A nickname?" he shrieked. "You think that's a nickname? Horseshit! It's just two capital letters with a couple of periods. Why don't you just use B.S. as your nickname instead? Because that's what your nickname is: bullshit! When I was growing up, people used to have nicknames that said something about them, like Slim or Red or Cocksucker, not pansy names like D.J."

"Sir," Payne interrupted. "I don't mean to be rude, but I was wondering what you saw this morning. David said you saw something that could help me find my girlfriend."

"Your girlfriend? Who's your girlfriend?"

Payne rolled his eyes in frustration. This was getting nowhere. "Ariane Walker. She lives upstairs in apartment 210."

McNally pondered the information for a few seconds before his face lit up in ecstasy. "Oh, you mean the brunette with the dark eyes and the nice rack? Yeah, I saw her bright and early today, about an hour ago. She was wearing a red top and a short skirt. It was so small I could almost see her panties." The elderly man cackled in delight as he pondered his memory of the beautiful girl. "That gal's a real looker."

Payne couldn't agree with him more. She was the prettiest woman that Payne had ever seen. The first and only female who had literally left him speechless, which was fairly unfortunate since he was in the middle of a speech at the time.

A few years back, Payne had volunteered to speak to a group of convicted drunk drivers about the tragic death of his parents. The goal of the program was to make recent offenders listen to the horrors of their crime in order to make them think twice about drinking and driving again. Payne was in the middle of reliving his nightmare—describing the devastation he felt when he was pulled from his 8th-grade algebra class and told about the death of his parents—when his eyes focused on Ariane's. She was standing off to the side, watching and listening with complete empathy. In a heartbeat, he could tell that she'd been through the same horror as him, that she'd lost a loved one in a similar nightmare.

He knew that she *understood.*

Payne managed to finish his heart-wrenching tale without incident, but when he started his conclusion, he found himself unable to take his eyes off of her. He knew he was supposed to be there to make a point, that he should have been focusing his anger and his rage on the thoughtless bastards in the crowd, but he was suddenly unable to. There was just something about her, something pure and perfect that made him feel completely at ease. In his mind, it was like something good had finally come from his parents' death, like god's master plan was finally starting to make sense. His parents' accident and her parents' accident had brought them together.

And the realization stole his ability to speak.

"Jon?" D.J. whispered. "Do you have some questions for Mr. McNally, or do you want me to take care of this?"

Payne blinked a few times, which helped bring him back to reality. "No, I got it." He turned towards the elderly man and said, "Sir, where did you see Ariane?"

"In my bedroom," McNally muttered.

Payne and Jones exchanged confused glances, trying to figure out what he meant. "Ariane was in your bedroom?"

The man cackled in obvious amusement. "If she was, do you think I'd be talking to you bozos? Hell no! I'd be inside eating Viagra like it was candy corn."

"So what did you mean when you mentioned your bedroom?" Jones asked.

McNally inhaled before replying. "Do I have to spell everything out for you young whippersnappers? I was in my bedroom when I saw her outside my window with a bunch of young fellows. And let me tell you what. . . ." He tapped Payne on his chest. "You need to get your woman on a leash 'cause she looked pretty darn snookered. They were practically dragging her."

"She was being dragged by a bunch of guys? What did they look like?"

McNally pondered the question for a few seconds, then pointed at Jones.

"They were black?" Payne asked.

"No, you dumb ass. They were butt-ugly and had stupid nicknames. . . . Of course I mean they were black."

"Could you tell us anything else? Were they tall? Short? Fat? Anything?"

"They were black. That's it. Everything about them was black. Black clothes, black hoods, black shoes. I don't even know how many there were 'cause they looked like shadows, for god's sake. Shoot, they even drove a black van."

Payne frowned at the information. He was hoping to uncover

something more helpful than a single hue. "I know this is unlikely, but did you happen to see a license plate on the van?"

"As a matter of fact, I did," McNally declared. "It was the only thing that wasn't black."

"You saw it? What did it say?"

"I have no damn idea," he answered. "The numbers were just a big ol' blur to me. But I do know one thing, though: The plates were from Louisiana."

Skepticism filled Payne's face. "How do you know that?"

"Well, I got me a lady friend that lives down in Cajun country, and every year I visit her for Mardi Gras. When the van first pulled up in front of the place, I saw the Louisiana plate and thought maybe she was coming here for a little lovin', but obviously, when I, uh . . ." The old man furrowed his brow as he tried to remember his train of thought. "What was I talking about again?"

"Actually," Jones lied, "you had just finished. So, is there anything else that you can tell us about this morning?"

"I'm kind of constipated, but I ate some prunes so I hope—"

"That's not what he meant," interrupted Payne. Even though he was sympathetic to McNally's advancing age, he just didn't have time to listen to him ramble. "David wanted to know if you had anything else to tell us about Ariane?"

McNally pondered the question, then shook his head.

"Well, I'd like to thank you for your information." Payne handed the man a business card, then helped him back inside his apartment. "And if you think of anything else, please don't hesitate to call me."

Once Payne had returned to the hall, he asked Jones what they should do next.

"I have to admit things are looking worse and worse for Ariane, but I don't think we can go to the cops quite yet."

"What?" Payne exclaimed. "Why not? You heard what the man said. A group of guys dragged her out to a van early this morning and no one's heard from her since."

"True, but Mr. McNally is not exactly what you would call an ideal witness. Don't get me wrong, I don't think he was lying or anything, but you have to admit he lost touch with reality a couple of times during our conversation."

"Shit!" Payne thought they had enough information to go on, but Jones knew a lot more about police procedures than he did. "So what do you recommend?"

"Honestly, I think we should go upstairs and snoop around Ariane's apartment a little bit. We can see if anything is broken or missing, plus we can see if the peephole video camera recorded anything before they covered the lens with tape."

"And how do you suggest we get into the apartment?"

Jones rolled his eyes at the question. "Remember, locks are my specialty."

"Yeah," Payne muttered. "As long as handcuffs and a desk aren't involved."

Chapter Seven

Inside the plantation house, Theo Webster stared at his computer screen and scrolled through page after page of his painstaking research. After removing his wire-rimmed glasses, the 31-year-old rubbed his tired eyes and stretched his skinny 5' 8" frame. The 150-watt track lighting that sat above him reflected off the ebony skin that covered his ever-growing forehead and highlighted the dark bags that had recently surfaced under his drooping lids.

"Man, I need a *siesta*," he yawned.

After cracking his back, Webster settled back into his seat while slipping his slim frames over his Dumbo-like ears. Once the rims were in place, he resumed his research, studying the in-depth genealogy of the island's most-recent arrivals. As he scrutinized Mike Cussler's family, Webster heard a creak in a floorboard behind him. "Shit," he mumbled as he reached inside his oaken desk.

Without looking, Webster fumbled through various items until his hand made contact with the object he was searching for: his gun. Slipping his fingers around the handle, Webster slowly pulled the .38 special from his desk while staring at the reflection of the approaching intruder on his computer screen. Creak. The floorboard whined again, but this time the sound was several feet closer.

It was time to make his move.

In a sudden burst, Webster dropped to the hardwood floor and spun towards his unsuspecting target. The move stunned the trespasser so much that he dropped the cup of coffee he was carrying and shrieked like a wounded girl.

The pathetic wail brought a smile to Webster's face. "Gump, what the hell are you doing sneaking up on me like that? Don't you know we have nearly two dozen prisoners on this island that would like to see me dead? Use your head, boy. God gave you a brain for a reason."

Bennie Blount lowered his head in shame, and as he did, his elaborate rows of dreadlocks cascaded over his dark eyes, making him look like a Rastafarian sheep dog. "I sorry 'bout that, sir. I was jus' tryin' to bring you somethin' to wakes you up."

Webster glanced at the brown puddle that covered the floor and grimaced. "Unless you have a straw, I think it's going to be pretty difficult for me to drink."

The 6' 6" servant stared at the steaming beverage for several seconds before his face broke into a gold-toothed smile. "For a minute, I thought you be serious, but then I says to myself, 'Master Webster ain't no dog. He ain't gonna drink his drink from no floor, even with a straw.' "

"Well, that's awfully clever of you, but before I congratulate you too much, why don't you run into the other room and get a mop?"

"That's a mighty good idea, sir. I guess I shoulda thought of it since it's my job to clean and all." Blount slowly backed away from the spill as he continued to speak. "Don't ya worry none."

Despite his improper grammar, Blount was hired by the Plantation for his strong work ethic and knowledge of the local swamps. Nicknamed Gump for his intellectual similarities to Forrest Gump, Tom Hanks' famous movie character, Blount lived in the guest wing of the three-story mansion. During the course of the day, he spent most of his time cooking and cleaning in the white-pillared masterpiece, but twice a week, he was allowed to journey to the mainland for food and supplies.

When Blount returned to Webster's office, he was disappointed to see his boss working again. He liked talking to his superiors every chance he got, but they often got upset when he interrupted them.

"Gump," Webster asked without turning around. "What are we having for breakfast?"

The question brought a smile to his lips, and his gold front teeth glistened in the streaming sunlight. "Well, I figure since this be a big day for all of you's, I should fix a big Southern meal likes my meema used to make. I makes eggs 'n' bacon 'n' ham 'n' grits 'n' biscuits 'n' fresh apple butter, too. Ooooooweeeeee! I think my mouth is gonna water for a week."

Webster nodded his head in appreciation, but as Blount's statement slowly sunk in, he turned from his computer to face the dark-skinned servant. "What exactly did you mean when you said this was a big day for us? What do you know about today?"

With the soiled mop in his hand, he shrugged. "Not much, sir, but I can tell somethin's up. There be an excitement in the air that's easier to smell than the magnolias in May. I figured maybe's yo' birthday or maybe's 'da approach of 'da Fourth of July."

Webster studied Blount as he spoke, and it appeared that he was telling the truth. "I think it's just the holiday that has everybody excited," he lied. "I know I'm looking forward to it."

"Well, I be too. In fact, I was wonderin' if I can go to 'da city for 'da fireworks show on Saturday night. I doesn't know why they on the 3rd, but they is."

"Let me ask the other guys at breakfast, then I'll let you know for sure. But as far as I'm concerned, that's fine with me."

"Thank ya, Master Webster. Thank ya. 'Dat'd be nice of ya." Blount picked up his bucket then backed towards the open door. "Oh! Speakin' of breakfast, I almost forgets to tell ya 'dat it's ready to eats."

*　*　*

While Payne looked on in fascination, Jones slid a skeleton key into Walker's lock and easily popped it open. So easily, in fact, he kind of surprised himself.

Jones asked, "I thought you increased the security on her place?"

"I did," Payne assured him. "I added a deadbolt and the alarms that I told you about."

"Well," he said as he pushed the door open, "it doesn't appear that she uses them."

At first glance, Walker's place appeared to be in order with the exception of a golf bag lying in the center of the floor. An off-white sofa sat against the wall to the left and faced an immense entertainment center that held a Sony television, stereo, and VCR. A leather beanbag chair rested in the corner of the room under a halogen lamp, which filled the otherwise dark room with an abundance of bright light.

"Looks clear," Jones whispered. "By the way, make sure you don't touch anything in here. If something did happen to Ariane, we don't want to mess up any potential evidence."

Payne nodded as Jones checked the kitchen, bathroom, and bedrooms for intruders. "Well?"

"I don't see any bodies or blood, so that's good. Since nothing valuable seems to be missing, I think we can rule out burglary. It doesn't look like there was a struggle of any kind so I would assume rape and assault can be crossed off, too. There is no obvious sign of a break-in like a broken window or lock. Therefore, we have to assume that if something happened to Ariane it was probably her fault."

"How so?" Payne demanded.

Jones instantly regretted his choice of words. "Sorry. That came out wrong. What I meant to say is this: Since there are no signs of a forced entry, I'd have to assume that if something has happened, then Ariane probably forgot to lock up or simply opened the door for the perpetrator."

"No way," he growled. "Ariane is an overly cautious type of person. That's one of the reasons that I installed all of this security in here. It wasn't for my peace of mind. It was for hers."

"Jon, I believe you, but that simply doesn't match up with the facts. If Ariane was as cautious as you say, then her alarms would've been set, her locks would've been locked, and she would've been safer than a virgin at an eunuch convention. Right?"

Jones walked to the security panel near the front door and pushed the button for a system check. Within seconds, the unit beeped and a digitized voice filled the room with sound. "The Centurion 3000 is currently off. . . . Push 1 to enable the system."

"See what I mean? The unit is working, which means she probably turned it off to answer the door. Either that or she forgot to turn it on last night."

Payne shook his head. "When I dropped her off last night, I made sure she got in and turned the system on before I left. In fact, I always wait until the damn thing beeps."

"Then she turned it off for some reason. And my guess is to open the door."

Payne swallowed deeply while opening the tiny black box that was mounted to the inside of Walker's front door. He removed the videotape from the peephole surveillance system and carried it to the VCR. "I don't know if we'll be able to see anything, but it's worth a look." After slipping the tape inside, he hit play, then patiently watched the screen as he rewound the tape.

"How does this thing work?"

"It's activated by movement in the hallway. That way it doesn't record hour after hour of nothing." Payne pointed to the screen to show Jones what he meant. "See, there we are when we gained entrance into the apartment a few minutes ago. Our movement turned the system on."

He continued to rewind the video until the image changed. "There I am right after I ripped the tape off of the camera."

The video continued to whir in fast motion until the screen went black.

"And let me guess. That's when the peephole was covered."

"I would bet on it. Since the aperture was blocked, the camera interpreted that to mean a presence standing directly in front of the door." Payne glanced at his watch, then looked at the electronic counter on the VCR. "What time did Mr. McNally say he saw Ariane?"

"He didn't. He said it was about an hour before we talked to him."

"Well, I got here about 7:30, and there was no black van in the parking lot, so I guess we're talking about 7:00 or 7:15, right?"

Jones nodded while Payne rewound the video to that point. When the counter hit the appropriate mark, Payne hit the play button and his own face filled the TV screen.

"When was that filmed?" Jones wondered.

Payne studied the image and recognized the clothes he'd worn the previous evening. "That's from last night, but I'm not sure if it was before or after my date." The faint beeping of the security system could be heard through the TV's speaker as Payne's image turned and walked away from the door. "See, I told you she set the damn system last night. I told you."

Jones was about to defend himself when a figure flashed across the screen. "Whoa. What was that? Go back." Payne had seen the image as well and quickly followed orders. "Use the pause button, Jon, then frame advance."

The picture crept by at a sluggish pace, but finally, after several seconds of non-action, a gloved hand emerged from the right of the screen. Moving an inch at a time, the arm eventually reached the lens of the peephole, and once it did, the picture immediately went black.

"Damn! Not a goddamned thing!"

"Hey, be patient." Jones grabbed the remote control from Payne and slowly advanced the image to the moment before the adhesive strip was applied to the door. "Just because we didn't see a face doesn't mean it's a total loss. There's more here than you think."

"Such as?"

"What color was the man who put the tape on the door?"

Payne stared at the screen. "I can't tell. He's wearing black gloves and long black sleeves."

"True," Jones muttered as he placed his finger on the image. "But look closer. There's a gap where the glove ends here, and the sleeve begins there."

Payne moved closer to the screen and stared. "I'll be damned. You're right. I can see the edge of each garment."

"The reason you thought they overlapped is because of his skin. Whoever put the tape on the door is black. Not coffee and cream like me, but pure black. I'm talking *hold the milk, hold the sugar, hold the freakin' water* black." Jones continued to study the monitor as Payne pondered the information. "Hey, what's that on his arm?"

"Where?"

"Right between the glove and sleeve." Jones stared at the image. "Is that a tattoo?"

Payne crouched in front of the TV and considered the question. Unfortunately, the image was simply too dark to distinguish anything conclusively. "Hang on a sec. Let me change the brightness. It might help." After twisting the dial, Payne backed away from the set and shrugged. "I can't be positive. It might be a tattoo, but I honestly don't know."

"Well, I know a way we can find out. I have a computer program at the office that enables me to blow up video images, alter color schemes, manipulate brightness, and so on. I'll take the tape over there and see if I can learn anything."

"Sounds good to me." Payne reached for the eject button, but before he pressed it, Jones surprised him by grabbing his arm.

"Listen," D.J. said. "I wasn't going to mention this, but I have to be upfront with you. There's still one thing we need to check. I was going to wait until later, but I feel you deserve to be with me when it's done."

"What are you talking about? What do you need to check?"

Jones placed his hand on Payne's broad shoulder and squeezed. "The peephole camera records image and sound, right? I mean, we heard the alarm system beeping, didn't we?"

"Yeah, so?"

Jones swallowed hard. "The video is obviously unwatchable because of the electrical tape on the lens, right?"

Payne nodded.

"But what about the sound? There's a good chance that we might be able to hear this morning's events even after the lens was blocked."

"Oh my god, you're right. Put it on."

"Jon, keep in mind if something did happen to Ariane, it might be painful to . . ."

"Put it on! I've got to know what happened. Just, put it on."

Jones sighed, then hit the button on the remote. After several seconds of silence, the faint sound of a doorbell could be heard from the TV's speakers, followed by a loud, rhythmic knocking on the door.

"You're early," Ariane complained from a distance. "I'm still getting ready." Silence followed her comment, then footsteps, then a faint giggle finally. "First you're early, now you're covering the peephole."

Beeps from the security system chimed in the tape's background.

"I'll tell you what, Jonathon, I'm going to kick your butt all over the golf course. There's no doubt about that."

Her comment was followed by the click of a deadbolt, the twist of the door handle, and—

Jones pushed the pause button, then turned towards Payne,

whose face was completely ashen. "Are you sure you want to hear this?"

"Yeah," Payne muttered, his voice trembling with emotion. In actuality, he had heard enough, but if he was going to help Ariane, he knew he had to listen to everything. "Play the tape."

"Are you sure?"

Payne shook his head from side to side. "No, but play it anyways."

With the touch of a button, Ariane roared like a banshee, sending chills through both of the horrified listeners. Then, as her wail echoed through the room, it was quickly replaced by heavy footsteps, muffled squeals, and the most frightening sound of all.

Silence.

Chapter Eight

While Holmes, Jackson, and Webster had breakfast in the comfort of the mansion, Hakeem Ndjai, an unmerciful man who'd been hired as the plantation overseer, took control of the captives.

Even though he was a valuable part of the plantation team, his foreign heritage excluded him from the decision-making hierarchy. He had been handpicked by Holmes, who'd heard several stories of his unwavering toughness, and was brought in from Nkambe, Cameroon, where he had been an overseer on a cacao plantation. Like most workers from his country, he had labored in unbearable conditions for virtually nothing—his average income was only $150 per year—so when Holmes offered him a job in America, Ndjai wept for joy for the first time in his life.

But that was several months ago, and Ndjai knew there was no place for joy while he was working. In fact, there was no room for any emotion at all.

In a cold growl that was tinged with the tongue of his native land, Ndjai reinforced the instructions that Jackson and Holmes had given during their cross-burning party, but he did it with his own special touch. "I am the overseer of this plantation, and out of respect for my difficult job, you shall refer to me as sir. Do I make myself clear?"

"Yes, sir," the naked group shouted.

"Each of you has been brought here for a reason, and that reason will eventually be revealed. Until that time, you will become a part of the Plantation's working staff, performing the duties that are about to be assigned to you."

Ndjai signaled one of the guards, and he ran forward, carrying a silver belt that shone in the sun. "While you are working, you will be positioned on various parts of our land, and at some point, you might be tempted to run for freedom."

He smiled under his dark hood. "It's something I do not recommend."

Ndjai took the metal belt and wrapped it around a cement slab that rested near the crimson-stained chopping block. After clicking the belt in place, he handed the cement to a nearby guard who immediately carried it fifty yards from the crowd.

"When your uniforms are given to you, each of you will have one of these belts locked around your ankle. It cannot be removed by anyone but me, and I will not remove it for any reason during your stay on this island." He reached into the pocket of his robe and pulled out a tiny remote control. He held the gadget into the air so every one could see it.

"This is what you Americans call a deterrent."

With a touch of the button, the cement block erupted into a shower of rubble, sending shards of rock in every direction and a mushroom cloud of smoke and flames high into the humid air.

"Did I get your attention?" he asked rhetorically. "Now imagine what would have happened if your anklet were to be detonated. I doubt much of you would be found."

A couple of the guards snickered, and Ndjai quieted them with a sharp stare. He would not tolerate disrespect from anybody.

"I'm sure some of you are trying to figure out how your anklets work, and some of you will probably try to figure out an ingenious way to disarm them. Well, I will tell you now: Your efforts will fail. We have buried a small number of transmitters on various parts of the Plantation. If at any time your anklet crosses the perimeter, your personal bomb will explode, instantly making you dead. Is that clear?"

"Yes, sir."

"One more thing I almost forgot to mention. If your device is detonated, it will automatically send a signal to the other anklets on this island, and in a matter of seconds, every other prisoner will share your brutal fate." Ndjai smiled widely. "Do you understand?"

They certainly did, and the mere thought of it made them shudder.

* * *

After returning to his office, Jones locked himself in his technology lab and got to work. The room cost a staggering amount of money to assemble and was filled with hi-tech equipment that many police departments would be envious of. The computer system was the most important component, and ironically enough, it was the instrument that cost Jones the least to acquire. Built by Payne's company, the computer was a scaled-down version of the one used at FBI Headquarters in Langley, Virginia, and was loaned to him by his best friend as an office-warming gift. And some gift it was. On the open market, the system would be worth millions of dollars.

Placing the surveillance tape into the unit, Jones quickly broke the video images into manageable data files, and from there, he was able to select a precise frame from the film and pull it onto his screen in microscopic clarity.

"What should I look at first?" he mumbled aloud.

Then it dawned on him. He wanted to see if the black mark on the assailant's right wrist was, in fact, a tattoo.

Jones scrolled through a number of frames until he found

the scene that fit his specific needs—one where the man's arm was perfectly centered on the monitor and the gap between the glove and the sleeve was at its widest. In order to improve his view, Jones highlighted the section of the scene that he wanted to examine and clicked his mouse button once. The computer's zoom kicked in and gave him a magnified close-up of the perpetrator's skin. Unfortunately, the image still wasn't clear enough, so Jones moved his computer arrow to the top of the screen and searched through his various options. Under the category marked TOOLS, he used the brightness feature, increasing the picture's effulgence by ten, then twenty percent.

Once the program had made the appropriate adjustments, Jones scrutinized the image while smiling in obvious triumph. His original hypothesis had been correct. The criminal had an elaborate tattoo on his right wrist. The three-inch design was in the shape of the letter P, and it started directly below the palm of his hand. The straight edge of the symbol was in the form of an intricately detailed sword, the blade's handle rising high above the letter's curve. At the base of the drawing, small drops of blood fell from the weapon's tip, leaving the impression that it had just been pulled from the flesh of a fallen victim. Finally, dangling from each side of the sword was a series of broken chains, which appeared to be severed near the left and right edge.

As Jones printed three copies of the image, his speaker phone buzzed, making him flinch with surprise. He took a moment to collect himself, then pushed the red intercom button.

"Yes?"

"Mr. Payne is on line one," his secretary stated.

"Thanks." Jones quickly switched lines. "Jon, any news?"

"I was about to ask you the same thing. I went to the police like you suggested and filled out the appropriate paper work. Since I have a couple of friends at the station, they assured me that Ariane would get top priority."

"Even though she's only been gone a few hours?"

"Well, the scream on the videotape and Mr. McNally's testimony have a lot to do with it."

"What did they tell you to do? Did they give you any advice?"

"I wouldn't call it advice, exactly. I think a warning would be more accurate. Like I said, these cops know me, so they automatically assumed that I would do something stupid to get in their way. Shit, D.J., why the hell would they think that?"

Jones smiled. The cops had Payne pegged perfectly. He was definitely the intrusive type. "Instead of giving you the obvious answer, let me tell you what I discovered." He described the tattoo in detail, then filled him in on a theory that had crossed his mind. "I think the tattoo we're looking for might be a Holotat."

"A Holo-what?"

"Holotat."

Payne scrunched his face. "What the hell is a Holotat?"

Jones, a graduate of the Air Force Academy, grinned. "I realize you went to an inferior school, but I assume they talked about World War II a few times while you were there."

Payne, who went to the rival academy in Annapolis, ignored the insult. "Go on, flyboy."

"Anyways, you might recall that many of the guards in German concentration camps branded their prisoners with numbers on their wrists in order to keep track of them. After the war ended, the people who survived these camps had a constant reminder of the Holocaust permanently etched into their flesh, marks that eventually became a source of inspiration. It showed the world that their people could overcome anything."

"Yeah, I remember that, but what does that have to do with Ariane?"

"About ten years ago, some members of *Los Muertos*, a Chicano gang from east L.A., decided it would be cool if they marked their homeys in a similar fashion. That way, they would have a constant reminder of their brotherhood everywhere they went. Well, the trend caught on, and Holocaust tattoos, known on the street as Holotats or Jew-toos, started popping up everywhere."

"And you think the P tattoo is a Holotat gang emblem?"

Jones nodded his head. "That's what it looks like to me. Of course, I could be wrong. It could be a jailhouse tat or the initial of his girlfriend's name, but my guess would be a Holotat."

Payne thought the information over, and a query quickly formed in his head. "You said it might be the initial of his girlfriend's name, right? Does that mean we're sure it's a guy?"

"That would be my guess. The thickness of the wrist in the photograph suggests a masculine suspect, but to be on the safe side, I wouldn't completely rule out a female. Of course, she would have to be a Sasquatch-looking bitch."

Payne laughed for the first time in several minutes. He felt better just knowing that D.J. was helping him through this. "So what now?"

"Well, if you have nothing better to do, why don't you come over here? I have a few more tests to run on the video, and I want you to take a look at the tattoo to see if you notice anything that I didn't."

"Sounds good to me. I'll be there in a few minutes."

Actually, it took Payne nearly an hour to reach Mt. Washington, and the drive was a miserable one. Holiday traffic was starting to pick up even though it was only mid-day. Payne used his master key to enter Jones' technology lab, and as he did, he noticed his friend hard at work on the computer.

"So, what's new?"

Jones handed him a printed copy of the tattoo and waited for him to study it. When he was done, D.J. filled him in on the latest development. "Since there wasn't a lot of visual stuff on the tape, I figured I should turn my attention to the sound. I know it's hard to believe, but sound can tell you so much."

"You mean like her scream?"

"No, I mean like background noise. You know, stuff that's

there but isn't really obvious to the naked ear."

Payne was familiar with the concept but wasn't sure how it could help. "Maybe you better show me."

Jones walked to the far side of the room and tapped his hand on a machine that resembled a small filing cabinet. "I call this device the Listener, and for the last half-hour, it's been our best friend."

Payne crossed the room for a closer look and watched as Jones typed a specific code into the unit's keypad. The Listener responded by extending its front tray six inches forward.

"This is where you slide in the tape, and as you can see, this morning's video is already in there." Jones pressed a few more digits on the keypad, and the front tray slowly disappeared into the depths of the circuitry. After hitting a few more keys, the Listener began to hum softly while data flashed on an adjoining screen. "This unit was designed to analyze sound and place it into specific categories. For instance, if we were to record our conversation, then put a tape of it into the machine, the Listener would easily be able to tell us that two separate people were talking."

"Wow," Payne remarked facetiously. "Couldn't a four-year-old do the same thing?"

Jones ignored the sarcasm. "In addition to our voices, it would also be able to analyze white noise, the hums and buzzes that people tend to overlook in day-to-day life."

"And how the hell could that be important?"

"It could tell us the type of equipment that was running in a room, the size of the room itself, the type of security system, the location of heating and cooling vents, the name of . . ."

"Wait a second," Payne demanded. "How is that possible?"

"Oh, I see how you are. A minute ago you were mocking me, now you want me to fill you in on how this works? Give me one good reason why I should."

"Because I paid for everything in this damn room."

Jones grinned. “As I was saying, it’s able to provide a pretty extensive auditory picture.”

“OK, let’s go over this one step at a time. I understand the theory behind the machine. It examines sound and let’s you know what it hears, right? But how the hell can it tell me how big a room is? A room doesn’t make noise if it’s just sitting there.”

“If the room is structurally stable, you’re right. It won’t make much noise. But that doesn’t really matter because the Listener takes advantage of something else in order to provide us with a picture: echoes. When something emits a noise, the sound travels in every direction, and when those sound waves hit an object, they bounce, causing them to disperse. If a sound returns toward its original source, an echo can be heard. Well, the Listener picks up these echoes, no matter how faint they are, and uses them to determine dimensions.”

“You’ve gotta be shittin’ me.”

“Not at all. As a matter of fact, the same basic concept is used in medicine all the time. For instance, an echocardiogram, better known as an EKG, is a picture of the heart that’s been formed by using the echo of high-frequency sound. The Listener does the same thing but on a bigger scale.”

Payne smiled. The technology in Jones’ room was amazing. “OK, I’ll take your word on it. Your machine can probably do everything that you claim, but how can it help us with Ariane?”

Jones took a seat in front of the computer and asked Payne to do the same. “Since we don’t need to know about the size of the room, I had the machine concentrate on a couple of things in particular. The first thing was Ariane’s voice. I wanted to see if I could understand what she tried to say after her initial scream.”

“You mean when her voice got garbled.”

“Yeah. My guess is they were probably gagging her at the time, but I was hoping the machine might be able to isolate the sound in a format that we could understand.”

“Did it work?”

"Actually, it worked beautifully. Unfortunately, it won't help our cause too much."

"Why not? What did she say?"

Jones picked up the transcript and read it aloud. "She said, 'Help me. Somebody help me.' "

Payne closed his eyes as Ariane's words sank in. He'd managed to stay relaxed while Jones explained the features of his computer equipment, but now that the focus of the conversation was back on Ariane, Payne felt the nausea return to his gut.

What would he do if he couldn't track her down? Or worse yet, if these bastards had already killed her? The thought of her death made him want to vomit.

"Jon?" D.J. called. "Are you OK? I asked you a question."

Payne opened his eyes and turned to his friend. "Sorry. What was that?"

"I wanted to know if you told the cops how many people were involved."

He thought for a moment, then shook his head. "I told them that Mr. McNally saw more than one person, but wasn't sure how many."

"Well, thanks to the Listener, I'd say that there were probably three of them."

Payne sat up in his chair. This machine was getting more and more impressive. "How did you figure that out?"

"Simple. I programmed the device to listen for footsteps when the door was opened, and after listening to the tape, I could hear three distinct sets of steps. But, as they were leaving, I could only hear two."

"You mean someone stayed inside Ariane's apartment?"

Jones shook his head. "At first, that's what I thought, too, but as I listened to the tape again, I noticed a scratching noise in the background. I filtered out all the other sounds, isolating the scratch, and this is what I got." He pushed his mouse button once, and a rough grating sound quickly emerged from his system's speakers. "What does that sound like to you?"

"Is that feet dragging on a carpet?"

"Bingo!" Jones was impressed that his friend had figured it out so quickly. It had taken him several minutes to come up with a hypothesis. "Remember what McNally said? It looked like your girlfriend was snookered because they were practically carrying her to the van?"

"Yeah, so?"

"Well, my guess is she was drugged or knocked out. The set of three footsteps that the Listener originally detected were Ariane's and the two assailants. They broke into her place, gagged her, drugged her, then dragged her out. That's the only thing that fits the facts."

"But I thought you said there were three guys involved? Where was the other one while the abduction was going on?" Before Jones had a chance to answer, the solution popped into Payne's head. "Oh, wait! They probably needed a driver to stay outside in the van."

"That's what most criminals would do."

"And you figured all of this out from the audio on the peephole tape?" Jones nodded while trying to conceal his large grin. "God, you were right. Sound can tell you a lot."

Chapter Nine

Payne and Jones gathered all of the information that they had and took it directly to the police. When they entered the local precinct, Payne headed for Captain Arthur Leyland's office. He'd met Leyland a year ago at a charity golf event, and since that time, they had stayed in touch.

"Do you have a minute?" Payne asked as he tapped on Leyland's glass door. The captain, who had a salt-and-pepper mustache that covered most of his upper-lip and a bald spot which started at his eyebrows and extended to the back of his head, waved him in. "By the way, have you ever met David Jones?"

Leyland officially introduced himself, shaking Jones' hand with a powerful grip. "Jon has told me so much about you. I almost feel like we've met. I understand that you served under Jon in special ops."

"Yeah," Jones answered as he took a seat. "We relied on each other so much we ended up attached in the real world as well. But from what I hear, that happens a lot."

"No doubt about it. There's something about life in the military that draws soldiers together—a kindred spirit that bonds all warriors."

Payne winced at the suggestion. "I don't know about that crap. I think D.J. stuck with me so I could get his ass a good-paying job."

Jones quickly nodded. "To be honest, Jon's right. I actually can't stand the bastard."

Leyland laughed loudly. "So, I take it from your comedy that Ariane's all right? Where was that gal hiding?"

The comment drained the humor from the room.

"Don't let our joking fool ya," Jones declared. "It's just our way of dealing with things. The truth is we're still looking for her."

Payne held up his cellular phone, showing it to Leyland. "I'm having all of my calls forwarded to this unit. If she tries to contact any one of my lines, it'll ring here."

"Good, then you won't have to sit at home, killing time."

Payne took a deep breath and nodded. To him, the waiting was the hardest part. "How are things on your end? Did you have a chance to send any officers to her apartment?"

"I sent a crew over. Unfortunately, we didn't notice anything new. You guys did a pretty thorough job this morning."

"I hope we didn't step on any toes by entering the scene."

"Heavens no. I would've done the same thing if a loved one of mine was involved in something like this. Of course, my answer as a police officer would've been different if I didn't know you, but you're professionals so I trust your judgment when it comes to the integrity of a crime scene."

Jones stood from his chair and handed Leyland all of the information from Walker's videotape. "We did get some data on one of the suspects that entered the apartment. He had an elaborate tattoo on the back of his right wrist. Looks like a Holotat to me."

Leyland pulled a close-up of the tattoo from the large stack of papers and studied it. "It could be, but I have to admit very few gangs in Allegheny County use them. They're a lot more common on the West Coast and down south."

"That makes sense," Payne muttered, "since this person's probably from Louisiana."

Leyland furrowed his brow. "I'm not so sure of that, Jon. If I were a criminal, I wouldn't use my own van as a getaway vehicle. And if I did, you can bet I wouldn't use my own license plate. I'd bet there's a good chance we're going to get a report of a stolen plate or an abandoned black van somewhere in the area. And when we do, we can go from there."

That wasn't what Payne wanted to hear. He was hoping the captain supported his theory on the van's origin, and when he didn't, he felt an unexpected burst of betrayal. "So what are you saying, that these clues are just bullshit? We worked all morning to find this stuff."

"I know you did, Jon, but I'm not going to lie to you. I respect you way too much to do that."

"Good. Don't lie to me. Tell me where we stand. I need to know."

Leyland stroked his mustache while searching for the appropriate words. "In a standard kidnapping, there's very little we can actually do until we get some kind of ransom demand. Sure, we'll continue to search for evidence and witnesses, but without some kind of miraculous break, the odds of us finding her *before* they call are pretty slim."

Jones glanced at his friend and waited to see if he was going to speak, but it was obvious he was done talking for the time being. "Captain? In your opinion, do you think this abduction was done for money?"

Leyland didn't want Payne to feel responsible for the kidnapping, but there was no denying the obvious. "To be honest with you, that would be my guess. Payne Industries is a well-known company, and Jon is generally recognized as one of the wealthiest men in the state. Since Ariane doesn't have a history with drugs or gambling or any other criminal activities, I can think of no other reason for her abduction."

"Thank you for your sincerity," Payne mumbled. Then, to the surprise of the other two men in the room, he stood up and headed for the door. "And if you find anything out, please let me know immediately."

"I will," Leyland promised. "The same goes for you. Give me a call, night or day."

Jones shook the captain's hand, then hustled after Payne, finally catching up to him in the parking lot. "Jon, what's going on? First you snapped at the man, then you bolted from his office without even saying good-bye. Now, when I look at your face, I can tell you're planning to do something drastic. What the hell do you have in mind?"

Payne shrugged. "I'm not really sure, but I'm not going to sit at home, waiting for some ransom demand."

"I kind of assumed that. You aren't exactly the sit-on-your-ass type."

He nodded as he pondered what to do next. Even though he valued Captain Leyland's advice, there was something about his opinion that bothered him. He couldn't place his finger on it, but he knew he didn't agree with Leyland's assessment of the black van.

While thinking things through, Payne pulled from the crowded police lot and turned onto a busy side street. He maneuvered his vehicle in and out of traffic until he got to McKnight Road, one of the busiest business districts in the area. After pulling up to a red light, Payne reached across Jones' lap and pulled out a small book from the Navigator's glove compartment.

"What's that?" Jones asked.

"It's my address book. I'm checking to see if I know anyone from Louisiana. I figured maybe a local would know something about the Holotat. You don't know anyone from down there, do you?"

"Sorry. My roots are up north, just like yours. How about you?"

"None that I can think of." The light turned green, and as it did, the word *green* clicked in Payne's mind. "I'll be damned," he said aloud. "I just thought of someone from New Orleans."

"Who?" Jones asked with a touch of skepticism.

"Did I ever introduce you to a guy by the name of Levon Greene?"

Jones' eyes lit up with excitement. Levon Greene was an All-Pro linebacker for the Buffalo Bills before a devastating knee injury knocked him from the NFL. Before getting chop-blocked by Nate Barker, a guard with the San Diego Chargers, Greene was a fan favorite, known throughout the country for his tenacity and his colorful nickname, which was taken from a famous Bob Marley song. "The Buffalo Soldier? You know the Buffalo Soldier?"

Payne nodded. "He lived in Pittsburgh for a year or two after the Bills cut him. The Steelers signed him and kept him on their injured list for over a season. During that time, our paths crossed on more than one occasion on the b-ball courts. He liked to play hoops for therapy."

"But that doesn't mean you *know* him. I see Steelers and Pirates all of the time, but that doesn't mean they're my boys."

"True, but I know Levon." He handed Jones the address book and told him to look for the phone number. Jones quickly flipped to the Gs and was stunned when he saw Greene listed.

"Holy shit. You do know him."

"I told you I knew him. What's Levon's home number?"

Jones glanced at the page for the requested information. "You don't have a home number. You only have a cellular listing."

"Yeah, that makes sense. When he gave me his number, he was getting ready to move back to New Orleans, and since he didn't know his new number yet, he gave me his cellular."

"He was moving to Louisiana, and he gave you his number? What, were you guys dating or something?"

Payne playfully slapped his friend on the arm. "You know I would never do that to you. You're my one and only man."

Jones shook his head and grinned. He'd always been amazed at Payne's ability to keep his sense of humor in the most tragic of times. Sure, his buddy would occasionally flare-up and reveal his true emotions during a crisis, but on the whole, Payne was able to conceal his personal feelings under a facade of levity.

Originally, when the two were first introduced, Jones had interpreted Payne's frivolity as a lack of seriousness, and he actually resented him for it. After a while, though, he learned that Payne's sense of humor was simply his way of dealing with things. He realized that Payne never mocked the tragedy of a situation. Instead, he tried to use humor as a way of coping with the fear and adrenaline that would otherwise overwhelm him. It was a good trick, and eventually Jones and the rest of the MANIACs learned to do the same thing. In fact, they were known for it.

"Seriously, Jon, what's the deal with you two? Have you known him long?"

"I met him playing basketball in North Park. We were on the same team, and the two of us just clicked on the court. He was still rehabbing his knee so he couldn't move like he used to on the football field, but he was a strong mother. He set some of the most vicious screens I ever saw in my life, and most of the time he did it to get me open jumpers."

Jones laughed at Greene's description. "It sounds like Levon plays hoops with the same intensity he displayed in the NFL."

"Oh god, yeah. Even though we were in the park, he had a serious game face on. In fact, some people were afraid to play against the guy."

"I bet, but that still doesn't explain why he gave you his number."

"We ended up making it a daily thing. We'd meet at the courts at the same time every day, and we'd take on all comers. Kicked some serious ass, too. Unfortunately, right before Steelers' camp started, he failed his physical and was released from the team. He told me, though, if I was ever in New Orleans I should give him a buzz."

"Wow, I must admit I'm kind of surprised. I thought I knew about most of your friends, and now I find out you've been keeping a celebrity from me. . . . So, are there any movie-star chums that I should know about?"

"Did I ever tell you about my three-way with Cameron Diaz and Heather Graham?"

Jones laughed at the comment. "So, what are you going to do with Levon?"

"It's not what I'm going to do. It's what you're going to do. While I'm driving, I want you to punch in his number for me."

"You want me to call Levon Greene? This is so cool." Jones punched the digits into the phone, then looked at Payne when it started to ring. "What should I say to him?"

Payne snatched the phone from Jones' grasp and put it to his own ear. "I don't want you to say anything. He's my boyfriend, not yours."

Jones looked offended, then playfully mumbled the word *bitch* under his breath.

As Payne laughed, Greene answered the phone on the fourth ring. "Who's dis?"

"Levon, I don't know if you'll remember me. My name is Jonathon Payne. I used to run ball with you at North Park when you were living up in Pittsburgh."

"White dude, nice jump shot?"

"Yeah, that's me."

"Yo, man, wazzup? I haven't heard from yo' ass in a long time. How ya doin'?"

"I'm fine, and you? How's the knee?"

Greene winced. It was one topic that he didn't like dwelling on. "It's still not a hundred percent, but it's better than it used to be. I'm still hoping some team needs a run-stuffing linebacker and gives me a look in camp. But I don't know. It's getting kind of late."

"Well, they'd be crazy not to take you, Levon. You're as fierce as they come."

"Thanks, man. I appreciate it. So, wazzup? Why the call out of the blue? Are you coming to New Orleans or something? I got a big-ass house. I can hook you up with a room. Won't charge you much, neither," he joked.

Payne wasn't sure what he was hoping to find out from Greene, but he figured the only way to learn anything was to be upfront with the man. "Actually, Levon, the reason I'm calling is an important one. You know how I told you I was doing fine?"

"Yeah?"

"Well, I lied. Something's going on up here, and I was hoping that you could give me a hand."

"I don't loan people money, man. You're gonna have to ask someone else."

Payne grinned. If Greene only knew how much money Payne actually had, he might be asking him for loan. "No, it's not about cash. Nothing like that. I promise."

"What is it then? What's the deal?"

Payne exhaled, trying not to think about Ariane. "I was trying to get some information about a gang that might be operating in Louisiana, and I figured since you play a lot of street ball, you might be able to find something out on the courts."

"Is that all you need? Shit. No problem, man. What's the name of the crew?"

"Actually, that's what I was hoping you could tell me."

"All right, but you gotta give me somethin' to go on 'cause there's a lot of motherfuckin' gangs down here, and every day a new crew pops up."

"Damn," Payne mumbled. He was naively hoping that New Orleans was a one-gang town. "Well, do any of the gangs in Louisiana have Holotats? You know, tattooed gang emblems?"

"Hell, yeah. A lot of the crews do. Just tell me what the Jew-too looks like, and I'll let you know what I know."

"Shaped like the letter P with a bloody knife sticking out of it."

Greene thought about the information for a full minute, then responded. "Off the top of my head, there's nothing that I can tell you, but I'll tell ya what. If you give me some time, I can ask around, and if anything turns up, I'll let you know immediately."

"That sounds great," Payne replied. "And I'd really appreciate anything you can come up with. It's a matter of life or death." Payne gave Greene his telephone number and, once again, stressed the importance of the information.

"Give me an hour, and I'll give you a buzz. I know a couple of brothers that know about this type of shit. Let me get ahold of them, then I'll get ahold of you."

"Levon, thank you. I'll be anxiously awaiting your call."

Jones, who'd been listening to the conversation, questioned Payne the minute he hung up. "So, he's going to help out?"

"He's going to try."

"And what if he does? If he tells you that this mysterious gang operates out of New Orleans, what are you going to do?"

Payne smiled as he put his hand on Jones' shoulder. "How does Fourth of July in Louisiana sound to you?"

Chapter Ten

The Kotto Distribution Center
Ibadan, Nigeria
(56 miles northeast of Lagos)

Most aspects of the sprawling complex were completely legitimate. Hundreds of Nigerian-born workers came to the Center each day to unload massive shipments of cacao, palm oil, peanuts, and rubber that had been brought in from Hannibal Kotto's various businesses. Because of these ventures and the numerous employment opportunities that he offered to the people of Africa, Kotto's name was known and respected throughout his homeland and in several other parts of the Dark Continent.

And it was that respect that allowed him to take advantage of the system.

As he sat behind his mahogany desk, Kotto waited for his assistant to give the go-ahead to start the conference call. When the female finally nodded, Kotto knew that everybody was ready to begin.

"Gentlemen," he said into the speakerphone. "I realize that English is not the strongest language for all of you, but since I'm trying to deal with a number of clients at once, I feel it is probably the most appropriate selection." Kotto took a sip of

Oyo wine, a local beverage that was made from the sap of palm trees, then continued. "In order to give everybody a sense of who you'll be bidding against, I'd like each of you to name the country that you're here to represent. Each of you has been assigned an auction number, and these numerals place you in a very specific order. When your number is called, please tell the group where you are from."

As Kotto's assistant read the numbers aloud, heavily-accented voices slowly emerged from the speakerphone, each announcing his country of origin. Algeria, Angola, Cameroon, Ethiopia, Kenya, Libya, Namibia, and Zaire were all represented.

"If you were listening," Kotto stated, "I'm sure each of you realize that Africa is the only continent that Mr. Drake and I are currently dealing with. We've had several offers from Asia and South America as well, but we're not ready to deal with their politics. At least, not yet."

"When do you expect to broaden the operation?" asked the delegate from Cameroon.

"That's a decision that we haven't made. If all continues to go well, and I am quite certain that it will, then there's the possibility of expansion within the next few months."

Kotto took another sip of wine while waiting for further questions. When none came, he changed the course of the discussion. "I realize that some of you were disappointed with the last shipment of snow. Mr. Drake and myself recently discussed that very issue, and I apologize for any problems it might've caused. I would like to assure you, though, that you'll have no such problems with the next delivery. It is the best snow that we've ever prepared."

The Kenyan spoke next. "What will that do to the price? I imagine we'll have to pay more for the increase in quality, will we not?"

Kotto grinned. He hadn't planned on raising the prices, but if his customers were willing to pay even more, then he would gladly take advantage of their generosity.

* * *

Jones settled into the soft leather seats of Payne's private jet, then closed his eyes for a moment of silent prayer. During his military career, he'd been on dozens of planes on hundreds of life-threatening missions, but this was the first time he'd ever felt hopeless before a flight. For one reason or another, he knew he was completely unprepared for what he was about to do—like a sailor heading to a whorehouse without his dick—and it was a feeling that he didn't like.

When he was a member of the MANIACs, they were always given advanced reconnaissance before they were dropped into enemy territory. Maps, guides, safe houses, and specific objectives were always provided before they were put into danger. But not today. On this mission, Jones was willing to forget everything that he'd ever been taught about safety and precaution because his best friend needed help. He was flying to a city that he'd never visited, to look for a girl that probably wasn't there, and the only thing that he had to go on was a tattoo of the letter P.

"This is crazy," he said to himself.

As he opened his eyes, he saw Payne hang up the phone at the front of the cabin, then make his way towards his seat, which was right across the aisle from Jones.

"Hey, pudding, how ya feelin'?"

Jones rolled his eyes in obvious displeasure. "Jon, are you sure that this trip is the wisest thing to do? I mean, don't you think it's a little bit impulsive?"

"Not really. As I told you, Levon talked to some of his boys in the city, and they assured him that the tattoo sounded like a Holotat that was used by one of the local gangs."

"Yeah, but that doesn't guarantee that Ariane's going to be down there. For all we know, the gang could have members in a number of cities, like the Crips or the Bloods. Heck, we could be looking for some local thugs from the Hill District."

"True, but that doesn't really explain the Louisiana license plate, now does it?"

Jones shook his head. He wasn't really sure how to explain that. "But don't you think that this is jumping the gun just a little bit? We have no idea what we're getting ourselves into."

Payne smiled. If he didn't know any better, he would've assumed that his friend was afraid of flying. "What's troubling you, D.J.? We've been to thousands of places that are more dangerous than New Orleans, and I've never seen you act like this before."

"Well, I've never felt like this before," Jones admitted. "I don't know how to explain it, but I can tell we're about to walk into a hornet's nest. And the fact that we weren't allowed to bring any weapons into the airport makes me feel very unprotected."

"I figured you'd feel that way. That's why I just gave Levon another call. Since he has a number of contacts on the street, I assumed that he'd have a couple of gun connections as well."

"Did he?"

"He said he'd see what he could do, but I think that's his way of saying he'll get it done."

"I hope so because I'm damn sure these gangbangers will be packin' some heat."

Payne pretended to be offended. "Why would you say that? The fact that these guys are black doesn't guarantee that they're criminals. In fact, I'm fairly certain that a preponderance of inner-city youths are simply misunderstood, and you, as a representative of the African-American race, should know that more than most."

Jones tried not to smile, but it was a nearly impossible task. There was just something about Payne that made most people laugh. "You're such an asshole," he chuckled. "Where do you come up with this stuff?"

"What stuff?"

"A preponderance of inner-city youths? Give me a break.

That's just a fancy way to say 'most niggers.' "

Payne quickly covered his mouth in mock horror. "I can't believe you just said the N-word. You're lucky the seatbelt sign is on, or I'd come over there and smack some manners into your black ass."

"Why don't you just wait until bedtime so we can consider it foreplay?"

Payne laughed as he tilted his seat into a reclining position. He needed to catch a nap before the plane reached Louisiana. "Thank god I know you're straight. Otherwise, I'd be afraid to fall asleep after a comment like that."

A few hours later, the jet landed on an auxiliary runway at Moisant International Airport in Kenner, Louisiana, which prevented Payne and Jones from dealing with the hassle of the main terminal. After grabbing their bags, they walked off the tarmac and followed a member of the ground crew to the nearest rent-a-car agency, where they picked up the fastest rental available, a Ford Mustang SVT Cobra Convertible.

Since the airport was only 15 miles west of the Crescent City, the drive to New Orleans was a short one. Following Interstate 10 all the way into Orleans Parish (Louisiana uses the term *parish* instead of *county*), Payne followed the directions that Greene had given him and before long they were navigating the streets of the Central Business District. A couple minutes later, they found the Spanish Plaza, the area where they were supposed to meet Greene.

Donated by Spain in 1976 as a Bicentennial gift, the Plaza was one of four foreign squares that paid tribute to the roles that France, Italy, England, and Spain played in the history and culture of New Orleans. The focal point of the site was a manmade geyser, encircled by an elaborate cut-stone deck and illuminated by a rainbow of bright lights that lined the scenic monument.

As Payne and Jones strolled down the Plaza's steps, they saw Greene, wearing a pair of white Dockers and a ice-blue Tommy

Hilfiger shirt, looking even larger than he did during his NFL playing days.

"Levon," Payne shouted to his old acquaintance. "Thanks for meeting me."

Greene, 6' 3" and 275 pounds of muscle, stood from the bench where he'd been resting his knee. "No problem, my man." He wrapped his massive arms around Payne in an enthusiastic hug, forcing the air from his unsuspecting lungs. "You're looking good. You still playin' ball?"

"Not as much as I used to," Payne gasped. "But I manage to work out whenever I can. Of course, I still have a long way to go before I'm a badass like you."

Greene smiled as he turned his attention to Jones. "By the way, my name's Levon Greene. And you are?"

Jones grabbed Greene's hand and shook it with vigor. It was a thrill to meet one of his biggest sports heroes. "I'm David Jones, a friend of Jon's and a big fan of yours."

"Wow, that's always nice to hear, especially since I'm a huge fan of yours as well. I can hardly believe that I'm actually talking to the lead singer of the Monkees."

Payne couldn't help but laugh. He occasionally teased Jones about his name's similarity to Davy Jones, the former lead singer of the Monkees, and it was something that D.J. couldn't stand. Payne had a feeling, though, that the remark would produce a much different reaction coming from Greene.

"Oh, I get it," chuckled Jones as he playfully punched Greene on his rippled biceps. "The Monkees. That's pretty damn funny, Levon. I bet I used to look a lot whiter on TV, huh?"

Greene laughed, then returned his attention to Payne. "So, have you guys eaten yet? There are a number of places in this city where you can get some traditional Louisiana food, like jambalaya or gumbo. Or, if you prefer, we can just head over to the French Quarter for a beer and some naked breasts. Trust me, whatever you want, I can deliver. Just name it and it's yours."

Payne glanced at Jones for a brief second, then back at

Greene. He'd been less than forward with Greene on the phone and decided it was time to give him a few details about their mission. "Levon, I have to tell you something. This isn't going to be a pleasure trip. We're down here for one reason and one reason only: to find out about your local gangs."

Greene grimaced, then asked the question that had never been satisfactorily answered. "Man, what is it about this damn tattoo that'd bring you guys all the way down here? What could possibly be so important?"

Jones noticed the look of anguish on Payne's face so he decided to answer the question for him. "Early this morning Jon's girlfriend was kidnapped from her apartment building. On the surveillance tape, we noticed the tattoo that Jon described to you on one of the suspects. In addition, there was a witness that saw his girlfriend thrown into the back of a van that had Louisiana plates. We're down here to try and find her."

Greene's face flushed with embarrassment. "Jesus, Jon, I had no idea. What did the police say?"

"Not much," Jones answered. "They're doing everything they can in Pittsburgh, but until we receive a ransom demand or find some conclusive evidence about the gang, they aren't able to do too much."

"So, you guys are here to investigate? What are you planning to do?"

With passion in his eyes and a lump in his throat, Payne finally rejoined the conversation. "Whatever it takes."

Chapter Eleven

Because of his size, Greene claimed the shotgun seat of the cramped Mustang, forcing Jones to sit in the back. Normally Jones would've bitched and moaned about losing his front-seat status, but since Greene would've needed the flexibility of a Russian gymnast to contort his 275-pound frame into the back seat, Jones didn't mutter a single complaint.

After getting into the car, Greene was the first to speak. "I was able to purchase the artillery that you guys wanted, but it cost me a pretty penny. If you want, we can pick it up now."

Payne agreed, and Greene directed him to the nearby parking garage where his black BMW 750iL was parked. The car was equipped with a 323-horsepower 5.4-liter V-12 engine, limousine-tinted windows, and enough speakers and sub-woofers to register a 3.0 on the Richter scale.

"This here is my pride and joy," Greene exclaimed. "It was the last extravagant gift I bought myself before my injury. Ain't she sweet?"

"She's a nice ride, and it certainly looks like you take care of her."

Greene nodded as he opened his trunk. "My father always used to tell me, 'If you take care of your car, your car will take care of you.' "

Jones slid up next to the ex-linebacker and glanced inside the spacious cargo hold. "My god, your trunk's bigger than the seat you're making me ride around in."

Payne rolled his eyes as he dismissed D.J.'s remark. "What did you get for us, big man?"

"You said you needed some reliable handguns so I picked you up a couple of Glocks. I didn't know what model you'd prefer so I got a 19 and a 27. The 19 uses standard 9 mm ammo, which many people like. Personally, I prefer the 27. In fact, it's the kind I carry for protection. It's chambered in .40 Smith & Wesson, which I think is ballistically better than the 9 mm."

Payne smiled his approval as he picked up the charcoal-gray 27 from Greene's trunk. The ridged polymer handle fit snugly into his experienced hand, and as he held it up to the overhead lights, he stared at the gun with the wide-eyed fascination of a kid with a new Christmas toy. "You made a nice choice. No external safeties to worry about. It's light, dependable. Perfect."

"I guess that means I'm stuck with the 19, huh?" Jones didn't have a problem with the weapon, but after riding in the cramped back seat, he was in the mood to complain about something. "Did you get us anything else?"

Greene leaned into the trunk and pulled out a large maroon suitcase. As he fiddled with the case's combination lock, he spoke. "You told me that money wasn't an object, and that you needed a couple of weapons with serious fire-power, right? Well, I hope this is what you had in mind." Greene opened the case, revealing a Heckler & Koch MP5K submachine gun and a Steyr AUG assault rifle.

Jones reacted quickly, grabbing the MP5K before Payne could get his hands on it. "My, my, my. What do we have here?" Jones admired it while Payne swore under his breath in jealousy. "German-made, three-round burst capability, 900 rounds a minute. A nice piece of hardware."

"That's not all," Greene declared. "I picked up the optional silencer as well."

"Great," Payne hissed. "Now you can kill a librarian without disturbing any readers."

"Is he always this envious of you?" Greene wondered, noticing the tone of Payne's voice.

Jones laughed. "His sexual inadequacies have led to his jealous nature."

Greene fought a smile as he attempted to appease Payne. "Jon, this Steyr AUG is one of the best assault rifles on the market. It has an interchangeable barrel so you can use it accurately from a distance like a sniper or up close like a banger. And the 5.56 × 45 mm cartridge can be bought in Wal-Mart for god's sake. It's very versatile."

Payne picked up the rifle and attached the scope with the skill of a soldier. Once it was in place, he held the eyepiece to his face and put a fire alarm across the garage in his site. He held the weapon steady, sucked in a deep breath, then paused. "Bang," he mouthed before dropping the AUG to his side. "You're right. This is a fine choice, and all the weapons appear to be in pretty good shape. What did the purchase run you?"

Greene pulled a handwritten invoice out of his pocket and gave it to Payne.

"Wow, I didn't think this stuff would cost so much, but I guess when you buy off the street, they can set their own prices." He tucked the sheet away and smiled. "What kind of a dealer writes out receipts, Levon? Does he have a return policy if we're not completely happy with our instruments of destruction?"

"Actually, I wrote the stuff down so I wouldn't forget 'em. I'm not that strong with numbers."

"Me, neither," Payne admitted. "That's why I try to avoid them at work."

"Oh, yeah? What do you do for a living?"

"I'm the CEO of my own multinational conglomeration."

Greene laughed in a disbelieving tone. "OK, whatever. If you don't want to tell me, that's fine. Besides, I'm too hungry to worry about it. Let's pack this stuff up and get out of here."

Jones nodded. "Sounds good to me. Should we take one car or two?"

"Two," Payne declared. "To be honest, I'm not really comfortable asking Levon to tag along. It's one thing to ask him for directions and a place to stay, but it's entirely different to put his life in danger for two guys he barely knows."

"Yeah, you're probably right," Jones agreed. "Things could get a little bit nasty if we meet up with the wrong people."

"Come on, D.J., let's put our stuff in the back of the Mustang, then we can follow Levon out of here."

Jones nodded, then walked towards the bright-yellow car with a handful of weapons.

"Hold up a fuckin' minute," Greene roared. "I can't believe you guys had an entire conversation about me and didn't even bother to ask my opinion about anything. What kind of Yankee bullshit is that?"

"Yankee bullshit?" Payne muttered. "I don't remember talking about baseball."

"I don't think you did. He must've misheard you. The acoustics down here aren't that great."

"Damn! Would you guys shut the hell up before I'm forced to use a Glock on your ass?" Greene shook his head in disgust as he walked towards Payne and Jones. "Listen, I realize I don't know you guys very well, but I'll be honest with you. This shit intrigues me. When I was still playing ball, I used to live for the adrenaline rush that I got on game day. The crowd calling my name, the speakers blasting my Bob Marley theme song, the feel of a quarterback sack. Man, those were the days."

Greene's eyes glazed slightly as he thought back to his All-Pro seasons with the Bills. "Unfortunately, that shit has changed. Since that faggot Nate Barker blew out my knee, I haven't been able to get too excited about anything. I've done my best to rehab and run and lift, but the truth is my career is probably done."

"So, what are you saying?" Payne asked.

"For the first time in almost three years, I can feel the adrenaline pumping again. When you called and told me to get enough weapons to overthrow a small Asian country, I nearly got a boner. Then, when you told me the reason for your visit, I got even more excited—an excitement I haven't felt in a long time. . . . In other words, if you don't mind, I'd like to come along for the ride. I'd like to help you find your girlfriend."

Payne turned towards Jones and grinned. He was hoping Greene was going to offer his services. "I don't know, man. I just don't know. D.J., what do you think?"

"Well, a New Orleans native with street connections might come in handy. And his nickname is the Buffalo Soldier after all."

"Yeah, that's true. I guess it'd be different if they called him the Pittsburgh Pussy or the Boston Bitch, but the Buffalo Soldier does have a certain military feel to it." Payne smiled and shook Greene's hand. "OK, Levon, you're on. But if at any point you feel like we're leading you somewhere you don't want to go, you just say the word and we'll understand."

Jones nodded his head. "Yeah, there's no sense getting killed in a fight where you have nothing to gain."

"Sounds pretty fair to me," Greene admitted. "But before we begin, I need to ask you guys for one small favor."

"You got it," Payne said. "Just name it, and it's done."

"Well, since there's a good chance that you might die on this trip, I was hoping you could pay me for the guns before you got killed."

Chapter Twelve

Robert Edwards laid on the dirt floor of the small cabin, trying to hold back his tears. He had never felt more exhausted in his entire life, yet the waves of agony that engulfed his body hindered his efforts to slip into a painless sleep.

His face was still scarred and scabbed from his unsuccessful escape attempt through the Colorado woods on Thursday morning. The flesh on his back was sunburned and slashed from the numerous whippings he had received in the field as punishment for alleged misbehavior. His hands were sore from pulling weeds, and his arms ached from crawling through the Plantation's untilled soil. But all of that paled in comparison to the unspeakable pain that he felt in his injured left leg.

The swelling in Edwards' foot and ankle was so severe that his limb no longer looked like a normal appendage, but instead appeared to be a severe birth defect or some kind of laboratory mutation. The bloated and deformed leg had turned such a deep shade of purple that its hue bordered on black instead of the peach color of his uninjured limb. Plus, enough blood had pooled in his lower leg that the subsequent pressure was cutting off his foot's circulation. His toes were ice-cold, and his foot tingled as if it were on the verge of falling asleep.

Edwards knew that something needed to be done, but his limited knowledge of first-aid was not advanced enough to deal with the severity of his injury. Without ice or an analgesic to reduce the pain and swelling, Edwards did the only thing that he could. He elevated his leg by resting it on the cabin's lone bench.

As he closed his eyes, trying to get the rest that his body required, he heard the rattling of the cabin's lock. He turned his head and watched the door inch open, then stared with unblinking eyes until he recognized the shadow that slid into the room. It was Master Holmes, and he was holding a sledge hammer in his tight grasp.

"What's that for?" Edwards cried, fearing the worst. "I've done everything you've asked of me. I haven't caused any problems."

"That's not what I've heard," Holmes growled. "My guards assured me that you were lagging behind in the field, you needed assistance on more than one occasion, and you objected to being beaten. Those sound like serious problems to me."

"I swear I was doing my best," he sobbed. "The pain in my leg was unbearable and it slowed me down at times, but I never quit. I never gave up. I swear to god I did everything that I could. Please don't hit me again, I swear I'll get better. Oh god, I swear."

Holmes considered Edwards' plea, then shrugged as he moved closer. "But I don't see *how* you can get better. You claim you were doing your best today, but my guards told me that your efforts weren't good enough. Now, you claim you're going to get better, but if you were already doing your best, I don't see how you could possibly improve."

Edwards tried to sit up, but he was unable to budge his elevated leg. "I promise I'll get better. If you could just give me a pain killer, then I wouldn't be nearly as hampered. I could crawl faster. I could work better. I'd be more efficient. I just need something for the pain."

The plantation master shook his head and sneered. "It's always something with you, Edwards. This morning you were complaining to the guards. Now you're claiming you can do anything if we get you some drugs. Well, as far as your pain goes, I don't give a fuck. Pain is something that everyone must deal with in life, and those that deal with it the best will succeed the most. Obviously you're one of those people that can't cope."

"I can, Master Holmes. I swear. I swear I can cope with the pain."

Holmes grinned as he tightened the grip on the wooden handle. "All right," he sneered as he lifted the sledgehammer into the air. "Let's see if you can deal with this!!"

Screaming like a medieval warrior, Holmes shifted his weight forward and swung the mallet's iron head with the dexterity of Thor. Edwards raised his hands and tried to deflect the blow, but his reflexes were too slow and Holmes' efforts were too determined. The hammer smashed into the bridge of Edwards' nose, splintering the delicate bones of his face with the sheer force of the weapon's fury. It continued downward, stopping for nothing until the cold steel collided with the floor's blood-soaked dirt.

"Can you handle that?" Holmes mocked. "Or do you need some Tylenol for the pain?"

Gasping for air, Edwards opened his eyes and lifted his head from the floor with a terrified shriek. He quickly gazed around the room, searching for Holmes with every ounce of energy that he could muster, but the powerful man was nowhere to be found. The tiny cabin was empty, except for the sound of a feminine voice that begged him to lie down.

"Honey," Tonya Edwards pleaded as she stroked her husband's damp hair. "You were just dreaming. It was just a bad dream."

Robert tried to catch his breath as he glanced at his wife's angelic face, but the image of Holmes' hammer still lingered in his mind. The dream had been so intense, so real, that his entire body was dripping with perspiration and his heart was pounding with urgency.

"Shhh," she begged, "just let me take care of you."

It took a moment to settle down, but Robert finally did as

she requested. He eased his weary head to the cabin's floor, then stared into Tonya's dark eyes, searching for answers. "How did you get in here? How did you find me?"

Tonya continued to stroke her husband's hair, doing everything in her power to calm him. "You collapsed when the guards brought you back from the field, and they didn't want you to die. They brought me in here to tend to you, and I've been waiting for you to wake up ever since."

Robert's eyes filled with tears as he tried to make sense of it all. The abduction, the brutality, the labor. What had he done to deserve this? He had never lived the life of a saint, but he'd never done anything to warrant this. He had never killed, robbed, or raped anyone. In fact, he had never purposely hurt a single soul in his entire life. And what about his wife? Why was she here? She was pregnant for god's sake. What could she have possibly done to merit her imprisonment on the Plantation?

"Sweety, did you hear me?" Tonya sobbed. "Can you hear what I'm saying?"

Robert did his best to focus on her lips, but he had no idea what she had just said. "How did you get in here?" he repeated, not remembering his earlier question.

She swallowed deeply, trying to stay strong for him. "The guards brought me in to take care of you. They want me to try and fix your leg."

"But you're not a doctor."

Tonya smiled, and the small movement of her lips temporarily lifted his spirits. "I know I'm not a doctor, but I'm the only person who's allowed to help. The guards told me what needed to be done, but I didn't want to do it until you woke up. I wanted to get your approval first."

"My approval?" Robert didn't like the sound of that. If it was a simple medical procedure like putting on a bandage, Tonya would've done it while he was asleep. "What exactly do you have in mind?"

Tonya clambered to her feet—a difficult task because of her pregnancy—and waddled to the bench where her husband was currently elevating his leg. Carefully, she sat next to his swollen limb, trying not to jostle the bench with her body weight. Then, with the tenderness of a new mother, she placed her left hand on his injured ankle.

"Robert, the guard told me two things. First of all, he said you have a displaced fracture. He said what that means is that your bone has been broken and the pieces shifted away from each other."

"And how could the guard tell that? Is he a doctor?"

His wife shook her head as she pointed to his leg. "No, he's not a doctor, but if you look right here, it's kind of obvious." Tonya took a deep breath before she was able to continue. "Your leg's pointing straight ahead, but your foot is turned about 150 degrees to the right."

Robert didn't need to look at his injury. The severity of his pain let him know that something was seriously wrong. "What are you supposed to do to fix it?"

Tonya gulped before answering. "Well, the guard told me if you want the bone to heal properly, I need to, ah, straighten things out for you."

He was going to ask how she was going to do that, but he knew the answer: She had to twist his foot until everything was aligned in his leg. "Dear Lord. . . . Do you trust his advice?"

She nodded. "Remember when I slipped on the ice and broke my finger two years ago? The first thing that the doctor had to do was to pop it back into place. That way, it was able to grow back together." She bent her right index finger back and forth in front of her husband's face. "And see? It turned out just fine."

Robert agreed with her logic. If he wanted the ability to walk without a limp, he knew that something needed to be done immediately. "Do you think you can handle this? I know how squeamish you can be."

"Yeah, I can handle it. If I'm doing it for you, I can handle anything."

He smiled. Despite the unpleasant circumstances, it was a nice sentiment to hear from his wife. "I want you to promise me something, though. When you do this, do it quick like a Band-Aid. Just make one decisive move and get it over with, OK?"

"You got it." Tonya stared from the bench, wanting to say something to her husband, but the appropriate words escaped her. "Are you ready?"

"Not really," he laughed through gritted teeth. "But I have a feeling I could never be ready."

She grinned, admiring his courageous sense of humor. "I think this will be easier if we did it on the flat ground. That way, I'll be able to anchor your upper leg with my body weight."

Robert closed his eyes as his wife lifted his swollen limb off of the bench and lowered it to the cabin's dirt floor. He winced as she placed it on the hard ground, but the pain wasn't nearly as bad as he had expected. "So far, so good."

Tonya leaned forward and gently kissed her husband on his forehead. After whispering soft words of encouragement, she turned away from him, placing her posterior on his left knee, anchoring his upper leg in place. Without pausing to contemplate the act that she was about to perform, she tilted toward his broken limb and grabbed his foot in her sweaty palms. Then, with a quick burst, she rotated his foot to the left. The violent twist filled the cabin with a series of sounds—first the grotesque snap of his leg as his bones shifted back into place, then the heart-stopping shriek of a man in agony, a horrific wail that seemed to last forever.

As his screaming continued, Tonya desperately wanted to face the man she loved and comfort him, but she could tell from the intensity of his writhing that her job as an anchor wasn't quite over. She was afraid if she moved her body even an inch, he might shift his leg just enough to jostle the bones out of alignment, and that was something that she just couldn't risk. There was no way that she wanted to put her husband through that type of pain again.

It took several minutes, but Tonya remained on her husband's leg until he stopped writhing. Then, before climbing off, she warned him to stay motionless until she had time to put a splint on the leg. "But before I do that," she stated. "There's something else that I need to do."

Robert groaned as he tried to recover from the last bit of treatment. "And what's that?"

"The guard told me that your swelling is so severe that it needs to be drained or it will never heal properly."

"That's what I was trying to do. I had my leg elevated to drain the blood from my ankle."

Tonya closed her eyes and shook her head in response. As she did, her face turned ghostly pale. "That's not what he had in mind. There's something else that I need to do."

The look on his wife's face told him all that he needed to know. If there was one thing that made her squeamish, it was the sight of blood, and if she was going to see blood while draining his leg, that could mean only one thing. "What are you going to cut my leg with?"

She struggled to her feet and retrieved a towel that was sitting by the door. As she returned to her husband, she removed a single silver instrument from the folds of the rough fabric.

"They gave me a utility blade to make the incision."

Robert swallowed hard as he contemplated his next question. "And where is this incision going to be exactly?"

She stared at her husband. "Actually, the guard didn't know."

"What?"

"He isn't a doctor, so he didn't know. He assured me, though, that it needed to be done."

"And if he isn't a doctor, how come he's so damn sure?"

"He's a soldier, and he knew medics that had done this in

the field. Unfortunately, he never watched the procedure because he was always preoccupied with other things."

"But I thought swelling was good for an injury? Isn't that the body's way to help it heal?"

Tonya shook her head. "I guess when the swelling is as severe as yours, the pressure can actually hurt more than it helps."

"And the guard told you this? One of the bastards that did this to me in the first place."

"Listen, if you don't want me to do it, I won't. As I said, that's why I waited until you were awake before I did anything."

He closed his eyes as he thought about the dilemma. On one hand, his injury would've never occurred if it wasn't for the members of the Plantation's staff. On the other hand, he remembered Master Holmes demanding treatment for the man who had his finger removed—and Holmes seemed sincere about it. For some reason, he wanted to hurt the prisoners but didn't want them to die.

"Fine," he finally relented. "If you think you can handle it, I'm willing to give it a shot. But if you think you're going to pass out in the middle of things, then it's not worth it."

"No," she muttered. "I can do it."

"Are you sure? Because if you pass out, I'll be bleeding all over the place with no one to help me."

She stared into her husband's eyes and smiled. "Like I said, I can do anything for you."

He grabbed her hand and kissed it softly. He knew how difficult this was going to be for her, and he appreciated the fact that she was willing to do it. It showed how much she cared.

"How do you want to do this?"

"Why don't you sit on the bench? That way you can hang your foot and ankle over the edge of the wood."

"And where are you going to make the incision?"

She shrugged, searching her husband's face for advice. "It's your leg. Any suggestions?"

He stared at his limb and looked for the area that contained the largest amount of fluid. But it was a tough decision. From his knee down, his leg had the basic shape of a small watermelon—bloated in the middle with swelling that tapering toward his lower-shin and upper-calf. His ankle was more than twice its normal size, puffed and purple, and his foot had the squishy appearance of a water balloon. "How do you feel about making more than one cut?"

"It depends. What did you have in mind?"

Robert leaned forward and touched the three areas that he felt needed help, marking his calf, ankle, and foot. "This way, you can control the flow a lot easier than if you make one big incision. Just start with the calf and squeeze as much fluid out of it as you can. After we stop the bleeding, move down to the ankle and do the same thing. Then, if it's necessary, we can drain my foot as well. Does that sound OK to you?"

The thought of it was already making Tonya nauseous, but she quickly agreed with the plan. "Slide forward a little bit so your leg's on a downward slope."

Robert did as he was told, and Tonya adjusted her position until she was practically underneath the bench.

"Where should I do this first?" she asked nervously.

"Mid-calf, just make sure you don't cut too deep. I don't want you to slice the muscle."

"Don't worry," she joked. "I don't even want to slice the skin."

Robert smirked as he gritted his teeth in anticipation. He knew it wasn't going to be nearly as painful as the straightening of his ankle, but he realized the insertion of a utility knife into his flesh was still going to be an unpleasant experience. "Let's get this over with."

With anxiety on her face, Tonya nodded and inched the cold blade toward her husband's bloated skin. She pressed the tip of the metal instrument against the swollen contour of his shin and waited for an explosion of blood or pus or something, but nothing happened. The knife sunk into his leg like a spoon into firm Jell-O, denting the swelling but unable to break the surface.

"I don't think this knife is sharp enough. They wouldn't trust me with anything shaper."

"It'll work. Just push harder."

After inspecting the blade with her finger, Tonya tried his leg again, shoving the metal tip into his calf with twice as much pressure as before. This time the scalpel pierced the bloated skin with a horrific pop. Blood and plasma immediately oozed from the incision like lava from a volcano, and the sight made Tonya want to vomit. It took a while, but after the stream started to subside, she was able to regain her composure.

"How are you feeling?" she asked her husband as she applied direct pressure to the wound with a clean towel.

"I've been better, but it wasn't as bad as I thought it would be."

"Good," she replied, "because I'm not done playing doctor yet."

"No," he groaned, "we're playing surgeon. If we were playing doctor, I think both of us would be having a lot more fun."

Chapter Thirteen

The last thing on Payne's mind was dinner, but Greene insisted that they stop for something to eat. They had to, he said. His stomach demanded it. As a compromise, Payne pulled into the first drive-thru he could find and ordered several ham 'n' cheese po' boys, a local specialty.

"Where to next?" Payne asked as they waited for their food. "Any ideas?"

Greene thought about it for several seconds. "The first thing we're gonna have to do is talk to some of my boys from the Quarter. They'd be more aware of things on the street than me."

"What kind of things?" Jones wondered.

"Everything. If it happens in the city, they'll know about it. They'll be able to fill you in on the tattoo that you're looking for. Plus, if you're lucky, they might be able to tell you something about the kidnapping. Of course, since that didn't happen down here, details might be limited."

Payne considered Greene's words carefully. "Will your friends be willing to talk to us?"

Greene scrunched his face. "That's something I don't know. Most of the time, they're pretty receptive about helping me out with information, but in your case, I don't know. You've got two things working against you."

"And those are?"

"You're white, and you're from the North. Some people down here don't take kindly to those two things."

Payne nodded. "I can understand that, and I figured as much. But at the same time, I have two things that I think will actually help my cause."

"Such as?" Greene wondered.

"First of all, I have you guys on my side, and since both of you are black, that might help us with some of the bigger racists that we come across."

"That's true, but it might not be enough . . ."

"And secondly," he said as he laid a thick wad of cash on the dashboard. "I'm filthy rich, and I'm willing to spend it all if it helps get Ariane back."

Greene eyed the stack of bills that sat before him. "You know, I have a strange feeling that you'll get along with my boys just fine."

"I had a feeling I would."

"But before we go anywhere, there are still a few ground rules that I'm gonna have to insist upon before we meet with my people."

Payne scooped up his money and nodded. "I'm listening."

"This is my hometown, the place that I've chosen to live for the rest of my life. And because of that, I don't want you doing anything that's gonna hurt me. That means I don't want you roughing up any of my contacts or making me look bad in any way. I have a reputation to uphold, and I don't want it ruined. Got it?"

Payne and Jones willingly agreed.

"And finally, if I'm gonna help you out, you need to promise me one more thing: absolutely no police involvement of any kind."

"Why not?" Jones asked, slightly suspicious.

"The people that we're gonna be dealing with aren't exactly friends of the law, and if word gets out on the street that I'm teaming up with the cops, then my sources will dry up. And trust me, that won't help you find the girl and it won't help me after you've left."

"No cops, no problem," replied Payne, who was willing to agree to just about anything. "Now unless there's something else, can we get this show on the road?"

* * *

After arranging a meeting with his best source, Greene directed his friends through the narrow streets of the *Vieux Carré*, a historic neighborhood that was better known as the French Quarter.

"Some people get pretty confused when they get down here because the term French Quarter is actually misleading. Most of the architecture you see around here is Spanish in design, built in the 18th century. Most of the original French settlement was burned during a rebellion a little more than 200 years ago."

From the back seat, Jones glanced at the buildings and noticed nothing but bars, strip clubs, and T-shirt shops, and none of them looked very old. "Levon? Are you telling me that Spain had nude dancing back in the 1700s?"

Greene turned around and laughed. "If they did, I doubt the conquistadors would have ever left their homeland. . . . No, this is the one part of the French Quarter that has been ruined by modern-day enterprises. If you want to experience the true character of this area, you need to explore the side streets of this neighborhood. That's where you'll find the flavor of the early settlers."

Payne suddenly looked at Greene in a whole new light. He always knew that Greene was intelligent, but he never realized the ex-linebacker had a passion for history. In the past, their playground conversations never got beyond street basketball and life in the NFL. "I have to admit, Levon, I'm kind of surprised. You never seemed to be the type of person who cared about the events of early America. Now, you sound like a freakin' tour guide."

"I'm not sure if that's supposed to be a compliment or not."

"Yes," he assured Greene, "it's a compliment."

"Thanks. I guess ever since I hurt my knee I've had the opportunity to do a lot of things that I wouldn't have done earlier in my career. One of those things is historical research. I've been reading a lot of books on the past, trying to picture what life used to be like down here before the 1900s. As you can imagine, it was a much different place back then."

Payne nodded as they pulled in front of The Fishing Hole, a nightclub that claimed to have the prettiest girls in *Nude* Orleans. The three men walked to the front door and were quickly greeted by a bouncer who recognized Greene. After chatting for a few seconds, the muscular employee allowed the trio to enter the club for free. Payne and Jones followed Greene into the smoke-filled lobby and were immediately taken aback by the first thing they saw: the couch-dance room.

Similar in design to the orgy rooms of the Roman Empire, the suite consisted of ten backless couches in two rows of five that were centered in the middle of a spacious chamber. For a $20 tip, an eager man was led to one of the black leather lounges by the hand of a naked vixen, and during the course of a five-minute song, she would rub, slide, and grind against his fully-clothed body while doing everything she legally could in order to seduce him into buying another dance. And it wasn't a tough sale. Mix horny men with inexpensive alcohol, naked women, and heavy petting, and there's a better chance that a guy will file for bankruptcy before saying no to a beautiful stripper.

While strolling between the couches, Payne and Jones gaped at the erotic scene that unfolded around them while Greene chuckled with child-like delight. "It's kind of hypnotic, isn't it? I always enjoy watching the crowd that stands along the walls. You'll see an awful lot of perverts with their hands in their pockets, if you know what I mean."

Both Payne and Jones knew what he meant, but that didn't mean they wanted to watch it.

"What are we doing here?" Payne eventually asked. "Is it for the scenery, or did we come here to meet somebody in particular?"

"Actually, both. The main guy that I wanted you to speak to is the owner of this club, and since I didn't want you fellas to come to New Orleans without having a chance to experience Bourbon Street, I told him that we would meet him here. I hope that doesn't bother you."

Jones continued to stare at the naked females and energetically shook his head. "Nope, doesn't bother me at all. In fact, I'm tempted to borrow twenty bucks."

Payne grabbed his friend by the arm and pulled him into the hallway. "Come on D.J., get your mind back in the game. If we start to lose focus, we could miss an important clue."

"Sorry," Jones muttered, his face flushed with embarrassment. "The only time I get to see stuff like this is late-night on Cinemax."

Greene led the two northerners through a back corridor, and before long, they were strolling through the dancers' dressing room. Interestingly, none of the naked women were bothered by the three men's appearance.

When they reached the back corner of the room, Greene spoke to the security guard who stood outside of the owner's private office. "Let Terrell know I'm here. He's expecting me."

The guard opened the thick metal door to get authorization from the club's owner but saw that he was currently on the phone.

"It'll be a minute. Mr. Murray is finishing up a call."

Greene nodded then turned his attention to Payne and Jones. It was time to give them some background information. "Terrell Murray is one of the most influential men in New Orleans, even though you'll rarely hear his name mentioned. He tends to stay out of politics and high finance and prefers to deal with the seedier side of the city—strip clubs, prostitution, gambling, and so on. Very few things of an illegal nature get done in Orleans Parish without his permission or knowledge, so there's a good chance that he'll be able to point us in an appropriate direction."

"And I take it you'll do all of the talking?"

"Definitely. Since you're a total stranger, he won't give a shit about you. Thankfully, he's a fan of mine from my playing days, so I'll be able to ask him anything you want. Sound good?"

Payne nodded as they went into Murray's private office.

The well-lit room was immaculately maintained and outfitted with French Neoclassical furniture from the late 1700s—definitely not what Payne and Jones were expecting. Four Louis XVI chairs, possessing the classic straight lines of the period, encircled a rounded wooden table that sat in the middle of the hardwood floor. Gold trim lined the walls, ceilings, and picture frames of the chamber, matching a breathtaking candle chandelier that dangled above the sitting area. The room's artwork was obviously influenced by the Roman Empire, a motif that reflected the French's interest in the designs of the ancient cities of Pompeii and Herculaneum, for a marble bust of Tiberius, the second Emperor of Rome, sat proudly on a pedestal in the far corner.

An elderly black man, dressed in a pale-gray suit and an open collar shirt, stood from his seat behind his Louis XVI desk and greeted his visitors with a warm smile. "Please come in. Make yourself at home."

"Thank you," Payne replied as he soaked in the office's ornate fixtures. "This is a very impressive setup that you have here, sir. It's like a museum."

Murray shook Payne's hand and thanked him for the compliment. "First of all, enough with the formalities. If you're friends of Levon's, there's no need to call me 'sir.' Please, my name is Terrell." Payne nodded in appreciation of his hospitality. "And as far as this room is concerned, antiques are a hobby of mine. I own a number of shops on Royal Street, but I'm afraid I deny my customers the opportunity to buy the best items. I tend to keep them for myself."

"And you've done a wonderful job," Jones added. "You truly have."

"Good, I'm glad you like it." Murray motioned for the men to be seated in the Louis XVI chairs, and he eagerly joined them. "So, Levon, what brings you here on a Friday night to see an old man like me? I know it can't be for companionship because most of my lovely employees would be more than willing to go home with you."

Greene smiled at the thought. "Actually, I'm here to take advantage of your connections. My friends and I are looking for a local gang, and we're hoping you could point us in the right direction."

Murray furrowed his wrinkled brow. "And should I guess the name of the gang, or would you like to supply me with that information?"

"See, that's the thing. We don't know the name. The only thing we know is the design of the gang's Holotat. It's in the shape of the letter P and uses a bloody dagger in the image."

"Yes," Murray replied with the blank face of a gambler. "I know the tattoo that you refer to, and its appearance is a recent one to this city. Unfortunately, I know very little about the men who wear them. I'm sorry I can't help you more."

Without saying a word, Payne pleaded for Greene to continue. He knew that Murray was hiding something, and it was up to Greene to get it out of him. At this point, it was their only hope.

"Terrell, I know that you're trying to stay out of this, but please, I beg of you, make an exception for me. Earlier today, a man with that Holotat abducted Jon's girlfriend. So far there's been no ransom demand and very little police activity. We're afraid if we don't do something quick we may be too late. Please, any lead that you can give us would be appreciated."

Murray considered Greene's plea for several stress-filled seconds. "Above Rampart Street, near St. Louis Cemetery Number 1, there's a small tattoo shop that's operated by Jamaican Sam. He's the most talented skin artist in the city. Go there and talk to him. I bet he's the man who designed the Holotat that you seek."

Chapter Fourteen

Galléon Township Docks
(near Breton Sound)
Galléon, Louisiana

The driver of the Washington Parish ambulance stopped near the narrow dock, then made a three-point turn in the secluded gravel driveway. Once the vehicle pointed away from the Gulf of Mexico, he backed it carefully onto the secluded pier, causing the thick wooden planks to groan under its enormous weight. When he was satisfied with its positioning, he silenced the growling motor with a turn of his key, then stepped into the radiance of the wharf's lone streetlight.

Tension was evident on his face.

While listening to the lapping water, he nervously checked his watch and realized he was several minutes early. To kill time, he pulled a cigarette from the pocket of his EMS uniform and lit it with a single flick from his lighter. After putting out the flame, he took a deep drag of the smoldering cylinder, then blew a billowy puff of smoke into the sticky, nighttime air.

"Man, I needed that."

This would be his last delivery of the month, and for that he was quite thankful. He didn't know why, but he'd grown more and more anxious with each mission that he'd completed for the Plantation. At first, he attributed his feelings to the recent death of his aunt. He assumed her passing caused some sort of subconscious guilt since his duties centered around the shipment of cadavers for medical experiments. But lately, his concerns were slowly beginning to be supported by tangible pieces of evidence: snippets of overheard conversations, copies of phony death certificates, and deliveries that were scheduled for the dead of night.

But that was only part of it. The thing that freaked him out more than anything were the sounds. On more than one occasion, he could've sworn he heard noises coming from the back of his ambulance—loud thumps emerging from the sealed containers, muffled screams leaking from the crates of the dead.

God, the thought of it still made him shudder.

To calm down, he took another deep drag on his cigarette and stared at the warm waters of the Gulf. "Where's their damn boat?" he wondered. "I want to get this over with."

As he continued to wait, he pondered his role as a delivery man, thinking back to the day he was first hired. A well-dressed black man spotted him washing his ambulance and asked him if he was interested in making some extra cash. The man claimed he was operating a private medical center off the coast of Breton Sound and was looking for the quickest way to deliver his research from Lakefront Airport to his new facility. Since EMS vehicles were given special privileges on the roadway, he felt that an ambulance would be the most efficient mode of transportation. Plus, he pointed out, he was looking for someone that would be comfortable around dead bodies and felt a medical worker would be the type of person he was looking for.

"Damn," the driver muttered aloud. "Why did I say yes to him?" Then he smiled as he remembered his reason for accepting the job. "Oh yeah, I almost forgot. Cha-ching." He laughed to himself as he recalled the $200 per trip fee that he'd negotiated for his services. It was money that the IRS and his ex-wife would never learn about—funds to buy a new car or the big-screen TV that he'd always wanted.

Yeah, that's why he did it. The big bucks.

He glanced at his watch again and realized he still had a few minutes until the workers from the Plantation would arrive. If he hurried, he figured he could sneak into the back of his ambulance and secretly investigate the crates that he'd loaded at the airport.

"Why not?"

With quiet determination, he opened the door of the EMS vehicle and climbed into the front seat of the cab. Sliding through the narrow entryway, he crept into the back of the ambulance and grabbed the paperwork that had been attached to the top of the first container. It read:

Walker, Ariane
28 years old
Wexford, PA
July 2nd

"Wow," he mumbled. "She died earlier today. That's pretty quick for someone to be moved across state lines."

He continued to glance through the rest of the documents, hoping to find a cause of death or the reason she was going to be researched, but the sheets were filled with numbers and other data that he was unable to comprehend.

Taking a deep breath, he glanced nervously at his watch and made the reckless decision to push on. After dropping to his knees, he reached under the vehicle's narrow bench and pulled out the crowbar that he sometimes used at accident sites. With the device in his hands, he returned to his feet and immediately searched for an insertion point in the crate. It was then that he noticed the small circular holes that lined the upper and lower rims of the wooden box.

"What the hell are those? Jesus! That looks like ventilation."

With a renewed sense of urgency, he took the tool in his hand and rammed it under the lid of the crate. Using his weight as an ally, he forced the lever down with all of his strength, and as he did, the sealed container groaned and creaked under the steady duress.

"Come on," he urged. "Open up."

Inch by inch, the crate's lid raised higher and higher until finally, after a few minutes of strenuous work, it had moved enough for him to peer within.

"Man," he laughed nervously. "Why do I feel like Indiana Jones?"

After propping the lid open with a first-aid kit, he tossed the crowbar aside and reached into his jacket for his medical flashlight. With a quiet click, he turned the gadget on and pointed it into the depths of the box. Unfortunately, the awkward angle made it difficult for him to see much. If he wanted to view the contents, he needed to pry the lid open even further or slide his head inside for a quick peek.

"I can't believe I'm doing this."

Stuffing the penlight in his mouth, he turned his face sideways and slid it into the interior of the box, carefully avoiding the sharp nails that protruded from the wooden lid. Before he had a chance to examine anything, though, he heard a soft thud in the front seat of his ambulance, then watched in horror as the first-aid kit started to move. He wanted to protest, but before he could, a large black hand yanked the kit aside, causing the crate's heavy lid to drop upon the driver with sudden force. The wooden top pinned his neck against the edge of the box while the lid's sharp nails sank into his soft flesh.

As blood trickled from his puncture wounds, the driver tried to open the crate with his hands, but the visitor immediately objected to his efforts. The black man climbed upon the ambulance's bench, then imitated a professional wrestler by leaping onto the lid with amazing dexterity. The weight of the black man's body coupled with the sturdy edge of the wood instantly snapped the driver's neck, causing his paralyzed body to dangle lifelessly from the side of the crate.

And for some reason, the morbid image made Octavian Holmes smile with delight.

* * *

The small boat navigated the narrow channel of the cypress swamp, carefully avoiding any logs or stumps that would puncture its fragile bow. As it eased against the moss-covered dock, the captain of the vessel tossed a rope to one of the guards, and he quickly attached it to its anchoring post. The craft was now secured.

Holmes emerged from the shadows of the stern and shouted terse orders to the men on cargo duty. The workers, dressed in black fatigues and carrying firearms, hustled through the moonlit sky and swiftly carried the two wooden crates to a waiting truck. Once Holmes joined the freight, the driver started the motor and maneuvered the shipment through the thick camouflage of the island's foliage. A short time later, the flatbed truck burst from the claustrophobic world of leaves and into the neatly manicured grounds of the Plantation.

"Stop here," Holmes growled with authority.

The workers lifted the wooden crates from the vehicle and placed them on the charred remains of the burned cross. As Holmes watched closely, they tore into the crates with reinforced claw hammers, and within seconds, the boxes were reduced to shreds. Cautiously, the men lifted the two unconscious prisoners from the tattered containers and placed them in the cool grass.

"They're all yours, sir."

Holmes nodded while studying the paperwork of his new arrivals. When he was satisfied with the information, he bent over to examine their sleeping forms and immediately liked what he saw. The first captive was an elderly man with a strong jaw, thinning white hair, and a deep surfer's tan. He was in amazing physical shape for his age, possessing great muscle tone despite his 71 years of life. His wrists were thick, his shoulders broad, and his stomach carried little flab.

"Jake Ross," he mumbled as he nudged the man's hip. "I bet you're still a pit bull, huh?"

When he was done with the senior citizen, he turned his attention to the drugged female, and her beauty instantly overwhelmed him. Her chestnut hair flowed over her rosy cheeks, cascading down her neck and onto her slender shoulders like a tropical waterfall. Her bosom, concealed under a bright red golf shirt, danced with each life-sustaining breath, and the image stirred something deep within Holmes' soul. Her legs, tanned and athletic, were in full-view since her white skirt had been torn during her cross-country journey, but even in rest, they possessed the fragile grace of a master ballerina's. And her face—ah, her face!—was more majestic than any he had ever seen.

After taking a minute to catch his breath, Holmes dropped to his knees and kissed the girl softly on her lips. "Ariane Walker," he whispered, "what a pleasure it is to have you on my island."

With a look of satisfaction, Holmes scooped her off the turf, then gently folded her frame across his left shoulder. As her arms dangled against his muscular back, Holmes carried the unconscious girl towards her cabin with very little effort. His eighteen years of work as a mercenary, which required stamina, strength, and discipline, guaranteed a level of physical conditioning that few men could ever hope to achieve. His missions had taken him through the severe warmth of the equator, the extreme cold of the Arctic Circle, and all the milder climates in between. In the process, he learned how to survive anything that this world was capable of throwing at him.

And because of that, invincibility radiated from Holmes like heat from a flame.

When he reached Walker's assigned cabin, he paused briefly, letting one of the guards unlock the exterior deadbolt. "You go in first," Holmes ordered. "Make sure her roommates are facing the back corner of the room." The guard did what he was told, threatening Tonya and Robert Edwards until they were properly positioned.

"All clear, sir."

Holmes walked into the cabin and eased Walker onto the hard ground. Then, before either captive could see his face, he turned from the room and disappeared into the dark night, leaving Tonya to worry about yet another family member—her unconscious baby sister.

Chapter Fifteen

Saturday, July 3rd

In New Orleans, St. Louis Cemeteries No. 1 and No. 2 are referred to by the locals as 'cities of the dead.' Designed in the 18th century, both graveyards feature elaborate above-ground vaults and French inscriptions that are both poetic and charming. Unfortunately, an unsupervised visit to either burial ground is liable to add to the body count of the sacred lands.

Located west of Louis Armstrong Park, this area is known as one of the most dangerous in the city. Gangs and criminals control the territories to the north of Rampart Street, and like the sweet nectar of a Venus flytrap, they use the popularity of the graveyards to ambush unsuspecting tourists.

Before leaving the safety of their car, Payne, Jones, and Greene gazed at the terrain like antelopes surveying a water hole. They carefully searched the shadows of the land, looking for predators that lay in wait, hunting for a clear passage to their intended destination.

"Let's do this," Payne grunted. "We're wasting time."

The men walked in silence until they saw a neon sign that blinked *Sam's Tattoos.* Greene paused to read the historical plaque that was fastened to the front of the building, then pushed the glass door aside. As he did, chimes from a small bell announced their presence.

A tall white man, dressed in an elaborately tie-dyed shirt and baggy blue jeans shorts, emerged from behind a wall of dangling plastic beads and greeted his customers with a nod of his head. As he did, his braided orange hair fell across his pale-green eyes while his shaggy beard bunched up in the folds of his neck. Tattoos covered the tanned flesh of his arms and legs.

"What can I do you for?" he asked in the jumbled syntax of a California beach bum.

As Payne studied the multicolored character in front of him, he realized it looked like a box of Skittles had thrown-up on the guy. "We're looking for a man by the name of Jamaican Sam. Can you tell us where to find him?"

"Dude, you're in luck. Sam, I am."

The three men looked at each other in confusion. They were expecting their contact be a little bit more, uh, Jamaican, not a mutant Dr. Seuss.

"You mean you're the owner?" Payne demanded. "You don't look like I pictured you."

"Is it the nickname, dude? People always get thrown off by my nickname." The three men nodded at the walking rainbow and laughed. "Damn, I gotta get me a new nickname."

Jones knew he was going to regret asking it, but for the sake of curiosity, he had to know. "By the way, how did you get the name Jamaican Sam?"

"Well, dude, the Sam part was easy because, you see, that's my name. But the Jamaican part, well, dude, that's a little more complex. A couple years ago, a bro from the Islands came in to get some ink done. I did this bitchin' drawing of a naked bitty and put it on his back. Once I finished, he was pretty stoked about the final product. In a heavily-accented voice, the dude said, 'Ja makin' Sam's name known t'roughout 'da city, mon.' Well, some customers overheard it, and they lumped 'ja makin' with the Sam, so people started calling me Jamaican Sam." He inhaled, then sighed with a satisfied grin on his face. "Pretty bitchin', eh?"

As fascinating as the story was, Payne realized he wasn't there to learn this dude's colorful history. He had more important things to find out—things that could possibly save the life of his girlfriend. "I don't mean to be rude, Sam, and I'm sorry if I cut your tale short, but I was hoping you could give us some help."

With his left hand, Sam brushed his braided orange locks from his eyes and shrugged. "Like I said in the beginning, what can I do you for?"

"Actually, you can help me out with a tattoo. I recently saw an elaborate design on this guy on the bus. The moment I saw it I knew I wanted to have it. I just knew it. Unfortunately, before I had a chance to ask the man where he got it done, we arrived at his stop and he disappeared. Do you think you could tell me who drew it for him?"

Sam shook his head violently, trying to clear his head. "OK, dude, let me see if I understand your quandary. You caught a shimmer of a slammin' tat, and the thing that caught your peeps the most was its dope design. Now you expect me, even though I've never peeped this ink in my entire existence, to picture it in my mind, then tell you who chiseled it into flesh? Whoa! That's some challenge, dude."

"But can you do it?" Payne demanded.

It took thirty seconds for Sam to reply, but he finally shrugged his shoulders. "I don't see why not, but it'll cost ya twenty bucks." Payne handed him the money, and Sam quickly stuffed the crisp bill into his multicolored boxers, which could be seen above the waistline of his torn blue jeans shorts. "What did this skin Picasso look like, dude?"

"It was in the shape of the letter P. The straight part of the P was a dagger, and . . ."

"Whoa!" Sam gasped, suddenly sounding like Keanu Reeves. "Was there, like, blood dripping from the dagger, dude?"

Payne stared at the kid—he couldn't have been any more than 24 or 25—and nodded. "Yeah, it had blood, but how did you know that?"

Sam walked over to his counter and flipped through a picture album of some of his most impressive designs. When he reached the page he was looking for, he handed the book to Payne. "Dude, the tat you're looking for is one of mine. How cool is that? Kind of a small globe, eh?"

"Yeah," Jones grunted, who suddenly didn't like the precision of Terrell Murray's advice. "Way too small for my taste."

Payne picked up on Jones' tone and instinctively patted the gun that he'd concealed under the flap of his shirt. "What can you tell me about its design?"

Sam scratched his bright orange beard for a brief moment, then shook his head from side to side. "It just ain't worth it, dude." He reached into his boxer shorts and withdrew Payne's bill. "Take your money back, dude. I've got nothing for ya."

Payne looked at the money with disapproval. He wasn't willing to touch something that had been stored next to Sam's crotch. "A deal's a deal," he argued. "You accepted the cash, now it's time to give me some info."

"Sorry, dude, but I just can't do that." Sam laid the money on the counter and slowly backed away. "I made a previous deal with the group of brothers that requested my work for that particular job. I told them my lips were *el sealed-o* if anyone asked me about that tat."

"How many people were in their group?" Jones asked.

Sam shrugged, then let out a weaselly little laugh. "Sorry, bro, I don't remember getting any money from you, so I don't owe you any info. You dig?"

Payne grinned at Sam and waited for the orange-haired freak to return his smile. When he did, Payne pulled his firearm into view and nestled it under the artist's hairy chin. "First, you referred to some black men as 'brothers,' and then you referred to my friend as your 'bro.' Now, you're going to test my patience even further by refusing to answer a simple question? Sorry, bro, that's not the way my friends and I operate."

"Wait a second," Sam gulped, as the color drained from his face. "Did you guys come in together? Oh, dude, I didn't know that. If I had known that, I wouldn't have been so shady."

Payne nodded, but refused to lower his gun. "Tell us about this group, Sam, before my finger gets a twitch and I add some red to your obnoxious shirt."

"Well, a bunch of brothers, uh, I mean, Africans came here one day."

Jones quickly corrected him. "The appropriate term is African-Americans."

"No, dude, not in this case, it isn't. These dudes were African."

Payne raised an eyebrow at the information. "Continue."

"Anyways," Sam stuttered, "they told me they were looking for a Jew-too. They told me the name of their gang, what they were looking for, and left the rest up to me. They gave me some cash and told me to have a tat design by the next day." Sam pointed to the picture in the album. "This is what I came up with, dude. Honest."

"What was the name of the gang?" Payne demanded.

"Dude, I can't tell ya that. I just can't."

Payne pushed the barrel of his gun even harder against Sam's throat, and as he did, he noticed Sam start to tremble with fear. "Sammy, I have a policy that prevents me from killing the mentally challenged, but since we're in a hurry, I might be willing to make an exception."

Sam took a trouble-filled breath, then answered. "I've got a problem, dude. When the group came to get their tats, they threatened to kill me if I told anyone about their posse. Now, here you are, and you're threatening to kill me if I *don't* tell you about their posse. Well, you don't have to be Alex Trebeck, dude, to see that I'm in jeopardy."

"Jeez," Payne chuckled. "That jeopardy comment was pretty cute."

"Did you like that?" Sam asked, hoping to lighten the mood. "I just made that up, dude."

"You did?" Payne grunted. "Well, unless you want it to be the last clever thing you ever say, I think you should start talking. What's the name of the gang?"

Sam closed his eyes and sighed. After giving it some thought, he realized it was better to possibly die later than to definitely die now. "The Plantation Posse."

Payne winked at Jones while lowering his weapon. "And what can you tell us about this Posse? Describe them for us."

"I don't know," Sam mumbled. "They were young, and black, and very athletic-looking."

"Wow," Greene remarked. "You just described every basketball team in the NBA. You gotta do better than that."

"And some of the guys had thick African accents."

"Come on," he objected. "My NBA comment is still accurate."

Sam glanced angrily at the ex-football star, but after a moment of concentration, his glare faded. A flash of recognition suddenly crossed his face. "Whoa, dude, I know you. I know who you are."

Greene immediately cursed under his breath. He knew going into this partnership that there was a good chance that he was going to be recognized, but he didn't think it would be so soon. "Who I am is not important, you box of crayons-looking motherfucker. What *is* important is my boy's original question. What did these guys look like?"

The rage in Greene's voice and the cold look in his eyes was enough to silence Sam. There was no way in the world that he wanted to infuriate the Buffalo Soldier. "OK, dude, I'll tell you anything you want to know, just don't hurt me. I've got a low threshold for pain."

Greene nodded. "I appreciate your honesty, Sam, and in return I promise not to test that threshold. But instead of talking to me, I want you to talk to my friends. And while you're telling them everything that they need to know, I'm gonna go through your Brady Bunch-looking wall of beads and hunt for your pisser." He turned towards Payne and looked for permission. "That is, if you guys can handle things alone for a couple of minutes."

Payne patted Greene on his muscular arm. "Thanks, I think we can take over from here."

"While you're back there," Jones added, "check to see if anybody is hiding or if there's a back way into this place. I'm not in the mood for any surprises."

Greene hustled into the rear room, and did what was requested. "Things look fine," he yelled to Payne and Jones. "There's nothing back here that can hurt ya."

Payne grinned as he leaned against the counter. "Sorry, Sam. Since you're all out of allies, it appears that you're kind of stuck. You have no choice but to tell us about the Posse."

"Dude, I swear, I can't describe them any better than I have. The only thing in my cranium is their black gear and the roll of large bills that they were toting. Other than that, nothing."

Slowly, Payne was beginning to believe Sam's claim. He realized that it would be tough for anyone to remember specific details about a group of men that had visited him several weeks ago, especially if they were foreigners. One face would blend in with the next. "Fine, let's get off their appearance for a while. Why don't you tell me about the tattoo itself? What did the image symbolize?"

Sam scratched his thick orange beard while studying the picture from his album. "Well, dude, the P obviously stands for Plantation Posse, but I bet you figured that out, huh?"

"Come on," Payne demanded. "Tell us something that might actually help."

"Fine," Sam growled. "I'll tell you what you want to know, but I'm warning you, dudes, you're forcing me to sign my own death warrant. My blood's gonna be on your hands."

And in a blink of an eye, Sam's words became prophetic.

Chapter Sixteen

Thunder echoed from across the street as the sniper pulled the trigger on his Heckler & Koch PSG1 rifle. His first bullet shattered the window of the tattoo shop, sending thousands of knife-like shards in every direction. As they fell to the floor in a melodic song, the hollow-tipped projectile entered the right eye of its victim, obliterating Sam's brain and skull in a single flash.

Without pausing to think, Payne and Jones reacted to the situation—their experiences with the MANIACs had prepared them for far worse—like it was an everyday occurrence. Payne dashed for shelter in the front corner of the shop, for it was away from the broken window and allowed him to take a clean shot at anyone that attempted to enter the front door. Jones, on the other hand, headed in the opposite direction, running to the back of the parlor and taking refuge behind the front counter.

"Are you all right?" Jones yelled while pulling out his Glock.

"I'm not perfect, but I'm sure as shit better than Sam."

Jones glanced around the corner of the ledge and stared at the near-headless victim. Crimson gushed from the gaping hole where his face used to be. Hair, brain, and bone clung to the back wall like chunky spaghetti sauce.

"We're dealing with a serious weapon, Jon. Whatever it is

tore right through his skull."

Payne surveyed the scene before offering his summation. "Possibly a hollow-tip bullet or a shell sprayed with Teflon. And from the looks of it, I'd say the shooter had an elevated position."

"How do you know that?"

"Look at the window if you can. The very top is the only part that's broken, and the only way a bullet can do that and hit a man in the head is if it was discharged from above."

Jones nodded in agreement. "If that's the case, this wasn't a drive-by. The bastard's probably on a roof or in a tree. No way we can nail him from this angle."

"You're probably right. That's why we have to go outside and get him."

Jones put his finger in his ear and attempted to open the auditory canals that had closed up during his flight to Louisiana. "I'm sorry, man, I must've misheard you. Did you say we should go out there and get him?"

"Yes, princess, that's what I said."

The statement did not sit well with Jones. "But we don't know what we're up against. Hell, we don't know a damn thing, and you want us to go outside with our weapons blazing?"

Payne chuckled at his friend's reaction. He expected something a little more soldierly from an ex-MANIAC. "Wow, wait until I tell all the fellas about this at our next squad reunion. They won't believe how quickly you've lost your nerve."

"I haven't lost my nerve, Jon. I've gained some common sense. What good could it do to go outside and face a sniper?"

"What good? Going out there could save Ariane's life."

"What the hell are you talking about? How can going outside save Ariane's life?"

"Think about it, D.J. Why was Sam killed? What purpose could that have served?"

Jones shrugged. "I don't know. Somebody wanted to keep him quiet, I guess."

"Exactly! Sam must've known something, and it must've been

pretty damn important."

"Like what?"

"I have no idea. Maybe he could identify someone, or had a billing address in his files, or maybe, just maybe, he knew something about Ariane. Truthfully, I don't know. But if we don't go outside, our odds of getting an answer go down considerably. And you know it."

"Shit," Jones grumbled, finally realizing what Payne had in mind. "You're hoping to take this guy alive, aren't you?"

Payne nodded at the query. "How else is he going to be useful?"

Jones knew that Payne was right, that they needed to talk to the guy, but he also realized the high level of danger that would be involved. If the sniper was still outside, he was probably waiting for them to make a move. And the moment they did . . . BANG!

Simply put, that's the way that snipers operated. They patiently waited for their targets to do something stupid, then they took full advantage of it.

"So," Payne asked in a less than pleasant tone, "are you coming or not? 'Cause if you aren't, I gotta start looking for a new best friend."

"Ah, man, why did you have to go there? Any time you need a favor, you always pull out the best friend card. Fine, I'll help you out, but I'm not doing this because of your stupid threat. I'm doing this to burn off dinner."

Payne grinned in appreciation. "The first thing we have to do is figure out how to get out of here. Since the door is glass, he'll pick us off before we even open it. We'll need to find a different exit."

"How about the window? If I knock out the bottom half, we could scurry behind one of the cars outside with little exposure time. Plus, it'll let this guy know we're armed."

"Sounds good, but before we go, let me get the lights. The less this guy sees, the better."

Jones liked the idea. Darkness would improve their odds

even more. "Can you reach 'em from there, or should we shoot 'em out?"

Payne leaned out from his hiding place and stared at the small panel of switches near the door. It would take some doing, but he felt he could reach the buttons without risking his life.

"No problem," he lied. "Piece of cake."

Moving quickly, Payne dropped to his hands and belly, then slithered across the vinyl floor in a military crawl. He did his best to avoid the broken glass in front of him, but since there were chunks of it everywhere, he found himself bleeding almost immediately.

"Looking good," Jones whispered as he peered out from behind the counter. "In about two feet, you'll be directly under the . . . OK, stop."

Payne tilted his head back and tried to reach the metal panel above him, but the damn thing was a foot too high, which meant he'd have to leave the safety of the floor to reach it. No matter. The advantage he'd gain with darkness outweighed the risk of going for the lights. So, while keeping his torso parallel to the floor, he stretched his bloody right hand upward, inching it slowly along the wall until he felt the cold surface of the switch in his grasp.

"Let's see if you like the dark, asshole."

The gunman replied with a bullet-filled blitzkrieg that tore through the tiny shop with the force of a tornado. Glass, wood, and plaster erupted in the air as the sightless sniper relied on blind luck and sheer volume to hit his targets. A second wave followed quickly, which shattered the front door and showered the room with a stream of razor-sharp confetti, but Payne remained calm, keeping his face covered and his body against the base of the thick front wall.

"I guess not," he sneered.

When the violence finally subsided, Payne risked a quick peak into the back of the shop. Things were blurry at first due to the lack of light, but after a few seconds, he realized what had taken the brunt of the sniper's barrage: The counter that shielded Jones had taken more hits than a hippie at Woodstock.

"D.J., are you all right?"

"Yeah and very lucky. I don't know how he missed me."

Payne glanced around the confined environment and realized they couldn't stay inside much longer. "We have to get out of here. If we stay put, he's eventually going to hit us with a blind shot."

Jones agreed. "He did us a favor by knocking out the door and the window. If you want, I can fire a few clearing shots, and that'll give you time to get outside."

Payne nodded. Even though D.J. wouldn't be aiming at the sniper, he would minimize the risk of return fire, which would allow him to reach the street. Of course, the drawback to the plan was the possibility of more than one gunman. If a second Posse member was lying in wait near the door, he'd nail Payne rather easily.

Unfortunately, it was a chance that they had to take.

"Are you ready?" Payne asked as he peered through the darkness. "On the count of three, shoot through the window as I head for the door."

"You got it."

"One," said Payne as he adjusted the Glock in his sweaty right hand.

"Two," muttered Jones as he peered at his glassless target.

"Three!" they yelled in unison, just like old times.

With a burst of adrenaline, Payne leapt from the ground and sprinted out the door while Jones aimed his gun at the window and fired. Or at least tried to. Unfortunately, nothing happened when he squeezed the Glock's trigger, which left his friend in a very precarious position.

The concrete under Payne's feet exploded in wispy puffs of smoke as the gunman opened fire from the roof across the street.

With nowhere else to go, Payne bolted sharply to his right and dove behind the closest car he saw, a maneuver that broke the cellular phone in his pocket and tore most of the skin from his knees. But in Payne's mind, it was a fair trade. He had always preferred scabs to bullet holes.

"Are you all right?" Jones wondered.

"I'm fine," Payne snarled. "Where the hell was my covering fire?"

"I'm sorry, man, but the freakin' gun jammed. The damn thing wouldn't shoot."

"What do you mean it wouldn't shoot? You have to pull the trigger, you know?"

Jones grinned, countering the insult with a fact that Payne had overlooked. "Don't be mad at me, be mad at the source. Remember, you got your gun from the same place as me."

Growling softly, Payne focused his attention on the weapon in his hand. If it had the same malfunction, he didn't have a chance against the sniper. The truth was he had pretty slim odds to begin with, but with a broken firearm, he had none.

"Shit," he mumbled to himself. "Only one way to find out."

Payne pointed his Glock towards the building across the street and squeezed the trigger, yet nothing happened. No lever movement. No discharge. No explosion. Obviously, his gun was suffering from the same disease as D.J.'s: *piece-of-shititis.*

"Well?" Jones yelled from inside the shop.

"We're so screwed we should be wearing condoms."

Jones grinned while peering out into the streetlight. "Don't give up yet. What kind of shot is this guy? Any good?"

Payne glanced at the holes in the sidewalk and sighed at the damage. "Not really. If he was, I wouldn't be talking to you right now."

"And he's probably working alone, huh?"

"If he wasn't, his partner would've nailed me by now."

"If that's the case, then what are we afraid of? Are we going to let some redneck knock off two of this country's best soldiers, or are we going to come up with a plan to take this guy out?"

"If I was a betting man, I'd put my money on the redneck."

"I'm serious. We've been in several situations worse than this, and we always made it out. Come on. If we put our minds to it, I'm sure we can come up with something."

Payne grunted as he stared at his broken Glock. "Fine, let's list everything that we have besides our experience, and maybe a plan will become obvious."

Jones nodded. "As far as I can tell, we have two defective handguns and . . ."

"And?" Payne muttered, hoping that he was forgetting something.

"And that's about it. As far as I can tell, we have two broken Glocks."

Payne leaned his head against the Chevy Celebrity and groaned. Their current inventory wouldn't even stop a mugger, let alone a well-placed sniper. "Is there anything else in there that can be used? A gun behind the counter? A telephone? A flashlight?"

"Oh shit," Jones yelled. "I just thought of something huge that could help us."

"Oh yeah, and what's that?"

"Levon!"

The answer stunned Payne. He had completely forgotten about the third member of their party. "Holy hell. Why don't you see where that bad-ass brother is hiding?"

"Be back in a flash."

"If you don't mind, I'll just wait here until you get back."

"I don't blame you one bit."

Payne snuggled up against the car the best he could, trying to conceal his body under the maroon frame. He realized if the sniper attempted a ground assault, the only way he could protect himself was by hiding under the car, and he was prepared to do that if necessary. Hell, he would shit on the carburetor if he thought it would help, but thankfully it never came to that.

Before he was forced to do anything ridiculous, Payne detected a sound in the far-off distance. At first he wasn't sure if he was imagining it or not, but after a few seconds of listening, he knew that he wasn't. It was the wail of sirens, and they were headed his way.

"Jon?" Jones shouted from the back of the shop. "Is that what I think it is?"

Payne peered under the Chevy and saw several squad cars pull onto his street. "Yes, Mr. Jones, the cavalry has arrived."

"Thank god."

"You said it, my man." Payne laid back on the sidewalk, his legs still underneath the car for protection. "By the way, how's Levon doing?"

Instead of shouting his response, Jones scrambled out of the store and quickly took a seat next to his friend. Once he was safely behind the maroon car, he turned towards Payne and looked him dead in the eye. "You're not going to believe this, Jon. You're really not."

"What now?"

"I don't even know how to start, but . . ." Jones struggled for the right words to break the news to his friend. "Levon is gone."

Payne bolted upright, the color draining from his face. "Oh my god. How did he . . ."

"No," Jones said as he grabbed his best friend's arm. "He's not dead-gone. He's gone-gone. I don't know how he did it, but that slippery son of a bitch has managed to disappear."

Chapter Seventeen

As the police pulled to a screeching stop in front of Sam's Tattoos, Payne stared at Jones, trying to determine if his best friend was being serious. After several seconds of eye contact, Payne decided that he was. "Levon has disappeared?"

"Yep. He's gone."

Payne shook his head in disbelief. "How is that possible? He's like eight-feet tall and weighs 500 pounds, and you're telling me you managed to lose him in a room that's roughly the size of a closet."

"That's what I said."

"I thought you were supposed to be a professional detective?"

"I am, and I'm telling you he's not in there."

Payne leaned closer to his friend and tried to smell his breath. "Have you been drinking?"

Jones grinned. "I wish I was."

Payne was about to reply, but before he had a chance, a booming voice shattered the stillness of the night.

"We see you behind the car," announced a patrolman through his intercom system. "Put your hands where we can see them and come out very slowly."

The two of them did as they were told and were quickly frisked by a team of gun-toting officers.

"Gentlemen," barked Sergeant Baker, the lead officer at the

scene. "I'm sure you realize that y'all have a lotta explaining to do."

Baker was in his mid-40s and possessed the face of an ex-boxer. His nose was crooked, his teeth were fake, and his face was dotted with several scars. His thick black hair was splashed with gray, but his navy-blue police hat covered most of it.

"Before I throw you guys in cuffs and haul your ass down to the station, I was hoping you could tell me what happened here. It'll make my report so much easier to write."

Payne cleared his throat and began speaking before Jones had a chance. "My buddy and I just flew into New Orleans earlier tonight for a little R & R. We rented a car, got something to eat, and then decided to do something out of the ordinary. A local told us that Jamaican Sam drew the best tattoos in the whole darn state . . ."

"A lovely state, I might add."

"It sure is, D.J. Anyway, we decided to come here to check out his craftsmanship."

"We were impressed. Very colorful stuff."

"But we were here for less than ten minutes when somebody shot Sam from across the street."

"We think from that rooftop there," Jones exclaimed, pointing. "Possibly with a sniper rifle."

"We wanted to fight back."

"But we didn't have any weapons."

"I hid in the corner for protection, and D.J. dove behind the counter."

"When I was back there, I found two guns. I tossed Jon one and kept the other for myself."

"We tried to use them when he started shooting at us."

"But neither of them worked."

"I left mine on the sidewalk," Payne volunteered.

"And mine is inside."

"You can check for yourself. Neither of them is capable of firing a round."

"Yep," Jones seconded. "I squeezed the trigger, but it wouldn't make a bang or nothin'."

Payne paused in thought, then turned towards D.J. "Anything else you can think of?"

Jones shook his head. "Actually, Jon, I think that covers it."

Payne nodded in agreement. "That's about all we've got, sir."

"We hope it makes your report pretty easy to write."

Baker studied the two men and smiled. He wanted to comment on the conversation, but he was simply too fascinated to speak. Even though Payne and Jones' statements were coming from two different voices, it was like they were coming from the same mind. When Payne started a sentence, Jones finished it. If Jones started, Payne ended it. Baker had been on the job for over twenty years and had never seen anything like it during his career.

"OK," he muttered, emerging from his trance. "We'll take a look around and see if your story checks out. If it does, y'all have nothing to worry about. I'll have you back on your vacation by sunrise. However, if it doesn't, then you might be staying here in our state . . ." He turned toward Jones. "Pardon me, in our 'lovely' state, for a lot longer than you were planning. In the meantime, why don't you guys show me some ID? That'll give me a chance to see if y'all have recently escaped from a mental-health facility, which is a distinct possibility in my book."

*   *   *

After searching for an hour, Baker decided that the two men from Pennsylvania were telling the truth. Before he let them go, though, he decided to discuss the facts of the case with his second in command. "Richie, can you think of any reason to hold these two any longer?"

The second cop, white and overweight, glanced at his notes and shook his head. "Nah. From what we've found, these guys couldn't have been the shooter. The bullet that killed Sam matched one of the empty casings that was found on the roof across the street. The two Glocks that were found at the scene possessed no serial numbers, probably bought by Sam for protection. And just like the guys said, the damn things didn't work."

"On top of that," Baker added, "Payne and Jones were covered in cuts and scratches, which looked like they were caused by flying glass. That means they were both in the shop when the shooting started."

"Yep, and the initial 911-call mentioned a sniper as well."

"What about their histories? Any warrants?"

"We checked their backgrounds, and neither of them have any prior convictions. Both of them had an academy education, and both are currently employed by a reputable company, Payne Industries. In fact, the white guy in your car is CEO of the corporation."

"You mean it's *his* corporation?" Baker demanded.

"Yes, sir. He's the head honcho. Flew down here on his private freakin' jet."

"I'll be damned. What the hell is a rich man from Pittsburgh doing in a New Orleans ghetto in the middle of the damn night?"

"Apparently getting a tattoo."

Baker laughed at the suggestion. "Kind of unlikely, huh?"

"Yeah, but I'll be honest with you, sir. I don't think he flew all the way down here to kill Jamaican Sam, either. A rich man like that doesn't commit his own crimes. A millionaire pays to have them done."

Baker nodded. "True, but we've already decided that Payne and Jones didn't kill anyone, right? So what brings them here at this hour?"

"Drugs?"

"I doubt it. I ordered a background check on Jamaican Sam Fletcher, and the man had no record. The cops that normally patrol this neighborhood claim he ran a clean place. In fact, his artwork was so admired by the local gangs that the thugs went out of their way to protect him."

"So where does that leave us?"

Baker didn't want to admit it, but he had no choice. "Honestly, it leaves us without a case. We can't hold these two without just cause, and we can't prove that these guys did anything wrong. We could hold them for 24 hours of questioning if we wanted to, but I guarantee that Payne would have a fancy-pants lawyer down here in the blink of an eye causing a big stink about something. No thank you. It just wouldn't be worth it."

"So we're kinda forced to let them go, huh?"

"Yeah, but that doesn't mean we're gonna forget 'em."

The cop looked at his superior and grinned. "What do you have in mind? Some kind of tail?"

Baker laughed at the suggestion. "Nothing that drastic, at least not yet. I'm gonna do some more digging when I get back to the station and see if I can turn up anything that makes sense. If I do, I'll nail these guys before they know what hit 'em." Baker groaned as he stared at the captives in the back of his squad car. "Let 'em loose, but tell 'em I want to have a brief chat with them before they leave."

While waiting for the prisoners to be released, Baker leaned against a nearby building, ready to verbally pounce on the men at the first opportunity. Payne and Jones barely had time to stretch their legs when the veteran cop started his lecture.

"Gentlemen," he said in the voice of an angry teacher. "You guys should know better then to be roaming around this type of neighborhood in the middle of the night. Violence is pretty common here, and the idiot that told you to visit Sam's shop after dark should've known better. You guys are pretty lucky to be alive."

Payne nodded his head in agreement. "Thanks to you, we are. If you guys didn't show up when you did, we would've been capped by the sniper for sure."

"Don't thank me," admitted the cop. "Thank the person who called 911. He was the one that made us aware of the shooting."

"Actually, I'd like to. Is the guy around?"

Baker shrugged while staring at the crowd that had gathered across the street. "Probably, but I don't know where to find him. The person used a cellular phone to report the incident, but refused to leave his name."

Jones smiled to himself, wondering if Levon Greene had made the call. If he had, they probably owed the Buffalo Soldier their lives. "If you manage to find out who it was, please thank him for us, OK?"

Baker shook Jones' hand and smiled. "You got it." The cop let go, then turned to shake Payne's. "Oh yeah, one more thing: If I happen to hear your names mentioned in connection with anything else during your stay in New Orleans, I might be forced to reconsider your involvement with this case. Understand?"

Both men nodded their heads even though they realized that their search was far from over. In fact, the damn thing was just beginning.

Chapter Eighteen

Lightning bolts. The pain felt like lightning bolts surging through her brain.

Ariane did her best to ignore it—tried to open her eyes, tried to fight through the jackhammer that thumped inside her skull—but the agony was too overwhelming. God, she wondered, what's wrong with me? She'd never felt this bad before. Ever. She'd suffered through hangovers, migraines, and a skiing accident that left her with a severe concussion, but in all her years, she had never come close to feeling like this.

Hell, it felt like she was giving birth through her nose. The pain was *that* intense.

To escape the pounding, Ariane was tempted to fall back asleep. She figured if she got a little more rest she'd have to feel a whole lot better than she did now. Then, if all went well, she'd roll out of bed like she'd planned and whip Jon's butt in a round of golf.

Golf? Wait a second. Something about that didn't seem right. Not at all. She tried to figure it out, struggled to put her snippets of memory together in an orderly fashion, but was unable to. She could vaguely remember waking up and brushing her teeth and getting a shower and . . . the door. Something about the door. She could remember someone pounding on her door.

Or was the pounding in her head?

Wow, she honestly didn't know. The details were hazy, like a painful childhood incident that had suddenly crept back into her consciousness. Why couldn't she remember the door? What was it about her door?

Ariane tried to open her eyes, fought to pry her lids apart, but the pain was too intense to overcome. Wave after wave crashed inside her head, causing her to lurch forward into the fetal position, but when she did the maelstrom of agony surged towards her gut, inducing the worst muscle spasms of her life. So back she moved, trying to find sanctuary from the suffering, but all that did was make her feel like she was going to throw up. And not just ordinary vomit. No, to her it felt like her innards were exploding upward. Her gallbladder, her liver, her intestines—they all felt like they were inching their way towards her mouth, swimming ever so slowly up the back of her throat on a viscous river of bile.

"What's wrong with me?" she called out, hoping God would provide her with some kind of answer. "Why do I feel like this?"

"Shhh," a motherly voice answered. "Just relax. The pain will soon pass. I promise."

The sound of a strange voice sent shockwaves through Ariane.

"Who are you?" she shrieked, now trying to open her eyes with twice the urgency of before. "What are you doing in my bedroom?"

The voice sighed at the query. "You're not in your bedroom."

That was news to Ariane. She honestly couldn't remember leaving her apartment all day. "I'm not? Where am I then? What's wrong with me?"

"Actually, I'm not sure where we are. Hell, I wish I did. And as to what's wrong with you, you're having a reaction to the drugs. But don't worry, it'll pass quickly."

"Drugs?" Ariane mumbled.

"Yeah, sis, I said drugs." The female paused for a moment to let the information sink in. "I could've sworn I always told you to just say no."

Sis? Did she say *sis*? Why in the world would this person call her *sis*?

Oh, damn! The reason suddenly dawned on her.

"Tonya?" she shrieked. "Is that you?"

Tonya Edwards looked down at Ariane and attempted to smile. "Of course it's me—unless you have another sister that you've been hiding."

"No, but . . ." The presence of her pregnant older sister only added to Ariane's confusion. Tonya lived in Colorado. What in the world was she doing in Pittsburgh? "Why are you here? Is something wrong?"

It was the understatement of the year.

"Yeah, kid, I'd say something's wrong."

Ariane swallowed, the bitter taste of bile still in her mouth. "Is it the baby?"

"The baby, Robert, you, me. Pretty much everything." Tonya tried to lower herself to the floor, but her belly prevented it. "I'm not sure why, but our family's been kidnapped."

* * *

Slightly banged-up but happy to be alive, the two friends walked to their rented Mustang in silence. As they strolled past the ancient cemetery, Payne shuddered slightly, realizing how close he had come to his own funeral. If the sniper had been a little more accurate, Payne and Jones would've been returning to Pittsburgh in wooden crates, not in the comfort of a private jet.

"You're being awfully quiet," Jones mumbled, studying his silent friend. "Are you all right?"

Payne nodded his head as he slid into the car. "As good as can be expected."

After strapping himself in, Payne allowed his mind to drift

back to the incident at the tattoo shop. Even though the shooting was unexpected, Payne realized that Ariane's kidnappers were bound to become aware of his presence eventually. But the big question was, how? How did they find out about him so quickly? Was there a spy at the airport? At The Fishing Hole? Or was the late-night gunplay an unlucky coincidence? Maybe Sam's death had been ordered several days before, and the sniper just happened to show up at the same time as them. Sam was the first one eliminated, so maybe he was the number one priority of the hit. Maybe the Plantation Posse, or some unrelated gang, had been planning to silence the tattooed-freak for an entirely different reason. Even though it seemed unlikely, it was a possibility.

Hell, in New Orleans, anything was possible. One trip to Mardi Gras would prove that.

"By the way," Jones wondered, "where are we going? Or are you planning on driving around this city until someone starts shooting at us again?"

"That's not what I had in mind, but now that you mention it, that's better than anything I can come up with."

"Stumped already?"

"I wouldn't say stumped, but I'm pretty confused. There are too many variables floating around in my mind right now, and I can't figure out which ones are important."

"I was thinking the same thing myself. There are lots of questions and very few answers."

"You're right about that, but two are bothering me more than anything else. I can't figure them out for the life of me."

"And they are?"

"Number one, if Ariane was kidnapped for money, why the hell would the Posse try to kill me? I'm the one with the big bank account, the man with the golden checkbook. Why eliminate me? My death would instantly take away their chance of a big payday."

Jones nodded. It was a thought that hadn't entered his mind, but one that made things even more confusing. "You're right. That's a pretty big issue, and one that I can't answer. So, what's number two? Maybe I can help you with that."

"Oh, that one's even more confusing. Where the hell is Levon?"

* * *

Because of his size and the weapon he carried, Levon Greene showed no fear as he walked through Louis Armstrong Park. Like most major cities, New Orleans had a policy against large, gun-toting black men walking in its city parks after midnight, but Greene knew he was in no danger of being stopped. Every cop in a half-mile radius was at Sam's Tattoos, trying to solve that shooting.

As he emerged from the darkness of the tree-lined sidewalks, Greene tucked his pistol in the waistband of his white Dockers, concealing it under his ice-blue Tommy Hilfiger shirt.

Despite the early-morning hour, up-tempo funk leaked from Donna's Bar and Grill, a famous jazz club off of St. Ann Street, while a group of well-dressed men and women waited to show the bouncer their IDs. Greene didn't have the patience to linger in line, so he shook the hand of the starstruck guard, then slipped inside without delay.

Celebrity had some privileges.

Since the sniper had prevented him from using the bathroom at Sam's, Greene quickly made his way to the rear of the club while trying to conceal his identity from as many people as he could. He simply didn't have time to sign autographs for anyone at the moment. There were more pressing matters on his mind—and in his lower colon—to deal with. After making his way into the restroom, Greene found himself angered by his phone, which started to ring the moment he turned the lock on his stall door.

"Who's dis?" he demanded.

"It's D.J.," he said with relief. "Are you all right?"

The call was completely unexpected, like hearing the voice of a ghost, and it took Greene a minute to catch his breath from the shock. "Am I all right? I think the better question is, Are you all right? I thought you were dead for sure. Jesus H. Christ. I can't believe you're alive. How's Jon?"

"He's fine, too. He's sitting right here next to me."

"Hey, Levon," Payne yelled. "I'm still alive."

"I'll be a son of a bitch," Greene muttered. From the number of bullets that were fired, he assumed nobody in the front room of the shop could've survived the assault, and if someone had, he assumed they'd be bleeding all over an intensive care unit by now. "How about the freak? Did Sam make it, too?"

"Nah, I'm afraid not. The first shot took him out, clean. He didn't have a chance."

"What about the next 100 shots? What the hell did they hit?"

"Everything but us," Jones admitted, suddenly realizing how fortunate he was. "I guess our military training helped us escape."

"Training?" he asked incredulously. "What the hell kind of training teaches you to dodge bullets? Are you guys fuckin' ninjas or somethin'?"

"I swear I never fucked a ninja in my life." Jones chuckled, hoping that Greene understood his joke. "The truth is that luck probably played a bigger role in our safety than I'm willing to admit."

"Man, how lucky can two guys get?"

"Speaking of lucky, how did you get out of the damn shop? I could've sworn we left you in Sam's bathroom, then when we went to save you, you weren't there. How did you pull that one off?"

Greene smiled as he thought about his easy escape, but it was a secret that he wasn't quite ready to share. He wanted Payne and Jones to ponder the mystery for a little while longer. "D.J., I'll tell you in a little bit, OK? But I'm in a public restroom as we speak, and I don't know if there are people in the other stalls listening."

"What did you do? Flush yourself to another part of the city?"

Greene laughed. "No, nothing like that, but you'll have to wait a few more minutes for the details. Where are you guys now?"

"We're on Conti Street."

"Well, that's pretty close to me." Greene gave Jones directions to Donna's Bar and Grill and told him that he'd be waiting outside when they got there. "But first," he insisted, "I've got some urgent business to attend to, and I'm not willing to do it while we're on the phone."

* * *

The bright yellow car screeched to a sudden stop in front of the club, then pulled away with its new passenger just as quickly. As the Mustang picked up speed, Greene greeted Payne and Jones, shaking their hands like they were long-lost friends, then buckled his seatbelt with a click.

"Military? You guys never told me you were in the military. What branch were you in?"

Payne answered first. "I went to the Naval Academy, but before I served my mandatory five-year stint, I got selected by the government to work on a Special Forces unit."

"That's where I met him," Jones added. "I was assigned to the same team as Jon even though I was from the Air Force. We were placed on a special crew that the government assembled, and unfortunately, we've been side-by-side ever since."

"I'll be damned," Greene muttered. "I'm sitting here with two Rambos. No wonder you guys were able to escape the tattoo parlor. I'm surprised you didn't kill the shooter in the process. What, are you guys rusty or somethin'?"

"Actually, we wanted to get the bastard, but weren't able to because of you."

Greene looked at Payne, confused. "Because of me? What did I do?"

"It's what you didn't do. You didn't get us guns that worked."

"They didn't work?" Greene demanded. "What do you mean they didn't work?"

Jones jumped into the fray. "Just like he said. We pulled our triggers several times, and nothing came out—like a guy with a vasectomy."

Payne grinned at the analogy. "Tell me a little bit about your gun dealer. Has something like this ever happened before?"

"No," Greene assured them. "He's got a first-class rep on the streets of Orleans."

"Maybe so, but his faulty products almost got us killed." Payne slowed to a stop at a red-light. Then with blazing eyes, he turned towards Greene. "I'd love a chance to meet this guy. You know, to see if I get a good feeling about him. Do you think you could set something up?"

Greene glanced at Payne and shrugged. "I guess I could, but I don't know what good it's going to do. You guys already met him, and you seemed to trust him just fine."

"Terrell Murray?" Payne asked. "The owner of The Fishing Hole?"

Greene nodded. "The one and only."

"Why didn't you mention that before we talked to him?" Jones demanded.

"Terrell is very hush-hush about his disreputable activities. He just doesn't like outsiders knowing about his business. If he sells something illegal, he deals with a restricted list of clientele, and if they betray him, he gets very upset and cuts them off immediately. That's why I purchased the weapons by myself, and that's why I didn't mention his name earlier. Can you understand that?"

"Sure," Payne admitted. "That makes plenty of sense to me.

So, why tell us now? If Terrell is so secretive, why risk his confidence by mentioning his name?"

"Sometimes you must betray one trust to gain another."

Payne and Jones pondered the philosophical comment, then shook their heads in admiration. For an ex-jock, Greene possessed a pretty good understanding of human nature.

"And besides, when we go to get your refund, I want you to do the talking. I'd prefer if you pissed him off instead of me."

Actually, a *great* understanding of human nature.

Chapter Nineteen

As they drove to The Fishing Hole, Jones patiently waited for Greene to answer the question that he'd asked earlier, but it was apparent that Greene had completely forgotten about it—or was trying to avoid it. "Levon, since you're out of the john now, can you please tell me how you escaped from Sam's? That's been bugging me for the past hour."

Payne glanced at his friend and smiled. "You must've been reading my mind. I was getting ready to ask him the same thing. How did you do that? Magic?"

Realizing that he was the center of attention, Greene grinned mischievously, his eyes twinkling like a small child's at a birthday party. Then, when he could hold it back no longer, he spurted the secret with a quick burst, like a geyser. "I went through the back wall."

Jones laughed at the information with a disbelieving tone. "Who are you, the Kool-Aid guy? I don't remember seeing any Negro-shaped holes in the back room."

But Greene stuck by his story. "How hard did ya look?"

"Pretty damn hard."

"Apparently not hard enough," Greene chuckled, "because I got my ass out."

Payne joined him in laughter. "He's got you there, Sherlock. I guess you aren't the infallible detective after all, huh?"

Jones leaned forward to object. "Yeah, but . . ."

"Actually," Payne interrupted, "why don't you listen for a second and let him explain things? Maybe you can learn a thing or two."

Jones rolled his eyes while waiting for Greene to start his lecture.

"Thank you, Jon. I'd love to help D.J. out. When I got into the back, I did as you asked. I looked for anything suspicious, but there was nothing but a bathroom and a closet."

"Right," Jones blurted. "That's what I found, too."

"So, like I said, I went into the bathroom to take care of my business, and BOOM! CRASH! I heard a gunshot then glass breaking in the front. I wanted to come out to check on things, but my pants were around my ankles and that slowed me down a great deal."

"I bet it did," Jones muttered.

"By the time I got my pants up, I heard a number of shots. Bang-bang-bang-bang! Glass was breaking, walls were shattering, chaos. At that point, I assumed that both of you guys were dead. I mean, come on. How was I supposed to know that you were freakin' commandos in a former life? Anyway, at that point I figured I needed to get out of there without using the front door, right? Well, I remembered when I walked into the shop there was a historical-landmark plaque on the front wall, and it said the building used to be a part of the Underground Railroad."

"Sam's place was a part of the Railroad?" Jones remarked in a doubting tone. "You've got to be kidding me."

"Not at all," Greene replied. "Like I told you guys before, I've been doing a lot of research on my hometown, and one of the things that has fascinated me the most was New Orleans' role in America's slave-trade. A number of ports on the Gulf of Mexico were notorious for bringing slaves into this country, but at the same time, there were a number of ports that were used to smuggle slaves out. Shit, there was so much diversity in this city during the 1800s that people often confused the slaves with their masters. In fact, there was one period in 1803 where ownership of New Orleans passed from Spain to France to the United States in less than a month's time. . . . If a city doesn't even know what country it belongs to, how's it gonna keep track of the people?"

Jones tried to absorb all of the information—historical facts and local folklore normally fascinated him—but in this case, he wanted to get to the important stuff. He wanted to know how Greene got out of the damn shop without being seen. "Levon, not to be rude, but . . ."

"I know, I know. You want to know how I did it." Jones and Payne both nodded their heads. "Fine, I'll tell you. The landmark plaque clicked in my mind, and I remembered going on a tour or two where I'd seen the same thing before. In each of those places, there was always a trap door or a hidden set of steps that allowed fugitives to slip out of the place undetected. And guess what?"

Jones was about to respond, but Payne answered for him. "You found something."

"Exactly." Greene's eyes lit up once again. "The rear wall of the closet was actually a well-concealed door, a back way out of the place. I don't know if Sam even knew about it because it was in pretty bad shape, but at that point, I wasn't about to bitch about its condition."

"What did you do when you got outside? Did you try to get the shooter?"

"To be honest with you, no. I don't have much experience with killing people, and I thought you guys were already dead."

"We probably should've been," Jones added. "A well-trained gunman should've picked us off clean. If, of course, that was his goal."

Greene turned to look at D.J. "What does that mean? You don't think he was aiming for you?"

"At this point, we don't know. What would be the purpose of

killing Jon if he hasn't paid any ransom yet? The kidnappers aren't in his last will and testament, so if they want his millions they better not kill him. Right?"

The comment took Greene by surprise. "You've got millions? I thought you were some kind of unemployed, street basketball wannabe. You really got that many Benjamins in the bank?"

"If you mean money, yeah. I have a nice nest egg stashed away."

"I'll be damned. A rich Rambo. What the hell did you do? Auction your soldiering skills to the highest bidder? Or, did you just sell a stolen nuclear warhead to Iraq?"

"Nothing that dramatic. Actually, my grandfather passed away, and when he died, he left the family business to me."

"Like a family restaurant or somethin'?"

Payne shrugged, trying not to smile at the understatement. "Something like that."

Greene nodded his approval. "As I was saying, I didn't have the expertise to take out the shooter, so I did the next best thing. I called the cops."

"So, that was you," Jones remarked, happy that his old sports hero had come through for them. "The police said that someone had reported the crime to 911, but they weren't willing to give a name."

"I told you, I don't like dealing with the fuzz. Plus, I don't want to buy tomorrow's newspaper and see my name linked to a bad part of town in the middle of the night. That wouldn't be good for my image."

"Amen." Payne laughed as he thought about the irony of Greene's statement. "Now let's go inside this nudie bar and bitch to the owner about the defective guns that you bought for us."

* * *

Despite the approach of daylight, The Fishing Hole was still crawling with semi-aroused men and naked women, a sight that surprised Payne and Jones. Neither man was a huge fan of the skin-club scene, so they were unaware that most dancers did their best business just before closing time—due to the intoxication and horniness of their fans.

"Let me see if Terrell's still here," Greene stated. "It's nearly 4:00 a.m., so there's a good chance he might've gone home for the night."

"Should we go with you?" Jones wondered.

"Probably not. Like I told you before, Terrell's pretty skittish around new faces. If the three of us go charging back there, he's liable to get pissed. And trust me, you don't want to see him pissed."

Payne nodded while receiving a skeptical glance from Jones. Once Greene had entered the club's back corridor, D.J. spoke up.

"What's your gut say about Terrell Murray?"

"It's undecided. Earlier tonight he seemed pretty hospitable, but it could've been an act. I find it pretty suspicious that he sold us defective weapons and recommended our visit to Sam's shooting gallery within a 24-hour period. That's a pretty big coincidence, don't you think?"

"But what would he have to gain from our death? Like you said, if the kidnappers want your money, your death does not help their cause."

"I know. That's why my gut is undecided on the guy. I can't figure out why he'd want to eliminate us. Shoot, maybe all of this was just a fluke."

Jones continued to ponder Murray's role as he watched The Fishing Hole's crowd. "You know, maybe he doesn't want to kill us, Jon. Maybe he has to."

"What do you mean by that?"

"I'm sure in a perfect world the people that captured Ariane would want to take your money, but maybe our presence in New Orleans has everyone spooked. Maybe the kidnappers figure it's better to cut their losses before they get caught. You know, live to play another day."

"Possibly," Payne admitted. It was a thought that hadn't crossed his mind. "But to be honest with you, I didn't get the sense that Murray was surprised by our visit. If, in fact, he is the ringleader of all this stuff, you would think that our appearance would've flustered him."

"True, but if Levon had inadvertently mentioned our names when he purchased the guns earlier in the day, then Murray would've had plenty of time to gather his senses, right?"

"Right."

"And arrange faulty weapons for us."

"Mmmm, hmmm."

"And arrange our death."

"I see what you're saying, but for some reason that last part just doesn't seem to click. If Murray wanted us dead and he knew that we had broken guns, then why didn't he have someone walk into Sam's and shoot us at close range?"

"Ah shit. That's a good point. So where does that leave us?"

Payne glanced at Jones and shrugged. "Confused and very tired. I'm sure there's something staring us in the face, but in my current condition, I can't think of it. Give me a little shut-eye, and I'm sure things will be a lot clearer."

"Then let's get out of here," blurted Greene. His approach had been so silent that he startled both Payne and Jones. "Terrell's not here, so I think our refund is gonna have to wait a few hours."

"That's OK," Jones muttered. "I think all of us could use some sleep before we face our next batch of confrontations."

Payne nodded in agreement. "And trust me, fellas, my gut tells me that there are some big ones headed our way."

And, unfortunately, he wasn't talking about the stripper with the 34DDs that was walking towards them.

Chapter Twenty

Hakeem Ndjai ordered the captives out of their cabins at the first sign of daylight, then led the bruised and battered group, still dressed in the same sweat-soaked work clothes as the day before, across the dew-covered grass to the far end of the field. The walk was a brisk one, forcing the prisoners to maintain a pace that they were barely able to keep, but at no point were they tempted to protest. The captives realized any complaint would've resulted in a swift and vicious beating at the hands of the guards, compliments of the braided cowhide whip that each of them carried at their side.

Not exactly the way the prisoners wanted to start their day.

When they neared the tree-lined edge of the field, Ndjai ordered the group to stop, waiting for everyone to gather around him before he started his speech. After clearing his throat, the African-native spoke to the prisoners, lecturing on the torture device that they were about to see, an invention that he had constructed himself.

"What I am about to show you is a contraption that I was never allowed to use on the cacao plantations of Cameroon because the land owners felt it would be too destructive to the moral of the workers. Thankfully, Master Holmes views things a little bit differently and has given me permission to use some of Ndjai paused dramatically, staring into the scared eyes of his my toys on the people that need to be disciplined the most." prisoners. "I like to call it the Devil's Box."

Then, just as quickly as he had stopped, Ndjai started walking again, leading the group along the edge of the forest, taking them even further from the cabins where they spent their terror-filled nights.

As they continued their journey, the sights, sounds and smells of nature became more obvious than on the cultivated land near the plantation house. Ducks, geese, and brown pelicans waddled on the marsh's edge, carefully avoiding the foxes that guarded the land and the alligators that patrolled the water of the cypress swamps. White-tailed deer darted amongst the fallen timber like a scene from a Disney movie, while beaverlike rodents called nutrias scoured the hard ground, searching for food. Doves, egrets, and wild turkeys squawked and sang in the dense groves of oak trees to their left, which dripped with thick blankets of Spanish moss. Small pockets of flowers—lilies, orchids, honeysuckle, jasmine, and azaleas—dotted the terrain, filling the air with a sweet fragrance that overpowered the horrid stench that covered the prisoners, temporarily giving the group a reason for hope.

But five more minutes of hiking ended that.

The soft sounds of nature that had calmed them a moment before had been replaced by the distant howl of a man. The echoing scream was muffled at first, like the sound of a crying baby that had just run out of oxygen, but it slowly increased in volume and intensity with every step that the group took.

"A little further," Ndjai chuckled as he listened to the melodious sound of torture. "Then you will see why my friend is so unhappy."

With tired legs and shortness of breath, the group mounted one of the few slopes that this part of Louisiana had to offer. A few of the prisoners struggled with the climb, stumbling on the loose sand and gravel that covered the steep mound, but the guards showed them no mercy, flogging the fallen captives with punishing blows from their braided whips. The loud cracks of cowhide, followed by the sharp shrieks of pain, only added to the horrific sound of terror that emanated from the crest of the hill. In unison, the combination of cruelty, agony, and torment created a noise that was so sinister, so evil, that some of the guards even shielded their ears from the heinous symphony.

When the last captive reached the apex of the bluff, Ndjai ordered the prisoners to study his invention—for he wanted their full attention when he introduced them to the torture device—but his command was anything but necessary. No member of the pilgrimage had ever been more wide-eyed in their entire life. The concentration of each person was focused solely on the wooden cube that had been anchored into the rich soil of the hilltop, waiting for a detailed explanation of Ndjai's masterpiece: the Devil's Box.

Standing four-foot tall and four-foot wide, the cube did not appear threatening at first glance. Made out of thick slabs of oak, the device was secured in place by a number of sturdy metal cables that had been pounded into the rocky turf. The outside surface of the box had been sanded to a smooth finish, then painted with several coats of black waterproof sealant, giving the device the look of a giant charcoal briquette. Solid on all sides but one, the center of the top layer had been carved in an intricate tic-tac-toe pattern, allowing fresh air into the cube without giving the occupant a view of anything but the blue sky above.

"I know what you're thinking. The Devil's Box does not appear very dangerous, but don't let its simplicity fool you. It can be nasty in so many ways. And if you don't believe me, you can always ask Nathan." Ndjai put his face above the box and laughed. "Isn't that right, Nathan? You thought you were pretty tough when you were out here, but now that you've been in there for a while, you don't feel very tough, do you?"

The incarcerated man answered the taunt with a torture-filled grunt, but the words he tried to pronounce were indecipherable.

"You'll have to excuse Nathan. He's been in my box since long before your arrival on the Plantation, and it seems that his tongue has swollen to twice its normal size due to dehydration." Ndjai turned his attention back to Nathan. "Isn't that right? You're a little bit on the thirsty-side, aren't you? Well, you should've thought of that before you hurt one of my bosses, you stupid man."

The guards laughed in amusement as they watched the taunting.

"But don't worry, Nathan. I won't let you die of thirst. I'll keep you like this for as long as I possibly can, teetering on the edge of life and death, contentment and pain."

Once again the captive screamed in agony but this time with a far greater intensity, causing each prisoner to shiver with fear for his predicament and hatred for the man that had put him there.

"Before you get the wrong idea," Ndjai continued, "and start to think that this device is simply used to bake the bad attitude out of an inmate, let me point out your error. The Devil's Box is not used for dehydration, even though, I must admit, the severe loss of fluids is a pleasant side effect. In fact, that's why I painted this thing black: to draw in the intense heat of the sun. You'd be surprised at how uncomfortable a person can get when they run out of liquid."

He moved closer to the group so they could see the emotion on his face.

"Obviously, in the beginning you feel an unquenchable thirst, but from there the human body falls apart, oh so quickly. The tongue starts to balloon, followed by the drying of the throat-lining and nasal passages, making it difficult to talk or even breathe. Lips start to crack, and skin starts to separate, painfully pulling apart with the slightest movement of any kind. Intense cramps surface in your arms and legs, causing agonizing spasms that you cannot stop. Your bladder swells from the lack of moisture in your body, making you suffer through the severe urge to urinate, but the joke's on you because there's no liquid in your system to squeeze out. From there, your kidneys fail, followed by the rest of your body's systems including your brain, causing extreme hallucinations and eventually insanity. All in all, not a pleasant way to go."

Ndjai caught his breath while enjoying the horrified look of the crowd that surrounded him—children clinging to their parents for support, strangers holding hands for comfort and unity, fear and desperation in the eyes of everyone. It was a sight that Ndjai truly enjoyed.

"But as I pointed out to you, dehydration is not the main purpose of the Box. It is merely a bonus, heightening the effects of the device's original purpose. And what purpose is that, you may ask? Well, let me tell you. The purpose is agony."

Ndjai approached the box again, but this time one of the guards accompanied him. When they reached the device, the guard handed him a plastic container that was no larger than a box of tissues, then quickly stepped aside.

"When we placed Nathan in here several weeks ago, he was covered in cuts and scratches, wounds that I personally administered with the aid of a metal-tipped bullwhip. Since that time his body has been unable to heal the torn flesh because of his severe thirst and lack of a balanced diet. In fact, I'd guess that his wounds are probably in worse shape now than the day that I created them due to the variety of infections that were bound to develop in these unsanitary conditions. Tsk, tsk. It's really a shame, actually. Nathan used to be such a large man. We even had a difficult time squeezing him inside the box because of his girth. But now, due to his lengthy stay in my device, he has been sapped of much of his size and strength—like Superman in a Kryptonite cage."

Ndjai grinned like a dominatrix as he held the small container above the grid-like opening in the top of the box, taunting the imprisoned man by swooshing the object back and forth with a flick of his wrist. Without delay, Ndjai's gesture instantly increased the intensity of Nathan's screams, turning his moans and wails of discomfort into terrified shrieks of torment. The sound, which filled the warm air with unspeakable dread, emerged from the wooden cube with the ferocity of a jungle cat, quickly bringing goose-flesh to everyone on the ridge.

"One of the most difficult things to deal with in the Devil's Box is the loneliness. The heat is bad, the thirst is horrible, but the solitude is what gets you. Without companionship, the mind tends to wander, leaving sanity behind while looking for ways to amuse itself. It's a terrible thing, but it eventually happens to each of my victims."

Ndjai peeled open the container's cover and slowly started dumping its contents into the Box.

"Since I worry about my friend's sanity, I do my best to occupy his intellect with tangible things. Instead of letting his mind drift off to a fantasy world, where it's liable to get permanently lost, I try to keep his brain focused on real-life issues. Each day it's something new, and each problem gets more and more difficult for Nathan to solve. You're probably wondering, what is today's problem?" He laughed softly while answering his own question. "Fire ants."

Ndjai drained the container into the Devil's Box, then glanced through the cube's tiny slits to see how Nathan was handling things. His intense screams proved that he wasn't enjoying himself.

"As you can probably tell from my friend's reaction, the sting of the fire ant is very painful. The poison isn't life-threatening, unless, of course, a person has an allergic reaction to it or gets stung by several dozen ants in a short period of time. Oops! Do you hear that, Nathan? Don't let them sting you if you can help it."

Ndjai chuckled as he redirected his attention to the group. "Unfortunately, that task might be pretty difficult for Nathan. You see, fire ants are actually going to be drawn to the taste of blood, and since he has a number of open wounds all over his body, they are going to get pretty wound-up, like sharks in a sea full of chum. Then again, look on the bright side: If he's able to eat the ants before they eat him, he'll get his first dose of protein since his captivity."

The guards smiled at the remark, displaying their approval of Ndjai's presentation.

"At this point of my lecture, I'm sure you're all wondering why I brought you up here to start off this glorious day. That is what you are wondering, isn't it? Well, the reason is quite simple. I wanted to show you how good you currently have it." Ndjai paused for a moment to let that comment sink in. "Is the heat of summer intense? Sure it is. Is working all day in the field tough? No doubt about it. Is sleeping on the ground of your cabin uncomfortable? Of course."

Ndjai moved closer to the group, narrowing his reptilian eyes to tiny slits before he finished his speech. "But keep this in mind. If you mess with me or my staff, I could make things so much worse for you. I could make your stay worse than hell."

* * *

For one reason or another, Hannibal Kotto had the sudden urge to phone Theo Webster at the Plantation for some assurances about their operation. Unfortunately, because of the time difference between Africa and Louisiana, he was forced to wait several hours before he could make the call in good conscience.

It was a considerate thought, but Kotto's restraint wasn't necessary. From the moment the current batch of prisoners had reached the Plantation, Webster's sleeping patterns had been thrown into a nasty loop. He wasn't sure if it was work-related stress or some kind of rare insomnia virus, but Webster hadn't been able to get any rest for more than a week, a phenomena that could be easily detected with one glance at his haggard face.

When Kotto's call finally came in on his private line, Webster slipped his wire-rimmed glasses off of his donut-sized ears, then set the spectacles on the mouse pad to his right. After rubbing his blood-shot eyes, Webster grabbed the phone. "Yes?"

"Theo, is that you?"

Webster smiled, quickly recognizing the distinct accent of his associate. "Hannibal, it's been a few days. How are things in the Motherland?"

"The sun is shining. The birds are singing. The giraffes are tall."

He laughed as he studied the clock and date on his computer screen. "Am I mistaken, or is this an unscheduled call?"

"No, you are correct. We weren't supposed to speak until tomorrow, but there were a few things on my mind so I decided to contact you a little bit early. Do you have some time?"

Webster grinned while sliding his glasses back on. "Since this $5 per minute call is on your bill, I have all the time in the world. What's on your mind?"

"Surprisingly, money."

"I would've been stunned if it had been anything else. What's troubling you now?"

"Nothing's troubling me, but things *would* be easier if I got your input on something."

"Just name it, and I'll try to help."

With the sleeve of his purple shirt, Kotto dabbed the perspiration from his upper lip. The next few minutes would ultimately determine how much money the organization would earn during the next month, and to Kotto, the bottom line was almost as important as the political statement that they were trying to make. "Yesterday, I had a conference call with our African distributors, and the topic of price was broached. They wondered how much we were going to charge per unit on our next shipment of snow."

"And what did you tell them?"

"Nothing conclusive. I said that a price wouldn't be set until after my people had a chance to sample the product. That seemed to quiet them for the time being, but . . ."

"But you'd still like to have an answer, right?"

"Exactly. And since I don't know what kind of quality we're dealing with, I figured your input would be most useful when setting the price."

Webster hastily contemplated the numbers, trying to get a rough estimate of the soon-to-be-made shipment. "Correct me if I'm wrong, but our last unit price was $50,000 per and the quality was pretty poor, right? Then I guess our goal should be to raise the bar significantly and see how many people are willing to jump."

Kotto's eyes narrowed as he ran his fingers through his graying hair. "How high is significantly?"

"Do you think your customers would be willing to accept double?"

"Double? Are you crazy? I truly doubt that anyone will be willing to pay that much."

Webster leaned back in his chair and sighed. Even though he felt that $100,000 per unit was in the ballpark, it was obvious that Kotto had given the question plenty of thought. "If you have a figure set in your head, Hannibal, I think it would expedite things if you just mentioned it."

"I was thinking $70,000 per, possibly $75,000 if you can assure me that the quality is outstanding."

"I think I can give you that assurance, but before I do, let me speak to the others. Each of them has a large stake in this game, too."

Chapter Twenty-One

Wearing nothing but a pair of gym shorts, Jonathon Payne opened his eyes and gazed at the ceiling in confusion. He knew he'd spent the night on somebody's couch but couldn't remember whose.

"Damn," he moaned, "I think Alzheimer's is setting in."

After cracking his back, Payne climbed to his feet and looked for something that would jog his memory, but the windowless den had no pictures or clues of any kind. Thankfully, he noticed two doors on the far side of the room and figured the hallway would provide more answers. Without delay he trudged to the nearest one and opened it.

Oops. It wasn't a hallway, but rather a closet filled with his clothes. "Man, I hate mornings. I swear to god I do."

After grabbing his toothbrush and a T-shirt, Payne shut the door and turned towards the next one. Unfortunately, before he had a chance to open it, he noticed the brass handle starting to turn on its own.

"Son of a bitch. Who the hell is this?"

Nervously, Payne glanced around the room, looking for somewhere—anywhere—to hide, but the lack of furniture made it virtually impossible. So, with little time to think, Payne opted to stand behind the swinging door, brandishing his toothbrush as the unlikeliest of weapons.

Finally, after a lingering pause, the door opened.

The wiry black man entered the room with careful steps, trying to be as quiet as possible. While holding a Glock in his right hand, he slid across the tan carpet, staring with bewilderment at the empty couch.

"Damn," he cursed. "I guess I'm too late."

"Too late for what?" Payne demanded as he jammed his toothbrush into the gunman's back. "Too late to shoot me in my sleep?"

The man sneered as he sized up the situation.

"Answer the question," Payne ordered, pressing the instrument even harder into the man's flesh. "Too late for what?"

"All right, I'll tell you. Just promise me you won't use that thing. I'm allergic to fluoride." David Jones laughed and turned toward his best friend. "Actually, I came up here to wake you, but I guess I'm too late. How long have you been up?"

"A couple of minutes," Payne admitted. Suddenly, most of the details of the situation—Ariane's abduction, New Orleans, the shooting of Sam—came flooding back to him. "How about yourself?"

"Several hours now. I had time to eat, read the paper, borrow this gun, write my will, raise a barn, milk a—"

"OK, I get your point. You couldn't sleep, so you're going to make me feel guilty."

"Actually, I slept fine. I'm just not able to crash like you."

"Crash? Why, what time is it?"

"It's nearly noon."

"Noon? Why in the world would you let me sleep that long? There are things to do."

Jones shook his head. "Jon, relax. Levon and I were able to get a lot of stuff done while you were sleeping. Besides, after yesterday's trauma, we felt you needed your rest."

"Maybe so."

"Plus, I know how you are when you're tired. You aren't worth your weight in shit."

"Yeah, but . . ."

"But nothing. Go get cleaned up, and when you return, I'll fill you in on everything."

* * *

A shower was just the thing that Payne needed, for when he returned, he was a changed man. His mind was clear, his body was re-energized, and his appetite was borderline ferocious. It was like the bathroom's steamy water had magically transformed him into a completely different person. Of course, it was a change that Payne had expected. He'd been this way his entire life and often referred to himself as a shower addict. Some people relied on caffeine in the morning; Payne relied on a bar of soap.

"Hey, buttercup, what's up? Did you need me for something?"

D.J. stood from the couch and grinned. "Since I know there isn't a chance in hell that you'll remember anything from before your shower, I'll start at the beginning."

Payne thanked him with a simple nod of his head.

"Levon and I went over last night's activities, and we came to one major conclusion: Levon messed-up bad."

"Why do you say that? Am I forgetting something?"

"Actually, it was Levon that forgot something, and that's the problem."

Payne leaned against the wall as he slid a pair of dress shorts over his scab-covered knees. "OK, I'm intrigued. What did Levon screw up?"

"Our guns."

"Our guns? How did he do that?"

"As you know, the Glocks we bought have no external safeties."

"Yeah, that's one of the reasons I like 'em."

"Me, too. However, the guns *can* be fitted with a special internal safety, normally used as a safeguard during demonstrations."

"And how does that affect us? Did we buy demo units?"

"No," Jones answered, "but Levon told me that Terrell sometimes sets the internal safeties on his guns before he sells them. That way, there's no chance a customer can use his new weapon to rob Terrell's men right after a sale."

"And Levon knew this?"

"Yeah, but he told me his gun was ready-to-shoot when he bought it, so he assumed ours would be, too."

"Of course you realize his assumption could've gotten us killed."

"Yeah, and he knows it, too. In fact, the big baby's been pouting all morning."

"Well, there's nothing he can do about it now. It's not like we would've been able to save Sam even if our guns had worked."

"That's what I told him, but he's still taking things kind of hard."

"Well, he shouldn't," Payne stressed. "He's not used to combat situations like we are. Mistakes should be expected."

"I know. I told him that."

"And he's still upset?"

Jones gave a short nod. "Very."

Payne sighed as he slipped on his shoes. "Don't worry, I'll go talk to him. Where is he? Hopefully, in the kitchen because I'm starving."

"Actually, he's at Terrell's. While you were sleeping, he made an appointment to get us some new guns."

"And you didn't go with him?"

Jones shook his head. "Levon assured me that things would go much smoother if he went alone."

"He's probably right." Payne realized that their names were probably mentioned in the local newspaper in connection with Sam's death, which wasn't the best thing to be known for when buying a gun. "I'll tell you this, though. I'm not taking any more chances with our weapons. I want an opportunity to fire at least a dozen rounds before we head out today. No more of this blindly going into combat bullshit."

"Sounds good to me. Of course, there's one problem. We're currently in the middle of a large city. What the heck are we going to shoot at?"

Payne grabbed Greene's gun, then flashed a wicked smile. "Have I ever told you how much I hate squirrels?"

* * *

As Payne looked for something to eat, he noticed movement on one of Greene's security monitors. Intrigued, he inched towards the screen. "We've got company."

Jones, who was building a meat-loaf sandwich, frowned at the news. "What kind?"

"Black car to the front." Payne watched in earnest as the iron gate slid open and the vehicle entered the driveway. "Whoever it is has the code."

"Is it a Beamer?" Jones asked casually.

"Could be. Why?"

"Because Levon drives one. Duh!"

Payne threw D.J. a nasty look, then returned his full attention to the screen. Thankfully, his tension melted away when he noticed Greene behind the wheel of the car.

"Guys!" Greene shouted the moment he walked into the house. "Where are you hiding?"

Payne and Jones made their way from the kitchen, following the sound of Levon's excited voice as it echoed through the front foyer. When they found him, they could tell that something positive had happened.

"What's gotten into you?" Payne wondered.

"Yeah," Jones mumbled as he chewed on his sandwich. "You seem happier than before."

"That's 'cause I am. You know how I went to get you guns? Well, I came back with more than that. Something much better."

"I hope you didn't buy a tank," Jones teased, "because Jon doesn't carry that kind of cash."

"No," Greene laughed. "I got some news on the Posse."

"On the Posse?" Jones blurted as chunks of meat loaf flew from his mouth. "What kind of news? What'd you hear?"

"Calm down, man. I'm getting to that." Greene wiped the front of his shirt, trying to knock off any morsels that clung to it. "As I was saying, I went to The Fishing Hole to talk to Terrell about that internal safety thing. I figured if I bitched enough I could get him to cut us a deal on some new pieces. Unfortunately, he was on the phone when I rolled in and his boys said he'd take a half-hour to finish. So instead of waiting back by his office, I strolled out front to check out the Saturday dancers. And that's when I saw him."

"Him?" Jones questioned. "You saw him? What the hell were you doing watching a guy dance?"

Greene rolled his eyes. "The guy I saw was a customer."

"Well, thank god for that. I thought maybe you were—"

"Knock it off," Payne ordered. In his mind, there was a time and a place for jokes, but this wasn't one of them. "Let Levon speak. This is important."

Jones growled softly, but did what he was told.

"Anyways," Greene continued, "I saw this guy leaning against one of the brass railings, his hand and arm just dangling over the side. And guess what I noticed?"

Payne answered. "A Posse tattoo."

"Give that man a prize. A fuckin' P tattoo. Can you believe my luck?"

"Did you talk to him?" Payne demanded. "Did you find anything out about Ariane?"

"Well, kind of."

"Kind of? What does that mean? Did you find anything out

or not?"

"I tried talking to him. I really did. But the bastard saw me staring at his wrist. I don't know how he noticed me—I mean, I was being really careful—but he did. Next thing I know, he's whispering something to the buckwheat next to him, then bolting from the club."

"So that's it? That's the great news? You saw a guy with a P tattoo but you let him get away? Damn, Levon. Weren't you a linebacker? You should've tackled him or something."

Greene frowned at the outburst. "Jon, you've gotta chill. There's still more to tell you."

"Then keep talking." Payne couldn't believe the methodical pace of Greene's story. Ariane was in grave danger, and Levon was spinning a yarn. "And get to the good stuff before we waste anymore time."

"OK, OK. Just give me a second." Greene, suddenly nervous, sucked in half the air in the foyer before exhaling. "As it turns out, the tall buckwheat at the bar knew everything that we needed to know. Well, maybe not everything, but he knew a lot."

"And trust me," Jones interjected, "we want to hear every last word, but before you continue, you've got to explain something. You keep saying 'buckwheat.' What the hell does that mean?"

"Sorry, man, it's a southern term. You remember that Little Rascals character, Buckwheat? You know, the one that Eddie Murphy played on Saturday Night Live?"

"O-tay," Jones chuckled, using Murphy's famous expression. "I remember."

"Well, there are brothers around these parts who are *really* rural. Nappy-looking hair, old work clothes, messed-up backwater language. Well, we call those brothers buckwheats."

Jones smiled. "Really? Up north they're called niggers."

Greene laughed at the term that only blacks were allowed to

use. "Yeah, well, us southerners use nigger, too. But when a guy's too dumb to know any better, we call 'em buckwheats. And trust me, this guy was a buckwheat-and-a-half. Fucked up dreadlocks, gold teeth, taller than me. Shit, I almost felt bad for the punk."

"Buckwheat, huh? I'll have to remember that term."

"Guys," Payne yelled, unable to wait any longer. "This isn't the time or place. What did this guy tell you?"

"Sorry, Jon." Greene gathered his thoughts before continuing. "I went up to him all cool-like, just watching the girls with him for a while. After a couple of minutes, he turns to me and starts talking. As luck would have it, he recognized me, and we started bullshitting about football. After five minutes or so, I decided to push my luck. I asked him about the guy with the tattoo."

It's about time, thought Payne. "And what'd he tell you?"

"He said he worked with the guy. He wouldn't give me many details, but said all the brothers he worked with had the same kind of tattoo. It was a requirement for their job."

Jones frowned. "I didn't know gangbangers had jobs, other than selling drugs and shooting rappers."

Greene shrugged. "Apparently these guys do."

"Or," Payne added, "maybe they aren't bangers. Maybe the tattoo isn't what we think it is. Maybe the P tattoo isn't a Holotat."

"Well, that gets me to the next part. This guy is pretty quiet about his friend, but he's unable to shut up about himself. He keeps ramblin' on about his job and stuff. He says that he cooks and cleans for a bunch of people every day, and the only time they let him leave is to pick up supplies. Then, he mentions the guy with the tattoo is the one who brought him to New Orleans. I guess he's his driver or something."

Jones groaned. "They're not from here? Damn! That'll make our job a lot more difficult. Or did this guy let the name of the town slip out during your conversation?"

"Nah, I wasn't that lucky. I asked him where he worked, but he kind of got rattled. Said it was top-secret stuff. Said he could get into all kinds of trouble from the state if he blabbed about it."

"From the state?" Payne blurted. "What kind of messed-up thing is that to say?"

"You've got me," Greene admitted. "Louisiana might be a little bit backward, but I've never heard of any traditions where state workers got branded for employment. Or any top-secret facilities that would hire a dumb-ass buckwheat like this guy."

"So what kind of place was he talking about?"

"I don't know, Jon. I asked him, but he said he had to shut up. I even offered to buy him a drink for his trouble, but he quickly turned me down. He said he had to buy a bunch of supplies before it got too late, said he wanted to get all of his work done before the fireworks started."

Jones raised an eyebrow. "Fireworks? Isn't it a day early for that?"

"You'd think so, huh? But the local shows are gonna be held on the Third this year. I don't know if it has something to do with the Sabbath Day, but if you fellas want to see fireworks in New Orleans, you better be looking at the sky tonight."

Payne didn't care for fireworks—there was something about the loud bangs and bright lights that brought back wartime memories that he'd rather forget—but due to the potential of that night's show, he was suddenly a big fan. "I'm sure I'm asking for a miracle here, but did this guy mention where he'd be watching them? Because, I'll tell ya, I'd love to talk with him."

Greene smiled at the inquiry. "As a matter of fact, he did. He said he'd be watching them at Audubon Park."

Chapter Twenty-Two

Payne dropped off his friends on opposite ends of the park, then focused his attention on the task at hand: finding a nameless witness in a sea of 60,000 people. Sure, Payne realized his chances were slimmer than Calista Flockhart with a bad case of the flu, but he figured he had three things going for him—his target's unique appearance (very tall, gold teeth, and more dreadlocks than a West Indies barbershop), his unwavering determination to find Ariane, and his two kick-ass partners.

Together, they made the three musketeers look like girl scouts.

With cell phone in hand, Payne parked his car on the Tulane University campus, then jogged for several blocks until he reached the spacious grounds that he'd been assigned. Greene had told him that the center of Audubon Park would be packed with partygoers—more people than you can count, he'd said—but when Payne arrived, he was greeted by the exact opposite. The scenic grove was empty.

Confused, he slid his gun from the constraints of his belt and inched along the concrete walkway, suspiciously searching the green boughs above him for signs of a potential ambush—a cracking branch, a glint of color, the smell of sweat—but the only thing he noticed were insects, dozens of chirping insects wailing their summertime song. Next, he examined the massive trunks of the live oak trees that surrounded him and the decorative cast-iron benches that lined the sidewalks, but everything in the vicinity seemed clear. Way too clear for his liking.

Puzzled by the lack of activity, Payne paused for a moment and considered what to do next. He was tempted to call Greene for advice, but before that happened, he heard the faint sound of horns seeping through the trees several hundred yards to the south. Relieved, he strolled towards the music and eventually found the scene that Greene had described. Thousands of drunken revelers frolicked on the banks of the Mississippi River, enjoying the hell out of the city's Third of July extravaganza.

"Damn," Payne grumbled. "This place looks like Gomorrah."

Clowns with rainbow-colored wigs trudged by on stilts while tossing miniature Tootsie Rolls to every child in sight. A high-steppin' brass band blared their Dixieland sound as they strutted past an elaborate barbecue pit that smelled of Cajun spareribs and grilled *andouille.* Vendors peddled their wares, ranging from traditional bead necklaces to fluffy bags of red, white, and blue cotton candy. And a group of scantily clad transsexuals, dressed as Uncle Samanthas, pranced in a nearby circle, chanting, 'We are gay for the USA.'

Yet somehow, Payne ignored it all.

With a look of determination on his face, he blocked out the kaleidoscope of diversions that pleaded for his attention—the gleaming streaks of light as kids skipped by with sparklers, the sweet smell of funnel cakes that floated through the air, the distant popping of firecrackers as they exploded like Rebel cannons on the attack—and remained focused on the only thing that mattered in his life: finding the Plantation witness.

Unfortunately, Payne had little experience when it came to tracking civilians on American soil. He was much more accustomed to finding soldiers in murky swamps than buckwheats at carnivals, but after giving it some thought, he realized his basic objective remained the same.

He needed to locate his target as quickly and quietly as possible.

To do so, he tried mingling with the locals, slyly shifting his gaze from black man to black man as he made his way through the festive crowd. But his efforts to blend in were almost comical. No matter what he attempted, the scowl on his face made him stand out from the lively cast of characters that surrounded him. He tried smiling and nodding to the people that he passed, but the unbridled intensity on his face made him look like a serial killer gone a courtin'.

After making a few children cry, Payne realized he needed to change his approach. Drastically. So instead of trying to hide in the crowd, he decided to stand out in it, making his anxiety work for him instead of against him.

Hell, Payne reasoned, why be cautious when there was little risk in being bold? The Plantation witness had never seen his face, right? So it made little sense for him to slink through the crowd, hiding. He figured, why not approach every Rastafarian in sight and just talk to him? To do so, he simply needed an excuse, one that would allow him to talk to strangers without raising their suspicion. But what could he use? What could he ask that would seem so harmless, so innocuous, that a person wouldn't flinch at the query? The question needed to be simple, yet something that explained the frazzled look on his face, a look with so much intensity that it actually scared kids. . . .

Kids. That was it. He could pretend like he lost his kids. He could move from black man to black man, pretending to look for his lost kids. Heck, in the few seconds it took for a suspect to respond to his query, Payne could study the man's face, hair, teeth, and height. And if that wasn't enough to eliminate him, Payne could listen to the man's voice and see if it possessed the backwater accent of a buckwheat.

Damn, Payne thought to himself. The plan was ingenious.

Bold, daring, creative and . . . completely unsuccessful.

Payne talked to every black man he saw, every single one, but most of them turned out to be way too short to be a suspect. And the few he found who actually stood over 6' 4" didn't have the Fort Knox dental work or the redneck speech pattern that Greene had described. In fact, nobody in the crowd even came close.

Yet, Payne remained undeterred. He had waited his entire life to find someone like Ariane—intelligent, witty, beautiful—so he wasn't about to give up hope after an hour. If he had to, he would stay in New Orleans for the rest of his life, spending every cent of his family's fortune, searching for the one witness that could bring her back into his arms.

But as it turned out, none of that was necessary, for his best friend was having a lot more luck on the eastern-end of the park.

Payne hardly noticed it at first. The sound was too soft, too timid, to be heard above the cacophony of the boisterous crowd. But when it repeated itself a second and third time, it grabbed his attention with a firm grip. It was his new cellular, and it was calling his name.

"Hello?" he mumbled, bracing himself for hundreds of possibilities.

"Jon, it's D.J. You're not going to believe this, but I nabbed the bastard."

"You what?"

"You heard me, man. I nailed the punk."

A huge smile formed on Payne's lips. "Are you serious? I was beginning to think that this was a waste of time."

"Me, too," Jones admitted. "But I got the Bob Marley clone right here." There was a brief pause on the line before D.J. spoke again. "Say something, you little prick."

For a minute, Payne thought he was being scolded, but before he could say a word, he heard a meek squeal on Jones' end of the phone. "Howdy, sir. How is you?"

The accent brought a smile to Payne's lips. "What's your name?"

"Bennie Blount."

"Well, Bennie, it's nice to meet you. Now do me a favor and put my friend back on."

Jones got on the line a second later. "Polite little bastard, isn't he?"

But Payne ignored the question. "Where are you? I want to chat with this guy *now.*"

"We're near the main road, about five minutes from the basketball courts where you dropped me off. How about you?"

"The same." Payne paused to collect his thoughts. "Listen, get to the courts as quietly as possible. I don't want our conversation to draw a crowd, and the courts should be deserted."

"No problem. And I'll give Levon a buzz on my way there."

"No," he growled. "I'll call Levon. I want you to keep two hands on this guy at all times."

Jones laughed at the indirect order. "Don't worry, Jon. This boy ain't goin' anywhere. I've got a gun shoved in his back. Plus, I'm using his hair as a leash."

Payne chuckled at the image. "Well, don't hurt him too much, you big bully. I want Bennie to be talkative, not comatose, when I meet him."

* * *

After calling Levon, Payne ran to the basketball courts to survey the territory before his partners arrived. As he'd hoped, the courts were completely deserted and far enough away from the crowd to attract unwanted attention, which would come in handy if they had to pacify Bennie with force.

As for the area itself, it was divided into two contrasting regions. Three concrete basketball courts with tattered nets and bent rims sat off to the left, next to a jungle gym and an old swing set that had clearly seen better days. A sandbox sat dormant, still decorated with a number of childlike structures which waited for their youthful architects to come back and complete their jobs. But if the sand castles were anything like the rest of the area, the odds seemed pretty good that they'd crumble into disrepair before anyone did a damn thing to fix them.

Surprisingly, in direct contrast to the first, the second region was in impeccable shape. Finished in smooth asphalt and recently painted with bright white lines, the full-length basketball court was tournament-ready, surrounded on all sides by metal bleachers and a large barbed-wire fence, which was designed to keep the ball in and vandals out. To get inside, a person usually had to show an ID to an armed park guard, but on this night, the only people who were armed were Payne and his friends.

"Yo, Jon!" called a voice in the night.

Payne turned from the metal bleachers and saw the massive form of Levon Greene jogging towards him. "Over here, Levon."

Greene lumbered closer, a limp fairly obvious in his stride. "Where is he? I want to make sure you got the right guy."

Payne shrugged as he watched Greene enter the main gate and approach the bleachers. "D.J.'s the one who has him, but he hasn't shown up yet. I hope he didn't run into any problems."

"None at all," Jones bellowed from the shadows. Payne and Greene whipped their heads sideways, searching for the source of the sound. "I was just waiting to make a dramatic entrance."

Payne struggled to find him, but after a while, two dark faces emerged from the night.

"Gentlemen," Jones announced, "let me introduce you to my new best friend and a future witness for the prosecution, Mr. Bennie Blount."

Chapter Twenty-Three

Jonathon Payne had seen thousands of people in his life, folks from hundreds of different lands, cultures, and villages, yet despite all of that, he could not remember a more unique character than Bennie Blount.

Standing 6' 6" with an elaborate web of dreadlocks that added an additional three to five inches of puffiness to the top of his pointed head, Blount looked like an exaggerated stick figure, created in the mind of a warped cartoonist. He lacked muscle mass of any kind; instead, resembling a limbo pole turned vertically, topped off with a poorly crocheted black wig. Gold front teeth were the only remarkable things about his face, and his dark eyes revealed absolutely nothing, resembling the lifeless props often found in a taxidermist's shop.

"How'd you find him?" Payne demanded.

"It wasn't very tough," Jones joked. "Some kids were using him to break open a piñata."

Payne smiled despite the seriousness of the situation. "And does our new friend know why you've brought him here?"

"Not yet." Jones released Blount's hair and pushed him forward. "I figured you'd want to provide him with all the details."

Payne nodded as he walked towards the witness. "So, Bennie, do ya know why you're here?"

Blount raked the dreadlocks from his eyes with his E.T.-like fingers, then responded. "I gets 'da feelin' it ain't to play no basketball."

"You got that right," Greene growled from the bleachers. "You're lucky I'm resting my knee, or I'd come down there and kick the shit out of you."

The color drained from Blount's dark face as he cowered from the angry voice. "Mr. Greene, is 'dat you? My gawd, 'dat is you. Did I do somethin' bads to you 'dat I don't remember?"

"It's not what you did," Payne interjected, "it's what you didn't do. You failed to tell Levon the things that he wanted to know during your earlier conversation."

Blount glanced at Payne and frowned. "Do I knows ya, sir? I don't mean to be rude none, but ya don't looks like someone I knows."

"My name's Jonathon Payne, and we talked on the phone a few minutes ago." He pointed to D.J. before continuing. "And that over there is David Jones."

Blount instinctively massaged the top of his sore scalp. "Oh yes, I knows him. We's already been introduced."

Payne tried not to laugh as he pictured D.J. using Blount's hair as a leash. "Bennie, as I mentioned, the reason that Mr. Greene is angry is because of your behavior earlier today at The Fishing Hole."

"But I didn't do nothin' wrong. I didn't drinks too much or cause no problems. Mr. Murray warns me mo' 'dan once about touchin' the gals, and I swears I didn't do none of 'dat today. I swears."

"That's not what I'm talking about. Mr. Greene is upset because you were unwilling to answer his questions about the man with the tattoo. He asked you some simple questions, and you refused to respond."

Blount glanced at Greene and shivered slightly. "Is 'dat why you's mad at me, Mr. Greene? 'Cause I wasn't in no talkin' mood?"

"I gave you an autograph, Bennie, and you weren't even

willing to help me with a little information. That was kind of disappointing, man."

"More like rude," Jones chimed in. "You should be ashamed, Bennie."

"Real ashamed," Payne added.

As Blount studied the men that surrounded him, guilt flooded his face. "I's so sorry Mr. Greene. I didn't know 'dat it meant 'dat much to ya. If I'd known things was that impo'tant, I'd've told ya everything I known. I promise I woulda."

Grinning, Payne slowly reached out his hand and placed it on Blount's rail-thin shoulder. "Well, Bennie, maybe it's not too late to make amends. If you act nicely, I bet Mr. Greene would give you a second chance. In fact, I know he would."

"Does ya think so, Mr. Payne?"

"I know so, Bennie." Payne stepped aside, allowing Blount to get a full view of Greene. "Go ahead, Bennie. Apologize to my friend."

Blount lowered his head in shame and looked at Greene's feet as he spoke. "Mr. Greene, I swears I didn't do nothin' wrong on purpose. If you gives me one mo' chance, I promise I make things up to ya."

Greene sighed deeply, as if he actually had to consider Blount's apology. "All right, kid. I'll let this one slide. But you better tell us everything that we want to know, or I'll never forgive you. Ever."

Blount's face erupted into a wide smile. "Anything, Mr. Greene. Just ask me and I'll tells ya. I promise, Mr. Greene. I don't wants ya to be mad at me. Really."

Greene grinned with satisfaction, enjoying every moment of this mini-drama. "I'm glad, Bennie. That's what I was hoping you'd say."

"Me, too," Payne interjected. He led Blount to the metal bleachers and asked him to sit down. "Now, I've got a number of questions that I'd like to ask you, Bennie, and some of them might seem a little bit strange. Trust me, though, each of them are really important to me and my friends."

"OK," he mumbled, slightly confused.

"First of all, what can you tell me about your friend with the tattoo? Where do you know him from?"

"Ya mean 'da P tattoo? I met him at work, Mr. Payne. Most of 'da people at my work have 'dat tattoo."

"And where is it that you work, Bennie?"

Blount paused for a second, not sure if he should answer the question.

"Come on," Greene urged. "You promised you'd help us."

"'Dat's true, I did," he admitted. "But it's not as easy as 'dat, sir. Ya see, I promised other peoples 'dat I wouldn't talk about this none."

Greene moved forward on the bleachers, flexing his massive arms as he did. "But those other people can't hurt you right now, now can they?"

Blount gulped loudly. "I guess you's right. 'Da place is called 'da Plantation. I work at 'da Plantation."

The word piqued the interest of all three men, yet Greene was the first to speak. "Plantation? What exactly is the Plantation?"

Blount frowned. It was obvious that he wasn't supposed to talk about the Plantation, but all it took was one glare from Greene and he started to speak freely. "'Da Plantation is 'da name of the place 'dat I be working for. It's a special jail 'dat the state puts in place less than a year ago."

"A jail? What kind of jail?" Payne demanded.

"'Da *secret* kind."

"What the hell is a *secret* jail?"

Blount exhaled before answering. "You know, 'da kind 'dat people are sent to fo' special crimes."

Payne grimaced. This was getting nowhere. "Special crimes? What the hell are they?"

"You know," he whispered, "'da kind that people aren't suppose to talk about."

Payne glanced at Jones, looking for help, but it was obvious that he was just as confused. "Bennie? Can you please tell me what type of people commit special crimes?"

"Not really, Mr. Payne. There've been too many people fo' me to keep track of over the past few months."

"Men? Women? Old? Young?"

"Yes, sir."

Payne lowered his voice, whispering to his companions. "I guess that means all of the above, huh?"

Jones and Greene nodded in agreement.

"Is there anything else that you can tell us about this place? Anything at all?"

Blount considered the question for a moment, then brushed the hair from his face. "Yes, Mr. Payne, there be one more thing I could tell you about 'da people at 'da Plantation."

"And what's that, Bennie?"

Blount pointed a long, bony finger at Payne. "All 'da people look like you."

It took a moment for Blount's comment to sink in, but once it did, none of the men knew how to respond. Finally, after a moment of silence, Jones spoke. "All of the people look like him? You mean everybody is ugly and has a small dick?"

The words brought a smile to Blount's face. "'Dat's not what I meant, sir. What I be tryin' to say is 'dey white. Ev'ybody at 'da jail is white."

"Levon?" Payne whispered. "Do you have any idea what he's talking about?"

"I wish I did, but I'm clueless." Greene turned his attention to Blount. "Bennie? What do you mean everybody's white? You're telling me there aren't any black people at the Plantation at all?"

"No, I ain't sayin' 'dat. There be plenty of black people at 'da jail. All 'da workers be black."

"What?" Jones screeched. "The prisoners are white and the guards are black? Holy parallel universe, Batman."

Payne glanced at his friend and grimaced. Sometimes he wondered if Jones was actually 36 years old. "Bennie, don't you think that's a little bit strange? Why are all of the prisoners white?"

"I don't know, sir, 'cause I ain't in charge of no prisoners. I just be in charge of 'da taters and 'da grits. My bosses don't be allowin' me to get near 'da people. They keeps me far away."

"And why do you think that is, Bennie?"

"My bosses tell me it be fo' my safety, but sometime I don't know. I jus' don't know."

"Why's that?" Payne wondered.

"'Cause some of 'da prisoners ain't 'dat scary, Mr. Payne. I ain't afraid of no girls, and I sure as shit ain't afraid of no kids, neither."

"Kids?" Nausea quickly built in Payne's belly. "What kind of kids, Bennie?"

"White ones."

"No, that's not what I meant. How old are the kids?"

"Well," Blount mumbled, suddenly realizing he'd probably revealed too much information for his own good. "It be hard to say. I ain't too good at guessin' no ages."

Payne moved closer, trying to intimidate Blount with his proximity. "This isn't the time to quit talking. How old are the goddamn kids?"

"I don't know," he whined. "I really don't. I just know that some of 'dem have to be young 'cause I have to make 'dem different chow to eat. I have to cut up 'deir food 'cause 'dey don't got big teeth yet."

"Jesus," Payne groaned. That meant the Posse had kidnapped kids under the age of five. "And you don't find that strange? Come on, Bennie, you can't be that dumb. What kind of prison holds toddlers?"

Blount lowered his head, too embarrassed to answer the question.

"Levon," Jones whispered, trying to take the focus off of Bennie. "What do you think? Could a place like this exist?"

Greene chuckled at the thought. "A state-run facility with black guards and white inmates? Hell no! The government couldn't get away with a place like that in Louisiana. There are way too many David Dukes down here to oppose it."

"How about privately?" Payne wondered. "Do you think a black-run facility, one that imprisons and punishes white people, could secretly exist in this state?"

"Now that's another story." Greene sighed, closing his eyes as he did. "Racial tension has always been big in this state. Always. For one reason or another, there are still thousands of people that are upset about the Civil War. I know that sounds ridiculous to a northerner, but trust me, it's true. White supremacists run some towns, while black militants control others. Then, to complicate things even further, there are places in this state that no one controls. The swamps, the forests, the bayou. Shit, I guarantee there are communities in Louisiana that don't even know what year it is—or even care, for that matter. Those are the areas where a place like the Plantation could exist. No visitors, no cops, no laws. Those are the areas where a place like that could thrive."

The possibility didn't make Payne happy. Until that moment, he had hoped that Bennie Blount was a simpleton who mumbled to strangers in order to get attention, but that seemed less likely now. If someone like Levon was willing to believe that the Plantation could exist, then there was a good chance that it actually did.

And if that was the case, then it was up to Payne to find it—before it was too late.

Chapter Twenty-Four

Sunday, July 4th
Independence Day

The Plantation Posse had waited several years—actually, several generations—for this day to come, and now that it was here, they could barely contain their enthusiasm. Originally, they were going to hold their ceremony an hour before dawn (the same time that they'd burned the cross) but they realized that their adrenaline wouldn't allow them to wait.

No, their big announcement would have to be pushed ahead.

Within minutes, Ndjai's battalion had assembled the prisoners, forcing them to stand in the field in a very specific order:

Group One: The Metz and Ross families
Group Two: The Potter and Cussler families
Group Three: The Edwards and Walker families

When they were ready for him, Holmes put on his cloak and rode his raven-colored steed across the lawn, like a shadow emerging from a black sea. The only thing announcing his presence was the patter of hooves, tearing up the soft turf in rhythmic bursts, and the occasional crack of his leather whip against the horse's dark flesh.

And the sound brought chills to the prisoners.

Once he reached them, Holmes stared through the holes in his black hood and sighed. "Well, well, well. A bunch of frightened white people. The sight kind of warms my heart." He turned his attention to Ndjai. "Is everyone here?"

"Everyone except Master Jackson and Master Webster."

Holmes nodded as he thought back to the days when he was the scared victim, when he watched the KKK ride in on horseback and terrorize his family with burning crosses and threats of violence. He could still remember the pounding of his heart, the knot in his gut, the way he trembled while clinging to his mom for safety.

"Will they be joining us?" Ndjai wondered.

Holmes blinked, then refocused his attention on the prisoners. He loved the way they quivered in the firelight. "My friends wouldn't miss it for the world."

* * *

Blount gawked at the interior of Greene's mansion, glancing into every room he passed. He'd never been in a house like that before and wanted a chance to investigate it while he had the chance. Unfortunately, his hosts had other ideas.

"Bennie!" Payne shouted. "Where are you hiding? Levon got off the phone ten minutes ago, and we've been waiting for you ever since."

"I sorry." He jogged toward the sound of Payne's voice. "I guess I gots a little bit lost when I left 'da toilet. I sorry."

Payne grinned at Blount's lanky form and easygoing country manner. "That's all right. But if we're going to finish, we've got to get back to work." He threw his arm around Blount's shoulder and squeezed. "And you're our star witness."

The concept made him smile. "Let's gets to it 'den. I been

waitin' my whole life to be a star." Blount and Payne joined Greene and Jones at the massive dining room table. Maps and sketches were scattered all over the flat wooden surface. "So tells me, what does ya need to know?"

Jones, who possessed the strongest background in military strategy, glanced at the information in front of him. He was a graduate of the U.S. Air Force Academy, where he'd studied computers and electronics at the Colorado Springs campus. After receiving the highest score in the Air Force's history on the MSAE (Military Strategy Acumen Examination), he earned his entrance into the MANIACs after a short stint in the military police. Once in the MANIACs, he served several years under Payne, planning a variety of successful missions.

"OK, now that we know about the Plantation, we need to talk about points of entry. How are we supposed to get onto the island?"

"'Da only way to gets to 'da island is from 'da Western Docks. Cypress swamps is gonna block every other way to 'dis place."

"Then tell me about the Docks. What's over there?"

Blount grimaced. "There be a clean path, right in 'da middle, and you needs to follow it to avoids trouble. If you goes to one side of the path, boom! You hits some stumps. If you goes to 'da other side, boom! You hits some trees. But, if you stays in 'da middle . . ."

"Boom! The guards see you coming and blow you out of the water."

Blount laughed at Jones' comment. "'Dat's right. We's gonna be gator stew."

But Payne wasn't nearly amused. This was Ariane's life that they were talking about.

"So," Jones continued, "if we can't use the docks without being seen, what do you recommend?"

"Why does you want to make 'dis so complicated, Mr. Jones? There ain't no reason to find no back door when 'da front door is working jus' fine."

"But I thought you said that there'll be guards at the Western Docks."

"Yep," he chuckled, "but 'da guards won't be expectin' what I has in mind."

"And what is that?"

Payne and Jones listened to Blount's idea, grinning. Even though they'd won dozens of military awards between them, had planned intricate missions through several of the world's most-hostile terrains, and had been in charge of the most elite fighting force in America's history, they were forced to admit that Bennie Blount, a dreadlocked, slow-talking buckwheat from the Bayou, had bested their military minds by devising the perfect plan all by himself.

And most importantly, it was simple enough that even he couldn't screw it up.

* * *

Dancing slightly with every crevice that they crossed, the headlights of the all-terrain vehicles looked like giant fireflies as they skimmed across the landscape of the Plantation. When the motors could finally be heard, the three groups of prisoners turned and watched the arrival of the two men. Wearing black hoods and thick cloaks, Jackson and Webster soared through the darkness, looking like supernatural beings on a mystical quest, their ebony wardrobes flapping in the great rush of air.

It was the type of entrance that nightmares were made of.

After stopping his vehicle, Jackson climbed off his ATV and walked toward Holmes, who was impatiently sitting on his steed. "Sorry we took so long. Right after you left, we got a phone call that we had to deal with."

"Is everything all right?" Holmes wondered, making sure that the prisoners couldn't hear the concern in his voice.

Jackson nodded. "It seems that we're going to be getting a few more captives, but it's nothing to worry about."

Even though he wanted to hear about the new arrivals, Holmes realized this wasn't the time or place to ask questions. He had more important things to deal with, like his announcement. "People, you've already met Master Jackson and myself. Now, it's time to meet the real brains of the Plantation, the man that issued your invitations. I want you to say hello to Master Webster."

Despite their hatred of the man, the group screamed in unison. "Hello, Master Webster!"

Webster laughed under his hood. When he'd started this mission of revenge several years before, he had dreamed of this moment, but now that it was here, he no longer knew how to react. His reality had somehow intersected with his dream world, and he could no longer discern which was which.

"Today," Webster said, "is the Fourth of July. Independence Day. A day to celebrate the freedom of this great nation." He took a deep breath while staring at the attentive crowd, wondering if they would understand the irony of their situation. "Unfortunately, some Americans weren't given their freedom in 1776. In fact, thousands of men and women from this country weren't given their emancipation until after the Civil War. And yet we, as a nation, celebrate our independence on this day and this day alone. Ironic, isn't it? A country celebrates their freedom on a day when only half of us were freed."

He cleared his throat as the prisoners thought about his words.

"Wait! You want irony? How about this? Independence means freedom, doesn't it? That's the basic concept, right? Well, what's the opposite of independence? Slavery! Back in the days, white people used to refer to slaves as indentured servants. Did you know that? That was the politically correct way to say slaves. Indentured servants. Has a nice ring to it, huh? Well, what does that term mean? If you're indentured, it means that you're bound to work for someone, literally forced to be a servant. *Forced.* In other words, slavery."

Webster could tell that his guests were getting confused, so he simplified things for their benefit. "I'm sure you're wondering, what's so ironic about that? Well, look the two terms up in the dictionary and guess what you'll find? The two words reside next to each other. First, you'll see indenture, then you'll see independence. Side by side, one after the other. Two words with completely different meanings, and yet, they're forced to be neighbors in the English language." He shook his head at the irony. "And if you think about it, it's kind of like us: We're independent, but you guys are indentured."

Holmes laughed loudly. He'd never seen Webster so animated before. Ever.

"And that brings us to the moment you've been waiting for. The answer to the one question on each of your minds: Why are you here?"

Under his dark hood, Webster smiled at the prisoners.

"That's what you're wondering, isn't it? Why have you been selected to join our festivities at the Plantation? Why, out of all of the people in America, did we bring you unlucky bastards here?"

He smiled again, loving the tension in the slaves' faces.

"Why? We chose you because of your past."

Chapter Twenty-Five

The boat inched from the private dock and slowly made its way through the dark waters that surrounded the Plantation. Dressed in a black robe, the muscular figure tied a rope around the white man's wrist and made sure that it was tight enough to pass inspection. After wrapping a thick cord around the next prisoner's arms, he completed the knot with a series of quick jerks, pulling the extra slack from the restraint with a firm tug.

"Watch it, big guy. You're pinching me."

Levon Greene stared at his captive, then yanked on the rope even harder. "We're playing for keeps here, D.J., and if that means you have to suffer, then so be it."

"Yeah," Payne shouted over the boat's motor. "You didn't hear me complain when Levon tied me up."

"True," Jones cracked, "but you've always liked the kinky stuff."

Normally, Payne would've laughed at the comment, but the tension of the moment prevented it. They were heading into battle, and the success of their mission was resting firmly on the shoulders of Bennie Blount, a simple-minded buckwheat from the Bayou.

And that scared the hell out of Payne.

"Bennie," he said in a calming voice. "If you don't mind, I'd like to talk about your plan one more time."

"Yes, sir. 'Dat's fine with me. I don't wanna be doin' nothin' that gets no one hurt—especially myself."

"Don't worry," Greene assured him. "Things will go smoothly."

"I be hopin' so."

It had taken several hours, but Payne suddenly realized how different Greene and Blount actually were. Sure, both men were black, but their physical appearance couldn't have been more different. Greene was thick and defined, muscle stacked upon muscle, veins literally bulging through his skin. His head was shaved, his nose was broad, and his teeth were pearly white. If he were a tree, he'd be the biggest, baddest, mightiest oak in all the land. Blount, on the other hand, looked like a sapling gone bad. His limbs sprouted from a thin and brittle torso, which appeared too feeble to support even the smallest amount of weight. His face, long and narrow, was topped with a haircut that resembled a rotting fern, black stems and roots tangled in every direction. And his teeth—his fake gold teeth—were straight out of the Mr. T. School of Dentistry.

"Trust me, Bennie. As long as you stay by me, you're not going to get hurt. I promise you that."

"Sounds good, sir."

"Bennie," said Payne. He hated to interrupt their conversation, but they were going to be at the island soon. "When we pull up to the docks, you said there'll be two guards waiting for us, right?"

"Yes, sir."

"Which means we have to make this look believable." Payne glanced at Blount and waited for a reaction. "Do you know what I mean by *believable*?"

"I think so, Mr. Payne. You jus' want me to play Bennie, right?"

Payne grinned. Things couldn't get much simpler for Blount. "That's right. Just be yourself and pretend that D.J. and I are your prisoners."

"You got it, Mr. Payne."

"And stop calling me, Mr. Payne. I'm your prisoner, remember?"

"Yes, sir."

Payne took a deep breath, then turned his attention to Greene. "Obviously, you have the most important role of all. You have to make the guards believe that you're one of them. Bennie claims that your black cloak is similar to the ones that they wear, but it's not a perfect match. So don't let them get a good look at it. Try to keep moving, OK?"

"Don't worry, I will."

"And always make sure that your hood is up. If they're sports fans and they see your face, the game's over. They'll immediately know that you're not a guard."

The ex-linebacker laughed at the irony. "You got that right."

"Then, once we get past the guards, you'll need to borrow one of their vehicles to take Bennie's supplies to the main house and us to the holding area. Halfway there, you'll cut our ropes and leave us in the woods. That'll give us a chance to do some recon on the island."

"But we'll get our weapons before then, right?"

Payne turned towards D.J. and nodded. "Yeah. One of the boxes with Bennie's supplies is filled with firearms. We'll take what we need and stash the rest in the trees. We don't want to be bogged down before we know what we're up against."

He turned back to Blount. "Bennie, this is when you execute your part of the plan. I want you to go into the house and start your normal breakfast preparations. While you're making the food for the guards, I want you to mix in the drug that I gave you. Pour half the bottle in the coffee, the other half in the scrambled eggs. That way, everyone's bound to get some whether they're eating or not."

"OK, Mr. Payne, I will . . . Oops. I mean, OK, prisoner."

Blount smiled with pride. He thought he'd done a good thing

by remembering his line, but his momentary blunder would've been enough to get everyone killed.

"Keep working on it, Bennie." Payne sighed, praying that Blount would improve quickly. "Where was I? Oh, yeah, within ten minutes of breakfast, everyone should be unconscious. That's when D.J. and I will make our move. We'll emerge from the woods in serious S & D mode."

Greene frowned. "S & D mode?"

"We'll *search* for the prisoners and *destroy* anything that gets in our way."

"You mean, you's gonna kill people?" Blount demanded.

Payne nodded. He'd already covered this at Levon's house and didn't feel like discussing it again. Unfortunately, he didn't have a choice. He had to keep Blount as calm as possible if this was going to work. "We don't want to, Bennie, but we might have to. That's just the way it is. Sometimes, the only way to help one group is to hurt another, and that's the situation that we're facing. In order to help my girlfriend and all the little kids on this island, we might have to hurt some of the guards. We'll try not to, but if it's us against them, they're the group that has to lose. I won't settle for anything less."

* * *

With the expertise of a riverboat captain, Blount weaved his way through the cypress swamp and coasted towards the moss-covered supports of the dock. As he approached, the guards rushed over to greet him.

"Gump, are you OK? We were expecting you a while ago."

"Did the fireworks run late?" asked the other.

But before Blount could say anything, Greene moved to the front of the boat and spoke for him. "It wasn't the damn fireworks," he growled. "There's been a security breach. Now quit your small talk and take our damn line before there's trouble. I have two prisoners on board."

The guards glanced at the large figure, then jumped to attention. After dropping their rifles to the ground, they ran to the dock and offered their assistance in any way possible. Greene nodded at them, then tossed them the boat's rope. The two guards snared the line and carefully pulled the craft against the side of the dock.

"It looks like they're buying it," whispered Jones.

Payne nodded slightly, but he wasn't nearly as positive. In his mind, something was fishy, and it was more than just the stench of the swamp water. "I hate to say this, D.J., but . . ."

The confidence quickly drained from his face. "Don't tell me. Your gut?"

"Or to put it in your cartoon lingo, my Spidey senses are tingling."

Jones rolled his eyes. "Can you be a little more specific?"

But before Payne could answer him, Greene rushed over and told them to be quiet. "Things are going well. Don't blow it by talking."

He followed his command by slinging Payne over his shoulder and carrying him to the dock. He repeated the process with Jones, then turned to the workers and shouted, "Don't just stand there. Start unloading the damn boat. We have a lot of work to do."

"Yes, sir!" they answered.

Greene smiled at Blount, then glanced at the two captives near his feet. "How was that? Authoritative enough for you?"

Jones tried rolling onto his back, but his bound hands hindered his effort. In a strange way, he kind of looked like a dyslexic turtle. He was currently on his stomach but wanted to flip over. "You sounded good to me, but I'm not the one you need to worry about. Ask Jon what he thinks. He's been paranoid since we docked."

Greene turned his attention to Payne. "Jon? Is there something we need to talk about before the guards return?"

"Not really. I can wait until they get back."

"Excuse me? What do you mean by that?"

"I mean, you're just going to tell them what I say anyways."

"What?" Greene lowered the hood from his head, then knelt next to Payne on the ground. As he did, his bad knee cracked several times. "What the hell are you talking about?"

"Yeah," Jones demanded. "What the hell are you talking about?"

Payne wanted to look his best friend in the eyes, but the position of their bodies made it impossible. "D.J., I'm sorry to say this, but if my guess is correct, Levon is one of them."

Chapter Twenty-Six

Holmes and Jackson had planned on speaking to the prisoners, but since Webster was doing such an eloquent job, they allowed him to continue.

"Independence Day is a holiday that's supposed to symbolize freedom in this country. Freedom? In America? What a joke! A country that turned its back on my people for decade after decade of neglect believes in freedom? Ha! My black brothers and sisters were smuggled into America in the hull of cramped slave ships in the most unsanitary of conditions, brought into this country like cattle, then purchased by the white man for their own personal use. And you call that freedom? They didn't have a choice in the matter. They were stolen from their homes in the dead of night, then forced to fight despair and depression as the only life that they'd ever known was ripped away from them in one malicious act. And if they somehow reached America, managing to survive the sickness and sadness and tumultuous seas, do you know what they got for their trouble? They were made into niggers. That's right, these people weren't born niggers; they were made niggers. They weren't allowed to read. They weren't allowed to write. For Christ's sake, they weren't even allowed to think. Generation after generation of black potential wasted by the sinister white race."

The prisoners listened, trembling.

"Take a look around you. This plantation was built several decades before the Civil War. Nice, isn't it? It's probably hard to imagine, but the people who worked this soil were my ancestors. Not black people in general, but my *actual* ancestors. That's right. Through painstaking research, I've traced my family tree back to this plantation. Isn't that amazing? My forefathers worked this land. They slept here, and ate here, and gave birth in the tiny cabins that surround us."

Webster shook his head, rage boiling inside of him.

"And because of you, my family was forced to die here, too."

A slight murmur rippled through the crowd. What did Webster mean by *you*?

"For the past few days, you've been subjected to unpleasantness. Long hours in the sun, a scarcity of food and water, nothing to sleep on but the ground itself. But guess what? That pales in comparison to what my relatives faced. Back in the 1800s, slaves were forced to live in these cabins year round. There was no heat. There was no air conditioning. Shit, there wasn't even insulation. In the winter, the frigid air would leak into their homes, stealing their health, killing their young. Were they allowed to complain? Hell, no! They had to endure. Ten, twelve, sometimes as many as fifteen people were thrown together into one cabin and forced to make do, huddling in the center of the cramped floor for warmth. And if they bitched, they were beaten.

"During the rainy season, the ground became so saturated that the moisture would rise up into their cabins, forcing my ancestors to sleep in the mud. The mud. Like fucking animals. These were *my* relatives, for god's sake, and they were treated like beasts. Can you imagine that? Hard-working people made to live like savages? Meanwhile, the Delacroix family, the white bastards that owned this property, slept in the comfort of the plantation house, fires roaring in every room. They had four-poster beds, pillows, blankets, mattresses. They didn't work, but they lived like kings. They ate vegetables, fresh from the ground.

Meat that was recently slaughtered. Bread, hot and fresh, baked in stone ovens. And wine, the sweet nectar of the gods, poured to their heart's content.

"Do you know what my relatives got to eat? Do you? At the beginning of every week, each person was given three and a half pounds of bacon from the smokehouse, and enough corn to make a peck of cornmeal. That's it. For the entire week. No coffee, sugar, or salt. Nothing. Just bacon, cornmeal and water for every meal, year round, for a lifetime. Think about that. No variety. No spices. And worst of all, no refrigeration. Can you imagine how many people got sick from eating spoiled meat? And if they didn't die from food poisoning or malnutrition, I wonder how many people were killed for their rations? Think about it. If you ran out of food on a Thursday and weren't getting more until Sunday, wouldn't you consider murder? You'd have to. If you didn't eat, there was a chance that you were going to die. Right? Murder would have to enter your mind. Wouldn't it? You're damn right it would!

"And what about punishment? Do you actually think we've been rough on you? Hell, you ain't seen nothing! The shit that occurred in the 19th century was far more brutal than anything we've done here. Yeah, some of you have felt the unpleasant sting of a leather whip, but back in the old days, slave drivers used to whip their niggers until they could see ribs. Motherfuckin' ribs. The gashes on the brothers' backs were so deep you could see their lungs. Have we done anything like that to you? Anything that brutal? Tell me, you bastards, have we?"

Despite his questions, the crowd remained silent, way too frightened to talk. But that didn't matter to Webster. He viewed their silence as insubordination, and that had to be dealt with immediately.

Turning towards Master Holmes, he said, "Can you believe that? They didn't answer me. Maybe you better show 'em what I mean about discipline."

Holmes grinned savagely under his black hood. He'd been on his best behavior since the finger-chopping incident on the first night, but now that Webster was encouraging him, he figured he could slide back to his sadistic ways.

He stepped forward, searching for a target, staring at the scared faces in the moonlight. Who should he choose? he wondered. Which person would be the most beneficial to their cause? Then he saw him, the perfect victim. He was the finest specimen in Group One. A middle-aged male, father of Susan and two other brats. What was his name? Oh yeah. Ross. Jimmy Ross. Yes, he would do nicely. An impeccable sacrifice.

Devastate the strong and the weak will crumble.

With unblinking eyes, Holmes focused on him, coldly, quietly selecting him as his prey. And Ross knew it, too. Holmes didn't even say a word, yet Jimmy dropped to his knees in fear, his entire body trembling with trepidation.

"Pick up the coward," Holmes growled.

And the guards obliged, pouncing on Ross like hungry wolves before they dragged him to the front of the crowd. Then, just as quickly as they had attacked, they backed away, leaving Ross at the feet of his master with nothing between the two but a palpable wall of hate.

"Master Webster?" Holmes continued. "Why don't you tell our guests about the white man's sacred temple? I think they'd enjoy that tale. I know I would."

Webster readjusted his glasses, grinning. "In the 19th century, the white man considered his body sacred. It was a divine and holy temple that was not to be defiled by the dirty black man. Sure, it was fine for Thomas Jefferson to run around having sex with all the black women on his plantation, but if a Negro ever touched a white man for *any* reason, the slave was legally allowed to be killed. Can you believe that? The courts actually allowed it. A brother could be killed for touching a white man. Of course, that didn't make much financial sense, so it was rarely done. I mean, why murder someone who is doing your chores for you?

Right? So the white man was forced to come up with a better punishment than that."

Jimmy Ross swallowed deeply, waiting for Master Holmes to make a move. But the black man didn't budge. He stood like a statue, not blinking, not breathing. Silent. Completely silent. Listening to the words of his friend.

"No one knows where the idea of the Post first came from, but its popularity spread quickly across the southern states during the early 1800s. In fact, it spread like wildfire."

Suddenly, without warning, Holmes burst from his trance and lunged in Ross' direction. The prisoner instinctively flinched, raising his hands to protect himself against the approaching target, but it was a mistake that he shouldn't have made.

"You tried to hit me!" Holmes screamed, stopping six inches short of Ross. "You white piece of shit! You tried to hit me!"

"I didn't, Master Holmes. I swear! I—"

"I don't give a fuck what you swear. I'm in charge of your sorry ass, so your words mean nothing to me. If I say you tried to hit me, then you tried to hit me." Holmes turned toward his guards. "Get me the Post! I need to teach this cocksucker a lesson!"

"In fact," Webster continued, like he was narrating an evil PBS special, "even if the threat was an implied one—a swing that never landed, a hand being lifted for protection, or a tip of a cap to a white woman—slave owners were encouraged to administer this punishment."

The guards carried a seven-foot wooden post, approximately six inches in diameter, to the front of the group and slammed it into the ground. After straightening it with a careful eye, they drove the long peg into the pliable turf with several swings of a large metal hammer. Once it was securely into the ground, the device was ready for use.

"Now get him," Holmes ordered.

The men clamped onto Jimmy's arms much rougher than

they had before and slammed him against the Post. Then, before he could move, the larger of the two black men forced Jimmy's cheek against the rough wooden surface, holding his face against the Post with as much strength as possible. And Holmes was pleased by the sight.

While watching his prey quiver in fear, Holmes slid in behind him, pulling a claw hammer out of the folds of his own dark cloak. The sight of the small instrument brought a smile to his lips. Even though he enjoyed chopping fingers, there was nothing that Holmes enjoyed more than the Post. The fear. The blood. The disbelief in the eyes of his victim. He loved it. For one reason or another, it satisfied something inside of him that most people couldn't understand—the desire to be violent.

Reaching into his pocket, Holmes fumbled for a nail. He knew that he'd placed one inside his cloak before his ride from the plantation house, but now that he needed it, he . . . Ah, there it was. Four inches in length, silver in color, sharpened to a perfect point. He lifted the tiny spike behind Jimmy Ross' head, then studied it with a suspicious eye. It was so small, yet capable of producing so much pain. God, it was beautiful. Holmes breathed deeply, thinking of the impending moment of impact. The smile on his face got even broader.

"The Post," Webster stated, "was a two-step process. Step one was the attachment phase. In order to prevent a messy scene later on, the slave needed to be attached to the Post in the most appropriate fashion. According to the journals that I've read, there was one method in particular that was quite popular."

Holmes lifted the tip of the spike and ran it through the back of Jimmy's hair, tracing the ridges of his skull with the sharp point of the nail, looking for the proper insertion point. Once it was located, Holmes raised his hammer, slowly, silently. The crowd, realizing what was about to be done, gasped with fear and pleas of protest, but to Holmes, their murmur of shock sounded like a symphony, only adding to his enjoyment of the moment.

"Showtime," Holmes laughed.

With a flick of his wrist, he shoved the nail through the elastic tissue of Ross' outer ear, piercing the tough cartilage with a sickening snap. Before the victim could even yelp in pain, Holmes followed the attack with a swift swing of the hammer, driving the nail deep into the wood, anchoring the ear to the Post.

After a silent pause, Jimmy screamed in agony, then made things worse by trying to pull his head away from the wood. What a horrible mistake. The more he pulled, the more flesh he tore, causing sharp waves of pain to surge through his entire skull. Blood trickled, then gushed down the side of his face. Warm rivulets of crimson flowed over the traumatized skin of his cheek, adding to the gore of the moment.

And the sight of it was too much for his family to take.

In the crowd, Jimmy's 16-year-old daughter, Susan, fainted from the gruesome scene. The image of her battered father was simply too much for her to handle. Tommy and Scooter, his two boys, vomited, then dropped to their knees in a series of spasmodic dry heaves, their bodies on the verge of convulsions. They had never seen anything that horrible in their young lives. Not even in their nightmares.

Unfortunately, the brutal part was yet to come.

With the broad-side of his left forearm, Holmes slammed Ross' face against the Post. "Stop your fuckin' squirming. You're just causing more pain."

"OK," Ross sobbed, willing to do anything to stop the agony. "OK."

"I promise if you stop moving, I'll let you go. I'll free you from the Post."

"All right, whatever you say." He took an unsteady breath, wanting to believe the vicious man. "I will. I swear. I'll stay still."

Holmes nodded contentedly. Things were so much easier with a calm victim. "Good," he hissed, "because you're ruining my souvenir."

From the constraints of his belt, Holmes pulled his stiletto, slipping the five-inch blade behind Ross' head. Then, while calming his victim with words of reassurance, Holmes lowered the razor-sharp edge of his scalpel to the tip of Jimmy's pinned auricle, pausing briefly to enjoy the scene. God, he loved this part: the quiet before the storm, the silence before the screams. There was something about it that was so magical, so fulfilling, that it just couldn't be explained.

Finally, when the moment felt right, Holmes returned his attention to Jimmy Ross.

It was time to finish the job.

With the confidence of a surgeon but the precision of a lumberjack, Holmes severed the ear with a single chop, severing the mass of cartilage from the side of his victim's head in one swift slash, like a movie on the life of Vincent Van Gogh.

A wave of pain crashed over Ross, knocking him off of his feet. As he hit the hard turf, blood oozed from his open wound and flooded his neck and shoulder with a sea of cherry liquid. That, coupled with his loud screams of torture, caused his wife to burst from formation. She rushed to his side, crying, hoping to administer as much first-aid as possible, but there wasn't much she could do. Her husband was missing his ear, and she didn't have a sewing kit.

In time, Webster was finally able to finish his lecture. "Then, as a sign of power, the ear was usually left hanging right outside of the slaves' cabins. And as I'm sure you can imagine, it was a mighty effective way to get across a simple message: If you do something wrong, you will pay for it in pain."

Holmes stared at his souvenir, which dangled from the wooden pole like a freshly slaughtered pig, and grinned. "And that, my friends, is how the listening post was born."

Chapter Twenty-Seven

Payne wasn't sure about Greene until that very moment, but one look into his eyes told him everything that he needed to know. The Buffalo Soldier was a member of the Posse.

"Were you always with them, Levon, or did they get to you after we showed up in New Orleans?"

Jones' eyes widened as he attempted to stare at Payne's face, but the angle of their bodies prevented it. "What are you talking about?"

But Payne ignored him. "Just answer me that, Levon. From the beginning or just recently? I've got to know. It'll make all the difference in the world to me."

Greene continued to stare at Payne, no emotions crossing his face.

"Come on, Levon, just one little answer. Which was it? Before we arrived or after?"

Greene refused to dignify the question with an answer, and to Jones, the silence was maddening. Because of his current position on the ground, he couldn't see what was going on.

"Bennie!" he called, desperately trying to get involved in the conversation. He strained his neck trying to find the dreadlocked servant. "Bennie, help a brother out! Kick me closer to the action! Anything!"

"Be quiet," Payne ordered. "If my guess is correct, Bennie's one of them, too, so he won't help you out."

Jones' eyes got even larger. He had no idea where Payne's theories were coming from, but the mere possibility that any of it was true was mind-blowing. "Bennie? Levon? Guards? Will somebody please tell me what the hell is going on? I'm supposed to be the detective here, for god's sake. Someone throw me a crumb."

Payne shook his head in disgust. "D.J., just shut up and listen. Levon's about to tell us everything."

Greene glanced at Jones, then returned his gaze to Payne. "I can't believe you, man. How can you think that after all the things I've done for you? I showed you New Orleans. I let you sleep in my house. I let you eat my food—"

Payne interrupted him. "You gave us faulty guns. You tried to have us shot. You took a bunch of my cash. . . . Should I go on?"

"No," Greene growled, "you shouldn't. I've heard all that I'm gonna take. You called me up out of the blue, and I went out of my way to help you, and this is how you're gonna repay me? You accuse me of trying to have you killed? Get real, get fuckin' real."

In a burst of rage, Greene kicked a nearby rock, then stormed away, which was fine with Payne, for it gave him a chance to talk to Jones.

"Do you believe me?" he asked.

Jones tried to shrug. "I know you too well not to believe you, but I've got to admit I'd love to hear something that supports your theory."

Payne nodded. "Bennie, do you want to tell D.J. about it or should I?"

Blount glanced at the two men near his feet, then stared at Greene in the distance. "I thinks you better do 'da talkin', Mr. Prisoner. I don't wanna make Mr. Greene mads at me."

Payne smiled. Blount was a hard man to read, but if Payne's theory about Greene was correct, then Blount had to know more than he was willing to reveal. He simply had to.

"Remember how things started bugging me on the boat? How my gut knew something was amiss? Well, it was the guards. The guards acted wrong when we showed up."

Jones scrunched his face. "The guards? You came to this conclusion because the guards acted wrong? Jesus! I could barely see the guards from the boat, but you could tell that something was wrong? What, are you psychic or something?"

"When we pulled up to the dock, the guards approached the boat expecting Bennie, right? They called to him, immediately asking about the fireworks. Well, before Bennie could say anything, Levon moved to the front of the boat and told them that there was a security problem. Right?"

Jones nodded his head, remembering.

"What did they do after that, D.J.?"

"They jumped to attention."

"And then?"

Jones thought back, trying to remember. "I give up. Tell me."

"What did they do with their guns?"

It took a moment, but the solution eventually popped into Jones' head. "I'll be damned. They threw them to the ground, didn't they?"

"Even though Levon's a stranger to these guys, he tells them that there's a security problem, and they throw their guns away. How in the hell does that make sense? Even mall security guards wouldn't have done that. Unless . . ."

"Unless they were told what to expect ahead of time."

Payne shrugged in agreement. "That's kind of what I figured."

Jones nodded, admiring his friend's theory. "I have to admit, Jon, that's pretty good. In fact, I'd give you a round of applause, but . . ."

"You can't because we let Levon tie us up?"

"Exactly."

"Probably not the brightest thing we could've done, huh?"

"Nope. Probably not."

"Right there with the handcuffed to the desk episode, isn't it?"

Jones smiled. The last few days had suddenly become cyclical. "Were the guards the first thing to tip you off, or did you have doubts about Levon before then?"

"No, the guards woke me up, but then I started to think back over the past couple of days. The broken guns, his rule against police involvement, his escape from Sam's, and so on. I figured all of that was too coincidental to be a coincidence."

"Yeah, you're probably right. Detective work should *never* be as easy as it's been for us. I mean, two days ago, we were in Pittsburgh with a license plate and a tattoo, and here we are on the threshold of finding Ariane? Please! I mean, I know we're good and all, but we should've realized something was up a while ago."

"Well, to be honest with you, I wasn't even 100% sure until I mentioned it to Levon. There was a look in his eye that told me everything. He looked like a big ol' dog that was caught sleeping on the nice couch—guilt all over his face."

"It wasn't guilt," Greene remarked. He had circled in behind them to listen to their conversation. "It was stunned surprise. I couldn't believe that you caught onto me. I thought I'd done everything right."

"Don't kick yourself," Payne sighed. "It was the guards' fault. They ruined the entire scene. They should be fired immediately."

"I must concur," Jones echoed. "In fact, I think you have a very big future in acting, just like that other ex-football player from Buffalo. Hmm? What was his name? O.J. something, wasn't it?"

"Nah, Levon's too good for that. He decided to skip O.J.'s second career and went right to his third . . . a life of crime."

Jones laughed. Then, using the melody of the classic Bob Marley song, he began to sing. "He's just a Buffalo Convict . . . works for 'da Posse. He took a bunch of steroids . . . now he's their boss-y."

"That was pretty clever," Greene admitted. "Very clever indeed."

Jones gave him a big wink. "Thank you, Louisiana. I'll be here all week."

"Actually, you will be. Might not be alive the whole time, but we'll worry about that later."

Payne twisted his head and glanced at Jones. "I don't know about you, D.J., but I'm going to worry about that now."

"Me, too," he gulped.

"Jeez," Greene laughed. "You guys don't stop, do you? I thought this black humor, no pun intended, was just an act, but you guys are like this even in the most dire of situations."

"No pun intended?" Payne asked. "Hey, D.J., I think he just made fun of your skin color."

"I'm not black, Jon. I'm mocha."

"Sorry, my mistake." Payne twisted his head once again, but this time towards Greene. "Hey, Levon. Did you sell us out before we came to New Orleans or after?"

A sadistic grin crossed Greene's lips. Since his cover was blown, he figured the answer to one question wouldn't hurt, so he crouched to his knees and stared Payne in the eyes. The friendly gleam that had been present during the past few days had been replaced by a cold, hard glare.

"Jon, if it makes you feel any better, I didn't sell you out. I've been involved with the Plantation from the very beginning. And just so you know, if I knew why you needed my help during your initial phone call, I wouldn't have invited you down here. Can you imagine my surprise when you finally told me about your bitch? I almost shit a Buick. But, hey, what was I to do? You were digging, and I had to stop you. It's as simple as that."

"Then why not kill us? Why take the time to lure us here?"

Greene sighed. He was getting bored with the inquisition and knew that his partners were waiting for him. "I wish we had more time to talk, but I'm afraid my friends are about to make a big announcement, and I don't want to ruin their surprise."

Chapter Twenty-Eight

The ringing of the telephone brought a smile to Harris Jackson's face. He'd been expecting a phone call for several minutes now, and when it didn't arrive, his anxiety began to rise. But now that the call was here, he was finally able to relax.

"Master Jackson, this is Eric down at the Western Docks. Master Greene and Bennie just left our area, and they're headed your way."

"And the prisoners?"

"They're tied-up and docile. I don't think they'll be causing any problems."

"Good," Jackson sighed. Since Payne and Jones had been a nuisance in New Orleans, he figured they might continue the trend on the island, especially since he'd learned of their military background. But now that he knew they were under control, he felt a whole lot better about their presence on the Plantation. "Very good indeed."

"What's good?" asked an eavesdropping Holmes.

Jackson hung-up his cellular phone. "Levon and Gump should be here any second, and they have two new prisoners with them. No problems."

Holmes patted Jackson on the back. "Nice work, Harris. It seems your guards have everything under control."

"It seems that way, but we'll find out for sure in a moment."

Jackson pointed to the truck as it emerged from the trees of the outer grounds. "Why don't you tell Ndjai to keep the captives busy while I check into things? Come on down when you're done."

Holmes agreed and went on his way.

"Master Webster!" Jackson shouted. "Join me for a minute, would you?"

The two men walked towards the truck not knowing what to expect, but the huge grin on Greene's face let them know that everything was fine. Holmes joined them a second later, and the three of them finished the trip in unison.

"Gentlemen," Levon crowed, "Gump and I should win an Oscar for this. We just put on a spectacular performance."

"And Gump helped out?" Jackson wondered.

"Help out? He practically carried it by himself. You should've seen the performance he put on. Unbelievable. His acting is even better than his cooking." Greene signaled for Blount to get out of the truck. "Come out here, Bennie, and take a bow."

"We heard you did a great job, Gump!"

"Congratulations, Bennie!"

Blount was flabbergasted. He had never been treated this nicely by his bosses before. "Thanks," he mumbled, barely smiling. He simply didn't know how to react to their compliments.

"So," Greene asked, "what are we going to do with them now?"

"You mean the new arrivals?" Holmes glanced into the flatbed of the truck and saw Payne and Jones, bound. "You know 'em better than we do, Levon. What do you think should be done?"

Greene considered the question, but it was obvious that he already had a plan in mind. "Once you guys are done with your big announcement, I think it would be best if my friends were eliminated. I figure, why take any chances with men like these?"

* * *

Earlier, Webster had lectured the captives on freedom, slavery, and punishment, yet there was no way that any of them could be prepared for what he was about to reveal next. No way at all.

"The concept of this plantation was born when I was in college. I was taking a class in American history, and we were discussing the Civil War. Don't ask me how, but my professor somehow went an entire week without mentioning black people once. How is that possible? The Civil War was fought over slavery, and this white asshole avoided the topic completely. After class I asked him about his oversight. I figured he'd tell me that an upcoming lecture would be devoted to slavery, or I'd learn more about it in a future reading. But do you know what this fucker had the balls to say? He said, 'Over the years, the impact of slavery has become greatly overrated.' Can you believe that? We're talking about the cause of the Civil War, and he tells me that slavery was overrated. Well, right then and there I knew what I wanted to do with my life: I was going to spend it emphasizing Black history in our so-called Land of the Free.

"But how does one do that? I wasn't really sure, but I knew I needed to get America's attention. I needed to find something that would grab people by their balls. That's why I ruled out things like papers or projects. Why? The majority of people won't pay attention to academic shit like that. No, what I needed was something spectacular, something unforgettable, something that would get this issue noticed. But what?

"Before I made my decision, I thought it was probably best if I did some extensive research on the topic. I started reading books and journals and manuscripts—anything I could find on the topic of slavery—and before long, one common theme started to stand out: plantations! Everything I read about slavery in America mentioned plantations as the focal point. Plantations were the place where slaves lived, worked, birthed, and died. It's where they escaped from when they could, and where they were returned when they were caught. For better or worse, plantations were the center of the black man's world.

"Now, before you get bored with my ramblings, let's move onto the good stuff. How does any of this involve you? I'm sure you're asking that question right now. Why is this nigger making us stand in a dark field in the middle of the night to listen to this lecture? That's what you're thinking, isn't it? You don't think there's anything in this world that I could tell you that would justify your being here, do you? You think I'm just some kind of thug who abducted your families on a whim. That's what you're thinking, isn't it?"

Webster paused to let the tension build. He wanted to see the confusion in his captives' eyes as it slowly continued to grow.

"Then each of you is about to receive the shock of your lives because each of you were selected for a specific purpose, a purpose that we're about to reveal."

Harris Jackson moved forward, taking over the lecture. "During Master Webster's research, he compiled some extensive slave genealogy, an actual list of black family trees. Why is this significant? Because it was nearly impossible to do. Unlike white people, whose history is well documented in tax and property records, the history of the black man is often shrouded in secrecy—slaves rarely had last names, marriages weren't officially recognized, kids were often sold or given away as gifts. Shit, these were just a few of the drawbacks that Master Webster had to overcome in order to complete his work."

Octavian Holmes grinned. "And that's what brings us to you. Why are you guys here? It's the question you've been wondering for a very long time. Trust me, I know. I've seen it in your eyes. Why me? you constantly wonder. Why us? you plead. There has to be a mistake, you assure us. We've done nothing wrong."

Holmes grimaced, his eyes narrowing to slits. "Nope! There have been no mistakes. Each of you is guilty of crimes against the black race. Crimes that you're in the process of being punished for."

The captives glanced at each other, panicked. The sound of Holmes' voice told them that he truly believed what he said.

Holmes actually believed that they were guilty of something terrible.

"Group One," Holmes shouted, "step forward!" Members of the Metz and Ross families reluctantly inched ahead. "Jake Ross, age 71, make yourself known."

The old man, still in great shape despite his age, emerged from the center of the pack.

"You are the father of Alicia and Jimmy Ross, are you not?"

Jake Ross nodded his balding head. "Yes, Master Holmes, I am."

"After marrying Paul Metz, Alicia gave birth to Kelly and Donny Metz. Is that correct?"

"Yes, sir," Jake agreed. "They're my grandkids."

"And your son, Jimmy? He married Mary DaMico, and she eventually gave life to Susan, Tommy, and Scooter. Right?"

Jake was mystified by the line of questioning, but he still answered. "Yes, sir."

"Now tell me, what was your grandfather's last name on your father's side?"

It had been a while since the old man had thought about it, but the name quickly popped into his head. "It was Ross, same as mine. The Ross name has lasted for several generations now."

Holmes winced when he heard the pride in Jake's voice. The tone actually made him want to vomit. "According to Master Webster's research, the Ross family first surfaced in America shortly before the 1800s. They settled in Massachusetts, but slowly migrated south as this country expanded in that direction. Eventually, your great-grandfather purchased a large chunk of land in Georgia, where he grew peanuts until the age of 82."

Jake wasn't sure what Holmes was getting at, but he could tell that it was something big. "Yes, sir. That sounds about right."

Holmes nodded, contentedly. The Plantation had found the right family.

"Group Two," Harris Jackson shouted. "Step forward!"

The Potter family followed directions, taking an immediate

stride toward Jackson.

"Richard Potter, I'd like to speak to you."

Richard groaned softly, then stepped ahead. "That's me, sir."

Jackson took him through the same line of questioning as Master Holmes, and when he was satisfied with the results, he nodded at his partners.

"Group Three," shouted Webster. "Step ahead and join the others."

Ariane Walker moved forward and was followed by her sister and her injured brother-in-law, Robert Edwards.

"Since you're the youngest group here, you might not be able to answer these questions. Therefore, I will give you a rundown of your family's history. If you disagree with anything, let me know immediately."

They nodded, not knowing whose family he was actually referring to.

"Ariane, since you're the healthiest one here, you will be the spokesperson."

"Yes, sir."

"Two years ago your sister married Robert Edwards and she is currently carrying their first child. Your parents, both of them only children, died in a car crash. Each of your grandparents died at an early age, leaving this planet before you were even born. You have no cousins, no aunts, and no uncles. It's just the three of you and the fetus on the way. Is that correct?"

Ariane agreed with everything. "Yes, sir."

"Excellent," he mumbled. "As far as I can tell, your father's parents were raised in North Carolina, but your father's grandparents had roots that grew much deeper south. In fact, they stretched all the way to Louisiana."

Ariane shrugged. "If you say so. As you pointed out, most of them died a while ago."

Webster smiled. "And they're lucky they're dead. 'Cause if they weren't, they'd be standing here right next to you."

The statement made Ariane wince. She knew her presence

had something to do with her family's background, but what? Her parents were both law-abiding citizens. Her sister was never in trouble, so it couldn't have anything to do with her. And as far as she could tell, her brother-in-law was one of the sweetest guys in the world. So, she wondered, what the hell could it be?

"I can tell by your face, Ariane, that you are deeply confused. Your face is flushed. Your eyes are darting. Anger is boiling inside."

In a moment of reckless courage, she decided to voice her feelings. "Yes, sir, I'm angry. My family's done nothing wrong, yet for some reason, we're here, suffering in this dark field. But why? What possible explanation could you have that would explain our presence?"

Ariane could tell from Webster's eyes that she had spoken too harshly. In order to soften the request, she continued. "That is, if you'd like to tell me, Master Webster, sir."

Webster glared at the girl for a tense moment, then eventually grinned. "As fate would have it, bitch, we were just getting ready to tell the entire group that very thing. And for that, you are quite lucky. Otherwise, I would've been forced to punish you severely."

Ariane nodded, relieved.

"Master Holmes?" Webster continued. "Would you care to tell old man Ross and the rest of his family why they are here?"

For a brief moment, Holmes thought back to his own childhood, one that was filled with threats against his family, degrading racial nicknames, cross-burning ceremonies, and the violent antics of the KKK. This was finally his chance to pay the white man back for their crimes against his ancestors, to get even for generations of pain and abuse. "With pleasure."

Holmes turned towards the 71-year-old slave and grinned savagely. "During the course of Master Webster's research, he stumbled across a fact that I found quite interesting. He located the name of the man that was responsible for much of the pain in my family's history. My ancestors, after they were brought to America in the belly of a wooden ship, were sold to a peanut farmer in rural Georgia. There, they worked, day after day, under some of the most horrible conditions imaginable. They were beaten, tortured, and sometimes killed for the tiniest of infractions. And what does any of that have to do with you? Their owner's name was Daniel Ross, and he was your great-great-grandfather, you wrinkled motherfucker."

Jake's head spun as he took in the news. Even though he knew his family had a farm in the south, the thought that they had once owned slaves never crossed his mind. It should've, since it was a typical practice of the time, but it never did.

"And Group Two," Jackson growled. "We've already discussed your heritage, but I left something out. Before your family owned and operated a warm and cuddly farm, they ran one of the strictest cotton plantations in the entire south. The Tanneyhill Plantation was known for its harsh guards and inhumane treatment of slaves. In fact, some black historians refer to it as the Auschwitz of Mississippi."

Richard Potter took a deep gulp as he waited for Jackson to finish.

"For the record, many of my kin were murdered on that plantation. Their innocent blood drips from the hands of your relatives, and I will never forgive or forget that."

Richard, and the rest of his family, lowered their eyes in shame. Even though they were never a part of the horrendous events of the Tanneyhill Plantation, they still felt guilt for the actions of their ancestors.

"And that brings us to you, Ariane." Webster glanced at Tonya, then Robert, then looked around the land of the Plantation. "Remember how I told you that your ancestors stretched way down to Louisiana? Well guess what, bitch. Your family used to own the land that we're standing on."

The color drained from Ariane's face. She had no idea if the information was accurate or not, but she knew that Webster believed it.

"Yes, that's right. The family that you claimed was so innocent, so pure, used to own this plantation and all of the people that worked on it. A group of workers that included my ancestors."

Webster, breathing heavily, moved his cloaked face next to Ariane's ear. "And that's why you're here, bitch. You're here to make up for their sins by giving us your lives."

Chapter Twenty-Nine

After the announcement ceremony, Hakeem Ndjai checked on the status of Payne and Jones. The guards assured him that neither man had put up a fight while being transported, and both of them had been switched from rope restraints to handcuffs as ordered. The news was pleasing to Ndjai. Because of the prisoners' background, he realized that these two men would pose a special problem if they ever escaped from custody, a situation that he'd rather not deal with.

Payne had been locked in the smallest cabin on the Plantation, one that was reserved for solitary confinement of the island's troublemakers. It possessed a low-beamed ceiling, a rock-covered floor, 8' × 8' of living space, and the lingering odor of urine and vomit. All things considered it was like the hazing room of a typical college fraternity.

Jones, on the other hand, was given the Taj Mahal of slave cabins, a room that was usually used by one of the guards. A narrow mattress filled the left-hand corner of the room, nestled between a sink and a small lamp that had been mounted to the thick wooden wall. A white porcelain toilet sat next to the basin, giving Jones a luxury that no other captive was afforded. To make up for it, though, they'd strapped an explosive to his leg, the same device used on the other slaves.

"Hakeem?" called a voice from behind.

Ndjai turned and was surprised to see Levon Greene. He wasn't used to the big man being around. "Yes, Master Greene? Is there a problem?"

He shook his head. "I need to have a word with David Jones. Can you let me in to see him?"

The African nodded, inserting the key into the cabin's lock. "I'll be right outside if you need me."

"Don't count on it," he said dismissively. "This boy's all mine."

Greene threw the door open and scanned the darkness for Jones. He was resting in the corner of the room, his hands bound behind him.

Jones sat up quickly and said, "Levon, is that you?"

Greene closed the door behind him. "How ya doin', D.J.? Are the guards treating you all right?"

"I'm still waiting for room service, but other than that, I can't complain. How about yourself?" Jones paused for a second. So much had happened during the last couple of hours, he wasn't sure if Greene's presence was a good or bad thing. "Oh, yeah. That's right. You're one of them, you bastard."

He ignored the insult. "I came to get you out of here."

Jones' eyes widened in the dim light. "Excuse me?"

"You heard me. I came to get you out. Let me see your hands."

This wasn't something that Jones was expecting. When Payne had first warned him about Greene, he was skeptical. He couldn't believe that the Buffalo Soldier was playing for the enemy. After thinking things over, though, it started to make sense. The broken guns, Sam's death, Levon's escape. Everything fit into place. Greene had been pulling their strings from the very beginning, treating them like wealthy tourists in a game of three-card monte. But now this. One minute he's Benedict Arnold, the next he's George Washington.

"Come on, D.J. Let me see your hands and be quick about it."

Despite his skepticism, Jones leapt off the mattress and turned his back to Greene. "What's going on, Levon? What are you doing?"

"This!"

With a quick burst, Greene forearmed him in the back of the head, sending him face-first into the corner of the cabin. Then, before D.J. could catch his balance, Greene attacked him further, pummeling him with a series of vicious blows to his ribs and kidneys. Punch after punch, elbow after elbow, landed solidly on Jones' back, causing him to sink to the floor in anguish.

"You have to be the dumbest, most gullible brother I've ever met. Did you actually think I was gonna set you free?" Greene punched Jones once again, landing another blow to the back of his head. "What good would it do anyways? As far as I can tell, you've already chosen a life of captivity. David Joseph Jones: house nigger for Jonathon Payne."

Greene chuckled as he climbed off of his victim. "You know, of all the types of people in this world, I hate your kind the most. You've been given so many advantages that other brothers would kill for, and you waste them by working for a white man. You take his charity. You call him boss. You kiss his ass."

He cleared his throat, then spit a giant wad of saliva onto the semi-conscious Jones. "You make me sick. Absolutely sick."

The large man turned and walked back towards the door. When he opened it, he was surprised to see Ndjai standing right outside.

"Is everything all right?" Greene asked.

The African glanced at Jones and frowned. "Did he cause you any problems?"

Greene flexed his hands briefly, then smiled. "My knuckles are kind of sore, but other than that, things went well."

Ndjai nodded his head in understanding. "Is there anything else I can do for you?"

"As a matter of fact, there is. I understand you have my good friend, Nathan, in the Devil's Box."

His eyes lit up with fatherly pride. "Yes, sir, I do. Would you like to see him now?"

"Maybe later. How's that bastard doing? I don't want him to die, you know."

"Yes, sir, I'm aware of that. He's still hurting after a run-in with some fire ants, but other than that, he's fine."

"Can he talk?"

"Not very well, sir. He is too dehydrated to speak."

Greene pondered things for a moment. "Pump him full of fluids over the next few hours. I want to talk to him later today, and it won't be any fun if I can't understand him."

"Yes, sir."

"One more thing. Once Nathan's out of the Box, I want you to replace him with Payne. It's supposed to be such a lovely day I'd hate to keep him inside. He is a guest, you know."

Ndjai smiled at the possibility. Let the torture begin.

* * *

Payne had always loved the sun. Whether he was golfing, swimming, or napping, he always tried to catch as many summertime rays as possible. He couldn't explain why, but there was something about the sunshine that made him feel good about himself, made him feel healthy.

But those views quickly changed as he baked in the Devil's Box.

"What the hell was I thinking?" he moaned. "Winter is so much better than this."

With his uncovered forearm, Payne tried to wipe the large beads of sweat that had formed on his cheeks and forehead. Unfortunately, since his hands were shackled to a metal loop in the floor, it was impossible, requiring the flexibility of a triple-jointed circus freak.

"Snow, ice, hypothermia. Man, that stuff sounds *so* good."

When Payne was dragged across the length of the island and up the thirty-degree slope of the hill, he wasn't quite sure what to expect. The possibility of a lynching entered his mind, but for some reason, he had a hunch that the Plantation was more about torture than death. He wanted to ask the guards that were towing him, but the four men weren't speaking English, mumbling instead in a rural, African dialect.

After reaching the hill's summit, Payne was actually relieved when he saw the Box. No guillotine, no electric chair, no gas chamber. Just a box, a simple, 4' wooden box that had been anchored to the ground.

Shoot, he figured, how bad could that thing be?

Then they opened it.

The figure that emerged was something from a horror movie, a grotesquely deformed zombie breaking from the constraints of his wooden tomb. Haggard and obviously dehydrated, the man's skin practically hung from his bones, like a suit that was two sizes too large. Payne wanted to turn from the scene—no sense getting a mental picture of the personal horror that was to come—but he knew it would be a mistake. He had to study the prisoner, investigate the guards, and analyze the device. He needed to know what was in store for the next few days, if there were any loopholes in the system. It was the only way he could plan an escape.

The first thing Payne noticed was the prisoner's size. Despite his malnutrition, the man was quite large. It took three guards to lift his massive frame from the tiny device, and even then, it took a concerted effort. In fact, the prisoner was so big, Payne was amazed that the guards had been able to squeeze him into the black cube to begin with. His limbs seemed too thick, too long to contort into such a confined space, but it brought Payne some optimism. He figured, if they could fit him in there, then there should be plenty of room to maneuver.

Once hauled from the Box, the victim tried to stand on his own, but it was a foolish mistake. He had been imprisoned far too long to stand unaided. Atrophy and disorientation took over at once, forcing him to the ground with a sickening thud, his once-proud body melting into the rocky turf that surrounded him.

The image of the tortured man, shivering and trembling at the feet of the laughing guards, made Payne flinch with fright, and that snapped him back into the world of reality.

He had been in the device for several hours now, and the intense heat of the Louisiana sun was already forcing his mind to wander. And things would only get worse as time wore on. The more he sweat, the more dehydration would occur. The more dehydration, the higher his body temperature. The more heat, the more illusions. And so on. It was a vicious ride, one that he desperately wanted to avoid.

"Hello," he yelled, hoping to find a compassionate ear. "Can anybody hear me?"

But the only reply was the sound of the breeze as it coyly danced around the Devil's Box.

Payne leaned his head against the oaken interior and stared at the bright sky above. The tiny slits of the lid's tic-tac-toe pattern gave him a limited view of the world, but he wasn't about to complain. He figured things could be worse: He could be rotting in a freshly dug grave right about now. Still, his current situation didn't offer much hope.

At least it didn't until he heard the sound.

At first, Payne thought it was his imagination playing tricks on him, the lack of liquid in his body causing the synapses of his brain to misfire. A heat-induced hallucination. But then he heard it a second time. And a third. Each more and more clear than the last. The sound, like a distant memory coming into focus, grew more distinct with each occurrence. Hazy, then muffled, then clear.

Footsteps, the sound of footsteps. Someone was coming.

Payne stretched his neck as far as it could reach, trying to peer through the intricate grate of the Devil's Box, but to no avail. The tiny slits in the device prevented it. "Who's there?" Payne called, not wanting to wait any longer for the mysterious guest to announce himself. "Hey, I'm in the box. Can you give me a hand?"

Yet there was no reply. In fact, the only sound that he heard was the whistling wind as it whipped over the crest of the hill—and that was baffling to Payne. He knew he'd heard movement only seconds before. No doubt about it. Someone was out there. Someone *was* near the Box.

But where were they now?

In order to listen more effectively, Payne turned his head to the left and placed his ear against the grate. From this position he hoped to hear things a little bit clearer, prayed that it would somehow make all the difference in the world. And it did. Despite the constant rumble of the wind, Payne was able to hear the sound again. But what the hell was it? It was loud, then quiet. Close, then distant. It sounded like breathing, labored breathing, like a fat man's in an aerobics class.

"Hello," Payne yelled, his voice cracking from severe thirst. "Come here for a second. I want to know who I'm talking to."

After a short pause, the movement started again, this time with calculated strides. But instead of approaching the Box, the footsteps circled it, like a hawk examining its prey, patiently waiting for its moment to strike. Payne took a deep gulp, pondering the possibilities.

What the hell was going on?

To find out, he shoved his ear closer to the grate, his lobe actually sticking through one of the tiny air holes in the Box. Someone was out there; Payne could hear him. Breathing and footsteps, nothing but breathing and footsteps. Why won't he say something? Someone was circling the device, faster and faster, building himself into a frenzy. What was he doing? Payne strained to catch a glimpse of him, struggled for any clue, but the only thing he could hear was breathing and footsteps, multiple footsteps.

Then it dawned on him.

"Oh, shit!" he screamed, pulling his head from the lid a split-second before the attack.

The beast, a snarling mixture of teeth and sinew, landed on top of the Box in an impassioned frenzy, drool spraying from its mouth like a rabid coyote. In an attempt to get at the prisoner, the animal clawed and chewed at the sturdy lid, hoping to find a way inside, but the device held firm, denying every attempt.

For the first time all day, Payne was happy to be inside the Box. He was actually thrilled that the contraption was so damn sturdy. Crouching as low as he could, he tucked his head between his legs like a passenger anticipating an airplane crash, and as he did, he felt the creature's saliva coating the back of his neck with burst after burst of slobber.

"Close your mouth, you drooling bitch!"

With his heart pounding furiously, Payne twisted his neck upward, hoping to identify the animal without getting in harm's way. Once he was safely into position, he stared at the snarling creature with a mixture of fear and amazement. He'd never seen anything like it in his entire life. He wasn't sure if it was a wolf or a dog, but it was, without question, the sleekest animal that he'd ever seen.

Covered in a sheer white coat, the level back and lean muscular frame of the magnificent creature glistened in the bright sun as it frantically clawed at the Devil's Box, trying to rip Payne into tender, bite-sized morsels. Its face, thin and angular, revealed a full set of spiked teeth, each quite capable of inflicting serious damage, and a pink nose, one of the few instances of color on the entire beast. The most prominent of its features, though, besides its unbridled ferocity and propensity for drool, were its ears. Long and light pink, they stood at attention like an antenna on an old TV.

As the attack continued, Payne gained confidence in the cube's sturdiness, which finally allowed him to take a relaxing breath. If the animal had somehow entered the Box, Payne realized he would've been screwed. Since his hands were bolted to the floor and his legs were severely restricted, he wouldn't have had a chance to defend himself against the anti-Lassie.

"Bad doggie," Payne scolded. "Go home! Shoo! Return to Satan!"

Surprisingly, the command worked. Just as quickly as the attack had started, it stopped. The animal suddenly leapt from the Box and scurried away.

"What the . . . ?" Payne's eyes grew wide from the surprising turn of events. He had never expected his request to work. In fact, he'd said it simply in jest. "Wow, is my breath that bad?"

But before he could determine an answer, a voice interrupted him.

"Hello, Mr. Payne. How are you doing today?" The words were English, but they were tinted with a thick, African accent.

Payne looked above, but he couldn't tell where the voice was coming from. He strained his neck in all directions but was unable to see who approached. "God? Is that you?"

"Very funny, Mr. Payne. Master Greene told me you were somewhat of a jokester. I guess he was right."

Payne grimaced. "Actually, I'm offended by that. I'm not *somewhat* of a jokester. I *am* a jokester. There's a big difference, my African friend."

Hakeem Ndjai leaned his face over the top of his box and smiled, revealing a set of decaying teeth that had obviously been neglected for some time. "Yes, I guess you are a jokester. Quite comical, especially for someone in your predicament."

"By the way, I meant to talk to you about that. You know, you have to do something about this box thing of yours. Your wooden-mesh roof is seriously messing up my sunlight. If I'm not careful, it's going to look like I tanned my face in a waffle iron."

Ndjai grinned once again. "Well, Mr. Payne, just write down your request and put it in the suggestion box back at the main house. Oh, I forgot. Your hands are tied and you're unable to get to the house. Too bad. I guess you're just going to have to deal with it."

Payne sighed. "I guess."

"Now, if we're done with the fun and games, I would like to ask you a simple question before I go about my duties. How did you enjoy your introduction to my pet?"

"Your pet? You mean the albino pit bull? Oh, yeah, it was just swell. I bet it's great around kids. Just make sure you get a head count beforehand."

Ndjai sat on the edge of the black device and chuckled. "Surprisingly, he is wonderful around children. He's only hostile when I want him to be. That's why he backed away from the Box when I called him. He's very obedient."

"You called him? Damn! I must've missed that. I was hoping it obeyed *my* commands. That would make my escape from the Box so much easier."

"Yes," he laughed, "I guess it would, but unfortunately for you, Tornado only listens to me."

"Tornado? That's a pretty stupid name for a dog. How the hell did you come up with that?"

Ndjai sneered. "If you hadn't noticed, Tornado has the tendency to circle his prey again and again until he's ready to attack. It's how he whips himself into a frenzy."

"Boy, that's kinda weird, don't you think? Why not call him Dizzy? That's a good name for a dog—at least better than Tornado. Or how about Retardo? That seems to fit. I mean, let's be honest, how smart can the dog be if it has to run in a loop to attack?"

"Quite intelligent," Ndjai argued. "Ibizan hounds are some of the smartest dogs in the world. They were originally bred for Spanish royalty."

"Well, they might be some of the smartest dogs, but I don't think yours qualifies. Did you get it at a clearance sale? 'Cause that would explain a lot."

Ndjai stood from the Box in a huff. He wasn't used to having arguments with his prisoners. Normally, they were too scared to even speak. "You have a lot of audacity for someone in your situation, Mr. Payne. Trust me, I will remember your words when it comes time for you to die. I will make sure you go slowly and painfully."

"You mean, like your teeth? You know, if you started brushing now, you might be able to save the two or three that you have left." Payne's words finally hit his mark, and Ndjai responded by slamming his fist into the top of the Box. "Oh, are you mad at me? Then why don't you let me out of this thing and kick my ass like a real man? Then again, you'd probably have to run around me like your fucked-up mutt, and by the time you were done, you'd be too dizzy to hit me."

Ndjai took a deep breath and finally understood the game that the prisoner was trying to play. Payne wanted Ndjai to become so infuriated that he'd do something irrational like opening the Box to get at him. It was a nice try, but Ndjai was too smart to fall for it.

"Don't worry about my aim, Mr. Payne. If I were to let you out of your cage—something I'm not going to do—I would be able to strike you. In fact, let me prove my accuracy to you right now."

Payne sat up in the Box, trying to view the exhibition that Ndjai was going to put on for him. Unfortunately, as it turned out, it was a show in which he was forced to participate.

With a grin on his face, Ndjai climbed on top of the cube and lowered the zipper on his pants. "The reason for my visit, Mr. Payne, was to give you your daily dose of water, but seeing how uncooperative you've been, I've decided to radically alter your menu."

A sudden stream of golden liquid fell from above, surging through the slits of the cube like a warm waterfall. By lowering his head and closing his eyes, Payne did his best to avoid the downpour, but his restricted mobility prevented much success.

"What do you think of my aim, now?" Ndjai laughed. "Or my dog? Do you have anything else you want to say about Tornado?"

Payne wanted to answer, desperately wanted to scream insults at the ornery guard, but he couldn't risk saying a word. The possibility of the yellow liquid seeping past his cracked lips and into his mouth was far too great to risk. Besides, he knew that he would somehow escape from the Devil's Box, and when he did, he would make Ndjai pay for his actions.

And the bastard would pay for them with his life.

Chapter Thirty

It was hard for Ariane to believe, but her seemingly perfect life was suddenly spiraling out of control. Two days earlier, she was a successful bank executive, preparing to spend a relaxing holiday with the man she wanted to marry. The only activities on her itinerary were golfing, swimming, and sex. No business. No stress. Just pleasure. She'd been looking forward to it all summer and had done everything in her power to plan the perfect weekend.

Unfortunately, her plans were altered.

In a matter of 48 hours, she'd been drugged, kidnapped, and smuggled to Louisiana, where she was being tortured for the sins of relatives that she never even knew existed. Her days, which used to be filled with meetings and paperwork in an air-conditioned office, were now occupied with grueling field labor and the stinging crack of leather whips in the sweltering southern sun.

If it wasn't for her inner-strength, a trait that was tested and fortified when her parents died several years before, she probably would've broken down from the duress. As it was, though, she stubbornly clung to hope, realizing that things were never as bad as they seemed.

Well, almost never.

Her current situation offered little hope, and because of that she decided to push her luck. While pulling weeds from the untilled ground, Ariane glanced around the spacious field, searching for someone to talk to. She knew that conversation of any kind was forbidden by the guards, but she had the feeling if she didn't do something soon, there was a very good chance she was going to end up dead. And she wasn't about to let that happen without a fight.

A young woman, no more than eighteen years old, stood fifty feet away from Walker, busily plucking rocks from the dark brown dirt. She tried to signal the girl from a distance, hoping to catch her eye, but the teen remained focused on her task.

Undaunted by the threat of punishment, Ariane moved her wicker basket to the east, carefully approaching the teenager.

"Hello," she muttered under her breath. "My name's Ariane."

The athletic-looking girl was stunned at first, surprised that someone had the guts to speak under the close watch of the guards, but after suppressing her shock, she whispered back.

"Kelly Metz." She wiped the dirt from her hands on her orange work pants, then brushed the brown hair from her eyes. "Where you from?"

Ariane glanced around again, but the closest guard was over one hundred feet away. "Pittsburgh. What about you?"

"Farrell, Missouri." As she spoke, she continued ripping rocks from the soil. "Heard of it?"

Ariane shook her head. There was no sense speaking when a simple gesture would do. "How old are you?"

Now it was Kelly's turn to be cautious. Like a student trying to cheat on a test, she made sure the coast was clear. "Seventeen." She carefully checked a second time, then continued. "Are you new? I don't remember seeing you in the field before."

"I think I got here yesterday. I'm not sure, though. Everything's kind of foggy."

Kelly nodded in understanding. "The drugs will wear off, you know. Don't worry. Just hang in there. You'll get through this."

Ariane smiled at the optimism. She found it amazing that a girl of Kelly's age would be holding up so well in such adverse conditions. "You here alone?"

Kelly searched for the guards. They were busy hassling one of the male slaves. "Me and my family are a part of Group One. Ten of us in all."

Ariane thought back to earlier in the day, back when it was still dark. If she remembered correctly, that meant Kelly was in Master Holmes' group. "Are you the one with the cute little brother?"

For the first time in a long time, Kelly wanted to laugh. "I've heard my brother called a lot of things, but certainly never cute." She looked over her shoulder, paranoid. "The cute one is Scooter. He's my cousin."

"But you have a brother, don't you?"

"Yeah," she whispered. "His name's Donny."

Something about Kelly's voice worried Ariane. She wasn't sure why, but she could tell something was wrong. She quickly looked for the nearest guard, but he was still occupied with the men.

"What's going on? Is something wrong with your brother?"

She sighed, then brushed the hair from her face one more time. "He's not, what you would call, er, tough. I kind of get the feeling that he isn't holding up too well."

Ariane found that hard to believe. If Donny was anything like his sister, he was probably cutting down trees with his teeth. "Are you sure? 'Cause you seem to be doing great."

Kelly grimaced, but the compliment was appreciated. "I guess, but I'm used to this stuff. I play sports year round, so physical stuff doesn't really bother me. Donny, on the other hand, is in the band. The most exertion he gets is playing his trumpet."

"So, he's breaking down physically?"

"That, and mentally. My dad was kind of tortured the first night we were here. I think that got to him."

Ariane tried to picture the members of Group One, and she distinctly remembered a middle-aged man with a bandaged hand. "What'd they do to him?"

Kelly took a deep breath. She didn't want to relive the horror of the first night, but she felt obligated to talk about it. "They cut off his finger. He didn't even do anything wrong, but they still chopped it off. Probably to prove that they were in charge."

Ariane was stunned but nodded. She couldn't believe that the guards were so sadistic that they'd cut off a finger to make a point. Furthermore, she couldn't believe how well Kelly was handling things. In her mind, there was no way she could've witnessed a loved one tortured and remained so calm—especially back when she was a teenager.

"How about your cousins? Have you had a chance to talk to them?"

"Not really, but I can tell Susan's on the edge. She's real close to losing it."

"Which one is Susan?"

"She's about my age, maybe a year younger. She's petite, blonde hair."

Ariane tried to place the girl in her mind but couldn't. Too many faces, too little time.

"She was abused on the same night as my dad. Master Jackson cut off all of her clothes in front of everybody. I think that rattled her somethin' good."

"They cut off her clothes?" Wow, Ariane was glad she missed the opening ceremonies. There's no telling what might've happened if she'd been around. "What'd he do that for?"

Kelly shrugged. "Probably did it 'cause she's pretty. And she was wearing this tight, little outfit, so she kind of stood out."

"And you think she's in pretty bad shape?"

Kelly considered it briefly, then answered. "Yep, she's screwed."

That wasn't what Ariane wanted to hear. In her opinion, the only way to survive a crisis was to keep calm at all times. No matter what happens, if you can keep your wits about you, you have a chance to make it through anything. "Where is she now?"

Kelly looked around, then casually pointed to a girl who was tossing pebbles into a small wicker basket. "Why? What are you gonna do?"

"I'm not really sure," Ariane admitted. "But once I get back to my condo, I'll give you a call and let you know how things went. Maybe we can do lunch and talk about it."

"Sorry. Getting my nails done later today. Maybe tomorrow."

* * *

Despite her best effort, it took Ariane over an hour to cross the Plantation's spacious field—her basket of weeds and the guards' careful scrutiny made her movement difficult—but in time she eventually made her way to Susan Ross.

As she approached the teen, the first thing she noticed were her eyes. They were striking; the color of the perfect summertime sky. But it was more than just their light-blue hue that made them stand out. It was also the tears.

Apparently, Kelly was right: Her cousin was close to losing it.

Ariane inched closer, hoping to comfort the girl with a kind word or two, but the move backfired. Susan sensed Ariane's approach and immediately tensed with fear.

"Get away from me!" she shrieked. "Just leave me alone!"

The outburst stopped Ariane in her tracks. She assumed the plea was loud enough to be heard by the guards, and the last thing she wanted to do was attract their attention. She'd seen how rough they were with the other slaves, and she desperately wanted to avoid similar treatment.

"Calm down," Ariane whispered. "You don't have to be afraid of me. I just wanted to see how you're doing."

"I'm fine," she screeched, not giving a damn if the guards heard her or not. "There! Are you happy? Now get away from me!"

Ariane was flabbergasted by Susan's behavior. Normally, she would've considered silencing the girl with a swift kick to the head, but under the circumstances, she was willing to cut the kid some slack. But not much. She wanted to help the girl, but not if it meant her own death.

"You've got to be quiet," she demanded. She glanced over her shoulder, half-expecting a stampede of guards to be headed her way. "I realize you don't know me and don't trust me, but your cousin, Kelly, sent me over here to check on you."

The frightened girl stared at Ariane, coldly. Her body language and icy glare suggested the word trust was no longer in her vocabulary.

"You know, I saw you and Scooter at the ceremony this morning. He sure is a cutie."

Susan blinked a few times, but didn't respond to the statement.

"How old is he?"

She licked her parched lips, giving the question a moment's thought. "Eight."

Ariane grinned, relieved that the girl was willing to talk—and in civil tones. "Well, he's just about the cutest 8-year-old I've ever seen. He looks like a future athlete."

Susan nodded, but refused to comment.

"How's he holding up? He seems like he's doing pretty well considering the circumstances."

She shrugged, never shifting her eyes from Walker's face.

"And you? What about you? How are you doing?"

Susan breathed deeply, sucking in the blistering air through her dry mouth. "What is it you want? There has to be some reason you're talking to me. You don't even know me."

Ariane smiled warmly. "Like I said, your cousin wanted me to check on you."

The answer didn't sit well with Susan. "Then why didn't Kelly come over here herself? Huh? Why'd she send you?"

Ariane moved closer, hoping her proximity would lower the volume of Susan's voice. "No reason. I'm trying to talk to as many people as possible, and when I talked to your cousin, she mentioned that she was worried about you."

"She's worried about *me*?" Her tone of voice suggested disbelief. "That would be a first from my family."

"Come on. Don't be silly. Your family's worried about you. They've got to be."

The statement brought a new batch of tears to the teen's eyes. "Ha! You don't know my family very well, do you? None of them have even asked how I'm doing. Not one of them."

"Well, I'm asking you. How are you doing, Susan?"

"How the hell do you think I'm doing? Every time I turn around one of the guards is touching me. Last night I saw my dad's ear cut off. And to make things worse, when I do get to see my family, all my parents seem to care about are my younger brothers. I mean, would it kill them to ask how I am?"

Ariane couldn't believe what she was hearing. Despite the gravity of their situation, Susan was showing signs of sibling jealousy. Jesus! How petty could someone be? "Don't take it personally," she offered. "I'm sure your parents are paying more attention to them because they feel they need it. You're older. They probably figure you can handle things by yourself."

Susan wiped the moisture from her face with her forearm. "Great! You're on their side, too."

"It's not about sides. It's about—"

"Just get away from me. I don't want to hear it."

"Susan."

"Get away from me," she repeated louder. "I don't want to talk to you anymore."

Ariane pleaded for her to calm down, but the teen refused to listen. "Susan, if you keep making noise, the guards are going to come over and punish us."

"Good. At least that'll get you away from me."

"Susan," she pleaded, "I'm just trying to help you."

“I told you. I don’t want your help.” Susan picked up her wicker basket and began walking away. “And if you follow me, I’ll scream for the guards.”

“Susan,” she begged.

“I swear to god, I’ll scream.” The fire in her eyes proved she wasn’t bluffing. “Stay away.”

Despite the threat, Ariane was tempted to run after her. In her mind, she figured Susan wasn’t a bad kid. She was just a traumatized teen, who was looking for someone to cling to, and if Ariane could be that person, she knew she’d be able to help.

Unfortunately, the Plantation wasn’t the best place to make friends, so her act of kindness would have to wait for another day.

That is, if both of them could last that long.

Chapter Thirty-One

After taking a short nap, Master Jackson strolled into the field to check on the current group of slaves. As leader of the guards, he had many important duties at the Plantation, but most of them occurred before any of the guests were even there. Jackson was in charge of training the guards, a task he shared with Ndjai since several of the men were straight off the boat from Africa. If it hadn't been for the language barrier, he would've preferred training the guards by himself, but as it was he didn't really have a choice. He was forced to work with Ndjai even though the African gave him the creeps.

Ironically, Jackson often elicited the same reaction from women.

It wasn't always like that, though. The bad vibe was more of a recent thing. As a youngster, he'd actually been very effective with the fairer sex. He was suave, polite, and romantic. But all of that changed in a heartbeat, one misstep that altered Jackson's life and his attitude towards women—and white people—forever.

He'd been a young associate at one of New Orleans' top law firms, and as his friends used to say, he had the world by its balls. He was handsome, athletic, intelligent, and personable. People often confused him with Wesley Snipes, but he was quick to point out their mistake. No, he used to tell them, my name is Harris Jackson, and before long, people will say *he* looks like *me.*

And he believed it, too. Jackson was on the fast-track to success, and he knew in his heart that he was ultimately destined for greatness.

But all of that changed when he met her.

A month before that fateful day, Jackson left his law firm to start his own business: The Harris Jackson Sports Agency. He figured with his legal mind, quick wit, and black skin, that he would be able to land professional athletes by the dozen. And he was right. Within two weeks, he'd signed Levon Greene, a college friend of his, and soon after several other stars in the world of sports started using his services.

As a token of his appreciation, Jackson invited his newest clients to New Orleans for a gala celebration and ordered everything that you had to have in order to throw a successful party: food, alcohol, strippers, Puff Daddy. Unfortunately, when he made the party arrangements, he didn't count on one unfortunate thing: the presence of the Anti-Christ. Oh, sure, she looked like a harmless exotic dancer—shoulder-length blonde hair, great face, see-through dress—but underneath that beautiful exterior lived the heart of the devil.

At the end of the evening, she begged Jackson for a ride home, and before he could say no, she was riding *him* in his limo. At the time, he figured it was just a one-night stand, a meaningless night of sex with a drunken vixen, but it turned into something more than that. It was the event that ended his career.

Unbeknownst to Jackson, the girl was young. Too young. An uninvited 16-year-old that had snuck into the party to meet some of the celebrities. After sobering up, she regretted her actions and quickly told the cops everything that had occurred. The liquor, the nudity, the sex, everything. In a flash, Jackson was arrested, convicted, and disbarred. Before he knew it, his legal career was over, and all because of the white bitch.

After his release from jail, Jackson realized that he needed to experience the sweet taste of revenge if he was ever going to put the past behind him, and he figured the Plantation was the perfect way to do that. One white whore had taken everything that he'd ever worked for in his life, and in his mind, this was his opportunity to get even with her and anyone like her.

Theo Webster had academic reasons for the Plantation.

Octavian Holmes had a childhood trauma to overcome.

But Harris Jackson was different. He was in it for personal revenge.

While he studied the female slaves, he tried to pick the one that he wanted to play with the most. But it was a tough choice, a lot tougher than the last group that they'd brought to the Plantation. In order to prepare for this current group, the Posse abducted 25 homeless people for a trial run, which allowed them to practice everything that they possibly could. They established the housing setup, perfected the guards' work schedules, and tweaked their kidnapping techniques.

All in all, it was a great success.

Unfortunately, it wasn't much fun for Jackson. The homeless group had only one good-looking female, a down-on-her-luck runaway, so he didn't have many playmates to choose from. Thankfully, the current crop of slaves was different, very different. As far as he could tell, there were five females in the bunch that would please him immensely. They were young, pretty, and white—just how he liked them. Now it was just a matter of time before he chose the one that he wanted to break first.

After figuring out the girls' names, Jackson told one of the guards to round up the following slaves: Kelly Metz, Jennifer Potter, Sarah Potter, Susan Ross, and Ariane Walker. As far as Jackson was concerned, the other females were too old or too pregnant to mess with.

"Ladies," he said to the five. "I'm sure you're wondering why I've pulled you from your work. Well, I'll explain that in good time. First of all, a question: How have you enjoyed working in this wicked heat?"

Not surprisingly, the women were too scared to speak.

"Ah," he sighed. "It seems that you've forgotten the policy that was established on day one. When I ask a question, you respond, or you will pay the price."

He looked at Susan, and she trembled at the sight. She remembered how Jackson had treated her on that first night: the sharp edge of his stiletto as it slid against her flesh, his erect penis as he rubbed it against the small of her naked back, his threatening words of terror. The memory of it all made her wince in agony.

"So let me ask you again. How have you enjoyed the heat?"

"We've hated it," Ariane admitted. "It's been brutal."

The comment made Jackson grin. "Thank you. Even though no one else had the courage to say it, I'm sure each of you agrees with Miss Walker's statement."

The group nodded their heads in agreement.

"Finally, a sign of life."

Jackson moved forward, glancing at the bodies and faces of the slaves, looking for the tiniest of imperfections. Sarah and Ariane were older than he usually preferred, but they did have the nicest figures of the five. Full breasts, great legs, firm bodies. And Ariane definitely had the prettiest face. She could be a model if she wanted to be. Unfortunately, he knew that neither of them were virgins. No doubt about that. Good-looking women don't reach their age without screwing someone, probably a lot of 'em, too. And to Jackson, that was a *huge* turn off. He preferred his victims innocent and pure, like the other three girls in front of him.

He wanted to ruin them for the rest of the world, to destroy a piece of their life, just like that whore had done to him.

It was his way of getting even.

"What I'm about to offer might sound too good to be true, but it's an opportunity that is steeped in southern tradition. Plantations used to have house slaves, people that assisted inside the plantation house instead of outside in the field. They cooked and cleaned and provided other indoor services that were requested, and as payment, they were given a bed to sleep in and a bath to soak in."

Jackson studied the faces of each of the women, trying to predict which one would jump at the chance first. "Keeping in mind that this house has air-conditioning, I need one of you to volunteer for the position at this time."

The females glanced at each other, reluctantly. Each of them had a feeling what the job was really about. Everyone, that is, but Susan Ross. After a momentary delay, she stepped forward.

"I'll do it," she said. "Take me."

"Splendid," he remarked. In his mind, he figured that she would be the one to volunteer. Of all the females, she was the one that had been struggling the most in the field. The tears in her eyes were another sign that she was looking for a way out. "Guards, take her inside so she can get cleaned up. I'll be in shortly to give her further instructions."

But as the guards moved toward the girl, Ariane did as well.

"Susan," she pleaded, "don't do it. This is about sex."

Jackson jumped forward and instantly slapped Ariane in the mouth. "Get back in line, bitch, before I have you whipped."

"Sir, she's just a kid. If you need someone to abuse, take me. At least I can handle it like an adult."

"Oh sure," Susan complained, not realizing Jackson's ulterior motives. "Use my age against me to take my spot inside. Great! That's just great! First you talk to me in the field and try to convince me that you're my friend, and now this. That's just great."

As the words sank in, Ariane took a step backwards. She knew that Jackson was going to strike her again. He didn't have a choice. She had broken one of his major rules, and he would have to punish her.

And he didn't let her down.

Jackson closed his fist into a ball and swung viciously, connecting with Ariane's face just above her jawline. It was a savage blow, one that knocked her unconscious before she even hit the ground. Then, as she lay there, he kicked her once in the stomach just to prove to the other women that he was still in control.

"Guards, while you're at it, take her inside, too. Now that she's broken one of my commandments, we're gonna have to dispose of her. But before we do, I think she can provide all of us with some entertainment."

* * *

Theo Webster answered the phone, smiling. If there was one thing in the world that he could count on, it was Hannibal Kotto's punctuality. "Hannibal, it's nice to hear from you again. I believe this is two days in a row for us."

"Yes, and for two days in a row I've been hindered by the time difference between our countries. I wish you Americans would finally wise up and start using the same clock as Nigeria. It would make my sleeping habits much more routine."

"Well, I'll see what I can do," he laughed. "So, how are things going? Did you run the new price by our clients?"

"I certainly did. I got the others to agree to an $80,000 per unit."

"80,000 American dollars?"

"Yes."

"Even though they haven't seen the quality of this batch?"

"Yes," Kotto chuckled. He sounded like a kid as he laughed. "Trust me, it's more than I could've ever imagined."

Webster quickly did the calculations in his head. He had 21 slaves on the Plantation ready for shipment. At $80,000 per, that meant the Plantation was on the verge of making $1,680,000 for less than a week's worth of work. Not bad for a plan that was originally based on revenge. And since Webster expected to get extra money for Tonya Edwards, the pregnant one, her fetus would push the total amount over 1.7 million dollars. "How soon do we get the money?"

"How soon can you make the shipment?"

"So it's as simple as that? When we're ready to ship, they're ready to buy?"

Kotto nodded. "The sooner, the better."

Webster finished the call, then sighed in amazement. The dollar amount that Kotto had quoted was beyond Webster's wildest dreams. Actually, in the very beginning, the concept of cash had never occurred to him. He wanted to establish the Plantation for revenge, not money. He planned to smuggle people onto his island, then treat them the way his ancestors had been treated. In his mind it would teach white people about the horrors of slavery while striking a blow for the black culture. Of course, since he'd never been an athletic person, he knew he needed help to make his plan a reality. He could control the bureaucracy by himself, but he needed someone to handle the brutality, someone that had been trained for it. But who?

While looking for assistance, Webster solicited the advice of Harris Jackson, his ex-roommate from college. Jackson wasn't very supportive of the idea at the time (this was before his legal problems had occurred), but he suggested the name of a client who might be willing to help. And it was the perfect recommendation.

Until that point, Octavian Holmes had made a good living as a mercenary, offering his military expertise to the highest foreign bidder, but he'd reached the point in his life where he was looking for a change of pace—guerrilla warfare in South America and jungle tactics in Africa were quickly losing their appeal. He was thinking about running a training camp for backwater militia types or opening his own paintball arena for weekend warriors, but he'd never gotten around to it.

When Webster called, Holmes was immediately intrigued. The concept of slavery was one that had always fascinated him, and the chance to actually have slaves was too great to pass up.

Of course, Holmes wasn't willing to do it for free. To coordinate something as large as the Plantation, he wanted to be compensated in an appropriate fashion. Webster was willing to pay what he could, but it simply wasn't enough to please a professional soldier like Holmes.

So, before it even got started, the Plantation had hit snag, a problem that threatened its very existence.

But not to worry. Holmes came up with a logical solution that saved the day. Why not make money while getting revenge? It sounded good to Webster, but he wasn't quite sure how it would work.

Holmes quickly clued him in. He told Webster about an African that had hired him for some military exercises in Nigeria. The man's name was Hannibal Kotto, and he was reputed to be as powerful as he was wealthy. Holmes claimed that Kotto was loved and respected throughout Africa despite his tendency to operate outside the letter of the law. In fact, while Holmes was in Lagos, he had heard rumors of a white slavery ring that Kotto was attempting to start.

The concept intrigued Webster. If the rumors were true, then they'd be able to take his slavery idea to a whole new level. Instead of just kidnapping and torturing white folks for revenge, he could actually sell them for money to the Motherland. It would be the original slave trade but in reverse: whites going to a black land instead of blacks going to a white one.

After checking with his sources, Holmes discovered that the rumors about Kotto were quite accurate. In fact, he had actually laid the foundation for the business. Kotto and Edwin Drake, an Englishman who lived in Johannesburg, had cultivated a long list of African entrepreneurs who were interested in buying white-skinned slaves. It seemed even though the Africans could hire black servants at a minimal price, the idea of having a white slave was too compelling to pass up. To them, a white slave would be a status symbol, like owning a Mercedes or a Ferrari. *If I'm rich, I can get a servant, but if I'm super-rich, I can buy myself a white one.* On top of that, many men planned on using white women as concubines, fair-skinned mistresses that they'd have at their sexual disposal, a fantasy shared by many African men.

But the concept wasn't perfect.

After several failed experiments, Kotto and Drake realized it was difficult to find a reliable supplier. Sure, the two men wanted to make money off of the white-slave trade, but neither of them wanted to get their hands dirty. They wanted someone else to do the hard stuff. Furthermore, even though there were thousands of white people scattered across Africa, neither man wanted to make enemies on the African continent. Kotto said it would be like shitting in his own backyard. In his mind, if they were going to get white people for the slave trade, they were going to have to smuggle them in from places where they had few ties: Australia, Europe, and North America.

And that's when the Plantation offered their services.

They were the suppliers; Kotto and Drake were the distributors.

A brutal partnership was forged.

Chapter Thirty-Two

The rattle of the door's lock made Ariane want to scream, but the gag in her mouth prevented it. She'd been tied to the bed with her arms stretched above her and her legs spread below her for over an hour, yet had no idea how she got there. The last thing she remembered was being dragged from the field and placed in a sexual lineup for Master Jackson. After that, she couldn't remember anything.

As the sound continued, she tried to free herself from her restraints, but her movement only resulted in brush burns on her wrists and ankles, meaning she'd be forced to stay in her current position, open and quite vulnerable, until someone had the decency to let her go.

But who?

As far as she could tell, she was the only female on the Plantation with any backbone, the others cowered in fear when the guards even looked at them. And the men were even worse, shaking and trembling at the first sign of trouble. Yet Ariane couldn't blame them. If she'd been around for the opening night of festivities and forced to watch the brutal acts of torture that were performed, her attitude might be different, too.

But as it was, Ariane's courage was higher than the other slaves, and for that reason she realized she might be their best hope for survival.

Then, the door opened.

With her limbs tied and her jaw aching, she watched helplessly as Master Jackson entered the room, naked from the waist up. Despite the darkness that clouded her vision, she could tell from the carnal look in his eyes why he was there and what he was planning to do.

He was there for her.

"I must admit, you look pretty damn good for a troublemaker. In fact, little darlin', you look good enough to eat." He punctuated his statement with a slurping sound that made her entire body erupt in goose flesh. "What do you think of that?"

Ariane wanted to vomit—that's what she thought. She desperately wanted to tell him how nauseous he made her feel, how disgusting she actually found him, but she couldn't. The gag in her mouth prevented it. Besides, Ariane realized insults would get her nowhere. If she attacked him with words, he'd attack her with fists, and in the long run, she'd be the one to suffer more.

"Go ahead, princess, admit it." Jackson stepped onto the bed and straddled her hips from a standing position. "You want me, don't you?"

Ariane closed her eyes and prayed that he'd be gone when she reopened them, like a nightmare that vanishes the moment the lights come on, but her prayer was not answered.

"You know," he purred, "from up here you look *so* inviting. Your arms way up above ya. Your legs spread open below. Combined, you're just a big ol' X. And you know what they say about the letter X, don't you?" He jumped from the bed and landed on the floor with a solid thump. "X marks the spot."

Terror flared in her eyes as Jackson turned and thrust his face against hers, scratching her nose with the stubble of his chin while licking the sweat that had formed on her forehead. As he did a thick wave of musk penetrated her nostrils, a scent so pungent that it increased the nausea in her stomach tenfold. In fact, her queasiness got so bad she could feel the vomit building in her gut like molten rock before a volcanic eruption.

Groaning slightly, Jackson slid downward, allowing his tongue to run across her eyebrow, her nose, and finally her cheek, leaving a thin trail of saliva on her ashen skin. Then he shifted his mouth to the right, nibbling and sucking on her earlobe for several seconds before he broke the hushed tension with an encore of his chilling phrase.

"X marks the spot, my dear."

Suddenly, without warning, he extended his left arm towards her groin and placed his hand on the soft flesh of her uncovered belly. Inch by inch, pore by pore, he slid his fingers downward, crawling across her exposed skin with the unstoppable determination of a worker ant.

"I wonder what it marks? What hidden treasure will I find in the middle of the X?"

Her stomach quivered, the liquid raging in her stomach like a maelstrom. God, she wondered, couldn't he see how disgusted she was? Didn't he realize how close she was to losing it? It had to be obvious. It just had to be. There was no denying it.

But his movement never ceased, continuing past her navel and her lower abdomen until he paused at the edge of her cotton panties to make one final remark.

"Will X reveal a pot of gold, or a bag of jewels? Or perhaps it'll show me something better, the entrance to a secret cave, one that will reward me with unspeakable delight?"

Thankfully, before he got a chance to find out, Ariane's body revolted, sending a great wave of bile from her gut to her throat in one violent spurt. The bitter fluid flooded her tongue and taste buds as she tried to open her mouth, but the gag prevented it from opening, keeping the liquid inside her cheeks like a giant water balloon.

Oh lord, she suddenly feared, what if it isn't the gag that's keeping my mouth closed? What if it's my jaw? Jesus, it's still throbbing from before. What if my jaw's broken and I can't open my mouth at all? What then? Will I be able to breathe through this stuff? How will I breathe?

Regrettably, there was only one way to find out.

With her mouth still full, she tried sucking oxygen through her nose, but the effort was less than successful. The greenish liquid had backed up so far into her throat that it clogged her nasal membrane, causing her to choke while sending her body into a series of violent spasms. The shaking didn't last long, but when it stopped she found herself filled with more than just vomit. She was also filled with panic.

Ariane suddenly realized if she couldn't discharge the fluid from her system, somehow purge it from her throat and mouth, there was no way to get air into her body. And without air, she'd blackout. And if that happened, she'd die—literally DIE!—half-naked and tied to the bed on this godforsaken plantation.

Screw that, she swore to herself. She wouldn't let that happen.

No freakin' way.

But what choice did she have? If she couldn't open her mouth, she'd drown in a puddle of her own fluid. She knew that. There was no doubt about that. So the one question that begged to be asked was this: Would Jackson be willing to save her?

Unfortunately, he didn't give her the answer that she wanted.

"Well, well, well," he teased. "What seems to be your problem? Are you sick? Ahhh, I'll tell you what, why don't I leave you alone for a while and give you a chance to get better? Unless, of course, you need my help."

The terror increased in Ariane's eyes, but she was unable to beg for his assistance.

"I guess your silence means you're OK, huh? Well, since that's the case, I guess I'll just go and do something else—like that bitch Susan Ross. I'll go do her."

Ironically, even though she despised Jackson and had prayed for his disappearance only a moment before, she suddenly felt like crying when he left the room. She had hoped that he'd display a hint of kindness and offer her a hand in her time of need. But that wasn't to be. Despite her desperation, he turned his back on her, leaving her to wrestle with death on her own. Hell, all he needed to do was remove her gag—that's all. She could've cleared her airway in a moment's time, spitting up everything that threatened her life with one burst of tainted air. Yet Jackson didn't even have the decency to do that.

But enough about him. She knew she didn't have time to worry about Jackson, not with death staring her in the face. *Death.* Good Lord! The word sent shivers down her spine. She didn't want to go out like this, not with so many things left undone in her life. She wanted to marry Jon. And have children. And grandchildren. And a life full of happiness. But she knew she'd never experience any of that if she didn't get free.

Ariane tried to quell her panic by concentrating on soothing thoughts, but it was a next-to-impossible task. Each second that slipped by meant she was a step closer to dying, and she knew it. There was no time to waste on images of rainbows and waterfalls. She needed to use her head on productive things and nothing else, or she was going to die. . . .

Use my head.

The words echoed in her head like a scream in an empty canyon.

Use my head.

What was it about that phrase that was so damn important? Why did it keep echoing?

Use my head. Use my head. Use my head. . . .

And then it hit her. It took a while, but she finally figured out what to do. She *did* need to use her head—not her brain, but her head. It was the only way for her to get free.

Despite the vomit that filled her cheeks, Ariane turned her head to the right and pushed the side of her face against her outstretched shoulder. Using her deltoid as an anchor, she forced the cotton gag against the fleshy ridge of her upper arm. Then, with a firm, downward motion, she rolled her neck and chin away from her armpit, trying to catch the restraint on her shoulder.

Her first attempt met with little success—the muzzle didn't budge, and the movement of her cheek actually pushed the vomit deeper into her throat. Gagging, she went into another mini-convulsion, her body shaking as if she was possessed by an angry poltergeist, but thankfully the fit stopped quickly.

The second try went smoother than the first. The gag wasn't pulled from her mouth, but she felt it twist like a wet gym towel that was about to be snapped. She hastily repeated the act a third and a fourth time, and each resulted in a slight tug of the restraint.

Keep it up, she thought. It's working. The cloth is definitely moving.

And it was, too. With each twist of her head and roll of her neck, the gag was pulled ever so slightly from Ariane's mouth. At first, it inched up to her bottom lip, exposing her chin for the first time since she'd regained consciousness, then after several more tries, she managed to free her lower lip completely. She hoped that would be far enough to open her mouth, but when she tried, nothing happened.

Undeterred, she turned her head back to the right and pushed the cloth restraint against her shoulder as hard as she could. Slowly, ever so slowly, she felt the restraint slide onto her upper lip, tantalizingly close to the target. A couple more tries and her mouth would be free.

Turn, push, drag.

God, she needed to breathe.

Turn, push, drag.

Her chest was burning, actually burning. To her, it felt like she had swallowed a lighter and the butane was slowly cooking her lungs.

Turn, push, drag.

She could feel the blackness of unconsciousness coming and knew if she didn't take a breath soon, she was going to pass out.

Turn, push, drag. Turn, push, drag. Turn, push, drag.

Finally, with her air supply completely ravaged, Ariane felt the gag roll above her mouth, stopping under her nose like a giant mustache. Relief instantly filled her body as she anticipated the sweet taste of oxygen.

With no time to waste, Ariane forced her tongue to the roof of her mouth and slid it between her teeth in order to pry her injured jaw downward. Pain gripped her entire face in a viselike clamp, but she knew if she wanted to live, she had to suffer through the agony. Finally, after several seconds of pure torture, a tiny fissure appeared between her two lips, allowing vomit to flow through the miniature crack like magma spewing from the Earth's core.

To assist with the purging process, Ariane turned her head to the side and hoped that gravity would help her out. The viscous green fluid oozed from her mouth and onto her shoulder at an alarming rate, but she didn't give a damn about the mess. The only thing that mattered was breathing, and breathe she eventually did, sucking in the life-sustaining air with the vigor of a hungry newborn.

Chapter Thirty-Three

If there'd been food in his stomach, Payne was confident that he would've vomited—the strong stench of urine that engulfed his body pretty much guaranteed that. But as it was, Payne only had to deal with dehydration, severe hunger pains, and intermittent episodes of dry heaves.

"Now I know what Gandhi felt like," he croaked, his throat burning from the simple act of speaking. But it didn't matter to Payne. He would continue to speak all night if he had to. It was the only way for him to stay in touch with sanity. "He probably didn't smell like piss, though. If he had, I doubt they would've made a movie about him."

He leaned his head against the Box, a position that he had been in all day, when he suddenly realized that his right hamstring was starting to cramp again. He hastily tried stretching, doing anything to prevent the muscle contractions from striking, but the shackles on the floor made it impossible to move. Once again, he was forced to ride out the wave of agony until the spasm passed.

As Payne suffered, Bennie Blount peered into the hole of the Devil's Box. "You ain't got enough *possium* in yo' body. 'Dat's why you crampin' like 'dat."

The voice stunned Payne, yet he replied quickly. "I'm cramping up like this because I'm locked in a Rubik's cube, not because I didn't eat enough freakin' bananas."

"I don't know. I still think it's the *possium*."

Payne continued fighting his cramp, in no mood to discuss the merits of potassium. "Nothing personal, but I have a policy about talking to traitors."

Blount turned on a small flashlight and placed it under his chin. He wanted Payne to see his face as he talked. "I sorry about 'dat, Mr. Payne, but I didn't have no choice. I wasn't allowed off 'da island unless I agreed to do it, and I really wanted to see 'da fireworks. . . . As it be, I didn't even get to see 'em."

Payne stared at the servant, then shook his head in pity. Blount was just a helpless pawn in this, caught up in something that he didn't know how to control or escape from. And even though Blount worked for the Plantation, Payne could tell he wasn't as sadistic as the others.

No, Blount was different. Much different.

"Hey, Bennie," Payne whispered. "I don't want to get you in trouble or anything, but I was hoping you might be able to give me a hand."

"You mean free ya? They'd never trust me wit' 'da key. I'd probably lose it."

"That's OK, Bennie. I don't need a key. There are other things you could do for me."

Blount lowered his face to the carved grill of the Box. "Like what?"

"Some food and drink would be nice."

Blount frowned, then suddenly stood from his perch.

Payne could hear him walking away and feared that someone was coming, or worse yet, that Blount had decided to abandon him a second time. "Bennie? What's wrong? Come back. Where are you going?"

The servant's face filled the top of the Box one more time. "I wasn't goin' nowhere. When ya mentioned you could use some vittles, it helped me remember somethin'. 'Da reason I came up here was to bring ya some chow, but with all 'da conversatin'

I forgot to gives it to ya."

Food. Mouthwatering food. Payne couldn't believe his luck. The image of a thick, juicy steak suddenly popped into his mind, causing his stomach to rumble like a subwoofer. "Thank you so much. What do you have for me?"

"First t'ings first. I heard 'bout what Master Ndjai did to ya, and I thought ya could use a bath." The dreadlocked servant held up a big pot of liquid, then explained what he had in mind. "Now don't ya be drinking this stuff while I pour it on ya. This ain't no tap water, you know."

"What the hell is it then?"

"Don't ya be worryin' none. I mixed up an ol' family recipe for ya, one 'dat we use to bathe babies when they be young. Not only will it makes ya clean, but it'll make ya smell like an infant."

"Thanks, but I already smell like piss."

Blount laughed as he readied the substance for pouring. "'Dat's not what I meant. You be smellin' April-fresh when I done with ya. I promise." He carefully tipped the pot until the liquid flowed over Payne. It surged through the Box's grate like a great flood, washing away the scent of urine and the lingering stench of sweat.

"I'll be damned," Payne chuckled, suddenly feeling a hell of a lot better. He took a deep whiff, breathing in the fragrance that filled the air around him. "And you're right. I smell like the goddamn Snuggle bear. What's in that stuff? It smells great."

Blount's smile quickly faded. "Trust me, Mr. Payne. You don't wants to know. I know it made me sick 'da first time I found out. Blahhhh!"

Even though he was curious about the marinade he was soaking in, Payne quickly changed the subject. He had more important things to worry about, plus he was a little concerned about the secret ingredient. "Bennie," he said, "now that I'm clean, what do you have for me to eat?"

"I gots ya lots of stuff, but 'da most important stuff be the liquids. We gots to get ya full of fluid or you's gonna melt away like lard in a black skillet."

Payne finished his meal of fruit and juices in no time, and when he was done, the smile of gratitude on his face said it all: Bennie Blount, the dreadlocked servant from the Bayou, had saved his life—if only for the time being. Technically, Blount had only provided Payne with food and a much-needed shower, but in reality he had brought Payne something even more important. He had given him hope. "Bennie, I can't thank you enough. I can't even begin to explain how much I needed that."

Blount smiled as he tidied the area around the Box. He needed to make sure that there was no sign of his visit or he'd get in serious trouble. "Well, I be feelin' bad about the trick 'dat we played on you and Mr. Jones. I figure it be 'da least I can do."

"Speaking of Mr. Jones, how is he doing?"

Blount took a deep breath, pausing ever so slightly before he answered. "I don't mean to scare ya none, but I heard 'dat Master Greene roughed him up somethin' fierce."

"What?"

"Now before ya get too worried, I didn't get a chance to find out if 'dat be true or not, but I just thought it be best if I done told ya what I heard."

Payne considered the information and realized it would make things doubly difficult. If he didn't have a healthy Jones by his side, he wouldn't be able to . . . Damn, he didn't even want to think about it. The task would be tough enough as it was. "Where's he being held? At the main house?"

"No, sir. He be in a utility cabin near 'da slaves. It kinda stands out from 'da others since it got plumbing and be much larger than 'da rest."

"Is there any way you can visit him? You know, to bring him some food and first aid?"

Blount shook his head. "Not without 'dem knowing. 'Da cabin is guarded, and it be locked from 'da outside. Since I ain't got no key, I can't get in without no permission." Blount frowned. "And I don't think I gonna be gettin' any."

"Is there any chance of him getting out? A window? A trapdoor? Anything?"

"You be watchin' too much TV. There ain't no such thing as trapdoors in 'da real world."

Payne immediately thought of Levon Greene's escape from the tattoo parlor, but he didn't have the time or the patience to explain the tale to Blount. "So, you're telling me he's screwed, right? No way in or out without the key."

"Yep. He be screwed."

"How about Ariane? Is she still in the same place as before?"

Blount winced in guilt. When he originally briefed Payne and Jones about the Plantation, he gave them bogus information. It was all a part of Greene's master plan of deception. "I been wantin' to talk to ya about 'dat. You see, the stuff 'dat I done told you before was a little off."

Payne leaned his head against the Box and groaned. "How off?"

"Well, ah, kinda completely off."

"Bennie," he sighed.

"I be sorry, sir, but Master Greene wasn't about to let me tell ya 'da real stuff. He's one of 'da bosses of 'dis place, so I didn't have no choice."

"Yeah, but . . ." Payne stopped his complaint in mid-sentence. He suddenly remembered that Blount had just saved his life, so there was no way he was going to make him feel worse about his earlier actions. "You're probably right. You didn't have a choice. But I'd certainly appreciate it if you filled me in on things now."

Blount nodded his approval. "We gotta do 'dis quick, though. I don't want to be gone too long from 'da kitchen. I might be missed."

"Fair enough."

"So, what do ya needs to know?"

Payne grimaced. There were tons of things that he wanted

to learn about the island, but before the opportunity passed, he needed Blount's assistance on a more important matter. "Bennie, I know that you've done a lot of nice things for me, and I really appreciate them all. But there's something that I need that's even more important than information."

Blount brushed the braided hair from his face, then gazed into the Box. "What be 'dat?"

"Well, I was wondering if you could scratch me."

"Huh?"

"I was hoping you could scratch me. You see, I've been in here for a pretty long time, and I got a number of itches all over my body that I can't reach, so . . ."

"You's bein' serious, ain't ya?"

Payne nodded, trying to look as pathetic as possible.

"You's crazy. I want to help ya and all, but I ain't touchin' no man. Besides, there ain't no way my arms can fit in 'dat thing. The holes on 'da top be too skinny."

Payne sighed, making sure that Blount could hear his disappointment. "Come on, Bennie, there has to be something you can do. These itches are driving me crazy. Every time I move, it feels like something is crawling on me—especially down *there.* It's horrible."

Blount examined the grate of the Box, but it proved his suspicions to be correct. There was no way to get his arm in the device. "Why don't ya do it yourself?"

"Trust me, if I could, I would. But as you can see, my hands are bound to the floor of this thing. I can't even crack my knuckles, let alone scratch myself."

Blount peered closer, shining the light inside. "Yeah, yo' hands is bound good. Unless . . ."

"Unless what?"

"Unless I can do somethin' with yo' hands."

Payne tried to suppress his smile, but it was tough. Blount had just suggested the one thing Payne was hoping for. In fact, it was the only reason that Payne had bitched to begin with. He was hoping he could trick the servant into freeing his hands. "Jeez, Bennie, what do you think you can do?"

Blount examined the shackles from several angles. Then, he peered at the outside structure of the Box. "Yo' hands is in handcuffs, right?"

"Yeah."

"Then 'da handcuffs is bolted to 'da floor, right?"

"That's right."

"So, if I release 'da bolt from 'da floor, you is still gonna be in cuffs, ain't ya?"

Payne knew he was, but he still examined the floor, pretending to contemplate the information. "Yeah," he said. "That sounds right."

"But you can scratch with cuffs, can't ya?"

"Definitely. And it wouldn't be like you were freeing me, Bennie. I'd still be in cuffs, and I'd still be locked in this thing."

Blount mulled the situation over. He didn't want to do anything that would give away his role in this. "All right. I think I can unscrew 'dis bolt from 'da outside. 'Den once you pull yo' cuffs from 'da hook in 'da floor, I be puttin' 'da bolt right back. 'Dat way it looks like you did it on yo' own."

Payne turned his head from Blount and grinned. The servant didn't realize it, but he had given Payne much more than an opportunity to scratch. He had given him a way to escape.

Chapter Thirty-Four

Monday, July 5

David Jones had no idea where Payne was being held or what was being done to him, but the racial overtones of the island suggested he was probably in serious shape. "Hang in there," he mumbled, still sore from his earlier beating. "I'm coming to get you."

He searched around the cabin for a way out, but there were no obvious choices. He probed the floor, walls, and ceiling, but each of them proved to be quite solid. After several minutes of intense examination, it became apparent that the heavily guarded front door was his only option.

Holding his tender ribs, Jones trudged to the wooden portal and studied it. Made of oak and finished with a light lacquer, the door was thick, too thick to knock down. It sat in a matching oak frame and was sealed from the outside with a steel, deadbolt lock.

When Jones was done with his investigation, he returned to his mattress and reclined, propping his tired legs on a pillow. "What would MacGyver do?" he wondered aloud, referring to the TV character who had a penchant for creative solutions. "He'd probably make a grenade out of his feces, then blow down the door like the Big Bad Wolf."

Jones chuckled as he said it, but as he stared at the door over his outstretched feet, two things quickly became apparent: one, a doorway explosion was actually within the realm of possibility, and two, he wouldn't have to build a device.

Why? The guards had actually given him one.

The idiots had strapped it to his leg.

Forgetting the pain in his back and ribs, Jones leaned forward to study his anklet. The mechanism that was attached to his lower leg was encased in a silver, metallic shell that was no thicker than his hand. The gadget was streamlined and carried very little weight, forcing Jones to conclude that the technology had to be pretty advanced.

"Unless," he mumbled, "this is a dummy."

Since the latest in incendiary gear was bound to be expensive, Jones wondered if the Posse had the finances to spend so much money on deterrents. If they didn't, he figured they might be tempted to put dummy devices on the legs of their captives. To him, it made sense. The prisoners would undoubtedly accept the guards' explanation of the anklets, and because of that they'd be too scared to run away or attempt to remove them.

To find out what he was dealing with, Jones looked for the safest way to penetrate the metal casing. He carefully explored the outside of the silver shell, deciding that there were only two practical choices: He could pick the lock on the front of the anklet, a difficult task without the proper tools, or he could pry the case open with some kind of wedge. The second option seemed the easier of two, but it also seemed much riskier. Even though there was a thin seam that ran along the top of the mechanism, one that could be pried apart rather easily, Jones figured it was bound to be booby-trapped. Most hi-tech explosives were.

"You don't have a choice," he said to himself. "You have to pick it."

But the question was how? If he had his lock-picking kit with him, Jones could open the clasp in less than a minute, but without it he had no idea how long the process would take—if he could do it at all. In order to have a chance, he needed to find something slender enough to fit in the lock but sturdy enough not to break inside. Jones scoured the walls for stray tacks or nails, but it was pretty obvious that there were none. Next, he examined his bed, hoping to find some iron springs on the inside, but the mattress was made of foam.

"Shit," he grumbled. "What can I use?"

Jones glanced around the room, unsuccessfully, for several seconds before his statement finally sank in. The word *shit* had pointed him in the right direction.

He could use a part from the toilet.

With a burst of energy that temporarily masked his pain, he rushed to the porcelain throne and removed the lid. Peering inside, he was glad to see the water in the tank was semi-clear, tainted slightly with the orange residue of rust but much better than he'd expected. Wasting no time, he plunged his shackled hands into the fluid, hastily searching for a tool that would fit into the lock of his anklet. After several seconds of exploration, Jones found the best possibility. The floater lever, which was shaped like an 8-inch long barbecue skewer, was thin and made out of a hard plastic.

Dropping to his knees, Jones sealed the main water valve with a few rotations of his wet hands, then lowered the handle on the commode. FLUSH! The murky liquid exited the tank and filled the bowl like a whirlpool before dropping out of sight. Jones climbed to his feet, grunting slightly as he did, then removed the plastic rod with a twist.

Jones didn't have the strength to walk back to his bed, for his ribs were starting to throb, so he chose to sit on the toilet seat instead. After taking a deep breath, he crossed his legs, bringing the anklet as close to his face as possible. Then with his hands chained, he tried sliding the slender piece into the lock, but it wouldn't fit. The part was just too wide.

Undeterred, he stood from the seat and slid the plastic lever into the toilet handle's interior chain. Using the metal links as a file, Jones rubbed his hands together in a back-and-forth motion, rolling the rod over and over like a drill. The repetitive motion did little at first, but after a while, it slowly started to wear down the edges of the lever, sharpening it to a point. When he was satisfied with his progress, he retook his seat and tried the lock again. This time it fit.

With his limited view of the anklet, Jones couldn't identify the type of lock he was dealing with. He knew it could be opened with a key, that much was certain, but he wasn't sure what kind of internal safeguards it would have. If it was a spring lock, he was confident he could pop it open rather quickly. Spring locks have very few safeties, making them a criminal's dream. They can often be picked with credit cards or other thin objects in a matter of seconds. If, however, the lock was tubular, then Jones knew he was out of luck. The multiple pins of the cylinder and the deadbolt action of the cam would require something more sophisticated than a sharpened piece of plastic. It would require something he didn't have: a key.

With the delicate touch of a surgeon, Jones jiggled the floater lever back and forth until he got a feel for the internal mechanism of the lock. A smile crept over his face when he realized what he was dealing with. It was a spring lock, just as he had hoped. After wiping his hands on his shirt, he slowly manipulated the lock in a circular fashion until it popped open with a loud click.

After sliding the device off of his leg, Jones was able to study the outer casing of the anklet in greater detail than before. The shell was silver in color, shiny and quite reflective, yet possessed an abrasive texture that was rough to the touch. It carried very little weight, one or two pounds at the most, but was quite durable, holding up to the rigors of his probing with nary a dent.

"What the hell is this?" he asked.

The alloy was unfamiliar to him, possibly a mixture of titanium and a lesser-quality metal, but definitely expensive—too expensive, in Jones' mind, for it to be a hoax.

"Ladies and gentlemen, we've got ourselves a bomb."

Now that he knew what he was dealing with, he had to decide the best way to use it. Sure, he could strap the explosive to the door and blow the sucker off its hinges, but what would that get him? Probably killed, that's what. The moment he ran outside, the guards would be all over him like the LAPD in the Rodney King beating.

No, in order to escape, Jones needed a way to take out the guards and the door at the same time. But how?

Jones went to work on the device as he planned a scenario in his head.

*   *   *

Even though he was trapped in the Devil's Box, Payne actually felt good about his situation. His hunger was gone, his thirst had vanished, and he smelled kind of pretty. So as soon as Bennie left the hill, Payne went to work on his shackles.

When his hands were bound to the floor, there was no way for him to remove his handcuffs. The thick bolt had prevented it. As soon as it was disengaged, though, he was able to use the maneuver that he'd learned from Slippery Stan, an escape artist whom he befriended while at a magic exhibit.

Unlike most magicians, escape artists rarely use optical illusions in their trade, instead they learn to manipulate their bodies in a variety of ways in order to escape from things like straitjackets or multiple layers of chains. And in the case of handcuffs, Payne was taught to turn his hands and wrists at a very precise angle, which allowed him to slide from the restraints like a hand from a glove.

Of course, the cuffs were only half the battle in this case. The next part of Payne's escape would be much more difficult, and he knew it. In order to get from the Box itself, he had to rely on some outside help. He wasn't sure where that was going to come from—perhaps Bennie, or a guard, or even an escaped captive—but he knew he was stuck until someone showed up.

And, unfortunately, it took nearly an hour before someone did.

The instant Payne heard movement outside he slid his hands under his chains, hoping to maintain the appearance of captivity.

"Are you still alive?" asked Ndjai with his thick accent. "I bet you're bored up here all by yourself, aren't you?" He lowered his face to the grate, smiling with his nasty teeth. "Well, I've got some company for you."

The wheels in Payne's head quickly started to spin. Was it D.J., or Ariane, or maybe even Bennie? None of the possibilities pleased Payne, and the grimace on his face proved it. "Who is it?" he croaked, trying to pretend like his was dehydrated. "Who's out there with you?"

"Ah, the question shouldn't be, 'Who?' The question should be, 'What?' "

Payne scrunched his face in confusion. He couldn't hear Tornado's panting so he knew it wasn't him. In fact, he didn't hear anything at all, except Ndjai's laughter. "OK, *what* is out there?"

"A couple of playmates to keep you company."

Payne didn't like the sound of that. "I appreciate the offer, but I'm actually all right. I've kind of enjoyed the solitude."

"You might get bored later, and I would hate for you to think of me as a bad host." He lifted a large shoe box above the grate then shook it a few times. An angry squeal emerged from the cardboard structure. The creature, whatever it was, did not like to be jostled. "Hmmm, he sounds mad. I hope you'll be able to calm him down."

"I hope so, too."

Ndjai rested the cardboard container on top of the Box and smiled. "Then again, that might be tough for you to do. My little friend tends to get upset around the other playmate that I brought for you." Ndjai lifted a large duffel bag into the air, then set it down with a loud thump. "You see, when this second guy is hungry, he has a nasty habit of wanting to eat the first guy. So, obviously, that makes the first guy nervous."

"Wait," Payne mumbled. "Am I the first guy or the second guy? You went so fast I got confused. Please say that again."

The African was ready to explain when he realized that Payne was making another joke, a reaction he hadn't expected from his prisoner. "I must admit I admire your courage. Too bad it is a feeble attempt to mask the fear underneath."

"It wasn't feeble," Payne argued. "I actually thought it was a pretty good effort on my part."

Ndjai ignored the comment, moving instead to the business at hand. "So, Mr. Payne, I will now give you a choice. Which would you prefer first: the bag or the box?"

"Well, it'd be a lot easier for me if you told me what they contained."

"Ah, but that would take away the fun part. The mystery, the intrigue, the fear."

"The fun part? Fun for who? Only a sick fuck like yourself could be enjoying this."

Ndjai laughed loudly. "Trust me, I am. And now, since you're being so uncooperative, I will make the choice for you. How about both at once?"

After sliding a glove onto his right hand, Ndjai carefully reached inside the container. Payne could hear the scratching of tiny claws on the interior of the box, then the squeals of anguish as Ndjai finally captured the creature. "I'd like to introduce you to the plantation rat, a breed that is indigenous to Louisiana."

Holding it by its tail, Ndjai dangled the rodent above the Box. Payne, who'd never heard of the species, marveled at its size. It was 16 inches in length, not including its tail, and weighed close to 20 ounces. It had a short snout, small ears, and was covered in coarse, reddish gray fur.

"Doesn't that thing do commercials for Taco Bell?" Payne wondered aloud.

"You can ask him yourself in a moment. He's about to become your roommate."

"Then I expect this and next month's rent in cash, plus I'll need him to sign a few waivers. Can the squirrel write?"

Ndjai smiled while lowering the rat to the Box's grate. As he did, the rodent squirmed, trying to free itself from the Ndjai's grasp. To punish the rat for its escape attempt, Ndjai squeezed its tail hard, causing the creature to snap its teeth and brandish its claws in anger.

"You're going to have fun with him. He isn't very happy."

Payne shrugged nonchalantly. "That makes two of us."

With his free hand, Ndjai reached into his pocket and removed a full set of keys. After choosing the correct one, Ndjai inserted it into the lock and opened it with a soft click. He removed the padlock with his left hand while dangling the shrieking rat with his right. "Are you ready?" he asked as he threw open the lid.

Payne grinned, knowingly. "Actually, I was about to ask you the same thing."

Before Ndjai could react, Payne leapt from his crouched position and struck his captor in the bridge of his nose with a quick blow. The African stumbled backwards, dropping the rat into the Box as he did, but Payne couldn't have cared less. Before the rodent could attack, Payne pounced from the wooden cage with the grace of a jungle cat, landing next to his stunned victim in a single stride. Ndjai raised his hands in defense, but he could do little against the infuriated MANIAC. In a quick burst, Payne pummeled the fallen man with several shots to his face and torso, beating him repeatedly until blood gushed from Ndjai's nose and mouth.

Once the African had submitted, Payne grabbed his legs and dragged him roughly towards the Box. "Let's see how you like this thing, Hakeem. We'll see if you can get the rat to calm down."

He pulled Ndjai to his feet, then bent him over the edge of the Box, dangling his upper body inside. The rat, still angry from before, reacted instantly, jumping and nipping at the crimson liquid that dripped from Ndjai's face.

"Oh, isn't that cute. I think he likes you."

Payne punctuated his comment by dumping Ndjai upside-down next to the appreciative rat and slamming the lid shut. As he reached for the lock, though, he suddenly noticed Ndjai's duffel bag out of the corner of his eye.

"Well, well, well. What other toys did Santa bring for the boys and girls?"

Payne tried lifting the bag with one hand, but was caught off guard by its weight. "I can't even imagine what's in here, but as you said, the mystery is part of the fun."

After emptying the bag inside the device, Payne closed the lid and broke the key in the lock with a sharp twist. Then, as he pocketed Ndjai's key ring, Payne took a moment to watch the terrified rat as it scurried over Ndjai while trying to avoid the jaws of the angry copperhead.

Chapter Thirty-Five

Moving silently in the darkness, just like he'd been trained to do with the MANIACs, Payne glided across the open fields of the Plantation, constantly searching for guards. Since he was unaware of Ariane's current location, he decided to head straight for Jones, hoping that his friend was in good enough health to assist him. If he wasn't, Payne realized he'd have to handle the Posse by himself. He had faced longer odds in the past and won, so he knew he was capable of doing it again, but all things considered, he'd prefer having his former lieutenant by his side.

When the cabins finally came into view, rising out of the flat ground like wooden stalagmites, Payne dropped to his belly and scouted the terrain for patrol patterns and sniper placements. He watched for several minutes, studying the tree lines and roofs, the bushes and walkways, but was unable to detect any movement.

"Where are you guys?"

His hazel eyes continued to scan the darkened landscape, probing every crevice and shadow of the compound, but the waning crescent moon and the lack of overhead lights made it difficult to see from his distance. Reluctantly, he moved closer.

With the stealth of a ninja, Payne sprang from his stomach and charged forward at full speed, the breath barely escaping his mouth, his feet rarely creating a sound. It was as if he was moving on a cushion of air, the clouds serving as silencers for each of his strides, softening the impact of his steps as he hustled across the hard turf. After closing the gap to forty feet, Payne found cover behind a large rock, pausing for a moment to feed his hungry lungs. When his breath returned, he carefully peaked over the light-brown boulder and scoured the immediate area for patrolmen.

"Come out, come out, wherever you are," he mumbled softly.

But no one did. The grounds were devoid of Posse members, leaving the front door of the nearest cabin without protection.

"This can't be right. There has to be guards here."

Taking a deep breath, Payne placed his hand in his pocket and removed Ndjai's keys so they wouldn't jingle when he ran. Next, after looking around again, he sprinted forward, heading straight towards the cabin that was closest to him. Upon reaching it, Payne crouched near the ground and made himself as small a target as possible while double-checking the terrain. When he was sure that no one was around, he shoved the first key in the lock and prayed it would let him inside, but he was unable to turn it at all. The same thing occurred with the next key, and the one after that, and the one after that. Finally, on his fifth attempt, with sweat dripping off of his forehead from a mixture of tension and physical exertion, he found the one that did the job.

With a sigh of relief, Payne opened the door as quietly as he could, then slid into the cabin with nary a sound. It took his eyes a moment to adjust to the darkened interior of the room, but when they finally focused, he realized his mission had just become a whole lot easier. He'd been hoping to find a cabin full of slaves or maybe a clue about Ariane, but what he found turned out to be even better.

He had hit the mother lode.

*   *   *

While still in handcuffs, Jones opened the silver shell of the explosive, then carefully probed the interior of the bomb for booby traps. He found several. If he'd removed the anklet's casing without care, the device would've exploded in his face, triggered in less than a millionth of a second by a series of tripwires that protected the outer core of the mechanism.

Thankfully, he noticed them in time.

After neutralizing the safeguards, Jones dug deeper, examining the hi-tech circuitry that filled the unit. "I'll be damned," he said, impressed. He had never seen a portable explosive filled with so much modern technology. Data microprocessors, external pressure sensors, satellite uplink capability, and digital detonation switches. The kind of stuff that couldn't be bought at Radio Shack. "Where the hell did they get this? This is some serious shit."

Using the sharpened lever from the toilet, Jones explored the interior of the bomb, searching under the electronic hardware for the actual explosive. In order to take out the door cleanly, Jones needed to understand how much force the device was capable of producing. He assumed that the component was filled with a relatively stable explosive, something that could handle sudden movements and exposure to body heat and/or static electricity, but he wasn't sure what. C-4, a commonly used plastic explosive, was a possibility, so were RDX, TNT, and pentolite, but because of the hi-tech craftsmanship of the anklet, Jones assumed that the manufacturer would use something newer, sexier. Perhaps even a synthetic hybrid.

When Jones finally discovered what he was dealing with, he gaped in horror and fascination. The device was unlike anything he had ever seen before. Two vials, three inches in length, sat tucked underneath the circuitry. Each plastic cylinder was filled with a liquid—one red, the other clear—and they were connected to a third vial, which was twice as wide as the others, through a series of slender plastic tubes, each one color-coded and approximately the width of a pencil.

The cylinders, the liquids, the tubes. All of them were new to Jones.

"What the hell am I supposed to do with this?" he demanded.

As the words left his mouth, his problems actually worsened, for he heard the distinct sound of keys rattling directly outside. Someone was about to enter the cabin.

Panicked, Jones searched for a hiding place but found nowhere to stash the equipment. The mattress was probably his best possibility, but Jones knew if he was forced to sit on the bed, there was a chance that his weight could detonate the device, and the thought of shrapnel being launched up his ass was a bit unsettling.

Finally, with nowhere else to turn, Jones scooped up as many parts as he could and ran towards the bed. He set the explosive on the floor, then turned his mattress on its side and angled it across the back corner of the room like a child's fort. He figured, if he timed things just right, he could throw the explosive at the guard the moment he entered the room, then duck behind the bed for protection.

The outside knob twisted with a squeak.

The plan wasn't perfect, but Jones realized this might be his only chance to escape before the Posse killed him. In his mind, he figured there was no way they could let him live—especially since he knew about Levon Greene's involvement—so why not take a chance?

The door swung open, and a man wearing black fatigues entered the darkness of the cabin.

After saying a short prayer, Jones threw the explosive and dropped to the floor behind his protective foam shield. Then, in anticipation of a powerful blast, he covered his face and ears, curling into the fetal position against the back corner of the room. And he was lucky he did. The cylinders ruptured on contact, creating a bright ball of flame that tore across the cabin in a tidal wave of heat and light. Thunder ripped through the enclosed space of the wooden cell with the ferocity of a jackhammer, stinging Jones' ears despite the sheltering presence of his hands. Shards of metal dug their barbed claws into the front surface of the mattress, narrowly avoiding the exposed flesh of his back.

Slightly dazed from the jolt, Jones managed to peek his head over the tattered barrier in order to see how much damage had been done. Large streaks of red and orange danced from the far wall toward the unprotected surface of the beamed ceiling. Billowy puffs of smoke filled the enclosed space, making it tough for him to breathe. The door, shaken free from the concussion of the blast, sat unhinged and heavily dented, covered in debris and awash in flames. And the guard was, er . . . where was the guard?

Jones knew he'd hit him—he had to have hit him, didn't he?—so despite the crackling flames that raged throughout the cabin, he climbed over the mattress and searched for a body. It didn't matter that the fire was quickly becoming an inferno, shooting tiny embers into the air like bottle rockets. He needed to find the guard. He had to get the man's gun and take his keys. He had to question the bastard about Payne and Ariane before it was too late.

Hell, he had to do something to help even the odds.

Unfortunately, the blaze was making his mission an impossibility. The smoke grew thicker and blacker every second, limiting his vision to a scant few feet. And the heat was becoming so intense that Jones felt like he was standing in the core of an active volcano, one that was getting angrier by the minute. But still he searched, heroically digging through scraps of plastic and wood, hunting for the guard until he could take no more, until the hair on his arms literally started to sear like ants under a magnifying glass.

At that point he fled the firestorm before he fried in its wake.

Covering his eyes with both hands, Jones ran from the burning cabin, shielding his head from the flames as he burst through the smoldering doorway. The nighttime air brought him instant relief from the blaze, but he wasn't able to enjoy it. Jones realized that the Posse would be arriving any moment to investigate, and when they did he needed to be gone. He probed the immediate area for cover, using the orange glow of the cabin as his torch, but his plans to flee were quickly altered. Before he was able to find a hiding place, Jones noticed the guard sprawled on the nearby turf, a weapon sitting on the ground next to him.

No time to waste.

He rushed to the man's side and grabbed his TEC-DC9 pistol. Then, in a moment of greed, he frisked him, looking for anything else that could help, but as he did he made a startling discovery: The man was alive and conscious.

Jones jumped back in surprise, completely unsure of his next move. In the old days, it would've been an easy choice. He would've shot him, searched him, and left before anyone else arrived. But things were different now. Jones was no longer the same man he used to be. He was no longer a soldier. He was no longer a MANIAC.

"Ah, screw it!" he muttered. He knew if he didn't kill the guard now, he'd be forced to do it later when the odds were a lot less favorable. "I'm sorry for this. I truly am."

While taking a deep breath, Jones aimed the semi-automatic pistol and prepared to pull the trigger. Just before he did, though, the man tilted his head upward and stared at him with familiar eyes. It took Jones a while to recover from the impact of his realization, but when he did, he instantly dropped to his knees in concern.

Surprisingly, the injured man wasn't a guard.

The injured man was Payne.

Chapter Thirty-Six

Because of the black fatigues and dark face paint that Payne had found in the first cabin, he looked like a Posse member in the darkness. It wasn't until Jones stared at Payne's eyes in the light of the fire that he recognized his best friend.

"Is there a reason you tried to blow me up?" Payne grunted. He staggered to his feet, shaken from the powerful blast but relatively injury-free.

Jones offered him assistance. "I thought you were a guard."

"If you don't want to hang out with me anymore, that's fine. But you don't have to blow me up."

Payne shook his head in mock anger, then sprinted from the cabin. He knew the Posse would be arriving shortly and didn't want to be there when they did. Once they were away from the scene, though, he turned back towards Jones.

"Yo, firebug, what was that stuff anyway? It had some serious kick."

"Some kind of hi-tech chemical explosive. Some African guy with bad teeth strapped the sucker to my leg to prevent my escape."

"Hakeem did that?" The thought of Ndjai in the Devil's Box made him warm with laughter. "Locking a soldier in a wooden cabin with a fire bomb? Pretty good thinkin' on his part, huh?"

"That was more than just a fire bomb, Jon. That was a first-rate piece of hardware. I'm not sure what we've stumbled onto, but the Posse isn't hurting for cash. Not with that kind of technology laying around."

"You don't know the half of it. Let me show you what I found a little while ago."

Payne led Jones to the first cabin that he had explored. Instead of containing prisoners like he thought it would, it was filled from floor to ceiling with military accoutrements: rifles, pistols, ammunition, explosives, detonators, camouflage paint, etc. All labeled and packed in crates for shipping.

"Whoa." Jones glanced at the gear in amazement. There was enough equipment to start a small war. "This is some kind of collection."

Payne corrected him. "This isn't a collection. This is a business."

"They deal arms? Where'd they get this stuff?"

"Where do you think?" Payne pointed to one of the invoices on the wall. The initials T.M. were highlighted at the top. "Does that ring any bells?"

Jones glanced at the sheet. "Terrell Murray? Mr. Fishing Hole?"

"You got it." Payne strolled through the stacks of weapons, looking to add to his personal stock. He needed as much firepower as possible if he was going to rescue Ariane and the others.

"So, the Posse sells Terrell all of his weapons?"

Payne corrected him. "Probably not. From the looks of Murray's office, he's way too established to be buying from a new group like the Posse. No, the odds are probably the other way around. The Posse gets their guns from Terrell."

Jones furrowed his brow while glancing through some of the crates. "But why would they need all of this stuff? I mean, jeez, this is like an armory."

"Not like an armory. It is an armory. And if my guess is correct, the Posse doesn't own these weapons. They're probably just holding them for Terrell. Remember what Levon said? Nothing goes on in New Orleans without Murray's involvement."

Jones pulled a Steyr AUG assault rifle from a box and showed it to Payne. "Boy, this looks familiar, huh?" It was identical to the one that Greene had supposedly purchased from Murray. "So this is where Levon got his stuff from? That son of a bitch! I can't believe he played us like that! I can't wait until I see him again. I really can't."

Payne glanced at the equipment and sneered, selecting a Heckler & Koch MP5K submachine gun as his weapon of choice. His face no longer displayed its normal warmth. The levity and twinkle that usually filled his hazel eyes had been replaced by the austere glare of a killer.

"The first thing we have to do is locate Ariane. Once I know she's all right, we can get as much revenge as we want."

Jones nodded, thinking mainly of Greene. "And who do you have in mind?"

Payne headed towards the cabin door. "There are too many on my list to name."

Chapter Thirty-Seven

Octavian Holmes roared through the trees on his ATV while two truckloads of guards followed closely behind. Out of all of the men on the Plantation, Holmes was the best equipped to handle military situations, for he was a professional soldier. He had worked for nearly two decades as a mercenary, renting out his services to a variety of causes, some good, some bad, but this was the first time that his skills would be used to protect something he called his own.

The Plantation was a part of him. He would not let it be destroyed if he could help it.

Holmes stopped his vehicle near the burning cabin, then watched his men attack the blaze with alacrity. There was little hope of saving the structure, but they needed to prevent the flames from spreading. The other cabins were close by and quite susceptible to damage.

As Holmes continued to watch their effort, he sensed a presence sneaking up behind him. He turned quickly, raising his gun as he did, but his effort was unnecessary. It was only Jackson and Webster.

"Any ideas?" Holmes asked calmly.

Webster nodded, slightly nervous. "It was the new guys. I was in my office and saw one enter the door with a key. Moments later it blew up."

Holmes frowned. "Which of you lost your keys?"

Both men showed Holmes their personal sets, proving they weren't to blame.

"Fine. Where's Hakeem? He's the only other possibility."

Webster shrugged. "I tried paging him on the radio, but he didn't answer. I tried all of you the moment I saw the guy enter the cabin, but there was nothing else I could do from my office. I swear, I did my best."

"Theo, don't worry about it." Holmes' voice possessed a scary calm. His presence was almost stoic. "You aren't here to do the dirty work. You're here to take care of our finances. We'll handle the rest."

Holmes moved closer to the blaze, still examining it. There was something about the flames that interested him. The way they moved. The way they danced. He had seen it before. "Theo? You said you saw the explosion, right? Tell me, what did it look like?"

"It was a mushroom-type blast. A big flash of light burst from inside. Flames spread quickly across the door and roof. An unbelievable amount of thick, black smoke."

Holmes grinned at the description. Things finally made sense. "If my guess is correct, we don't have to worry about any escapees. The blast you described sounds like one of the anklets was detonated."

Webster quickly disagreed. "Actually, I saw both of them survive. One of them went in, but two of them came out."

Holmes' grin grew wider. That meant the prisoners had discovered a way to remove the anklet without getting killed. The thought of two worthy adversaries immediately piqued his interest. He would take great pleasure in hunting them down. "What do you know about these two men? Anything?"

Jackson answered. "Levon said they were some kind of ex-soldiers. They were called the Crazy Men or somethin' like that. If you talk to him, I'm sure he can tell you more. He lived with the bastards for two days."

"Crazy men?" Holmes had never heard of a group that went by that name, and he considered himself an expert on the military. "Could it have been something else? Perhaps the MANIACs?"

"Yeah, that was it. Have you heard of them?"

"Yeah," he muttered. The smile on Holmes' face was no longer present. "I've seen their work. They're clean. Real clean. Some of the guys I've worked with referred to them as the Hyenas."

"The Hyenas? Why's that?"

"They liked to ravage their victims. I mean, rip 'em to fuckin' shreds from very close range. Then, they'd leave the scene in packs, laughing, like their job was the easiest thing in the world to do." Holmes shivered at the thought, an equal mixture of fear and excitement surging through his body. After all of these years, he would finally get to see how good he was. "They're the best-prepared soldiers in the world."

"Come on, how tough can they be?" Jackson asked naively. "We've got dozens of men, all well-armed, and we're fighting against these guys in a confined space, right?"

Holmes nodded gravely. The stories he'd heard about the MANIACs bordered on legend, military folklore. "True, but if these two are who you claim, we might be severely outnumbered."

* * *

After stealing gear from the armory, Payne and Jones hustled into the nearby trees to establish their attack strategy. Unfortunately, their planning process would be quite difficult since they still lacked one major piece of information: Ariane's current location.

While removing Jones' handcuffs, Payne updated his friend on everything he'd learned about the guards and the landscape. "I searched a few of the cabins before I reached you, but all of them were empty."

"Empty? Bennie said there were 20 to 25 captives on this island."

"Well, I didn't check all the cabins, but there didn't seem to be much guard activity around. Either the prisoners are being kept somewhere else, or they've been moved off the island."

"Or," Jones added, "there are several people in one cabin. In the old days, slaves used to sleep ten to a room, and I have a feeling the Posse isn't trying to make their guests very comfortable."

Payne nodded in agreement. "So tell me, what should we do?"

Jones smiled at the question. "I thought you'd never ask."

For as long as they'd known each other, this was how their partnership worked. Payne would name a place, and Jones would lead him there. It didn't matter if it was a top-secret mission into Cuba or a beer-filled trip to a Steelers game, Jones was the direction man. He was the planner. A strategy prodigy. It was his specialty. He was the best there was.

Payne, on the other hand, was the closer, the military's equivalent of a baseball relief pitcher. He'd come in when everything was on the line and finish the job. No, he was never pretty; in fact, most of the time his work was borderline savage. But things always worked out in the end. Always.

Give him a quest, and he'd make it a conquest.

Together, the duo was virtually unstoppable.

Let the games begin.

Chapter Thirty-Eight

There was no reason for the duo to wage battle in the open fields where a lucky shot could take them out. No, it was better to do their dirty work in the dark underbrush of the island, where they could control the game. The woods would be their playground. Search and kill, jungle-style.

Without speaking, Payne and Jones communicated their ideas through hand signals. It wasn't traditional sign language, but for them it was just as effective. They knew exactly what the other was saying without saying a word, and that was critical. During night runs, sound was the biggest enemy. On the other hand, sound could also be quite useful, the ultimate ally. By making a noise on purpose, a soldier could divert his enemy's attention. The crash of a thrown rock could confuse a tracker. A snapping twig or a well-placed scream could quickly draw attention away from an endangered colleague. And occasionally, it could also be used as a lure, a way to bring several people into an area at one time. It was a difficult thing to accomplish, but when done right, it was very effective.

Cows to the slaughterhouse, as Payne liked to say.

Eventually, this was the technique that Jones settled on. In order to make it work, they placed some charges near a small clearing that they found in the middle of a thick grove. A boulder, partially buried on a nearby plateau, would be used as the duo's nest. The goal was to draw as many men as possible into the open area below the large stone before Payne and Jones used their elevated position to commence target practice.

After climbing the bluff, Jones settled into position right next to Payne. Normally, they would've spread far apart, attempting to surround their victims with crossfire in hopes of cutting off their escape routes, but in this case it was completely unnecessary. This assault would be child's play, a complete blood bath. Two experienced soldiers facing a team of untrained men was as lopsided as a battle could get. Besides, the landscape didn't allow them to fan out over a wide range. The terrain dictated that both of them sit in the crow's nest from the get-go.

When Payne was ready, he glanced at Jones and nodded. It was time to begin.

BOOM!!! The sound of thunder shook the earth, and a flash of light brightened the nearby sky. Everyone near the burning cabin flinched, then turned their heads towards the trees. The prisoners were apparently in the woods. Holmes gave orders to pursue them.

Tat-tat-tat-tat-tat!!! Payne and Jones squeezed off a few rounds for additional attention, plus they wanted to make sure that their weapons were functional. The last time they'd used Terrell Murray's guns they were very disappointed with the results.

BOOM!!! A second charge exploded. Payne and Jones tried to lure the guards to a specific spot in the woods. They couldn't afford to have any strays sneaking up behind them. It would ruin their plans and possibly cost them their lives. No, they needed everyone to appear in the open area below the boulder, right where the guards would be most vulnerable.

BOOM!!! The last of the small charges was detonated. Neither Payne nor Jones wanted the woods to be too bright when the guards arrived. They wanted a soft glow, just enough light to see their targets, but not enough light to give away their own location. Candlelight to kill by.

"Do you hear that?" Payne whispered as he screwed the

silencer on his MP5K. His weapon was capable of spitting out 900 rounds a minute, and now that its silencer was in place, it would make less noise than a Walkman.

Jones smiled. He heard several footsteps approaching through the grove. "I think these are the first contestants on The Price is Life."

Payne nodded and focused on the area below him. He wouldn't fire his submachine gun until the small pocket of space was completely filled with victims. He needed to make sure he could get everyone at once.

One by one, the guards emerged from the trees. Two, then five, then six more. Thirteen in total. Unlucky thirteen. They glanced around, looking for the source of the commotion, but could find nothing. They stood there, confused, unable to choose their next move, for none of them had the experience or the authority to take control.

"Like cows to the slaughterhouse," Jones mumbled, stealing Payne's line.

Payne nodded again, his face devoid of emotion. "Moooooo."

There wasn't any time for the guards to react or to fire back. Hell, they never even knew what hit them. One minute they were standing, searching for the escaped prisoners. The next they were sprawled on the ground, marinating in each other's blood.

There were no screams, no tears, and no pleas of mercy. Death had been silent and swift.

*　　*　　*

Anticipating an easy victory, Jackson and Webster followed the guards at a leisurely pace. Thirteen men against two. With odds like that, they figured it would be a massacre, an absolute slaughter. It was. When they arrived at the scene, they found bodies, nothing but bodies. All of them black. All of them dead. Victims of massive gunfire. Head shots. Heart shots. Limbs completely tattered. Pistols still holstered. Rifles unfired. The smell of war lingered in the air. Crimson poured from gaping wounds, flooding the forest's floor. Death was everywhere.

And Webster couldn't handle it.

When he realized what had happened, he dropped to his knees and vomited. It was the first time that he'd seen a corpse outside of a funeral home, so the sight of a bloodied baker's dozen was too much for him to handle. Tears rolled down his face, dripping onto his puke-stained shirt.

"They killed them! Payne and Jones killed them all!" He staggered to his feet, wanting to confront Jackson, but was unwilling to walk amongst the gore of his fallen comrades. "Octavian was right. These guys are the best. Look what they did to your guards. Just look!"

"Be quiet," Jackson ordered. "They might still be around."

The thought had never crossed Webster's mind. The killers could be in the trees, watching him at that very moment. More vomit rose from his belly.

Jackson rolled his eyes in disgust. He didn't have time to baby-sit. He needed to focus all of his attention on the battle site. He needed to look for clues while the trail was still warm.

"Don't worry," he said. "I might not have their training, but I can be a warrior if I have to be."

As Jackson finished speaking, his radio squawked, causing him to flinch in surprise. The incoming voice said, "Harris, this is Octavian. What's going on out there?"

Jackson whispered, "Dead. Everyone's dead. Payne and Jones killed everyone. Theo and I showed up one minute behind the guards, and we found corpses. Thirteen fuckin' corpses. Blood everywhere. No sign of the prisoners, but our guys are dead."

"You're sure."

Jackson kicked one of the men; he didn't move. "Yep."

Holmes felt his pulse quicken, then noticed the hairs on his arms stand at attention. Thirteen kills in less than ten minutes.

My lord, these guys *were* good. "What did they use for weapons?"

"Guns," Jackson answered. "I don't know what kind, but they definitely possess rapid-fire capability. I don't see any shells near the guards, so I guess they didn't have time to fire back."

"Where the hell did they get weapons like—"

Holmes stopped before he finished his statement. Nervously, he turned to examine the cabin on the far end of the row. The door looked closed from a distance, but there was only one way to know for sure.

"Guards!" he shouted. Two men left the burning cabin and ran to his side. "Check the armory and tell me if anything's missing."

The men saluted crisply, then ran off.

As he watched them approach the storage shed, Holmes felt the tension rise in his body. If Payne and Jones had located the artillery, there was a good chance that they'd stolen enough equipment to wipe out the entire island. Instead of seizing the Plantation one guard at a time, they could do it one acre at a time.

The men reached the cabin within seconds, and glanced at the partially opened door. The armory had been violated. Drawing their weapons, the two men kicked the door aside and prepared to fire at the perpetrators. It was the last move that they ever made. Because of their haste and inexperience, the men failed to notice the wire that had been tied to the base of the door. When they bumped the cord, it triggered a fragmentation grenade, which exploded in their faces with deadly force. The *fragger*, designed to launch razor-like pieces of metal over an extended area of space without the impact of a large explosion, tattered the men with shrapnel, killing both men instantly. Meanwhile, the remaining contents of the shed were hardly disturbed.

Holmes grimaced as he heard the muffled blast, followed by the guards' silence. The sounds proved what he already knew in his gut: The Plantation's artillery had been compromised.

"Damn," he muttered.

He wasn't the least bit concerned about his men, but he was worried about the missing weapons. It was going to make his job so much harder to accomplish.

He grabbed his radio once again. "Harris? Theo? Are you there?"

"What do you need?" Jackson whispered. He was walking through the trees, trying not to make a sound. "We're on our way back now."

"Well, that's probably a good idea. Not to alarm you, but I just discovered that Payne and Jones got into Terrell's gear. That's apparently where they got their weapons, so there's no telling what other surprises they might have in store for us."

"What do you mean by surprises?"

"I don't know," Holmes admitted. He still needed to get someone inside of the armory to check the inventory. "Land mines, flame throwers, grenades, rocket launchers. Shit, they could have anything."

Without taking time to respond, the speed of Jackson and Webster's stride increased significantly.

Chapter Thirty-Nine

When Greene saw the site of the first explosion, it hit him like a punch in the gut. It was Jones' cabin, and there was nothing left of it. The wooden frame had collapsed, succumbing to the intense heat of the fire. Debris, spread from the power of the initial blast, littered the yard, cluttering the neatly trimmed grass in several directions. Clouds of smoke lingered in the air, making it tough to breathe or even see.

"Damn," he muttered. "This can't be good."

Holmes, Jackson, and Webster saw Greene's approach and immediately rushed to his side. Before they even said a word, Greene tried to ascertain the situation from their expressions, but was unable to do so because of the wide range of emotions that he saw. Holmes had the cold glare of a terrorist. Blank face, intense eyes, neither a frown nor smile on his lips. He had seen this type of shit before, and that was apparent from his confident stride. Jackson, though not as polished as Holmes, was still under control. His eyes showed some concern, like a sick man waiting for test results in a hospital, but he did his best to mask it with a broad grin. This was his first combat, and overall, he was holding up relatively well.

Then there was Webster. He was the complete opposite of the other two men. In fact, if he had been a horse, Elmer would've been negotiating for his glue rights. His face was pale and sweaty, giving him the appearance of someone who'd been caught in the rain. His body trembled, and his eyes were as big as pancakes. If not for the tragic possibilities of the situation, Greene would've laughed at the tiny man. Hell, he was thinking of doing it anyway.

"Why are you here?" Webster whined. "Who's watching the boat of prisoners?"

"Don't worry about it. The passengers are chained and surrounded by water. They aren't going anywhere." Greene turned towards Holmes. He knew that Octavian would give him the facts that he was looking for. "So, what happened?"

"It seems that your friend blew up the cabin and somehow managed to escape in the process."

"Jones escaped? How is that possible? Where was Hakeem when this happened?" The three men looked at each other but didn't know how to respond. "Shit, where's Hakeem now?"

Holmes shrugged. "We don't know, but we're assuming he's dead. He's been missing for quite some time, and Theo saw one of the prisoners with his set of keys. We figure that—"

"Prisoners," Greene blurted. "Are we talking plural?"

Holmes nodded. "Yeah, it seems that your other friend, Payne, unlocked the cabin door before Jones blew it up. At least that's what we've pieced together. Theo watched the escape from the house and thinks Jones made the bomb from his anklet."

All eyes turned to Webster, but it took a moment for him to notice. "What? Uh, yeah, I think he made the bomb himself."

Holmes shook his head at Webster's anxiety. "But I'm still trying to figure out why they blew up the cabin. It just doesn't make sense to me. I mean, why blow the thing up if you have a set of keys to get out quietly? Wouldn't the explosion just draw attention to your escape?"

Greene considered the question before responding. "Maybe that's what they wanted. Maybe they blew the cabin up for attention. You know, to draw us to this part of the Plantation for some reason." He paused as he fleshed out the theory in his mind. "What were the other blasts I heard?"

"Actually," Jackson answered, "you may be on to something there. Three charges were set off in the trees for just that purpose. Your friends lured thirteen of my guards to a spot in the woods, then waited for their arrival. When they finally showed up . . ." He finished his statement by running his thumb across the base of his throat in a slashing motion.

"They killed all thirteen?" Greene demanded. "How the hell did they do that?"

Webster groaned, and Jackson cleared his throat. Neither of them wanted to tell Greene about the carnage that they had witnessed. But Holmes didn't mind talking. In fact, he wanted Levon to know what kind of trouble he'd brought to the island. "It seems our escapees aren't your average, every day army grunts. These are two very talented men, special forces plus."

Greene furrowed his brow. "Special forces plus? What does that mean?"

"It means they're the best. They're capable of doing anything they want."

"Anything?" said a doubtful Greene. He'd fought Jones a few hours before, and D.J. barely put up a fight. He certainly didn't think of him as a killer. "Come on, they're just men. Two injured men. How tough can they be?"

"You don't understand. I've known about the MANIACs for a very long time. These guys ain't human. They're machines, military supermen."

"Get real," he laughed. "Don't you think you're exaggerating just a little bit?"

Holmes' face finally showed some emotion—not much, just a slight flare-up in his cheeks and eyes. "Exaggerating? You tell me. They slipped out of bondage, located Terrell's armory, stole a shitload of weapons, booby-trapped it, killed thirteen guards in the woods and two right in front of me, then mysteriously disappeared into the night. Now you tell me, Mr. Buffalo Soldier, do these guys sound normal to you?"

Greene took a deep breath. He didn't want to admit it, but from Holmes' description it did seem like Payne and Jones were pretty talented. Hell, he had underestimated them at Sam's Tattoos and they had escaped. Maybe these guys *were* something to worry about.

"So, they're still out there, huh?"

"Yeah," Holmes answered. "They're on the loose, doing god knows what."

"And what about Payne's girlfriend? Where's she? She's our insurance policy, you know."

Holmes turned towards Jackson. "Didn't you have her in your possession?"

"Yeah, but the bitch got sick before I could do her."

Greene's eyes flared with anger. The concept of rape wasn't one he was comfortable with. "Where's she now?"

"In the guest bedroom. I left her tied to the bed."

"Jesus," Greene growled. "You mean you left her in the house this entire time, and you didn't say anything. She's what they want, you dumb ass."

The thought of Ariane's escape made Greene tense with fear. She was his best chance at safety, and he knew it. As long as he had her, he had bargaining power and lots of it.

"We better retrieve the bitch before they find her. If we lose her, we're screwed."

Holmes nodded in agreement. "I'll go with you. I think we should bring the blonde out of the house as well. The less spread out we are, the better."

* * *

With a hollow reed in his mouth and a bag on his shoulder, Payne took his final breath of fresh air, then slipped into the warm water of the gulf. He wouldn't have to swim far, but the distance he'd travel would be done underwater in complete darkness, so the reed would guarantee a supply of oxygen if he needed it.

Using his hands as his only guide, Payne swam blindly through the intricate web of wooden poles that supported the Western Docks, then made his way towards the heavily-guarded boat. After circumnavigating the bow, he breathed through his reed and continued forward, hugging the underbelly of the ship as he successfully wove through a series of ropes before he emerged along the edge of the stern.

The toughest part was over. He was where he needed to be.

* * *

While peering through the scope of his semiautomatic sniper rifle, Jones swung his gun from side to side, searching for targets. He found several. It was a good thing that his weapon offered a deadly combination of precision and speed, or he wouldn't have a chance against so many men. And if he failed to complete his mission, Payne would probably die.

"Well," Jones yawned. "I guess I should get started."

The sound of the first blast pierced the night as the bullet struck the guard, exploding his skull in a mixture of blood, brain, and bone. Before the victim's partners could even react, Jones lined up his second target and repeated his deadly performance.

Another shot. Another corpse. Blood everywhere.

Shot three eliminated one more guard. Shot four did the same. Yet for some reason, the guards weren't hiding. They just stood there, scanning the trees for the source of the gunfire, hoping to see the discharge in the distant night. Jones couldn't believe his luck and their stupidity, but he was going to take advantage of both while they lasted.

"*Adios.*" Guard five, killed.

"*Sayonara.*" Guard six, dead.

If he'd had the chance, Jones would've continued shooting all night, but a few of the guards finally wised up and dashed into the woods to find him, which was his cue to leave. Before he departed, though, Jones blasted a few shots into the water—his signal for Payne to begin—then slipped deeper into the trees for safety.

He had done his part, now it was up to his partner.

*   *   *

And Payne was ready.

He'd been waiting for several seconds in the water, trying to remain completely silent near the stern, but now that he'd been signaled, he knew he could spring into action. Using a rope that hung from the deck, Payne quickly scaled the back edge of the ship. He draped his bare feet over the railing for support, then slipped his hand into his shoulder bag and grabbed his Glock. The powerful handgun, fitted with a silencer and a full clip of ammo, would allow him to kill with stealth. And that was crucial. He couldn't risk drawing attention to himself before he had a chance to leave the area.

As water dripped off his damp clothes, Payne strolled around the small boat, looking for the enemy. One stood by the instrument panel, his back facing the water. Another rested by the bow. And neither sensed the presence sneaking up behind them.

Pffft! The Glock whispered. Pffft! Pffft! Both men were dead.

The prisoners saw the guards fall, and immediately turned towards the sound of the muffled gunshot. Payne, covered in slime and water, raised his finger to his lips to silence them.

"Don't be alarmed," he whispered. "I'm one of the good guys."

Ten mouths dropped in wonderment. They couldn't believe that someone had found them.

"Are there any other guards?"

Ten people shook their heads in unison before a masculine

voice rise from the back of the crowd. "Jon? Is that you?"

The sound of Payne's name made his heart leap. Of course he realized it wasn't Ariane—the voice was too deep to be hers—but the question meant someone else knew him. But who? He frantically searched through the faces, looking for the source of the sound, but he couldn't figure it out until the man spoke again.

"Jon Payne?"

Payne nodded and moved closer to the man, desperately trying to recognize him, but his battered appearance made it difficult. Bruises covered his face and neck. Blood and dirt covered everything else. A makeshift splint was tied to his leg. "Robbie? Is that you?"

Robert Edwards, Ariane's brother-in-law, nodded his head with joy. He tried to stand up, but his ankle injury prevented it. "Oh my god, I can't believe it's you."

"Yeah, it's me," he gasped. The reunion with Edwards was so unexpected Payne didn't know what to say. "What are you doing here?"

"I was kidnapped. We were all kidnapped." Edwards clutched Payne's hand to make sure he wasn't dreaming. "And what about you? What are you doing here?"

"I heard the island served a nice buffet," he joked. It was the only way he could hold his emotions where they needed to be. "Actually, I'm searching for Ariane. Is she here?"

Edwards nodded. "Not on the boat, but somewhere on the island. I haven't seen her today, though." He took a deep breath of air. "I haven't seen Tonya, either. I hope to god she's all right. The baby, too."

Payne winced. He had no idea that Ariane's entire family was on the Plantation. What kind of bastards would drag a family, one with a pregnant woman, into this type of situation?

"Do you have any idea where they're at? Any at all?"

"I don't know. They might be in the cabins, but I don't know."

"No, they aren't. I already checked there." Payne glanced at the other nine slaves. "Does anyone know where the others are?"

All of the prisoners shook their heads.

"Damn." He had hoped that someone would be able to direct him to Ariane, but it was obvious that the two groups had been kept apart. "One last question, can you tell me how many other captives I should be looking for?"

Edwards shrugged. "Ten, maybe twelve. They rotated us around quite a bit."

"OK. I'll take it from here, but before I leave, I'd like to make a small suggestion: Why don't you guys go home? Does that sound all right to you?"

Ten sets of eyes started to get misty.

Payne continued, "Before you can, though, we need to get rid of those bombs on your legs."

"But how?" shrieked one of the women captives. "The guards said they'd explode if we tried to take them off. He said all of them would burst, one after another."

"And he was right. They would've exploded if you pried them off." Payne reached into his shoulder bag and retrieved Ndjai's keys. "That's why we'll use these instead."

The lady smiled in gratitude as he handed her the anklet key.

"Carefully remove the bombs, then place them in here when you're done."

While waiting for the bag to be filled, Payne walked over to the boat's instrument panel and was surprised to see a key in the ignition slot. He had assumed that he'd have to hotwire it. "Hey, Robbie, how are your navigational skills? Any good?"

"Not too bad. I've taken you water skiing a few times, remember?"

Payne should've remembered. He and Ariane had visited Edwards in Colorado on more than one occasion. "That's right. Good, then I'm making you the captain." He placed his arm around the injured man and helped him to the wheel. "Now, I want you to pull out of here very slowly."

"Slowly?" called out one of the kids. "Why slowly?"

Payne didn't have time to explain, but he knew he'd better do it anyway. The last thing he needed was a mutiny on the escape vessel.

"The area around the island is surrounded by fallen trees. It's a pretty thick swamp, clogged with all kinds of logs. If he goes too fast and hits one, the boat could sink." He smiled for the child's benefit. "And that would be bad."

The kid nodded his head in understanding.

Payne turned back to Edwards. "While you steer, make sure you have some people looking into the water. They can help you avoid some of the larger obstacles. Got it?"

"Sure, but what do you want me to do when I get to the open sea? Do you have backup waiting for us?"

"No, there won't be any backup. It's just me and my partner, no one else."

The looks on the prisoners' faces said it all. They couldn't believe that Payne and Jones had done so much—and risked so much—on their own.

"Once you hit the open sea, go north towards the closest set of lights. If you encounter any boats along the way, ask to use their radio. Call the Coast Guard, the police, NASA, anyone! The sooner I get some help around here the better."

Of course, while he waited for backup, there were a few things that Payne was planning to do.

And most of them would be violent.

Chapter Forty

The leaves and branches would have covered Jones completely, if not for the small gap near his eyes. It was the only spot of flesh that he risked showing, for it gave him his only view of the world. And if his mission was to be a success, Jones needed to know when someone was coming.

The shadow lurking in the distance told him that somebody was.

As he waited, Jones wrapped his fingers around the polymer handle of his gun, readying himself for action. If possible, he would eliminate the target from his current hiding place, but if necessary, Jones was prepared to do it on the move. It was the first thing he learned with the MANIACs: be ready for *anything*.

Jones continued to watch as the shade moved closer, slipping past the tall trees with a graceful stride, using the darkness of the woods to his full advantage. The lack of moonlight made things difficult, but in time Jones learned to distinguish his target from his surroundings. He wore black clothes, black leather boots, and a mask. A gun dangled from his right hand.

A grin appeared on Jones' face.

The more guards he killed, the better. It would make things easier when they rescued Ariane and the other prisoners. So far, by his count, he had been a part of twenty deaths—thirteen in the ambush, six more on the boat, at least one at the armory—and the number would continue to grow. Hell, number twenty-one was currently approaching.

Without making a sound, Jones shifted his weight slightly, sticking the barrel of his gun through his thick bed of camouflage. He would fire when he had a clean shot, and not a second before. No sense wasting a bullet on a maybe.

"Come to papa," Jones whispered. "Take another step. Come on."

His target finally came into view, no more than fifteen feet in front of him. But before Jones had a chance to squeeze the trigger, the man whistled softly—a sound that had a meaning only to D.J.

This man wasn't a guard. It was Payne.

"Jon," he called softly.

Covered in dark mud from the swamp, Payne glanced around, hunting for the source of the sound. He was supposed to rendezvous with Jones in this part of the woods, but his friend's concealment techniques were virtually impenetrable. There was no way he'd find Jones unless he accidentally stepped on him.

"Ollyollyoxenfree."

A large chunk of the forest's floor rose to the sky as Jones climbed to his knees. To Payne, it looked like an elevator rising from the Earth's core.

"You're lucky you whistled when you did," Jones admitted. "I was going to try to kill you for the second time today."

Payne shrugged. It seemed like everyone was trying to kill him. "Actually, you're the lucky one. If you'd killed me, you wouldn't have been allowed to fly home on my plane."

"Good point." Jones climbed to his feet, removing as many leaves from his person as he could. "How'd the boat mission go?"

"Just like you planned. I took out the remaining guards without any problems and got the boatload of slaves off the island."

"That's great." Jones studied Payne's face and could tell his friend wasn't happy. "What's wrong? We just saved several lives.

You should be thrilled."

"Not only did we save lives, but we knew one of the survivors."

Jones' eyes widened with surprise. "Ariane was on the boat?"

Payne shook his head. "It seems that the Posse kidnapped her entire family. Robbie was one of the captives on board."

"What?" He'd met Ariane's family on several occasions. "Was Tonya on the boat, too?"

"No, they still have her somewhere, and remember, she's pregnant." Payne paused as he thought about the situation. "That is, if all this hasn't brought on childbirth. You never know what stress can do."

Jones could tell his buddy was hurting—it was probably a future nephew or niece that he was talking about—so he tried to get Payne's mind back on the mission. "What did you find out about the others?"

"Not much, but something strange is going on. That boat was filled with families, nothing but families. Moms, dads, kids. These weren't just strangers picked at random. These were groups chosen on purpose."

"But why?"

"I don't know."

"And where were they taking them?"

"I don't know that, either."

Jones forced a chuckle. "Shit, you don't know too much, do you?"

"I guess not," Payne admitted. "But I do know this. If ten of the captives were on the verge of leaving this place, then there's a good chance that the second group will be leaving shortly. . . ."

"And if that happens, our odds of finding them goes down significantly."

"You got that right." Payne checked the ammo in his Glock and was pleased. "So tell me, Mr. Jones, you're the brilliant military strategist. What do you recommend in a situation like this?"

"That's easy. Let's go save some people."

*   *   *

Holmes and Greene were ready to enter Ariane's room when Jackson's voice appeared on Holmes' radio. They'd just left Jackson five minutes before, and he was already calling.

"What the hell do you want now?" Holmes barked.

"Well, hello to you, too," Jackson replied. "Sorry to disturb you, your highness, but we just heard some gunshots by the western dock. A bunch of them."

"Damn," Greene cursed. "They're going after the boat." In the back of his mind, he was kind of glad that he'd left his baby-sitting job when he did. He didn't want to face Payne and Jones until the odds were more in his favor. "We have to stop these guys before they ruin everything."

"How do we do that?" Holmes demanded. He had the most military experience of any Posse member, but he was clueless when it came to Payne and Jones. They were playing in a different league. "You know these guys better than I do. Do they have any flaws we can exploit?"

Without speaking, Greene pointed to the door in front of him. As far as he knew, their only weakness lay inside the room.

Holmes thought about the information for a moment, then pushed the button on his radio. "Harris, we're coming out with the two girls. In the meantime, gather up all the guards and arm them with the best weapons we have. As soon as I get outside, we're gonna storm the dock."

"You got it." Jackson's voice was a mixture of excitement and concern. "I'll see ya soon."

Greene raised his eyebrows in surprise. "Do you think an all-out attack is gonna work on these guys? Won't they see us coming?"

"Definitely, but that's exactly what I want. I'll have our guys make as much noise as possible, and I guarantee that Payne and Jones will try to slip through a crack and come to the house." Holmes pointed to the door. "If she means as much to them as you say, they're just killing time until we leave the home front open. As soon as we make a move, they'll seize the opportunity."

Greene nodded in agreement. The plan made perfect sense. "Out of curiosity, what are we gonna do with her?"

Holmes grinned sadistically. "We'll use her to set a trap of our own."

Chapter Forty-One

Just as Holmes had expected, Payne and Jones could hear the guards approaching, but it wasn't because of their military training. All it took was a good set of ears, for the African guards did everything in their power to make as much noise as possible. They'd been told to drive Payne and Jones towards the docks, where they'd eventually be trapped against the water. Sure, their technique might've worked if they were hunting a man-eater or some other type of game, but Payne and Jones were far more intelligent than a lion. Much more dangerous, too.

"Uh, oh," Jones joked. "I think somebody's coming."

Using the night as their ally, the ex-MANIACs slipped past the squadron of guards without any difficulty. They had the opportunity to kill a few men if they had wanted to, but they decided the risk wasn't worth it. They figured it was probably better if the guards continued their search in the woods while they crept unnoticed towards the main house.

No sense rattling their cage if they didn't have to.

Once the duo reached the edge of the Plantation grounds, Jones asked Payne to stop. He had something on his mind, and he needed to voice it before it was too late. "You realize, of course, that there's a good chance that this is a setup."

"Yep."

"And if Ariane's inside, she's probably surrounded by armed

guards."

"Mmmm, hmmm."

"And there's a pretty good chance that we'll get killed doing this."

Payne frowned. "You think so?"

"No, but I wanted to make sure you were listening. You tend to block me out sometimes."

"What was that?"

Jones laughed. "OK, let's do this."

The two men hustled to the nearest cabin and used it as temporary shelter. Then, by repeating the process several times, they slowly made their way up the row of cabins until they found themselves crouching near the blackened remains of D.J.'s blast site.

"Now what?" Payne asked.

From this point on, he knew their cover was limited. With the exception of a few moss-covered oak trees, there was nothing between their current position and the house.

"Front door or back?"

Jones studied the outside of the three-story plantation house and shrugged. He'd never been inside the white-pillared masterpiece and had no idea what kind of security equipment it possessed. Everything from this point forward would be blind luck.

"It's your girlfriend, you decide."

Payne didn't even bother to reply as he made his way towards the rear of the house. Jones stayed close behind, scouting for potential trouble. When they finally reached the back of the structure, they noticed something that made their choice a good one: Bennie Blount was sticking his head out of a downstairs window, trying to get their attention.

"Pssst," he called. "Over here."

The duo raised their weapons, then hustled over to Blount.

"What the hell are you doing?" Payne demanded.

"I was waiting for you. I saw your approach behind the cabins and watched as you paused by the burnt shed. That's when I realized you were coming to the house."

Payne and Jones looked at each other, puzzled. Something didn't seem right about Blount's demeanor, but they couldn't figure out what it was.

"How'd you see us from that far away?" Jones wondered. "It's pretty dark out here, and you're in the back of the house."

"Security cameras. The Plantation has them everywhere."

"Cameras?" Payne's interest was piqued. He realized that they could be helpful if he used them properly. "Where are they situated?"

"All over. I can't tell you where, though, because they're very well concealed. Shoot, I wouldn't have even known about them if I didn't break into the security office to hunt for you guys. That's when I saw all of the monitors."

Payne glanced at Jones and grimaced. Something was wrong, definitely wrong. He could sense it. He couldn't quite put his finger on it, but it was there, like a word on the tip of his tongue. Jones noticed it, too, and he showed his displeasure by frowning.

Something was up.

"Gentlemen," Blount said grinning, "is something amiss? You seem strangely distressed by our conversation. Perhaps it was something I said?"

Finally, after a few seconds, both men figured it out. Blount was no longer talking in the backwater language of a buckwheat. He was using the proper diction of a scholar instead.

"What the . . . ?" Payne couldn't believe what he was hearing. "You sneaky son of a bitch."

"Now, don't be goin' on like 'dat about my mama. She ain't no bitch, I tell's ya."

Jones' mouth fell wide open. As he stood there staring at the dreadlocked servant, he couldn't help but feel foolish. "The Academy Award for Best Actor in a criminal conspiracy goes to—"

Payne cut him off. They didn't have time for D.J.'s theatrics.

"Bennie, or whatever the hell your name is. Look me in the

eyes and tell me which side of this war you're on." Payne raised his gun and put it under Blount's chin. "I ain't shittin' you, man. Tell me right now or you'll die like the rest of the Posse."

Jones laughed to himself. "You best tell him, Master Bennie. He ain't bluffin' none."

Blount responded in perfect English. "I'm with you guys, I swear. I'm not a part of the Posse, never have been. I've just been biding time and gathering information. I swear to god."

"Information for what?" Payne demanded, pressing the gun deeper into Blount's throat.

"Tell's him, Bennie. Master Payne gots himself a nasty temper and an itchy trigga finga. And that ain't no good combination."

Blount shuddered as Jones' words sank in. "I've been gathering information for the authorities. I'm trying to get this place shut down, I swear, but I can't do it in both continents without the documentation to back it up. No one will listen to me until then."

"What do you mean by both continents?"

"The Plantation isn't just a torture site. It's a lot more complicated than that." Blount tried to swallow, but the gun pressed against his throat made it difficult. "This is business, big business. The Posse has ties all over the world, and if I want to shut everything down, I have to learn the names of the other people. That's the only way to do it properly. Get everybody at once."

Payne looked into Blount's eyes, and Bennie appeared to be sincere. But in this case, *appeared* was the operative word. For the longest time, Blount appeared to be an uneducated country boy, and Payne had trusted him. Now Blount appeared to be telling the truth a second time, and he was asking Payne to believe in him again. But how could he? Blount was such an incredible actor that there was no way Payne could separate his web of bullshit from reality.

"I'm still not sold. You're going to have to tell me something to convince me."

"Like what? I'll tell you anything, just don't kill me."

Jones stepped forward. "What kind of business is the Posse in?"

"You guys should know. You're holding some of their products in your hands."

"Guns?" Payne remarked. "But that doesn't make sense. Why bring all of these innocent people to this island if you're going to smuggle guns? There has to be more than that."

"There is," he grunted. "But you're going to like that even less."

Payne's eyes flared with anger. He was tired of being jerked around. "Why's that, Bennie? Why am I not going to like it?"

"Because you're white."

"OK, you racist bastard, what does that have to do with anything?"

"Hey, I'm not racist, but the Posse is."

"No shit. I kind of figured that out myself. You're going to have to do much better than that, Bennie. What does racism have to do with the Posse's business? Racism can't be sold, you know."

Blount stared Payne directly in the eyes. He wanted to make sure that Payne recognized the truth of his words. "That's true, but slaves *can* be sold. White slaves."

The concept made Payne quiver. If Blount was telling the truth, it meant that these people weren't just being tortured. They were being broken—housebroken—for their new master.

"And how do you know this?"

"I just know. I've been walking around this place for several weeks, and I've been able to overhear stuff. Everybody treated me like an idiot so they tried to talk over me. Nobody knew that I could put all of the pieces of the puzzle together. But I could. I've just been waiting for the right moment." Blount took a breath. "And that moment is finally here."

"Why's that?" Jones wondered.

"Because of you two, of course. You've killed most of the guards, you have the masters running for their lives, and as far as I can tell, you got rid of the cargo ship. This is the time to finish them off. We can end the Posse right here, right now."

"And why should we trust you?" Payne demanded. "You already dicked us once."

"But I couldn't help that. I couldn't risk blowing my cover to help you out. I couldn't. I tried to make it up to you, though. You know that. If it wasn't for me, you would've died in the Box."

Payne shook his head. "You're going to have to do better, Buckwheat. I wouldn't have been in that damn box if it wasn't for you."

"I know you don't trust me, Jon, but without my help, you won't be able to save your girlfriend. I can help you find her, and you know it. But we can't wait much longer."

The comment staggered Payne. With all of the fighting and arguing that was going on, Payne had forgotten about the one thing that mattered most: Ariane.

"How can you help?"

"I know the island much better than you. I can be your guide and an extra gun. And whether you know it or not, Ariane means an awful lot to me, too."

Payne pressed the gun even harder into Bennie's neck. He interpreted Blount's comment as some kind of sexual insult.

"Why is that, you little shit? And trust me, if your answer isn't a good one, I'll splatter your dreadlocks all over the wall." Payne took a deep breath to control his fury, but it didn't work. He was still fuming. "Why is Ariane important to you?"

"Why?" Blount stuttered. "Because she's my cousin."

Chapter Forty-Two

Ariane could hear heavy footsteps in the hall but had no idea who was there until the door burst open. Two large figures quickly entered the room.

"Well, well, well," Greene laughed. "If it isn't the troublemaker's bitch?"

Holmes followed him into the room, grinning. "All tied up and lookin' good. You know, if we had a little more time, I might be tempted to get a slice of her pie."

Greene shook his head. "Alas, we don't. And all because of Payne."

The sound of his name made her heart beat faster. Oh my god, she thought to herself. Was he actually on the Plantation? "Is Jon here?" she tried to ask, but because of the damage to her jaw, the query came out severely mumbled.

"Wow, I think she's trying to talk." Holmes moved closer and stared at her mouth. Dried vomit covered her lips and cheeks. "On second thought, I don't know if I want a crack at her. The bitch is covered in puke. Hell, she looks like some sorority chicks I used to know."

"Tease her later," Greene suggested. "We gotta move before the two soldier boys find us."

Two soldier boys? The sound was music to her ears. That meant D.J. was probably with Jon. Of course, that only made sense. They did everything together, especially when it came to the military. But how in the world did they find her so quickly? she wondered. Were they brought to the island the same time as her, or did they find her on their own?

"OK," Holmes said, "I'm going to untie you now, but I expect you to be on your best behavior while I do. Understand?"

Ariane nodded, even though it hurt her jaw to do so.

Holmes reached for the knot near her left wrist, but before he got ahold of it, a frantic voice came out of his radio. "Jesus! Is that Jackson again? What does he want now?"

"Don't worry about it," Greene muttered. "You take care of the girl. I'll take care of Harris." Greene pushed the reply button on his own radio. "Harris? Is that you?"

"Levon," Jackson answered. "Unless you guys are keeping something from me, we've got a major problem here."

Greene glanced at Holmes and frowned. "We're not keeping anything from you. What's going on?"

"I went down to the docks to check on the boat and . . . it's gone."

"What are you talking about?" Greene roared.

"All the guards are dead, and the boat is gone."

"You've got to be kidding me."

"No, I'm not kidding you. This isn't something I'd joke about."

"What about the slaves?" Greene demanded. "Where are the slaves?"

"They're gone, too. I don't know how, but the boat is gone."

"Fuck!" Greene shouted. "I don't believe this."

Ariane watched Greene carefully, waiting to see what he was going to do next. For one reason or another, she sensed that he might take his anger out on her, but thankfully that never came to pass.

"What should we do?"

Holmes shrugged as he unfastened Ariane's rope. "Your call."

Greene gave things another minute of thought before answering. "Just wait for us at the docks. We'll be there shortly. And try to find Theo if you can. I think it would be best if we all stuck together."

"Sounds good," Jackson replied. "And make it quick. I'm kind of in the open down here."

Greene closed his eyes as he turned off his radio. "I can't believe this shit. How can two guys cause this many problems?"

Holmes grinned at the comment. "You'd be surprised what two men can accomplish if they put their minds to it. . . . Like us, for instance."

"What are you getting at?"

"I realize you've known Harris and Theo forever, but under the circumstances, we need someone to take the blame for all of this, and I figure if the feds get a couple of suspects in custody, they won't be as likely to hunt for anyone else. At least not immediately."

Greene's interest was piqued. "So what are you proposing?"

"How much would it bother you if we left them behind? Hmm? Why don't we get off this island while we still have a chance?"

"Interesting," Greene mumbled. But after giving it some thought, he detected a flaw in the plan. "But we can't leave them here."

Holmes' eyes flared with anger. "Why not? I'm giving you an opportunity to flee, and you're not willing to seize it because of them. They'd leave your ass behind in a minute."

"Wait a second!" he yelled back. "I don't mind leaving them, but we can't. They'll name us, say we were the force behind everything, and preach their innocence. I guarantee they'll frame their stories to suit their needs, and they'll come out of things sitting pretty. Hell, they might even be given immunity to testify against us."

Holmes grimaced at the thought. "Damn, you're right. So what do you recommend?"

Greene smiled at Ariane, then glanced at his new partner. "We should leave the island ASAP. But before we do, we need to silence Theo and Harris—permanently."

* * *

Blount's comment was absurd, completely asinine. Perhaps, the most outrageous, preposterous, nonsensical thing that Payne had ever heard. But that's why he was tempted to believe it. It wasn't the type of thing that someone would make up to save his own ass.

"OK, Bennie, my interest is aroused. But I promise you, if I smell bullshit at any point of your explanation, Boom! Understand?"

Blount nodded. "As you know, I'm not a dumb hick, but I *am* a local. My family's lived in these parts for generations. In fact, when this place was owned and operated by the Delacroix family, my ancestors worked the land."

"As slaves?"

"Yes, sir, as slaves. It's the only work black folk could get around these parts back then. You know, working on the farms, doing manual labor . . ." Payne signaled for him to continue. "For the past few years I've been working on my Master's degree at LSU and recently started work on my thesis. I planned to show the effect that the abolition of slavery had on black families using my family tree as an example. I hoped to prove that . . . well, I guess you don't need to know all of the specifics."

Payne shook his head.

"A few months ago, I came to this island to look around. This place had been abandoned for the longest time, and I thought a few photos of the plantation would look good in my project."

"So, what happened?"

"I bumped into a team of black men doing all kinds of work: painting the house, mowing the grass, digging in the fields. I assumed that someone had bought the estate and was going to move in. So I went up to one of the brothers to ask him a few questions about the new owner, and I discovered that he couldn't speak any English. Actually, none of them could. These guys were right off the boat from Africa."

Jones joined in. "Everyone?"

Blount nodded. "I didn't want to get anybody into trouble, including myself, so I left quickly. It's a good thing, too, because if one of the owners had seen me, I would've never been allowed to come back later."

"Why'd you want to come back?"

"Curiosity, I guess. I wanted to see what they were going to do to the place. Of course, I also thought it could help my research. You see, during my studies, I came across a very old family journal from the 1860s. It was like finding a gold mine. It gave me a first-hand account of slave life on this plantation from a distant relative. Simply fascinating stuff."

"I'm sure," Payne said, "but I'm beginning to get a little impatient here. My hand's starting to fall asleep, and if that happens, my trigger finger might accidentally twitch." Payne playfully twitched. "Oooh! And if that happens, things might get messy."

"You want me to get to Ariane, don't you?"

"Is it that obvious?"

Blount nodded. "During the course of the journal, my distant grandmother admits to having an affair with Mr. Delacroix, her master. She said she did it for special treatment, but eventually, it turned into more than that. She fell in love with Delacroix and allowed him to impregnate her on several occasions. Shortly after that, the Civil War ended and the journal entries stopped."

"That's it?" Payne demanded. "What does any of that have to do with Ariane?"

"At the time, I didn't know, but I was bound and determined to talk with someone from the Delacroix family so I could get a look at their family tree. I figured if I was a direct descendant of

Mr. Delacroix, then I would technically be related to all of his white offspring."

Payne was beginning to see where this was going, and his eyes slowly filled with acceptance. He knew that Blount was telling the truth and couldn't wait to see how Ariane fit in.

"I went to the local courthouse and tried to find his relatives, but every path I found ended in a death. I swear, the Delacroix family must've been cursed or something because everyone in that family died so young. Anyways, I decided to come back here to look around again. I hoped maybe the new owners had bought the property from a distant relative of mine, and they'd be willing to give me my relative's address."

"Makes sense," Payne added.

"But when I came back, I got the shock of my life. The old plantation was back in business. Not just as a farm, but as an *actual* plantation. Crops in the ground and slaves in the field, but this time, unlike the 1800s, the slaves were white."

"What'd you do?" Jones wondered. He was supposed to be watching for guards, but he found himself wrapped up in Blount's historical tale.

"I tried to leave. I wanted to tell somebody what I saw, but before I could get my small boat out of the swamps, I was stopped by a big man named Octavian Holmes. He blocked my passage and demanded information from me at gunpoint. Obviously, I didn't want to tell him the truth. If he knew that I'd been digging around, he would've killed me. So I decided to play dumb. At that moment, I became a buckwheat by the name of Bennie Blount."

Payne smiled. "So that isn't your real name?"

"Not really. My real name is William Benjamin Blount, but I thought William sounded too formal for a buckwheat. That's why I chose to go with Bennie. I thought it sounded, you know, simple."

"Speaking of simple, I've got a simple fact for you. You're taking too damn long to tell this story." Jones turned towards

Payne. "Come on, Jon. We have to get going."

"One more minute," he replied, calmly. "Go on, Bennie, finish."

"I convinced Master Holmes that I could be useful around here. I could cook, clean, and show him around the local swamps. One thing led to another, and he decided to hire me. I figured it was perfect. I could make a little money, and at the same time, I could get to the bottom of things."

"Speaking of the bottom of things," Jones groaned.

"OK," Blount muttered. "I'll get to it, I promise. Up until recently, the Posse was bringing random groups of people onto the island, mostly street people. They'd beat them, train them, then ship them overseas for big money. It's been a very lucrative business. But all of that changed with this last group of slaves. The people that were selected were no longer random. These people were brought here for a reason. They were brought here for revenge."

"What kind of revenge?"

"Revenge for the black race. One of the men on the island, Theo Webster, did some genealogical research, and it was a lot more in-depth than mine. He traced the roots of the Plantation's four founders and tried to determine their family origins. Three of the men came from slave backgrounds, but Levon didn't. His family came to America after slavery had been abolished. Anyways, Webster determined the name of the slave owner that had owned the ancestors of the other three men. Then, tracing their family trees to the present day, he located the modern-day relatives of those slave owners."

"And the people that were kidnapped were the relatives?"

Blount nodded. "Ariane and her sister happened to be a distant relative of Mr. Delacroix, my great-great-great-great-grandfather. That's why they were brought here, and that's why I'm related. I realize it doesn't exactly make her my first cousin, but she is my relative. I swear. I even have the data to back it up."

Payne shook his head. "Don't worry about it. I actually believe you."

"Great," muttered a relieved Jones. "Now that this Ebony and Ivory reunion is over, do you mind if we get our asses out of here? We've got some people to save and not much time to do it."

Payne lowered his gun from Blount's chin. He was finally convinced that Bennie was on his side. "Mr. Blount, would you please show us the way inside the house?"

Bennie grinned. It was the first time in his life that a white man had ever called him Mister.

Chapter Forty-Three

When the truck arrived at the docks, Harris Jackson was finally able to breathe a sigh of relief. Even though he knew he wouldn't be safe until the MANIACs were caught, he felt a lot better with Holmes and Greene by his side.

"Hey, Harris," Holmes called, "where's Theo? I thought he was supposed to meet us here."

"He'll be here any minute. He said he had to go to the house for something."

Holmes nodded as he searched the dock for a trace of the missing boat. There were no clues except for a number of dead guards that littered the ground.

"These guys are good," he admitted. "Real good."

"So what are we gonna do?" Jackson wondered. "The boat's gone, half the slaves have escaped, and Payne and Jones are still running around killing our men. Is there any way we can salvage this?"

Greene gave Holmes a quick smile before speaking. "Sure, we can. Remember, that's the reason we wore our masks at all times. None of the slaves can identify our faces. Once we leave this place, we're home free."

A flash of panic crossed Jackson's mind. He'd revealed his face to Ariane, right before he was about to molest her.

"What's wrong, Harris?" Holmes noticed the tension in Jackson's eyes. "You look upset."

"Oh, ah, nothing. It's just that I took my mask off in the bedroom, and one of the whores saw me."

"You idiot," Greene laughed. It was just like Jackson to do something stupid around one of his young females. "Thinking with your wrong head again, huh?"

Annoyed, Jackson took a step towards Greene. Even though Levon outweighed him by sixty pounds, he wasn't about to back down. He had to stand his ground, or Greene would tease him forever. "What's your problem, man? Why do you have to ride me so damn hard?"

"Because I feel like it," he chuckled.

"And why's that? What's your problem with me? Huh?"

Greene smiled, reveling in the thought of a confrontation. "Here's my problem, bitch. I'm fed up with all your perverted games, your groping and raping. That shit is wrong, and it's gotta stop."

"Oh yeah? And who's gonna stop me?"

"Who's gonna stop you?" Greene glanced at Holmes and smirked. They had discussed this moment back at the house, and Greene had volunteered for the duty. "Me, my Glock, and I."

The thunderous blast echoed off the water and the surrounding trees as the bullet struck Jackson in his right eye and plowed through his brain with the finesse of a bulldozer. Then, as if in slow motion, his body slumped to the edge of the dock and hung there for just a second before it tumbled into the water with the splash of a belly-smacker.

"Nice shot," Holmes remarked. His nonchalant tone suggested that Greene had just made a free throw in a game of H.O.R.S.E. "Try to keep your elbow in more. It'll improve your accuracy."

"Thanks. I'll remember that the next time I kill one of my friends."

Holmes glanced at his watch and realized time was running short. “That might be sooner than you think. We have to take care of Webster before we leave. Why don’t you give him a call and see what’s keeping him?”

Greene nodded, the adrenaline from Jackson’s murder still surging through him. The experience was so intense it practically made him giddy. “Breaker, breaker, one nine. Theo, do you read me?”

There was a slight delay before Webster answered. “I’m here, Levon.”

“Where’s here? We’ve been waiting for you at the docks for several minutes.”

Another pause. “I’m up at the house. I figured we’d have to get out of here soon, so I wanted to pack a few things up before we left. Sorry.”

“Hey, no problem.” This would work out well for Holmes and Greene. They needed to stop by the house before they left the island anyway. “I’ll tell ya what, why don’t we swing by the mansion and help you out with your things?”

Relief filled Webster’s voice. “That would be great. I wasn’t looking forward to going down to the docks by myself. I’m not very good with guns, you know.”

A grin returned to Greene’s face. “Don’t worry, Theo. I am.”

* * *

Payne patted Webster on his balding head, then took the radio from his hands. “You did great, Theo. You sounded very natural.” But Webster refused to say a word. Instead, he slumped in his chair and pouted about getting caught.

“What now?” Jones asked as he chewed on his first food in a long time. “We got them coming here, but what are we going to do with ’em when they arrive?”

Payne flicked Webster on his very large ear. “I say we make a trade. I’ll gladly give up Dumbo here if they give us Ariane. As far as I'm concerned, anything we get after that will be icing."

Jones swallowed a mouthful of apple and decided it was the best goddamned piece of fruit he had ever tasted. "Speaking of icing," he said as he searched the pantry for anything that resembled cake, but a box of Twinkies was the only thing he could find. "Once we get Ariane to safety, will we have any time to hunt down Levon?"

"I don't care what we do as long as you understand that she's the number one priority. After that, I'll back you on anything that your heart desires."

"Cool," he mumbled as he stuffed an entire Twinkie into his mouth.

While Jones chewed the yellow cake, Blount entered the kitchen from the security office and spoke. "They'll be here any second. I just saw them pull their truck onto the road from the docks."

Webster stared at Blount in disbelief. It was the first time he'd heard Bennie speak English.

"What kind of truck?" Payne wondered.

"Flatbed. Both guys are in the front, but it appears they have some hostages in the back."

Payne prayed one of them was Ariane. "Were they guys or girls?"

Blount shrugged. "Kind of looked like females, but I don't know."

Jones continued eating Twinkies as he ran several different scenarios through his mind. Finally, he came across one that he liked. "OK, fellas, this is how we're going to play it. Instead of picking these guys off from a distance—which I could do with my eyes closed—I think it'd be best if we dealt with them up close and personal."

"Why's that?" Payne demanded.

"First of all, if I kill these guys long-range, there's no one to stop their speeding truck. I mean, the last thing we want is for Ariane to smash into a tree with a bomb strapped to her leg."

"Good point."

"Secondly, I get the feeling Holmes is running things, and if that's the case, it'd be foolish to kill him without interrogating him. Heck, there's no telling where the slaves are, and if we shoot him right away, there's a chance we won't be able to find them for a very long time."

Payne groaned at the possibilities. "Isn't a face-to-face confrontation kind of risky?"

"Definitely. And if you'd prefer, I'm still willing to pick these guys off with a scope. Of course, keep this in mind: Ariane *might* be one of those hidden slaves."

* * *

The truck pulled across the grass of the main yard and drove straight to the house. Once they stopped, Holmes honked the horn, hoping Webster would come to the front door. It worked. He immediately swung the door open, sticking his head out of the narrow crack.

"Can you guys come inside and give me a hand? I'm not strong enough to carry all this stuff."

Greene looked at Holmes and frowned. He didn't have a clean shot from his current position, and by the time he raised his weapon, Webster would be able to duck inside the house.

"Before we do," Greene countered, "we want you to give us a hand with something."

"Really? What do you need?"

Greene glanced at Holmes and shrugged. He hadn't thought that far ahead.

Holmes quickly jumped to his rescue with the first thing that popped into his mind. "The guards have Payne and Jones cornered by the swamp, and we want you to help us flush 'em out. You're the smartest guy here, so we figured you could come up with something that might work."

A grimace filled Webster's face. He didn't know what to make of Holmes' comment, but he realized something strange was going on. "Guys, I'd hate to waste my time for nothing. Are you sure that you have them cornered?"

"Oh, yeah," Greene claimed. "We got 'em trapped all right. I made the I.D. myself. We just need some help flushing 'em out."

Payne sensed Webster's desire to make a break for the truck so he tightened his grip on him before he could move.

"Don't even think about it," he whispered. "Tell them you can't leave until they come inside and give you a hand. Insist if you have to."

Webster quickly obeyed. "Guys, I can't help you right now. I've got other things to worry about *inside*." He tilted his head towards the door, hoping to signal Holmes and Greene, but they didn't understand what he was pointing to. "I think it would be best if you gave me a hand."

Greene growled softly as he watched Webster twitch his head. He couldn't believe how swiftly he was becoming unglued. "I don't know what your deal is, Theo, but we need you in the truck right now. Time is running out, so let's go."

"Come on," Holmes shouted. "We need your help immediately."

Webster tried to move towards the truck, but he wasn't strong enough to tear away from Payne. In fact, the only thing that he managed to do was piss him off.

"Don't do that again," he warned, "and I'll blow your fucking head off."

"Come on," Holmes repeated. "Let's go. Now."

"I can't come," Webster assured him. "I'd like to, but I can't. I really can't."

Greene had heard enough. The cops were probably on their way, and he realized the only thing that stood between him and freedom was a 150-pound computer geek. Angrily, Greene threw his door open and climbed out. "I'm sick of this, Theo. Come out here now before you really piss me off."

He accented his statement with a slam of the truck door.

And that was the sign that Jones and Blount had been waiting for. They quietly opened their windows on the second floor of the plantation house and thrust their weapons outside. Once they had settled into comfortable positions, they aimed their guns at their targets. Jones focused on Greene. Blount pointed at Holmes, who remained inside the truck.

After counting to five, Payne threw the front door open while using Webster as a shield. "Show me your hands," Payne shouted. "Show me your fucking hands."

Greene stopped dead in his tracks and slowly raised his two closed fists into the air.

"Surprised to see us?" Jones teased from above. "You must be since we're currently trapped down by the swamps. That's why you're turning white, isn't it?"

"Something like that."

"Don't turn too white," Payne muttered, "or someone around here might make you a slave."

Greene tried to take a breath, but his chest was too tight to inhale. "What do you guys want?"

"Revenge!" Jones laughed. "A shitload of revenge!"

Payne wrapped his arm around Webster's neck and pulled him closer. "And you know what I want. I want Ariane."

"Then this is your lucky day, Jon. She's in the back of our truck with another girl. If you want, you can come over and see for yourself."

Payne shook his head. "No thanks. I kind of like where I'm standing. But my partner can take a look. Hey, D.J.?"

"Yeah, chief."

"Can you see into the back of the truck?"

"Sure can. Looks like a couple of chicks to me. Not sure who they are, though. They're tied up, and their heads are covered."

Payne grimaced. "Do they look alive?"

"They sure do. I see lots of squirmin'."

Payne returned his attention to Greene. "So, what's next?"

"Well, you're obviously in control of things. You've got a gun pointed at my heart, and your arm around my best friend's neck. So you tell me: How do you want to resolve this?"

"I say we shoot him," Jones suggested. "Then we just take the girls."

Greene chuckled. "Oh, you could do that, but if you shoot me, Octavian is gonna speed off before you have a chance to grab 'em."

"No, he won't," Jones retorted. "Before he moves ten feet, Bennie will pump him like a gay porn star."

Greene quickly looked at the other end of the house and spotted Blount, who had an unobstructed view of the truck. "That's a pretty colorful image, especially from a soldier like yourself."

"Thanks. I learned it from your dad."

Greene smiled, trying to remain as calm as possible. He had played football in front of millions of fans on TV, so he was used to keeping his nerves during times of pressure. "Hey Octavian, do you have a clear shot at Ariane?"

Holmes thrust his muscular arm out the back of the cab and pointed his gun at the tied-up hostages. "Yeah. There ain't much that can stop a bullet from three feet away."

"That's true," remarked Payne. "But the same can be said about my distance. And I promise you this: I won't miss."

"And I believe you. But you know what, Jon? I've got a strange feeling that you're not going to shoot me. You know why? 'Cause if you do, a lot of people are gonna die."

"Really. And how do you expect to pull that off?"

"Oh, it's not what I'm gonna *pull.* It's what I'm gonna *push.*"

Greene slowly lowered his left hand and revealed the tiny detonator that he'd been concealing in his massive palm. "One touch of this button, and every anklet on this island goes boom!"

He accented his statement by making the sound of a large explosion, then followed it with a defiant smile. "So, let me ask you again, How do you want to resolve this?"

Payne remained stoic, showing Greene the ultimate poker face. He didn't laugh, grin, or frown. Nothing was going to crack his concentration, not even the threat of a blast. "It's simple as far as I'm concerned. I get my girl, and you get your bitch." He tightened his grasp on Webster's neck. "Simple swap."

"I don't know. What's to prevent you from shooting us the minute you get Ariane?"

"Nothing," Payne admitted. "But what's preventing you from doing the same? And remember, Levon, you're the one with the history of reneging."

"That's right," Jones cracked. "You're a re-*nigger.*"

Greene allowed his eyes to float upwards. He saw nothing but the barrel of Jones' gun. "You know if you weren't black, I'd kick your ass for that comment."

"Yeah, but you'd put me in handcuffs before you even tried."

Greene lowered his gaze back to Payne and smiled. "So, you want to make a trade, huh? Tell me how to do it." He bent into a pronounced bow. "And I shall oblige."

"First of all, I need to make sure that's Ariane."

Greene clicked his tongue a few times in thought. "That's gonna be kind of tough. She's currently gagged, and I'm not about to let you get near her."

"Not a problem, Levon. Just let me see her face. If it's her, we can continue, but if it isn't, I'm gonna let D.J. show you his Lee Harvey Oswald impersonation."

"Don't worry," he assured him. "You can trust me on this one. I'll remove her hood, and you'll see that it's her. OK? Just don't shoot me."

As Greene strolled towards the rear of the truck, he studied the upstairs window out of the corner of his eye. He hoped that Jones would relax for just a moment, giving him enough time to make his move, but D.J. was too good of a soldier to slip up. The barrel of his gun followed Greene wherever he went.

"That's far enough," Jones ordered. He was afraid that

Greene would sneak to the far side of the truck, and if he did, he would no longer have a shot at him. "Climb into the bed from the back bumper. And if you flinch, you die."

"Bennie," Payne called. "How's your shot at the driver?"

"Clear. I can take him at any moment."

"Stay on him, Bennie. Never let him leave your sight."

Greene stepped onto the back bumper as directed, then pulled himself up with a quick tug of his arm. After stepping over the hatch, he moved slowly towards Ariane, keeping his eyes on Jones while looking for a chance to get free.

"D.J.," Payne shouted, "you still got him?"

"No problem. In fact, I'm tempted to take him now just for the hell of it."

Despite the boast, Payne felt uneasy about the situation. There was something about the cocky look in Greene's eyes that made him nervous. Payne wasn't sure what was going on, but his gut told him that something bad was about to happen. As a precaution, he moved forward, keeping the hostage directly between himself and Greene.

"Do this nice and slow," Payne ordered. "No mistakes." Greene nodded as he pulled Ariane into a sitting position. Next, he placed his hand on the cloth that covered her face while crouching down behind her.

"D.J.?" Payne screamed.

"Don't worry, Jon. On your command, I can put a hole in his brain—if he has one."

Payne felt temporarily better, but his anxiety returned when Greene started working on the rope around her throat. "Careful."

"You gotta chill," he growled. "If I hurt her, I know you'll hurt Theo. And trust me, I don't want you to do that. You know why? Because I want to do it myself."

While using Ariane as armor, Greene pulled a gun from the back of his belt and fired two shots towards Payne. As he did, Holmes punched the gas pedal hard, which sent Ariane and

Greene tumbling backwards in a web of body parts, an act that kept Jones from shooting. Sure, he could've fired, but the risk of hitting Ariane—and the possibility of Levon pushing the detonator—was simply too high for his taste. Instead, he figured he'd rely on his backup.

"Bennie," he screamed. "Get the driver."

But Blount was too late to react. He fired a number of shots at the front windshield, yet the only thing that hit Holmes were shards of broken glass.

Jones cursed as the truck continued forward and did his best to stop it by shooting out the back right wheel, but the angle of the flatbed protected the exposed tire like an iron shield. Next, he shifted his aim to the rear window, hoping to nail the driver in the back of the head, but Holmes anticipated the move and made a sudden turn toward the side of the house.

"Son of a bitch!" Jones yelled. He couldn't believe that so many unexpected things had happened in such a short amount of time. Greene's hidden gun, his lack of compassion for Webster, the detonator, and Ariane's interference. "This can't be happening."

Jones immediately abandoned his position and ran towards the front steps where he came across Blount in the hallway. The two of them sprinted down the stairs together, hoping to run outside and hit the truck with some kind of long-distance shot, but when they burst out the front door, they noticed something that suddenly changed their priorities.

Two bodies were sprawled on the columned porch.

One was Webster; the other was Payne.

Both were covered in blood, and neither was moving.

Chapter Forty-Four

While Blount searched for a first-aid kit, Jones rushed to Payne's side, then probed his unconscious friend for wounds. Unfortunately, Payne's black clothes made locating his injuries quite difficult.

"Bennie, get out here! I need your help!"

Blount returned a moment later, medical supplies in hand.

"Help me get his shirt off. I don't know where he was hit."

Expecting the worst, the two men carefully cut off the bloodied garment, exposing Payne's chiseled but scarred torso. Thankfully, his chest and stomach were free of new wounds.

"The blood must've been Webster's," said a relieved Blount.

"Not all of it." Jones pointed to a gaping hole in Payne's arm. One of Greene's bullets had torn through Webster's body and imbedded itself in Payne's left biceps. "It's not life threatening, but I have to patch him up before he bleeds too much."

"What do you need me to do? Get you some towels? Boil some water?"

Jones frowned. "He's not having a baby. He's been shot."

His face flushed with embarrassment. "Does that mean I can't do anything?"

He pondered the question for a moment. "Actually, you can. The second Jon's up he'll want to find Ariane. Do you think you can find us some transportation?"

Blount nodded. "Consider it done."

While waiting for Blount's return, Jones tried to focus his concentration on Payne. Under these conditions, there wasn't much he could do other than sterilize the wound and wrap it, but he realized that might be enough to save Payne's life. Right now the two biggest concerns were blood loss and infection, but if he did a good job of applying a field dressing, he knew he'd be able to prevent either from happening.

As Jones searched for the proper supplies, Payne opened his eyes. Still groggy, he blinked a few times, absorbing his surroundings.

"Excuse me, Miss Nightingale? I think you need to re-apply your makeup."

A slight smile crossed Jones' lips. He didn't care what Payne said as long as he was able to talk. "How are you feeling, buddy?"

"Not great." He blinked a few more times, trying to remember everything that had occurred. "I think my arm hurts."

"Well, that might have something to do with the bullet that's in it." Jones knelt beside him, trying to comfort him in any way possible. "And when you fell, I think you hit your head on the steps. That's why you blacked out."

Payne winced as he touched the back of his head with his right hand. He felt a large lump slowly emerging from his scalp. "Where's Ariane?"

Jones frowned. He didn't want to upset his friend before his wound had been treated, but he wasn't willing to lie. "To be honest, Jon, I don't know. They all got away."

"What?" He immediately tried to sit up, but Jones restrained him. "How did that happen? I thought you had a shot at Levon."

"I did, but Ariane blocked it. When the truck started to move, she tumbled on top of him. I couldn't risk pulling the trigger."

"What about the driver? Did he get hit?"

"Bennie hit the front windshield more than once, but Holmes kept driving." He paused for a moment as he considered the events of a few minutes before. "I don't know if he hit him or not."

Payne took a deep breath, trying to calm his rage. He wasn't mad at Jones or Blount—they'd done their best considering the circumstances—but he was upset at the unfortunate turn of events. Ariane was within his reach, something that he'd hoped and prayed for since her disappearance, but he blew his chance to retrieve her.

"We have to catch them before they leave the island. If they get away, there's no telling where they'll go."

Jones could see the desperation etched on Payne's face. It showed in the color of his cheeks and the glare in his eyes. But that wasn't all that he noticed. He could also see his pain. There was something about the tightness of his jaw and the grimace on his lips that revealed Payne's physical agony.

"Let's take care of you first. Then we'll worry about them."

"D.J., I'm fine." He tried to sit up a second time, but Jones pushed him down again.

"Jon, we can't chase them until we get a vehicle, and Bennie's getting us one right now. So just calm down and let me patch you up while we wait for our limo to arrive."

Jones cleaned and wrapped the wound in less than five minutes. Then, as he put the last layer of elastic tape around the sterile gauze, he heard the rumble of an approaching motor. He gazed across the field, trying to identify the motorist, but was unable to.

"We better take cover."

Both men climbed to their feet, Payne still groggy from his injury, and waited in the nearby bushes until they spotted Blount. They realized it was him when they saw his dreadlocks flapping in the breeze of his ATV. As he pulled up to the front door, Payne and Jones reemerged on the porch.

"Jon! You're OK!"

"Yeah, I'm all right." He glanced at the yellow and white Yamaha Blaster and realized it was too small for three people.

"Is this all you could find?"

"Actually there are two more where I found this, but I couldn't drive 'em all. If one of you comes with me, we can figure out a way to bring 'em both back."

Jones looked at Payne. "Let me go. You should rest up for another minute."

"No arguments from me."

As Blount and Jones sped away, Payne scanned the immediate area, making sure that no one was watching from the trees. When he was confident that he was alone, he walked towards Webster. In the aftermath of the shooting, he never thought to ask about his condition—he just kind of assumed that he was dead—but one quick glance proved that he wasn't. Blood pulsated from the wounds in his upper torso and that meant his heart was still beating.

Surprised, Payne crouched next to him and examined his injuries, but they were way too severe to be fixed with a Band-Aid. There was nothing that Payne could do except offer him comfort—something he was reluctant to do considering his role in Ariane's abduction.

"Theo," he said in a soothing voice. "Can you hear me?"

Unexpectedly, Webster opened his eyes.

"Hey," Payne whispered, "how are you feeling?"

"P . . . p . . . p." Webster was trying to say something, but his lack of strength made it difficult to pronounce the words. "Come here."

But before he did, he checked Webster for weapons—the last thing he needed was a knife in his gut. When he was confident that Webster was unarmed, he moved closer. "I'm here, Theo."

"Paw . . . paw," he stuttered. "Paw . . ."

He looked into Webster's eyes. They were glassy and starting to droop. Payne knew he didn't have much time left. "Theo, you have to repeat that. I can't understand you."

"Paw . . . paw . . . it," he managed to mutter. "Paw . . . it."

"*Paw it*? What does that mean? Theo? What's *paw it*?"
But this time there was no reply.
The bastard died before he could finish his message.

* * *

On the eastern side of the island, far from the plantation house and the Western Docks, sat a small inlet, filled with warm water from the nearby Gulf. At first glance, it seemed like an impassable marsh. Bald cypress trees clogged the waterway in sporadic groves. Jagged stumps and fallen timber, remnants of recent hurricanes, rose from the water like icebergs, waiting to shred any boat that dared to travel by. But in reality, it wasn't impassable. It was actually a path to freedom.

"Where the hell are we going?" Greene screamed from the back of the truck. "There's nothing back here but swampland."

Holmes answered cryptically. "It seems that way, doesn't it?"

"Yeah, so what's the deal?"

"Don't worry. Everything will become apparent in a few minutes."

Greene didn't like the sound of that, but he realized he didn't have much of a choice. Holmes was currently in control of the situation, and he was just along for the ride. "Fine, but keep something in mind. I am armed."

"I know that, Levon. And so do Theo and Harris."

Greene grinned as he thought about his two fallen friends, but that smile turned to a grimace when he felt the truck slowing to a halt. "Why are we stopping?"

"I want to show you something," he said through the back window. "But before I do, I think you and I need to reach some kind of an understanding."

Greene instinctively raised his gun. "The ball's in your court, huckleberry. Just make your move, and we can dance."

"I'm not talking about violence. I'm talking about a partnership. If we're going to stick together, we need to discuss what each of us is able to contribute."

"Contribute? What exactly does that mean?"

Holmes got out of the truck and tried to explain. "For this to work, each of us has to contribute something of value. I, for instance, am going to get us out of the country. Then, once we get to Africa, I'll be able to provide us with a network of contacts who will set us up with fake identities and a place to stay." He paused for a few seconds to let Greene absorb all of the information. "What about you?"

"Me? What the hell *can* I contribute? All my money is tied up in my house and this place, and I'm gonna have to abandon them both."

"True, but you'll be able to get some of your cash back."

Greene grimaced. "How do you figure that?"

"You never did anything illegal in your house, did you?"

"No."

"Then the FBI won't be able to take it. When Payne and Jones tell them that you were involved, they'll be able to search your house, but they won't be able to seize it. A year from now you'll be able to sell it through a local Realtor and have all of the money wired overseas. Several million if I'm not mistaken."

Greene hadn't thought of that, and the realization made him ecstatic. "But this investment is down the tubes, right?"

"Not necessarily. If you play your cards right, you might be able to collect a shitload of insurance money on it."

"Insurance money? For what? The burned log cabin? My deductible is probably more than that thing was worth."

Holmes shook his head. He'd planned for this contingency from Day One. "I'm not talking about the cabin. I'm talking about the house. You'll be able to collect on that."

Greene raised his eyebrows in confusion. "How do you figure? With the exception of a bullet hole or two, that place is in great shape."

"If you want an explanation, just follow me." Holmes walked into a grove of trees and removed a small metal box from an azalea. “Take a look inside. It’ll answer most of your insurance questions.”

Greene held the box with childlike fascination. He couldn’t imagine what Holmes had stored so far away from the house in a tiny crate. “Actually,” he laughed, “I’m not really in a trusting mood. Why don’t you open it?”

Holmes grabbed the box and pulled out a small radio transmitter, one that was commonly used for mining detonations. “Think about it, Levon. We wore masks the entire time we were here, but we didn’t always wear gloves. Our finger prints are all over that house. If we don’t do something about it, the FBI will be able to gather enough evidence to put us at the top of their hit list.” He shook his head decisively. “And there’s no way I’m gonna let that happen.”

“But won’t it happen anyway? With Payne, Jones, and Blount still alive, won’t they be able to tell the FBI everything?”

“Yeah, but without physical evidence, there’s no way they’ll be able to convince an African government to extradite us. At least that’s what Harris told me. He said witnesses won’t mean dick in a situation like that. Plus, if we’re careful, the American government won’t even know where we are. We’ll disappear from their radar forever.”

Greene smiled. He kind of liked the sound of that. “But what about the money? Won’t they be able to find me when I collect on my house?”

“Not if we follow Theo’s business plan. He set up a number of off-shore accounts using the names of bogus corporations. If you use them to filter all of the funds, the FBI won’t be able to touch you.”

“Are you sure? That sounds kind of risky, especially without Theo to walk me through it.”

“Hey, it’s your money not mine, but if I were in your shoes, I’d try to collect every cent that I possibly could. ’Cause if you don’t, you’re gonna be forced to work for the rest of your life.”

Greene grimaced at the thought of that. He was accustomed

to a life of luxury and didn't relish the thought of returning to the workforce—especially the one in Africa.

"Either way," Holmes continued, "I'm blowing this joint up. The explosives are set, and I can do it with a touch of a button."

"Bullshit," Greene growled. "I paid for it, so *I* get to blow it up. At least I'll get some kind of enjoyment out of this place."

Holmes smiled. He was glad that Greene wasn't going to fight him on this. "Good! You can do it in a minute, but before you do, you still need to answer my earlier question. I need to know what you're gonna contribute to this partnership."

Greene rolled his eyes. "You're obviously looking for something, so just tell me. What do you need from me? Money?"

Holmes nodded. "I was expecting us to make close to two million dollars off of the current batch of slaves." He turned back towards the truck and pointed to Ariane and Susan. "We're down to two. Granted, they're exceptional and will probably get us top dollar, but it won't be enough to live on for the rest of my life. That's why I want some guarantees from you, right here, right now."

"Octavian, if you expect me to give you two million dollars, you can fuck off. But if we're talking about some kind of reasonable settlement for getting me to safety, then there's no problem. Consider it done."

Holmes extended his hand, and Greene shook it eagerly.

"There's one thing, though, that kind of confuses me. As far as I can tell, we still have about a dozen slaves left in storage. Why don't we take them with us? It would net us a cool million."

Holmes signaled for Greene to follow him again, and he did so willingly. The two men walked ten feet deeper into the woods when Greene saw their getaway vehicle, buried under some brush. It was a hydroplane, capable of seating no more than four people at one time.

"If we had a way to transport 'em, I'd be all for it. Unfortunately, at this point, we'll have to settle for what we have: a boat ride to safety and your money to live on."

Chapter Forty-Five

It took several minutes for Blount and Jones to return, but they finally arrived at the house with three ATVs. Blount drove his unattached while Jones lagged behind, towing the third one.

"What took you guys so long?" Payne wondered. "I thought maybe you ran into trouble."

Jones shook his head. "It just took a while to figure out a towing system. We didn't have much to work with."

"Well, while you were busy playing engineer, I was stuck here talking to Webster. You should've told me he was still alive before you left."

Blount and Jones exchanged glances, then looked at the dead body near the porch. Webster was lying in the same position as before. "Jon, are you feeling all right? You took a blow to the head and I think maybe you were hallucinating."

Payne adamantly denied the suggestion. "I'm fine, D.J. My arm hurts, but my head's fine."

"You talked to him?"

"Yes."

"And he talked back?"

"Yes. He was alive, for god's sake. I swear!"

"You know," Blount admitted, "we never checked to see if he was dead or not. I think we both kind of assumed that he was a goner."

"He wasn't dead," Payne insisted. "Honest. He was alive."

While Jones struggled to remove the towing cable, he considered Payne's claim. "So, what did Lazarus have to say? Is the light as bright as they claim?"

Payne ignored the comment, concentrating on the first question instead. "That's the strange part. He kept repeating the same thing over and over, but it didn't make any sense to me."

Intrigued, Blount moved closer. "I knew him better than you. Maybe it'll make sense to me. What did Theo say?"

Payne frowned as he thought back on the urgency of Webster's statement. "*Paw it.* He kept repeating the phrase *paw it.* Does that mean anything to you?"

"Not off the top of my head, but give me a second to think."

"Are you sure he didn't say, Rosebud?" joked Jones. The mysterious word had been whispered in the famous death scene of the movie, *Citizen Kane.* "Maybe *Paw It* was the name of his sled."

"I doubt it," Blount countered. "Louisiana isn't exactly known for its snow. Hell, I can't even remember the last time I put my hands in my pockets let alone in a pair of gloves."

Blount's statement instantly triggered a smile on Payne's face. In a moment's time, he had gone from confused to enlightened, and all because of Bennie. "I'll be damned. I think I got it."

"Got what?" Jones questioned.

"The point of the message. I bet Webster was trying to say 'pocket' but couldn't pronounce it. I bet he has something in his pocket that he wanted me to see."

Since Blount was the closest to the body, he reached into the dead man's clothes, looking for anything of value. Even though it was soaked with blood and tattered with holes, he probed the garment for objects or clues, carefully trying to avoid the fluid that saturated it.

"Nope. Nothing."

"If you want to be thorough," Payne urged, "you should check to see if he's wearing a pocket undershirt. I know whenever I get a business card that I don't want to lose I put it in there."

After taking a deep breath, Blount slowly unbuttoned Webster's dress shirt, pulling back the blood-soaked garment like he was peeling a bright red apple. Once he exposed the undershirt, he placed his hand on the crimson-stained pocket and felt for anything of value. "I think there's something in here." With newfound excitement, Blount reached into the pocket's inner lining and removed a flat, black disk. "I'll be damned. You were right, Jon. He wanted you to go into his pocket."

Jones, who'd just finished his work on the ATV, rushed over to Blount's side. He was eager to see what had been found. "What is it?"

Blount stared at the object in the dim light. A look of absolute joy engulfed his face. "Oh my god! It's his disk. Theo's special disk."

"What do you mean by *special*?" Payne asked.

"I overheard him talking about it. I walked into his office while he was talking on the speaker phone. He said, 'If anything ever happens to me, I want you to look for a disk that I labeled with the scarlet letter.' " Blount showed Payne and Jones the disk. The letter *A* had been written on the label in bright red magic marker. "He said, 'The disk will contain financial records that will be helpful to your business.' "

Blount stared at the disk for a few more seconds then handed it over to Payne. "The other guy, whoever he was, asked him what type of records he was referring to, but Theo assured him that the information would only be important if he died."

Payne studied it, making sure that the blood from Webster's wounds hadn't seeped inside. "Well, Theo's dead, so I guess it's up to us to see if it's helpful—even though I have my doubts."

"Why do you say that? I heard him talking about this thing."

"I'm sure you did, but how much information can one little disk hold?"

"You don't get it, do you?" Blount frowned as he pointed to the disk in Payne's hand. "That isn't an ordinary disk. It's a Zip disk, which means it can hold the data of over 75 normal disks. Plus, Theo was the man in charge of the Posse's finances. If the Plantation spent or received money on anything, he would've been the one to keep track of it."

Payne and Jones smiled, finally understanding the significance of the find. If Blount was right, then they had just acquired the evidence that they needed to nail anyone who was associated with the Posse. Holmes, Greene, Jackson, Terrell Murray, and the slave buyers themselves. All of them could be linked to the crimes of the Plantation through Webster's data.

* * *

As he drove the truck across the island, Octavian Holmes shook his head at his own stupidity. He couldn't believe that Levon had actually convinced him to trade passengers for their journey to freedom. They already had enough money to live on for the rest of their lives, and if they'd left the Plantation immediately, they would've easily escaped from the island. So, why take the chance of getting caught? To him, it just didn't make any sense.

But Greene was passionate about it. In fact, he wouldn't take no for an answer. "There are four seats on the hydroplane," he had said. "An extra person means extra cash. Your cash, Octavian. You can keep all the money that we get from the sale. All of it. Think of what you can buy in Africa with $80,000. And all you have to do is trade Susan Ross for my special captive."

And that had done it. Holmes' greed had taken control of his common sense and convinced him to make the switch. He was risking his own life, his freedom, everything, for $80,000. Holmes shook his head repeatedly, thinking of the mistake that he was making.

"You're a greedy bastard," he said to himself. "A complete

idiot."

As he pulled his truck to a screeching halt, Holmes studied the concrete shed in front of him. It appeared to be in the same condition that he'd left it in. The door was still locked from the outside, the ground was unblemished with fresh footprints, and Ndjai's dog could be heard patrolling inside. Just like it should be.

The sound of Susan's whimpering and Holmes' keys caused the dog to erupt with even more ferocity than before. The barking, which had been relatively restrained, was quickly replaced by bloodthirsty howls as the canine flung itself against the door in an attempt to strike. Time after time, the creature repeated the process, hoping to quench its animalistic cravings with a savage battle, trying to get at the intruder before he had a chance to set a foot inside.

The dog's effort made Holmes smile.

"Hey Tornado, it's your Uncle O. How are ya doing, fella?" The Ibizan hound quickly responded, going from a ferocious killer to a friendly pet in less than a second. "That's a good boy. Your daddy trained you well, didn't he?"

Holmes cracked the door, allowing Tornado to smell his hand.

The inside of the structure was filled with darkness and the overwhelming stench of imprisonment, created by the bodily functions of the eleven terrified prisoners. There weren't windows, vents, or toilets, which meant the unsanitary conditions were bound to get worse as the hours passed. The majority of the room was enclosed by a large cage, made from thick barbed wire and massive wooden posts that had been placed there for two reasons: to keep the slaves from the exit and to keep Tornado away from the slaves.

Before he stepped into the room, Holmes grabbed a flashlight from above the door and shined the light into the huddled group of prisoners. He moved the brilliant beam from slave to slave, studying the dirty faces until he saw the man he was looking for: the chosen one.

Nathan was standing in the back corner of the room, far from the others, his face covered in layers of coarse facial hair. If it wasn't for the prisoner's 6' 5" frame, Holmes never would've recognized him, for he was just a shell of his former self. His body weight had dropped by at least fifty pounds in the preceding weeks, and his face was haggard and sickly. But his failing health was easily explained. He had arrived long before the current crop of slaves and had spent most of his time within the sadistic world of the Devil's Box. All told it had taken longer than anyone had expected, but the harsh treatment had eventually broken his spirit. One look into his eyes revealed it: Nathan was no longer the same man.

The peculiar thing, though, was the reason that he'd been brought to the Plantation. He wasn't kidnapped because of his ancestry or because of his race. He was there to fulfill one man's obsession with revenge, and as long as the Posse continued to flourish, his imprisonment would never end. Ever.

And cruelly enough, Nathan had never been told why.

Chapter Forty-Six

Even though he had a hole in his left biceps the size of a quarter, Payne wasn't about to give up. If he was going to rescue Ariane, he knew he had to endure whatever physical pain he was currently feeling. He simply had to, for he realized the agony in his arm could never approach the sorrow he'd feel if he lost Ariane forever.

The body mends quickly. The mind and heart do not.

"Bennie," Payne yelled over the roar of his motor, "where do you think they took her?"

Blount started his ATV, the lead vehicle in the pack, then answered. "One day when I was exploring the island, I found a boat hidden in the weeds. I'm not sure if the Posse put it there, but I think there's a chance that they did. It was in pretty good shape."

Jones started the middle Yamaha, completing the thundering chorus of engines. "That sounds like the place to start. Take us there."

With a twist of their accelerators, the three machines sprang into action, tearing up the soft turf in long strips and tossing it high into the air. After getting accustomed to his controls, Payne increased his speed until he was nearly even with Blount, choosing a position near Bennie's right shoulder. Jones, on the other hand, swung wide and settled on the opposite side of the pack, hoping to protect Blount from any outside threats.

Of course, there was nothing he could do to prevent the explosion.

Instantaneously, the sound of thunder overpowered the roar of the ATV motors as an invisible specter slammed into the backs of the bewildered drivers. In a moment of stunned confusion, the three men skidded to a grassy stop then turned to locate the source of the shock wave: It was the plantation house, and it glowed like Mount Vesuvius.

As they stared at the destruction, a second explosion tore through the remnants of the 18th-century structure with the force of a hurricane, sending antique meteorites into all directions. Fireballs sprang into the air like popcorn, spreading the inferno to the nearby trees and cabins, igniting them like they were made out of gasoline.

"The detonation is too precise to be an accident," Payne screamed. "Either the house was on a timer or it was set off by hand. And if it's the latter, that means our friends are still on the island."

Blount and Jones turned from the fireworks display and studied the surrounding terrain, using the glowing nighttime sky as a giant spotlight.

"Is that the truck up there?" Blount shouted.

Jones looked in the direction that Bennie was pointing and tried to identify the object. "I don't know if it's the truck we want, but it's definitely a truck." He patted the weapon that hung from his hip like a sheriff from the Wild West. "Let's saddle up, fellas, and teach them boys a lesson."

* * *

Despite Tornado's barking and the loud rumble of the truck engine, Holmes heard the house's detonation and quickly pulled over to investigate. Looking back, he saw the bright orange flames as they shot towards the sky and felt the concussion of the blast as its shock wave rolled across the tiny island like an invisible stampede.

With a large smile on his face, Holmes climbed from the vehicle and strolled towards the back of the truck. Tornado emerged from the front seat as well, and the two of them gazed at the light of the artificial dawn. "Did you like that, boy?"

The dog remained silent, staring at the horizon with sustained interest.

"You liked that, didn't you?"

Tornado answered the query with a low, menacing growl. Then, after a few seconds of obvious displeasure, it began pacing back and forth across the grass of the open field.

Holmes stared at Tornado with fascination. The only time he'd seen the dog act this way was when Ndjai was preparing him for an attack. "Hey, fella, it's gonna be all right. The fire isn't gonna hurt you. It's too far away to bother us."

A guttural moan emanated from the dog's throat as it continued its frenzied movement. Back and forth. Back and forth. Again and again.

"What is spooking you, boy? What's wrong?"

Then, as if answering the question, Tornado hopped onto the truck and growled at the nearby trees.

"What's wrong, boy? Is there something . . . ?"

And then Holmes heard it. Softly, just below the whisper of the wind, there was a rumble. It wasn't the sound of the fire as it devoured the evidence of the plantation. No, the sound was more manmade—like a machine. Yeah, that was it. Like an engine that was headed his way.

Without delay, Holmes jumped behind the wheel of the truck and hit the accelerator. Driving as quickly as the terrain would allow, he glanced in his sideview mirror and searched the darkness for his enemies' approach. He hoped that they wouldn't be back there. He prayed that he was just being paranoid, but the mirror gave him indisputable proof.

The MANIACs were behind him, and they were gaining ground.

"Son of a bitch. I can't believe those guys." He turned back and looked at Tornado, who was still growling fiercely at the noise. "Hang on, boy. This could be an interesting ride."

* * *

Blount shouted from the lead ATV. "I think he saw us."

Payne nodded, even though he had no idea what Blount had screamed. All of Payne's concentration was focused on the driver of the truck. It wasn't on Blount, the explosion, or the pain in his arm. No, everything—every thought, every breath, every beat of his broken heart—was devoted to the man that threatened his lifetime of happiness.

He would make the man pay for his transgressions.

But he had to catch him first.

Little by little, second by second, Payne gained ground on the vehicle he chased. He wasn't sure how it was possible—the pickup truck had more horsepower and quicker acceleration than his ATV—but he was getting closer.

"I'm gonna try to cut him off," Blount yelled.

Jones nodded his head in understanding as Blount pulled ahead like a marathon runner using his final kick. Five feet, then ten. His lead quickly lengthened while his dreadlocks flapped in the wind like a tattered flag in a tropical storm. Jones stared in amazement as Blount, whose speed approached 60 mph, inched closer and closer to the truck.

"He's gonna catch him," Jones shouted. "Holy hell, he's gonna catch him."

* * *

Holmes looked in his sideview mirror with great displeasure.

Even though he drove the fastest vehicle, the trio was still gaining on him. "Come on, you piece of shit truck. What's wrong with you?"

He tried pressing the gas pedal even harder, but it was already on the floor. There was nothing else he could do to increase his speed.

"Tornado, attack those men!"

The dog, who'd been watching the approach of the four-wheelers with fascination, barked excitedly in response. After locking its gaze on the nearest target, Tornado obtained top speed in three quick strides, then launched itself from the back of the truck with as much force as its muscular legs could generate. The dog flew through the air like a white missile, aiming its sleek and powerful body at the closest threat it could find: Bennie Blount.

Tornado crashed into Blount's face with such force that it shattered his nose and cheekbones on contact, knocking him from his vehicle at a highly precarious angle. Then, as Blount slumped to the ground, his leg snagged on the underside of the handlebar, forcing his vehicle to turn sideways. The awkward movement was too extreme for his Yamaha to handle, causing the four-wheeler to flip over in a series of exaggerated somersaults until the spiraling vehicle burst into a massive ball of flames.

Lucky for Blount, he was thrown free of the ATV before the explosion occurred, but his bloodied and broken body skidded helplessly until it slowed to a stop in Jones' path.

With the reflexes of a NASCAR driver, D.J. leaned hard to the left and slipped past his fallen ally by less than a foot. Unfortunately, as he surged past Blount, he found himself heading for a catastrophe of a different kind. Blount's out-of-control vehicle, still tumbling in a pronounced spin, sprang sideways and landed squarely in front of him. The two ATVs smashed together with a metallic scream, launching Jones over the handlebars of the Yamaha and onto the hard ground beside the fiery wreck.

Payne saw the accident out of the corner of his eye—the gruesome collision of the two vehicles and his best friend's violent spill—but realized there was nothing that he could do to help. As much as he wanted to offer his assistance, he knew he couldn't afford to. It pained him to be so selfish, so uncaring towards D.J., but he realized if he turned around now, he might lose track of Ariane forever. And he just couldn't handle that possibility.

*   *   *

Despite the thick layer of fog that clouded his mind, Bennie Blount was able to recall many details of the accident. The truck, the ATV, the vicious impact of the dog.

God, he suddenly realized, it was a miracle that he was even alive.

While giving his body a moment to recuperate, Blount tried to clear the cobwebs in his brain, but was unable to snap out of his accident-induced haze. His head throbbed with every beat of his pounding heart, and his vision came and went at unannounced intervals, making it all but impossible to concentrate on anything. He tried to focus on something simple—the names of his family members, his childhood home, what he ate for dinner—but his concentration was distracted by the warm sensation that slowly engulfed his face.

The feeling, unlike anything he had ever experienced, started in his cheeks and gradually crawled towards his eyes at a slow rate. At first, Blount wasn't sure what was causing it. A swarm of insects? the blowing wind? a hallucination? But in time, he realized what was actually happening: His entire face was filling with fluid.

As he laid there, twisted and grotesquely mangled, Blount could feel his cheeks as they expanded and swelled at a hideous rate. Blood flooded his taste buds as the copper-flavored liquid surged from his nose like a waterfall and drained into his open mouth below. His orifice quickly filled with the warm fluid, and as it did, he tried to purge it with a quick burst of air but shockingly realized that he was unable to. Regrettably, he had bitten his tongue during his fall, and the severed tip floated in his mouth like a dead fish in a crimson pond.

He tried to roll onto his side by using his arms and hands, but nothing happened. His limbs didn't respond, and he remained completely stationary. Blount then attempted to pull his knees towards his chest, hoping to see or detect movement of any kind from his lower body, but his legs remained planted on the ground. In a final test, Blount tried to wiggle his fingers and tap his feet, but they remained lifeless. Completely lifeless.

He wanted to do something, anything, to prove that he was making a mistake, that he was simply overreacting to the situation, that he wasn't paralyzed, but his body was unwilling to cooperate.

It kept letting him down, over and over again.

Chapter Forty-Seven

Despite the agony in his arm, Payne managed to close the gap between himself and the surging truck to less than five feet. Once he matched the truck's speed, Payne pulled his right leg from the ATV and placed his foot on the vehicle's seat. After doing the same with his other leg, he found himself steering the Yamaha in a catcher's stance, a position that would allow him to leap onto the back of the truck.

But Holmes wasn't about to let that happen.

Using the view from his passenger-side mirror, Holmes spotted Payne in pursuit. In an effort to thwart him, Holmes swerved the truck violently to the left, trying to shake free of the high-speed pest, but Payne adjusted quickly, gliding adjacent to the right edge of the pickup. Without delay, Holmes whipped the steering wheel to the right, trying to flatten Payne with the violent impact of the two vehicles, but the maneuver quickly backfired.

Since Payne was anticipating Holmes' move, he was able to use the approach of the truck to his advantage, jumping from the Yamaha a split-second before impact occurred. Holmes laughed when he heard the metallic crunch of the two vehicles and quickly glanced in his mirror to examine the wreckage, but the darkness prevented him from seeing much. The only thing he could see was the spiraling glow of the ATV's headlight as it turned over and over again in a series of violent flips.

"It was nice bumping into you," Holmes howled.

Little did he know that Payne was still along for the ride.

* * *

The initial sound came from behind, and it made Blount's heart leap with fear. It wasn't a distinct noise like a bark or a howl, but Blount still knew what had produced it. It was Tornado, the hound from Hades. The bloodthirsty dog had paralyzed him and was coming back for more.

Blount knew if he remained stationary he wouldn't stand a chance against the blood-crazed beast. The dog would pin him to the ground with its thick, muscular body and thrash him to death with its razor-sharp teeth. He had seen the animal in action during its training sessions with Ndjai, so he knew what it was capable of doing. If he was to survive, Blount knew he needed to get to his feet and find some kind of weapon to defend himself. But how could he? He couldn't run or even twitch. What chance did he stand against something like Tornado?

Realizing he couldn't put up a fight, Blount tried to scream for help, hoping that Payne or Jones would hear him, but his severed tongue and mouthful of blood restricted his effort. Instead of a shout, all that he was able to produce was a muffled whimper, and no one was close enough to hear it but Tornado, who heard the plea and sprang forward to investigate.

Once the dog was confident of Blount's helplessness, it began its customary attack pattern, circling its victim at a dizzying rate. Around and around, over and over again, the beast whipped itself into an impassioned frenzy while waiting for the right moment to strike.

* * *

If he had wanted to, Payne knew that he could kill Holmes

immediately—all it would take was a bullet to the back of his head—but there was a slight problem with that approach: Who was going to stop the truck? The vehicle was going too fast to slow on its own, and since Payne was in the back of it, the thought of it ramming into a tree or plunging into a swamp wasn't very appealing. No, if Payne was going to take out Holmes, he had to do it with a great deal of finesse.

It was the only way to guarantee his own safety.

Payne pulled the Glock from his belt, then studied the back of the truck, hoping to find something useful, but the bed was pretty bare except for a tool chest, a tire, and a thick military blanket. Payne thought for a moment, trying to figure out how he could use any of these things to his advantage. Suddenly, an idea hit him: He could use the blanket to obscure Holmes' vision.

With a quick tug, Payne slid the blanket across the bed and readied it for use. All that he needed to do was take it towards the cab and toss it over the front of the—

"Oh my god," he gasped.

He stared at the object on the other side of the truck and couldn't believe what he saw. How had he been so blind when he first climbed aboard? How could he have missed such a large lump under the blanket? It just didn't seem possible. But there it was, or more accurately, there he was. The captive who'd been pulled from the Devil's Box before Payne had been placed inside. The man, who was covered in insect bites and facial hair, was handcuffed, unconscious, and lying no more than five feet away.

Payne crawled across the truck bed and tried to examine him, hoping that he was still clinging to life. His skin was ashen, completely colorless from a lack of sun and a severe shortage of food and water. His eyes, even though responsive, were quite lethargic—possibly from dehydration, maybe from an illness or infection of some kind.

"Hang in there," Payne whispered.

He glanced at the open terrain of the surrounding field and realized that he needed to make his move immediately. He didn't want to abandon the sick prisoner, but if he struck now, he knew there was no chance of the truck slamming into anything solid.

"Everything's going to be fine."

With blanket in hand, Payne crept towards the driver, carefully moving in the back of the speeding truck. Pain ripped through his biceps as he struggled with the blanket, but he realized he had no other choice. He had to use his left arm to complete the job.

After taking a quick breath to ease the agony, Payne thrust his arms through the back window and arched the blanket over the face of the stunned driver. Holmes instantly released the steering wheel and used both of his hands to tear at the thick blanket, but Payne wasn't about to give in. In fact, he felt like a rodeo champion clinging for dear life on the back of an angry bull.

"Stop the truck," he demanded. "Stop the truck now."

Holmes responded by pushing on the gas pedal even harder while screaming, "Fuck you!" through the rough cloth of the blanket.

The vehicle's speed continued to increase until Payne tugged on the blanket again, this time in a series of rapid bursts. "I . . . said . . . stop . . . the . . . truck . . . NOW!"

Thinking quickly, Holmes gave into the request, but not in the way that Payne had hoped for. Instead of easing his foot from the gas pedal, Holmes slammed on the brakes as hard as he could. The sudden shift in the truck's momentum did the trick, flinging Payne over the top of the roof like a drunken gymnast, legs and arms flailing in every direction while he tried to stop his slide, but nothing could prevent him from tumbling in front of the screeching truck.

* * *

While trying to shake off the effect of the ATV crash, Jones pulled himself to a sitting position, then studied his immediate surroundings. He saw two four-wheelers, both of them damaged and overturned, and the closest one to him was on fire. Using the light from the blaze, Jones checked himself for blood but was surprised to find very little.

Sure, he had a wide assortment of scrapes and bruises, but he didn't have any gushers like he had feared.

After rubbing his eyes for several seconds, Jones climbed to his feet and looked for the other driver. He wasn't quite sure who he was looking for—his head was still groggy from the accident—but he reasoned if there were two vehicles, there should be two bodies.

At least, that seemed to make sense in his current state.

Jones wandered to his left and stared at the flaming wreckage, making sure that no one was on fire. "Hello? Can anybody hear me?"

There was no response.

Jones limped to the second ATV, the one that he'd been driving, and pushed it over onto its wheels. Even though it was dented and fairly banged-up, Jones didn't notice any major damage. There were no obvious leaks or stray parts lying on the ground, and despite the collision the wheels seemed to be intact.

"Takes a licking and keeps on—"

A deep growl broke Jones' concentration. He immediately stared in the direction of the noise and searched for the source of the sound.

"Hello?" he shouted, but this time with a little more apprehension.

Once again, there was no response.

As he studied the darkness, Jones placed his hand on his belt and felt for the cold touch of his gun. He was thankful when his fingers curled around the rough texture of the handle. It gave him a sudden burst of confidence.

"Who's out there?" he demanded.

Another growl. Softer, angrier.

Jones took a few steps forward, holding his gun directly in front of him. He was in no mood for games and planned on punishing the first person he came across. "If you're out there, I recommend you answer me. Otherwise, I have a bullet with your name on it."

He took another step, moving closer to the source of the sound. The light of the fire helped show him the way. In fact, he relied on it.

"I'm telling you," he warned. "You're really pissing me—"

But Jones wasn't able to finish his statement. In fact, he literally choked on the words as he tried to say them.

Bennie Blount was sprawled on the ground, twisted and contorted in a puddle of his own blood. Hovering above him, like a monster from another world, was Tornado, its face and claws dripping with the crimson liquid that surged from the open wounds that it had created.

When the animal saw Jones, it lifted its head and growled in an effort to protect its dinner, and while it did, chunks of flesh dropped from its mouth and fell onto the red dirt below.

The bloody display made Jones nauseous, yet it only added to his determination.

He instantly raised his Glock and pointed it at the snarling beast.

BANG! The first shot entered the animal mid-shank, knocking it away from Blount amidst a series of yelps. But Jones refused to stop. He wouldn't be content until this creature had suffered.

BANG! The next bullet ripped through Tornado's back hip, sending a spurt of blood into the air and onto the ground where the dog collapsed with a loud thud.

BANG! BANG! BANG! Tornado danced spasmodically as Jones pummeled its body with shot after well-aimed shot, and he wasn't about to stop until he was sure that this beast would never breathe again.

"Enjoy your trip to doggy hell," he sneered. "Tell Cujo I said hello."

Chapter Forty-Eight

When Payne opened his eyes, he was unable to see anything except two blazing orbs of light, one shining on either side of him. He tried leaning forward, using his good arm to lift him from the ground, but the front bumper of the truck restricted his movement.

"Wow," he gasped, noticing that most of his body was actually underneath the frame of the vehicle. "Thank goodness for tall wheels."

Using the front grill for support, Payne scrambled backwards, freeing himself from the undercarriage as quickly as possible. He realized he didn't have time to plan any elaborate strategy—Holmes would be looking to strike hastily—so Payne decided to follow his gut instinct: And it told him to attack.

With the confidence of a medieval knight, Payne lowered his right hand to his hip and snatched his weapon in one quick movement. As his finger curled around the metal trigger, Payne glanced under the motionless vehicle, looking for Holmes' feet. If he had seen them, he would've blasted them immediately, but Payne's search turned up empty.

That meant that Holmes was either inside the truck or on it.

Since the front windshield was missing, Payne knew he'd have an unobstructed shot if Holmes was in the front seat. He realized, though, that the windowless space would be far more beneficial to his opponent. The gap would give Holmes more room to maneuver inside the cab and an extra way to escape. But Payne wasn't about to let *that* happen.

No, the only way that Holmes was going to get away was through Payne, not through a window. Unfortunately, that's what Holmes had in mind.

While recovering from the sneak attack, Holmes noticed Payne's silhouette on the ground ahead, created by the effulgence of the headlights. The shadow gave Holmes all the information that he was looking for: Payne was still alive and directly in front of him.

Without delay, Holmes slammed his foot on the gas. The truck charged forward at full speed, but Payne, using his well-honed instincts, sensed what was about to happen. With mongoose-like quickness, he fell backwards, doing the Nestea plunge on the hard ground in order to avoid the mechanical beast. A split-second later, the truck roared above him like the Blue Angels at an air show, its high undercarriage protecting Payne from injury.

The instant the truck passed Payne flipped onto his belly and burst forward like an Olympic sprinter at the start of a race, but he quickly realized that the vehicle had too large of a lead for him to make up. Stopping immediately, he aimed his Glock at the truck's back tire and discharged three quick rounds in succession. The second and third bullets hit their mark, piercing the right wheel and causing Holmes to temporarily lose control of the truck. The vehicle fish-tailed, skidding sideways on the dew-filled grass, yet Holmes didn't panic. He coolly compensated for the loss of air pressure, allowing the back end to straighten itself out, then continued forward as fast as the vehicle could carry him.

*　　*　　*

"Where the hell have you been?" Levon Greene growled. He'd

been standing by the boat for several minutes, impatiently waiting for Holmes' return. "I was getting ready to leave you behind."

Holmes stepped from the heavily damaged truck with a look of annoyance on his face. "Where the hell have I been? I've been doing your dirty work, that's where I've been." He opened the hatch with a slam, then climbed onto the back of the truck. "If it wasn't for your selfishness, we'd already be in the Gulf by now. But no! You just needed to have your pet slave, didn't ya?"

Greene moved forward, glancing into the flatbed. He wanted to make sure that Holmes had returned with Nathan. "He's gonna fetch you an extra $80,000, so I don't know what you're so pissed about."

Holmes glanced down at the slave and gave him a swift kick in the mid-section. He was completely fed up with Greene's shit, and he needed to take it out on somebody.

"You don't know why I'm pissed? You brought two MANIACs to my island, then when they get loose, you run and hide while I'm forced to deal with them." Holmes pushed the slave towards Greene. "I mean, this is *your* guest, right? So why did I have to risk my life to get him?"

Greene shook his head at Holmes' ignorance. "Because I'm the one with the money. If your name was on the bank account, then I'd be doing stuff for you. But as it is, I'm the one with the cash, so you're the one with the job."

* * *

Payne knew he had a lot of ground to make up—probably too much to do on foot—so he decided to take a chance. He wasn't sure if his four-wheeler had survived the vicious jolt from Holmes' truck, but he decided to run back to the crash site and find out. Thankfully, the gamble paid off. The Yamaha had overturned, but it was still working fine.

After putting it on its wheels, Payne jumped on the ATV and rocketed ahead with a touch of the accelerator. The yellow vehicle reached 20, 40, then 60 mph as Payne urged the machine to catch Holmes. He realized if Ariane was taken from the island, the hope of finding her would go down significantly. No, it wouldn't be an impossible task—hell, Payne would devote his entire life and all of his corporate resources to finding her—but he knew it would be a difficult undertaking.

"Come on," he implored, digging his heels into the side of the metallic horse. "Go faster!"

But the vehicle was going as fast as it could, vibrating rapidly from the strain. The darkened scenery of the Plantation whipped by in a blur. The trees, rocks, and animals were all a part of the landscape that Payne ignored. His full concentration, every thought in his throbbing head, was focused on the love of his life and the bastards that had taken her away.

Oh, they would pay. They would fucking pay.

But he had to catch them first.

* * *

It wasn't until the hydroplane eased into the warm water of the inlet that Holmes was finally able to relax. Up until that moment, he was confident that Payne or Jones would appear at the last possible moment to foil his escape. But the instant he glided from the marsh's rugged shoreline, he noticed his anxiety start to fade.

He'd faced two MANIACs in battle and lived to brag about it.

As the boat moved deeper into the swamp, passing groves of cypress trees and several curious alligators, Greene noticed the difference in Holmes' appearance. His partner's face no longer looked haggard, and his body no longer looked beaten. In fact, he actually seemed to lose years as the boat continued forward.

"What's your deal?" he asked with a hint of curiosity. "You suddenly look like a new man."

"Feel like one, too." A full smile crossed his lips for the first time in hours. "My gut told me we weren't gonna make it, Levon. I don't know why, but something inside me warned me about Payne and Jones."

"What did it say?"

"It told me that they were gonna be our downfall." Holmes took his eyes off the water and cast a paranoid glance at the land. He just needed to make sure that the MANIACs weren't back there. "But I guess I was wrong, huh?"

Greene stood from his seat and looked back as well, but the hydroplane had traveled so far he could barely see the shoreline through the trees. "What does your gut tell you now?"

Holmes pondered the question as he increased the boat's speed ever so slightly. There was a faint glow in the water up ahead that he had a theory about. "Actually, it tells me that we're gonna make it to Africa and something good is going to happen to us along the way."

"Along the way? Why do you say that?"

Holmes extended his finger forward, causing Greene to turn towards the front of the hydroplane. When his eyes focused on the scene just ahead, he couldn't believe their good fortune.

Paul and Jake Metz were standing on a fallen cypress tree, trying to push the boat into the center of the channel, but their effort was completely useless. The duo, weakened from days of labor in the field, didn't have the strength to disengage the boat by themselves, and Robert Edwards didn't have enough experience with the craft to assist them.

No, the slaves weren't about to free themselves from the tree, and now that Holmes and Greene had stumbled upon them, they wouldn't be getting free at all.

* * *

Payne attempted to follow the truck's tire prints in the dew-covered grass, but the rocky terrain near the eastern shore limited his tracking ability.

Once the trail stopped, he decided to scan the swamp in both directions, hoping to stumble upon a clue in the soft light of the rising sun. With each passing minute, he knew the chances of finding Ariane on the island were getting smaller and smaller, yet he refused to give up hope while there was still fuel in his gas tank and ground to cover. It wasn't until he saw Holmes' truck, slowly sinking into the soft mud of the marsh, that he knew he was too late to make a difference.

The Posse had escaped from the Plantation.

"Son of a bitch!" he screamed while punching the leather seat in frustration. "I can't believe I . . ." He took a deep breath, trying to calm down, but it didn't work. The extra oxygen simply made him more agitated than before. "Fuck! Fuck! FUCK!"

After a moment of contemplation, Payne jumped from his four-wheeler and ran to the edge of the swamp. He was tempted to wade out to the sinking truck to search for clues, but the splashing of nearby gators eliminated the possibility.

"Think, man, think. What can I do? What can I do???"

Unfortunately, there was *nothing* he could do except watch the vehicle—and his chances of finding Ariane—slowly vanish.

Chapter Forty-Nine

Tuesday, July 6th
District Office for the Federal Bureau of Investigation
New Orleans, Louisiana

Jonathon Payne rubbed his eyes in frustration then glared at the agent across the table. He'd already answered more questions in the past few hours than he had during his entire four years at the Naval Academy, and it was starting to try his patience. He was more than willing to assist the FBI with their investigation, but enough was enough. It was time to speed up the process.

Payne stood from his chair and glanced at the large mirror that dominated the wall in front of him. If he was correct, the people in charge of the investigation were standing behind the glass, watching him give his testimony about the Plantation.

"Gentlemen," he announced, "I have reached my limit. I've done nothing wrong, yet I am being treated like a criminal. Well, that's it. I'm not saying another word until one of you assholes comes into this room and answers a few questions for me. Do you understand? Nothing else until I get some answers."

Payne accented his request by slamming his hand against the two-way glass—not in an attempt to break it, but rather to drive home the intensity of his message. The point apparently got through because less than a minute later, the door to the conference room opened and the local director of operations walked in.

Chuck Dawson was a distinguished-looking man in his mid-50s, and the power of his position showed in the confidence of his stride. He greeted Payne with a firm handshake and studied him for a moment before telling the other agent to leave the room.

"How's the arm feeling, Mr. Payne? Can I get you something for it?"

Payne glanced at his injured biceps and shrugged. It wouldn't get better without surgery, and he didn't have any time for a hospital at the moment. "A beer would be nice. You know, for the pain."

Dawson smiled at the comment. "If I had some in my office, I'd offer you a cold one. Unfortunately, I was thinking more in the line of bandages or a pillow."

"Nah, your doctors patched me up pretty good when I first came in. I don't think I'm ready for the golf course quite yet, but I'll be OK for our little chat."

"Well, if that changes, be sure to let me know. I don't want anything to happen to a national hero while you're under my care."

Payne raised his eyebrows in surprise. The recent line of questioning suggested that he was more of a suspect in the FBI's eyes than a hero. He'd been drilled on everything from Jamaican Sam's murder to his possible involvement with the Posse, and now he was being praised? That just didn't seem right. "On second thought, I might need a hearing test. I could've sworn you just called me a hero."

"But I did," Dawson assured him. He opened the folder that he brought with him and glanced at its confidential information. "From what I can tell, you and your partner, David Jones, saved the lives of ten prisoners—actually eleven if you include Tonya Edwards' baby—while killing more than twenty men in the process. At the same time, you managed to prevent the future abduction of countless others by shutting down a criminal organization that we didn't even know existed until yesterday."

Dawson noticed Payne trying to read the FBI data, so he hastily closed the folder. "Yeah, that makes you a hero in my book."

Payne leaned back in his chair and grimaced. "Well, Chuck, that seems a little bit surprising. I don't feel like a hero. In fact, I kind of feel like a second-class citizen around here. What was with all of the questions and accusations?"

Dawson's tanned face broke into a bright smile, revealing a full set of perfect teeth. "Come on, Jon. You're ex-military. You know the way things work."

"Yeah, you like to burn up valuable manpower by asking a ton of worthless questions just so you have something to put into your files."

The FBI director shrugged. "It's the government's way."

A grin cracked the frown that had been on Payne's lips. "Well, at least you're willing to admit it's worthless. That's more than the last agent was willing to do."

"Now don't be putting words into my mouth. I never said it was worthless. The questions weren't worthless. . . . OK, I admit some of our questions were a little far-fetched, but they weren't without worth. We often gather more information from a person's reaction to a question than we can from their actual answer."

Payne rolled his eyes at the comment. He couldn't believe that his entire morning had been wasted on psychological games. There were so many other things that he could've been doing with his time. "And that's why you've been harassing me? To see if my answers and my facial expressions stayed consistent?"

"Something like that. But it isn't just self-consistency that we look for. We also check a witness' claims against the claims of others."

"Like D.J.'s?"

"Sure, and Bennie Blount's, and the slaves, and anyone else we can dig up. We make sure everything checks out before we're willing to accept it. It's the only way to guarantee in-depth analysis."

"Well, Chuck, now that I've passed your little test, would you please answer some questions for me? I've been trying to get some information all morning long, but I keep getting shot down by your flunkies."

Dawson nodded. His men had been instructed to keep Payne in the dark, but now that they were confident in Payne's innocence, he was willing to open up. "As long as the questions don't involve confidential data, I'd be happy to fill you in. Fire away."

It was a poor choice of expressions, but Payne was willing to overlook the faux pas if it meant getting some answers. "You just mentioned Bennie Blount. How's he doing?"

"Mr. Blount is in serious but stable condition. He lost a hell of a lot of blood from the crash and the animal attack, but your buddy did a great job keeping him alive until help arrived."

"But what about his legs? Is he going to be able to walk again?"

"Regrettably, it's too early to tell."

"What kind of answer is that? Will he, or won't he?"

"Jon, I'm not a doctor, but from what I was told, he did sustain a spinal cord injury. They don't think it's a devastating one, though. God willing, he'll be as good as new after some rest and some rehab."

Payne closed his eyes and said a short prayer. For some reason, he was always more devastated by his partner's injuries than his own. "And what about the twenty-plus prisoners we saved? Are all of them all right?"

Dawson laughed. "Maybe I should ask you a similar question? Are *you* all right?"

"And what's that supposed to mean?"

"Twenty-plus prisoners? You must have double vision or something. Like I mentioned before, you helped save the lives of eleven captives."

"Yeah, I heard what you said, Chuck. There were eleven people on the island when you showed up and ten on the boat that I set free. If my math is correct, that would mean over twenty."

"Shit," Dawson mumbled. He suddenly realized that Payne hadn't been informed about the missing vessel. "I'm sorry to be the one to tell you this, Jon. We never found the slave boat that you and your partner talked about. The Coast Guard is currently conducting an all-out search of the Gulf, but as of right now, we don't know what happened to it."

"You've gotta be shittin' me."

"I wish I was, but it hasn't turned up."

Payne tried to process the new information as quickly as possible. "So the slave boat could be on the bottom of the Gulf somewhere? Ah, shit! What about Robert Edwards? Did you find Robert Edwards anywhere?"

Dawson shook his head. "He's one of the missing slaves. His wife and future baby are fine, but he's still unaccounted for."

"And what about the kids? How many kids have turned up?"

"So far just one. A girl named Susan Ross. We've been trying to talk to her for a while, but she's currently on another planet. Psych is trying to get through to her as we speak."

"Damn! There were four kids on that boat alone."

Payne tried making sense of the information, but the bad news caught him completely off guard. When he left the island, he thought he'd rescued everyone except Ariane and the unknown captive from the truck. Now he realized that he might've sent a boatload of inexperienced sailors to a watery grave.

"Jon?" Dawson whispered in a comforting voice. "Not to change the subject, but when you pounded on the mirror and called me an asshole, you said you had a bunch of questions. Did you want me to answer anything else, or is that all for now?"

It took Payne a moment to gather himself. "With the new

information that you just gave me, one suddenly leaps to mind."

"Go ahead, fire away."

Payne wished he'd stop using that expression. It seemed *so* inappropriate. "How the hell did you find us? Originally, I thought the people on the boat must've told you about the Plantation, but since they're still missing, I guess they couldn't have been the ones."

Dawson nodded. "As it turns out, a couple of planes noticed the house explosion from the air. They, in turn, notified the local authorities. Eventually, word filtered down to us."

"What about Levon Greene and Octavian Holmes? Any luck with them?"

Dawson shook his head. "We put out an APB and flooded the airports and local islands with their pictures. Unfortunately, if they decided to head south, we'll have little chance of getting 'em. Hell, a guy in a sailboat can fart and propel himself to Mexico from here. We're that close to the border, so it makes things kind of tough for us."

* * *

Once Payne was excused from the conference room, he rode the elevator to the main lobby, where he met up with Jones. The two greeted each other with a firm handshake, then walked into the bright sunlight of the Crescent City.

"How'd the questioning go?"

Jones smirked like an uncaught shoplifter. "Just peachy, and you?"

"Not too bad. When things started to get sticky, I made a big fuss, and they immediately backed down." Jones' smirk must've been contagious because it quickly spread to Payne's lips. "Did they ask you anything about the disk?"

Jones patted the pocket of his T-shirt and laughed. "Nope, and to be honest with you, I forgot to mention it." He suddenly stopped on the sidewalk and pretended to turn around. "Do you think I should go back and tell them? 'Cause I could—"

"Nah," Payne interjected. "It's probably not important. The damn thing's bound to be blank."

"Yeah, you're right. It probably won't tell us where to look for Ariane, or Levon, or the slave owners. And, hell, even if it did, it's not like we'd even care."

"Not at all. Not one freakin' bit."

* * *

The property in Tampico, Mexico, had been in Edwin Drake's family for four decades, yet he never had any use for it until recently. After several years of dormancy, the land was suddenly critical to Drake's slave-exportation business, serving as a makeshift airport in the middle of nowhere, a place where they could load people without governmental interference.

The boat of slaves, adroitly piloted by Octavian Holmes, reached the Tampico coast just before the break of dawn and was immediately greeted by two trucks of dark-skinned guards, all chosen from Kotto's plantations in Nigeria. The Africans loaded six slaves into each truck, then drove them to Drake's property, which sat ten miles northwest of the Mexican city. When they arrived at camp, the slaves were quickly herded into a containment building, where they were stripped, hosed, deloused, and then clothed, before being fed their first meal in over a day.

After eating greedily, the slaves were examined by Kotto's personal physician, who treated each of their injuries with urgency—these people were Kotto's property, after all—making sure that every wound was cleaned and every infection was attended to. Then, after certifying and documenting the health of each person, the doctor gave the slaves the immunization shots that they would require for their trip to their new homeland, Africa.

Once the medical details were taken care of, the slaves were led to Drake's homemade airfield, where the guards checked the names and ages of each:

Jake Metz (71)	Donny Metz (15)	Scooter Ross (8)
Paul Metz (45)	Mary Ross (35)	Ariane Walker (28)
Alicia Metz (43)	Tommy Ross (14)	Robert Edwards (32)
Kelly Metz (17)	Jimmy Ross (42)	Nathan (31)

Doubting the ability of the foreign guards, Levon Greene double-checked the list of passengers. He realized these twelve slaves would generate a million-dollar payday in Africa, so he didn't want there to be any mistakes.

"How do things look?" Holmes asked, no longer worried about Payne or Jones. "Are they ready for their trip across the Atlantic?"

Greene nodded with confidence. "As ready as they'll ever be."

"Well, to help them with their transition, we've selected *Roots* for their in-flight movie."

Chapter Fifty

Thursday, July 8th
Ibadan National Railyards
Ibadan, Nigeria
(56 miles northeast of Lagos)

The dark-skinned American looked in both directions, making sure that the tracks of the rail station were free of traffic. When the conditions met his approval, he continued forward carefully lifting his caftan (a robe of white cotton) from the grease-covered rails. After crossing the congested railyard, he turned left, walking parallel to the far track while trying to conceal the noticeable limp in his gait. It was the only thing about him that was the least bit conspicuous. Other than that, he blended in perfectly, resembling the rest of the peasants as they rode the trains back to their suburban homes after a hard day of work.

"May the peace, mercy, and blessings of Allah be upon you," said a passing Muslim.

The American nodded graciously, hoping that the loose-fitting Nigerian cap did not fall of the top of his head. "And also with you," he replied in Yoruba, one of the common languages in Ibadan.

With a watchful eye, the American continued forward, searching for the designated meeting spot. He had already completed his reconnaissance of the neighborhood: double-checking the security around the Kotto Distribution Center, studying the building blueprints, looking for weak spots in the perimeter of the industrial plant. Overall, he was quite happy with his findings, but his opinion mattered little in the greater scheme of things. He was simply a pawn in a very complex game, one that he knew very little about.

But that was about to change.

After reaching the rendezvous point, he glanced in all directions, making sure that he wasn't being followed. Everything looked clear to his well-trained eyes. Smiling confidently, he knocked on the rail car five times, the agreed-upon signal to gain access to the box car, which had been secretly commandeered for the current operation.

"Who is it?" called a high-pitched voice from inside.

This wasn't a part of standard protocol, but the dark-skinned man was more than willing to play along. It helped to lessen the tension of the moment. "Domino's Pizza," he chuckled.

"Your delivery took more than 30 minutes. I expect a large refund."

The American grabbed his crotch with both hands. "Open the door, lady. I've got your large refund, right here."

The cargo door slid open, revealing a white soldier in black camouflage. "Oooh," he exclaimed in a feminine voice. "And what a big refund it is."

Both men laughed as the black soldier climbed into the railcar.

"Any problems with your recon?" asked one of the soldiers inside.

"None, except for my damn gun." He reached under his robe, removing the weapon that had been strapped to his leg in case of an emergency. "I need to get a new leg holster. This thing cut off my circulation within ten minutes, and I've been limping ever since."

"Bitch, bitch, bitch," teased a familiar voice from the back of the car. His view was obstructed by a large stack of crates, but he knew exactly who he was listening to. "You were bitching when I first trained you, and you're still bitching now. Haven't you grown up yet?"

A grin instantly appeared on Lieutenant Shell's face. He removed the white cotton cap from his head as a sign of respect, then moved forward, searching for the source of the voice. "I'll be damned. Is that . . . Captain Payne! It is you!" Joy filled the soldier's face. He hadn't seen his former commander in a long time. "What are you doing here?"

"Listening to you bitch. I thought I taught you to be tougher than that. Complaining about a little cramp? How embarrassing."

The men hugged briefly, a touching reunion between two MANIACs, past and present.

"It's great to see you, sir. It really is. But I have to admit, ya look like shit. What happened?"

With scars all over his face and body, Payne glanced at his left arm, dangling lifelessly in its sling, then shrugged. "This is what happens once you reach your mid-30s. Your body starts to fall apart."

"Don't let him fool you," Jones interjected, moving from his hiding place on the other side of the boxcar. "He got into a disagreement with an exotic dancer, and she kicked his white ass. Breast to the face . . . breast to the face . . . high heels to the nuts . . . knockout."

Shell laughed like a little kid as he rushed to D.J.'s side. It'd been almost three years since they'd spoken, and the smiles on their faces revealed their love and admiration for one another. It was the type of bond that developed when two people had been through hell together—the type of stuff that the MANIACs were known for.

"How are you doing?"

"Pretty damn good," Shell declared. "But I'd like the right to change my opinion. I mean, if you guys are here, then something big is about to go down. Right?"

He looked at Jones, then allowed his gaze to drift to Payne. He noticed anxiety in both sets of eyes, something that was very atypical for them. "Damn," he groaned. "How big are we talking about?"

"Pretty big," Payne admitted. He tried to smile, but his effort was less-than-successful. "And quite personal."

The comment piqued Shell's interest. "Personal? As in off-the-books personal? As in the-government-doesn't-know-we're-here-but-who-gives-a-rat's-ass-about-them-anyway personal?"

Payne nodded. He knew that Shell got off on this type of stuff, so he was kind of looking forward to his response.

"It's about time we started doing this shit again. I was getting sick of all these military-run missions. It's about time we got the old gang back together and had some fun." He put his arm around Jones' shoulder and smiled. "What's it been, D.J.? Three years?"

Jones nodded his head in agreement but wasn't nearly as enthusiastic as Shell. "Yeah, it's been about that long, but I don't know if 'fun' is the right word to describe this mission. I don't think it's very appropriate."

"Oh, yeah?" Shell laughed, still not understanding the sensitive nature of the assignment. "Then what word would you use?"

Payne took a step forward, the intensity of the Plantation returning to his face. It was a look that Shell had seen several times before, and one that meant it was time to get down to business. "The word that I would use is desperate."

"Desperate?" Shell didn't like the sound of that, especially from a control-freak like Payne. "Did you say desperate?"

"Yeah, Shell, I said desperate, and once I tell you why I called you here, I think you'll understand why."

"*You* called us here?" Shell asked, dumbfounded. "But how

did you pull that off? Nobody's supposed to know where we are, yet you somehow managed to track us down? Don't get me wrong, it's great to see ya, but that doesn't make much sense to me."

Captain Juan Sanchez, the current leader of the MANIACs, cleared his throat and immediately got the attention of Shell. "It doesn't have to make sense to you, Lieutenant, as long as it makes sense to me."

Shell sprang to attention. "Yes, sir. Sorry, sir."

Sanchez winked at Payne, his former team leader, then smiled. "But since you'll bitch the rest of the night if I don't tell you, I'll be a nice guy and let you in on the little secret."

"Thank you, sir. I'm all ears, sir."

"As luck would have it, I stay in touch with Captain Payne on a regular basis, which is apparently more than you do. Anyways, I gave him a call after our last mission, just to see how he was doing, and he let me know what he and D.J. were up against. When he told me that he'd be making a trip to this part of the world, I offered to give up our much-needed R & R in order to help. That is, if it's all right with you."

"Once a MANIAC, always a MANIAC!" Shell shouted, passionately.

"You're damn right," Sanchez stated. He quickly turned his attention from Shell to the man that he faithfully served under for several years. "Captain Payne, at this point in time, I'd like to offer you control of the finest, fiercest, fighting force ever to walk the face of this fucking planet. We are the MANIACs, and we'll follow you and fight with you until death—their death—so help me god!"

Payne nodded in appreciation, then saluted.

It had taken a while, but he finally realized that everything was going to be all right.

* * *

The *Qur'an*, the spiritual text of Islam, requires all Muslim adults to pray five times a day—at dawn (*fajr*), noon (*zuhr*), midafternoon (*asr*), sunset (*maghrib*), and night (*isha*)—to prove their unyielding faith and uncompromising devotion to Allah. But these required sessions are not assigned to a specific hour, making prayer time a very difficult thing to agree upon amongst modern-day Muslims. In order to rectify this problem, most Islamic communities utilize a town crier (*muezzin*) to climb the local mosque tower (or *minaret*) and announce the beginning of each prayer session. When his voice is heard, echoing loudly throughout the streets of the city, all Muslims are expected to stop what they are doing and drop to their knees in prayer.

These breaks are their holy time, periodic moments of forgiveness and thanks. But in Payne's mind, it was also their biggest weakness, for it gave him five daily opportunities to catch the enemy with their guards down. Literally. And he planned to exploit it for all that it was worth.

As nighttime crept over the city, the MANIACs deployed silently along the outer perimeter of the eight-block Kotto Distribution Center, using the shadows as their cover while waiting for their signal to start the assault. Even though Payne had showed them the advantages of this unconventional approach, the twelve soldiers didn't like the lengthy exposure times that they'd have in the field. They were used to invading, dominating, and leaving, but rarely waiting. In this case, though, the MANIACs agreed that the benefits of Payne's master plan far outweighed the negatives. In fact, if all went well, they knew their battle with Kotto's men would be over within seconds, making it, perhaps, the easiest mission that they'd ever been involved with.

Unfortunately, it didn't feel very easy while they waited.

Dressed in black and trying to blend in with the landscape of Ibadan, the soldiers were unable to relax. They were nervous and eager, excited and scared, but not relaxed. Too many things could go wrong for them to be relaxed, especially since the start signal was in the hands of a stranger that they had never worked with before.

No, not Payne. They followed his advice like scripture. In actuality, they were waiting for the *muezzin*, the Islamic crier. They would go on his call, during the Muslims' moment of weakness: when the sun kissed the horizon and the guards least expected an unholy act of violence.

The voice rang out like a tormented wail, soaring from the largest mosque in the city to the smallest homes in the neighborhoods below. The *muezzin's* impassioned plea, like a hypnotic command from Allah himself, sent people dropping to the ground, causing all Muslims to set aside their nightly activities in order to give thanks.

And the MANIACs took advantage of it.

"*Gracias*," growled Payne, who was thankful for the opportunity to burst into the complex with a silenced Heckler & Koch MP5K in his hands. He knew when he reached his assigned territory, a small section in the center where the hostages were supposedly kept, that all of Kotto's guards would be on the floor, praying towards the distant land of Mecca. And once he found them, he would use them for target practice.

Payne was trailed by Jones, Shell, and Sanchez, and their path met no resistance along the way. No guards, no workers, no noise. The place was an industrial ghost town, and the lack of activity suddenly unnerved Payne. In confusion, he drew a large question mark in the air.

Responding in the silent language of the MANIACs, Shell touched his watch, made a counterclockwise motion with his finger, pointed to his eyes, then the room straight ahead. That meant, when he came through earlier, he had seen the guards in the next room.

Payne nodded in understanding.

If Shell's reconnaissance data was accurate, the massacre was about to commence, and it would take place in the chamber they were facing. Their goal was to eliminate as many guards as possible—the plant workers were already out of the building, so they didn't have to worry about innocent bystanders—and rescue the slaves from captivity.

After taking a deep breath, Payne calmly pointed to his watch, his foot, and then his own back-side before glancing back at his partners. The unexpected signal brought a smile to their anxious faces. In MANIAC speak, it meant it was time to kick some ass.

The four men moved forward, looking for the best possible opportunity to begin their assault. Thankfully, that moment occurred the instant they walked in the door. Ten guards, all assembled in the tiny area, were spread across the floor in prayer, each kneeling on individual straw mats while facing their holy city. And unluckily for Kotto's men, that direction was away from the door.

Wasting no time, Payne and Shell crept to the left while Jones and Sanchez slid to the right. Then, once everyone was in a secured position, Payne looked at his friends and nodded.

Pfffft! Pfffft! Pfffft! Pfffft!

Fury rained upon the Posse like a judgment from God, splattering the guards' innards all over the room like a slaughterhouse floor. The tiny bursts of gunfire, practically muffled by the silencers, continued at a rapid pace until the MANIACs were confident that Kotto's men were dead, each sprawled neatly on his very own place mat.

Then, just to be safe, Shell and Sanchez fired some more.

No sense in taking any chances.

When target practice was over, Jones tread through the carnage, inspecting bodies as he moved. After reaching the door, he examined the simple spring lock, then pulled the proper lock-picking device from his pocket. "The infrared that we used earlier proved that this room was full of people. And from what we could tell, there was no sign of weapons. Hopefully, they're who we're looking for."

Payne nodded, praying that Ariane was inside and

unharmed.

It had been nearly a week since he had last kissed her, since he had held her in his arms and confessed his love to her. But it was the first thing he was going to do when he saw her. He was going to grab her and tell her how much he cared, how much she truly meant to him, how lonely he had been without her. She meant the world to him, and he was going to make damn sure she knew it.

"Got it," Jones whispered.

The sound of his partner's voice brought Payne back to reality. After regaining his focus, he quickly moved to the left of the entrance and waited for D.J. to turn the silver handle.

Damn, Payne thought to himself, so much was riding on these next few seconds. His hopes. His dreams. His future family. Everything. Every damn thing came down to the next couple minutes of his life. Everything came down to saving Ariane.

"Jon?" Jones called as he stared into his buddy's vacant eyes. "Where were you just now? I've never seen you like this before."

Payne took a nervous breath before responding. "That's because this shit is personal."

Jones considered the response and nodded. "I know it is. So do me a favor and get your head out of your ass. If you keep dwelling on what's at stake, you'll screw everything up."

Payne couldn't believe what he just heard. He looked at Shell and Sanchez for help, but all they did was nod in agreement. "What are you talking about?"

"You heard me. Remember, you were the one who taught us how to keep our wits during war. Stay loose, you used to say. Joke around. Keep happy thoughts in your head until the mission is at hand, then flip your military switch on. And you know what? It works. But here you are, in the middle of this mission, and you're daydreaming about your woman?" Jones shook his head in disgust. "You need to practice what you preach, man."

Payne gave the lecture a moment of thought and realized

D.J. was right. If he kept thinking about Ariane, he was bound to screw up, and if he did, he was bound to lose Ariane. It was a vicious cycle that he didn't want to be a part of.

"OK. You're right. My head isn't where it should be."

"You're damn right, it isn't. But luckily, for your sake, I'm a loving and forgiving guy." Jones gave his friend a wink and a reassuring nod. "Now, before we go any further, let me ask you one important thing: Are you ready for some football?"

Payne smiled at the Monday Night Football reference. It was time for the big game to begin. "I sure as shit am."

Jones grinned. "Then what are we waiting for? Let's do this."

With a flick of his wrist, Jones swung the door open and calmly waited against the outside wall for gunshots. Payne and the others waited, too, knowing that inexperienced guards often charged forward to investigate the unknown. But when the four men heard nothing—no footsteps, no voices, and no gunshots—they realized they were either facing an elite team of guards or no one at all.

Payne did his best to raise his injured arm and slowly counted down for his men.

Three fingers. Two fingers. One. Showtime.

The MANIACs entered the metal chamber in a classic 2 × 2 formation. Jones slid in first, followed closely by Payne and the others. With their guns in a firing position, the men scoured the room for potential danger, but none seemed present at first glance. The only thing they saw was a scared group of hostages, gagged and tied up in the center of the floor.

"Is there anyone in here?" Jones demanded. "Did they set any traps?"

The heads of the hostages swung from side to side.

Shell and Sanchez didn't take their word for it, though. They carefully searched the corners, the walls, and the exposed pipes of the 20' × 20' metallic room, a room that had the feel of a submarine mess hall, but found nothing that concerned them.

When Shell gave the word, D.J. grabbed his radio and spoke rapidly into the powerful device. "The pigeons have shit, and the statues were hit. Send in the cleaners."

The reply came swiftly. "Cleaners on their way."

But Payne ignored all of that. His mind was on one thing and one thing only: Ariane.

He moved into the group of hostages and instantly recognized their faces from the Plantation boat. He couldn't wait to ask them how they managed to get caught—the last thing he knew they were motoring away from the island—but that would have to wait until after he found Ariane.

Damn! Where was Ariane? Why couldn't he find Ariane?

Out of nowhere, the face of Robert Edwards appeared in the crowd. Payne quickly rushed to his side. He removed the man's gag and attempted to untie his hands. "Are you OK?" he asked. But before he got a response, he continued. "Have you seen Ariane?"

"No," Edwards replied. "Have you seen Tonya? Have you seen my Tonya?"

At that moment, Payne could've kicked himself. Here he was worrying about his own needs when he should've been more concerned about the slaves. They were the ones who had been through the bigger ordeal. Shoot, compared to them, he'd been through nothing.

"Yes, I've seen Tonya, and she's fine, just fine. And the baby's still inside her, right where it should be."

Relief flooded Edwards' face. "Where *he* should be," he corrected. "We're having a boy."

Payne smiled at the information. "Right where he should be."

"And Tonya? Where is she now?"

"Don't worry about her. She's safe. She's in New Orleans, giving a statement to the FBI. And before I left town, I got her an appointment with the best obstetrician in the state. He promised me that she'd be in good hands."

"Thank god," Edwards mumbled.

Payne gave him a moment to collect his thoughts and count his blessings before he continued his questioning. "Robbie, I don't mean to be rude, but . . ."

"How stupid of me. You want to know about Ariane."

"Yes. Have you seen her?"

Edwards nodded. "She was on the plane with the rest of us, but once we landed, the two big guys grabbed her and a male slave and took them somewhere else."

"Two big guys? Was it Holmes and Greene?"

"Yeah, they got ahold of her as soon as we landed."

Payne couldn't believe the news. Why did they single her out from all the others? Was it because of him? Were they planning on torturing her because of his interference with the Posse? God, he hoped that wasn't the case. He prayed that he wasn't the cause of any of her suffering. That would be a tough thing to handle.

"Do you have any idea where they took her? Any at all?"

But Edwards stared at him blankly, unable to offer any help.

Chapter Fifty-One

Friday, July 9th
The Kotto Family Estate
Lagos, Nigeria

Ariane moved with trepidation towards the large man. They had shared a boat to Mexico, a plane to Nigeria, and a train to Lagos, but he had failed to utter a single word during the entire journey—not even when he was handcuffed, drugged, or beaten. It was like his body was there, but his mind wasn't. She hoped to change that, though. She wanted to undo the damage that had been done to him. That is, if he would let her.

"I'm not going to hurt you," she whispered. "I promise I'm not going to hurt you like those other guys. I just want to know your name." She studied his face, hoping to see a blink or a smile, but there was no sign of interaction on his part. "My name's Ariane. What's yours?"

Nothing.

"I heard some of the guards refer to you as Nathan. Is that your real name, or did they just make it up for you?"

Still nothing.

"I like the name Nathan," she said. "I think it's different, kind of sexy. So many people are named Mike or Scott that it gets monotonous. But not Nathan. No, that's a name that people will remember, like you. You're a big guy that people will remember, so you should have a memorable name." She gazed into his eyes, but they remained unresponsive. "What about my name? Ariane? Do you like it? I do, for the same reason that I like yours. It's different. In fact, I've never met another Ariane in my entire life. How about you? Have you ever met an Ariane before?"

For a brief instant, he shifted his eyes to hers, then looked away. It wasn't much, but it was so unexpected she took a step back in surprise.

"Well, I guess that means you haven't." She grabbed his hand and shook it enthusiastically. "Nathan, you can never say that again because we have just officially met."

A large smile crossed her dry lips as she tried to decide what she wanted to say next. "I'd ask for your last name, but I have a feeling that might take a little longer to figure out. Besides, we don't want to get too personal. This is our first date after all."

* * *

Levon Greene sat on the edge of his bed, trying to block out the events of the past few days, but it was an impossibility. Too much had happened to simply forget. Jackson and Webster were dead, murdered by his own hand. The Plantation was history, blown to bits with the touch of a button. And worst of all, he was a fugitive on the run, unable to return to the only city, the only country, where he'd ever wanted to live.

Greene tried to analyze things, tried to figure what went wrong, yet he kept coming up with the same answer over and over again: Payne and Jones. It was their fault. Everything could be traced back to them. If he had just shot them when they met at the Spanish Plaza or killed them while they slept at his house, then none of this would've occurred. The Plantation would still be in business, the second batch of slaves would be in Africa, and Greene would be enjoying a hot bowl of jambalaya in one of his favorite restaurants.

"Fuck," he mumbled in disgust. "I can't believe I let this happen."

With a scowl on his face, Greene trudged from his bedroom and looked for something to alleviate his boredom. Kotto and all of his servants were already in bed, sleeping peacefully in their air-conditioned chambers, but Greene was still on New Orleans time, unable to rest because of the difference in time between the two continents.

As he made his way down the ornate marble staircase, he heard the far-off mumble of an announcer's voice. Intrigued, he followed the sound to Kotto's living room.

"Couldn't sleep?" Holmes asked while glancing up from the game on the big-screen TV.

A smile quickly returned to Greene's lips. "Nah, it's late afternoon in Louisiana. My body won't be ready for bed for another ten hours."

Holmes nodded in understanding. As a mercenary, he'd been forced to work in several different countries, so he knew all about the inconveniences of travel. "Don't worry. Your internal clock will adjust to the sun. You should be good to go by the end of the week."

Greene settled on the couch next to Holmes and sighed. "What about the other stuff? When will I get used to that?"

Holmes raised an eyebrow. "Like what?"

"Food, culture, language, girls."

"Oh," he laughed, "you mean the stuff that makes life worth living. That might take a little bit longer, but I assure you, you'll learn to adapt. Every country has its advantages and disadvantages—if you know where to look."

"I'll believe it when I see it," Greene said while rubbing his knee.

Holmes instinctively glanced at Levon's left leg, staring at the series of gruesome scars that covered it. "So it still troubles you, huh?"

Greene didn't like talking about it, but he realized Holmes was the only American friend that he had left. "The pain comes and goes, but the instability is constant. And the doctors told me as I get older my joint will deteriorate, meaning I'll need knee-replacement surgery. Something to look forward to in my old age, I guess."

Holmes decided there was nothing he could say to soften the stark reality of Greene's future, so he decided to change the subject instead. "Levon, I've been meaning to ask you this for a while now, and since this is the first time we've talked about your knee, I was wondering if I could ask it."

Greene looked at Holmes and smiled. He knew what he was going to ask even before he said it. "You want to know about Nathan, don't you?"

"If you don't mind talking about it."

"Nah, that's fine. You deserve to know. You brought him here for me."

"That's true, but I don't want to overstep—"

"It's fine. Don't worry about it. What do you want to know exactly?"

A thousand questions flooded Holmes' mind, but only one word made it to his lips. "Everything."

A large grin engulfed Greene's face. He'd waited nearly three years to get back at Nate Barker, the player that had ended his magnificent football career. Thirty-three months of pain, rehab, and nightmares. One thousand days of planning and plotting his personal revenge.

"You know, I started to think about Barker as soon as they started wheeling me off of the field. It was amazing. There I was in unbelievable pain, listening to the gasps of horror from the crowd as they replayed the incident over and over on the scoreboard, but for some reason, a great calm suddenly settled over me. You could actually see it during the TV telecast. One minute I was writhing in extreme agony, the next minute I was borderline serene."

Greene shook his head at the clarity of his memory. To him, it felt like it had happened just yesterday. "The team doctor assumed that I had gone into shock, but I'm telling you I didn't. No way. It was Barker, fuckin' Nate Barker. The bastard that did this to me was also the person that softened the agony. I'm telling you, man, one thought and one thought alone allowed me to get through my pain and devastation. It was my thought of revenge."

"So you knew right then that you wanted to get even?"

"Hell yeah. The bastard took away my livelihood. He took away my leg. You're damn right I knew, and I've never regretted it. Never. From the moment we seized him to the moment I locked him in the cage downstairs, I've never looked back. In fact, I view his kidnapping as the crowning achievement of my life."

A bittersweet smile appeared on Levon's dark lips.

"Nate Barker ruined my life, now I'm getting a chance to ruin his."

*   *   *

The loud ringing startled Kotto, causing him to leap from the warmth of his purple comforter with heart-pounding fright. Nightmares had gotten the best of him lately, so he'd been sleeping in a state of uneasiness, flinching at the slightest hint of noise.

Well, the damn phone just about killed him.

After turning on a light, he realized what was happening and grabbed the tiny Nokia off of his nightstand. Few people had his cellular number, so he knew that the call had to be important.

"Kotto," he mumbled, slightly out of breath, his heart still beating abnormally fast.

"Hannibal?" Edwin Drake shrieked. "Thank god you're alive! When I heard the news, I thought perhaps they had gotten you, too."

"Edwin, what the hell are you rambling about? Do you know what time it is?"

"Time, I can't believe you're worried about the time. There are so many other things that we need to be concerned with."

Kotto glanced at his clock. It was nearly midnight. He would much rather be sleeping. "Have you been drinking, Edwin? You're not making any sense."

"Sense? *I'm* not making sense? You're the chap who isn't making any sense—especially since the incident happened in Ibadan."

The fog of sleep lifted quickly for Kotto. There was only one thing in Ibadan that Drake would be concerned with, and the thought of an incident sent shivers down Kotto's spine.

"My god, what has happened?"

Initially, Drake assumed that Kotto was kidding, but he quickly realized it was unlike Hannibal to joke during a time of crisis. "You mean, you haven't heard? It happened at your place for god's sake."

"What did? What's happened?"

"The slaves . . . they're gone!"

The four words hit Kotto like a lightning bolt, nearly stopping his heart in the process. "Gone? How is that possible?"

"Don't ask me. I sent one of my men to inspect the condition of the slaves, and when he got there, there were none. They were gone."

"But that's not possible. If the slaves had escaped, I would've been told. My guards would've called me. These were my best men. They would've called me immediately."

Drake remained silent as he thought about the ramifications of the information. "If these were your best men, Hannibal, then we are in trouble. Very grave trouble."

"Why? Why do you say that?"

"Because your guards are dead. Quite dead."

Lightning bolt number two hit, causing pain in his chest and left arm.

"Dead?" he groaned. "My men are dead."

Drake nodded gravely. "Quite."

"And you're sure of this?"

"Of course I'm sure! I wouldn't be so panicked if I wasn't sure!" Drake tried taking a breath, but his chest was tight as well.

"I'm sorry to doubt you, but it just seems so unlikely. . . . What are we to do?"

"That's why I'm calling you from my plane. I was going to check the plant myself, but since you're alive, I shall tell my pilot to land in Lagos instead. It will be easier to talk if we're face-to-face."

"I'll have my car and several guards meet you at the airport."

"I appreciate the gesture," Drake said, "but I doubt it will be necessary. Who in their right mind would plan a second attack so quickly after their first?"

*   *   *

Jones smirked as he continued to monitor their conversation from a car near Kotto's house. "These guys don't know us very well, do they?"

"No," Payne growled. "We'll have to make sure we introduce ourselves in our own special way."

Chapter Fifty-Two

Edwin Drake opened the front door to Kotto's home without knocking. He had no time to be polite at this time of the evening. All of his hard work was swiftly crumbling, and he was determined to save it before irreparable damage had occurred.

"Hannibal," he called, "where are you?"

The Nigerian rushed from the living room, where he'd been briefing Holmes and Greene on the slaves, and met Drake in the front parlor.

"Edwin," he said as he shook his pasty, white hand. "I'm so sorry that any of this is necessary. I truly am. Obviously, I'm just as shocked about the incident as you are."

"I somehow doubt that," he replied coolly. "It seems that you have been keeping some secrets from me."

The comment caught Kotto off guard. "Secrets? I have no secrets from you."

"No? I find that hard to believe with the information that I just acquired. Who is Jonathon Payne, and why have you been keeping him from me?"

Octavian Holmes heard the name as he emerged from the other room and decided to answer for Kotto. "Jonathon's a Payne-in-our-ass, that's who he is. Now, before I respond to your other question, I've got an even better one for you. Who the fuck are you?"

Drake was ready to spout a nasty comeback until he saw Holmes' size. When he saw an even larger figure approaching behind him, he decided it would be best to play nice. "I'm Edwin Drake, Hannibal's financial partner. And you are?"

"Octavian Holmes, Hannibal's supplier of slaves." He glanced over his shoulder and pointed to his large shadow. "This here is Levon Greene, and he's *my* financial partner."

"Ah, the American footballer. I've heard about you." Drake studied the two men and realized he desperately wanted to stay on their good sides. "Well, it's certainly a pleasure to meet our U.S. connection. I'm glad to see that Hannibal wasn't exaggerating when he told me that our snow was in some rather capable hands. Now that I see you two, I realize he was bloody right."

Kotto remained silent for a brief moment, waiting to see if Holmes responded to the obvious attempt at flattery. When he didn't, Kotto decided to ease the tension. "Edwin has flown in from South Africa in order to discuss the Ibadan incident."

"And to see how you're doing," Drake quickly added. "I know that you've lost a lot of men, Hannibal. You must be in shock."

In truth, Kotto was more stunned by Drake's quick change in tone than by the incident itself. It had gone from accusatory to sympathetic in a matter of seconds. "At first I was, but now that I've had some time to think about it, I'm fine with things. Saddened, but fine."

"Good," Drake stated. "I'm glad to—"

"Enough with the small talk," Holmes ordered. "You said something about Hannibal keeping secrets from you. What's that all about?"

Drake's complexion turned whiter than normal. He wasn't used to being bossed around by anyone. "As I was saying, I just received some information from the States, and it seems that you failed to let me know everything about the incident at the Plantation. You told me that there was some trouble, but you never told me that it was blown up."

All eyes shifted to Kotto, and he squirmed under the sudden spotlight. "It wasn't that I was keeping it from you, Edwin. I was just waiting for the appropriate moment to tell you. I didn't want to tell you on the phone. We've already discussed the danger of that. Besides, I wanted to design a backup plan and have it in place before I broke the news to you. I figured it would ease the shock of it all."

"Actually, it did quite the opposite. Instead of having time to make advanced preparations, I am now forced to deal with everything at once. The Plantation, the missing slaves, the murdered guards. That is a bloody lot to recover from."

"Yes, of course, I see that now. But I obviously couldn't have foreseen the incident at Ibadan. There was no way of knowing that they would find us here so quickly."

Drake winced at the statement. "What do you mean by they? Who are 'they'?"

"They," Holmes answered, "would be Jonathon Payne and David Jones. They single-handedly wiped out the Plantation and probably did the same thing at Ibadan."

"I really doubt that," Drake uttered. "Maybe they were behind the events at the Plantation—you were there, so you would know—but I do not see how they could've handled the Ibadan massacre. There was a variety of shell casings found, not just from one weapon but from several. And unless these are the type of men that would tote five weapons apiece into battle, then they couldn't have done it alone. They needed plenty of help to pull that off. Plenty, I tell you!"

"Damn," Holmes mumbled under his breath. "I hope . . ."

"What?" Kotto demanded. "What do you hope?"

Holmes glanced at Kotto, then at Greene, and both of them were surprised by the look in his eyes. The air of confidence that use to ooze from Holmes like bad cologne suddenly seemed to be gone. No longer did he carry himself with invincibility. In fact, the contours of his face suggested fear.

"I hope I'm wrong about this, but this sounds like the MANIACs."

The comment brought chills to every man in the room.

"Gentlemen," he finished, "I have the feeling that we may have pissed off the wrong guy."

* * *

The semi-tropical landscape gave the soldiers many hiding places as they made their way across Kotto's yard. They'd already eliminated a few of his guards and several of his security cameras, now they were going for his power supply. Once the electricity was cut, they would storm the house in a cloak of darkness.

"Sanchez?" Payne called. "What can you see?"

The captain of the MANIACs was in the midst of an infrared scan of the house, trying to determine the current number of occupants. When he was through, he lowered the hi-tech device and mumbled into his radio's microphone.

"I can't see anyone, sir. It's like the place is devoid of people."

"No one?"

"That's affirmative, sir."

Payne and Jones winced in confusion, trying to figure out where everyone was. The house had been under surveillance for the last several hours, so they knew that there were people inside. A lot of people.

"Sanchez," Jones whispered. "If you can't see anything upstairs, check the basement. Maybe there's something down there."

"I'll try, but the moat that surrounds the house might screw this unit up. It doesn't see well through water."

Payne crept a little bit closer to the house, trying to stay as low as he possibly could. There was no sense risking his life before they knew if Ariane was inside. "Try closer to the drawbridge. The water might be more shallow over there."

"You got it."

Payne and Jones waited while Sanchez attempted to get a better reading, but after more than a minute of scanning, he radioed them back with the bad news.

"Sorry, sirs. He's got something in the basement, but I can't get a readout on the damn thing. It might be a vault or possibly a bomb shelter of some kind, but whatever it is, it's too thick for me to see through."

"Well, keep us posted if anything changes."

"You got it, Captain."

After switching channels on his radio, Payne tried to get an update from Shell, who was in charge of knocking out Kotto's power lines with a small explosion. He remained silent, though, until the device had been set and he had hustled into the nearby trees for safety.

Once there, Shell turned his radio to an all-inclusive frequency and spoke to the entire squad using the tone and mannerisms of a commercial airline pilot. "Ladies and gentlemen, this is your lieutenant speaking. In exactly thirty seconds, we will be experiencing some violent turbulence, so I would advise you to don your nighttime goggles and put your firearms into their locked and upright positions." Shell smiled to himself before finishing. "And as always, thank you for choosing the MANIACs."

20 . . . 15 . . . 10 . . . 5 . . . BOOM!!!

The earth shook violently as the explosion ripped through the power station, tearing the privately owned generator to shreds in one blinding burst of heat and light. Payne and Jones were tempted to glance at the colorful display of sparks but realized it would ruin their night vision for the next several minutes. So they waited patiently, until the shower of orange light subsided and Kotto's entire estate fell under the blanket of a manmade eclipse, before giving the command to move.

Finally, when Payne felt the moment was right, he pushed the button on his transmitter and growled into the microphone, "Gentlemen, it's a go. Don't let me down."

With stealth-like silence, the platoon of soldiers converged on the Nigerian stone mansion and crawled across the structure's moat in groups of two and three, using wooden boards that they had stashed near the water's edge. Windows, doors, and skylights were the next targets on their list, and the MANIACs breached them effortlessly in a series of textbook military maneuvers.

"So far so good," Payne mumbled as he watched the assault from Kotto's yard. "I'd like to be inside, though, where all the action is."

Jones nodded his head in agreement. "Yeah, but there's no way you could've climbed over the moat with that bad arm of yours. And you know it."

"Actually, I *don't* know it. I think if I was given the chance, I could've—"

Jones squeezed his friend's injured biceps in order to prove his point.

"Jesus," he grunted in agony. "You didn't have to do that."

But Payne was secretly thankful that D.J. had, for it reminded him once and for all that he'd made the correct decision by sitting this one out. If he hadn't—if he had been stubborn and insisted on participating in the assault—he would've slowed down the team, and that was something that he couldn't risk. No, at this point the only thing that mattered was Ariane, and everything else—his soldierly pride, his lust for action, and his desire for revenge—paled in comparison.

"I hope you realize there's no reason to feel guilty about your decision. We've accomplished more in the last week than anyone, including myself, could've ever imagined."

Payne didn't respond, choosing to keep his attention on the mission instead.

"Plus, you set a wonderful example for the squad by letting them take over when they did. A man has to know his limits, and when he reaches them, he shouldn't be ashamed to ask for help."

"I know that, D.J. In fact, I might ask for some more of that help right now."

"Really?" The comment surprised Jones. "Why's that?"

Payne took a moment to adjust the focus on his night goggles, then calmly pointed over D.J.'s left shoulder. "Because if I'm not mistaken, I think our targets might've found a way out of the house."

Jones gazed in the direction of Payne's finger and was stunned by what he saw. Levon Greene was standing outside Kotto's iron fence, helping Octavian Holmes climb out of a well-concealed passageway—a tunnel that wasn't mentioned on the blueprints that D.J. had downloaded from a government database.

"Get on the com," Payne said coolly, "and tell Sanchez to send half the team out to secure the periphery. Have the others continue their sweep for the slaves but warn them about the tunnel entrance. I don't want Greene doubling back inside if we can help it."

Jones nodded as he reached for the radio. "And while I do this, what are you going to do?"

Payne smiled as he squeezed the handle of his Glock. "I'm going to play hero."

Chapter Fifty-Three

Using the darkness as his ally, Payne moved as quietly as he could towards the mouth of the tunnel with hopes of eliminating Holmes and Greene before they even knew what hit them. But as he approached the iron fence that surrounded the estate, he soon realized that there was more going on than a simple escape attempt. For some reason, instead of trying to slip away from the house unnoticed, Holmes and Greene were taking the time to smuggle several slaves out of Kotto's house, an act that seemed to defy common sense.

"D.J.," Payne whispered into his headset. "What's your position? I need your input up here."

A few seconds later Jones slipped into the bushes next to him. "You rang?"

"Take a look at this. Does this make any sense to you?"

Jones watched closely as the duo pulled two cloaked slaves from the tunnel and shoved them forcibly to the ground. Then, when Greene was satisfied with their positioning, he went back to the tunnel for two more while Holmes hovered over the first pair with a handgun.

"No sense at all," Jones answered. "They must be up to something, otherwise they'd be heading for the hills by now."

"That's kind of what I figured, but what?"

Jones shrugged at the query. "I don't know, but it has to be something creative. They aren't going to hold us off all by themselves."

"Something creative, huh? See, that's what I can't figure out. What the hell can these guys come up with on such short notice? I mean, it's not like they have a lot of experience with . . ."

Experience. The word sent shivers down Payne's spine, for he suddenly remembered what Holmes and Greene were experienced with. Of course. It made perfect sense. The reason they weren't leaving is because they needed to stay nearby in order to complete their plans—just like they had when they blew up the Plantation.

Without delay, Payne hit the button on his radio and spoke directly to Sanchez. "Juan, get out of the house! Do you read me? Clear the area!"

"But, sir, we haven't completed our main objective. Do you understand? We haven't—"

"Screw your objective, Juan. The house is hot. Get out of there at once."

Several seconds passed before Sanchez replied. "But, sir, Ariane might still be in here."

The notion hit Payne like a sucker punch, temporarily robbing him of his ability to breathe. God, how could he have forgotten about her? How was that possible?

It took him a moment to shake off the guilt—for forgetting about Ariane in her time of need *and* for the command that he was about to issue—but once he thought things through, he realized he couldn't allow his personal feelings to interfere with his duties as squad leader. No matter how much he loved Ariane and how willing he'd be to give up his own life for hers, he knew he didn't have a choice in the matter. This wasn't *Saving Private Ryan.* He couldn't risk the lives of several of his men in order to save one person. That just wouldn't be acceptable, especially since they were here as a personal favor.

So, after taking a deep breath to clear his mind, Payne turned his radio back on and said the most painful thing that he ever had to say. "What is it about my order that you don't understand? Get out of the house now!"

* * *

Greene helped Kotto to his feet then gave Drake a much needed hand. Neither of the businessmen had been thrilled with the idea of sneaking to freedom through the mansion's basement, but once they were assured that it was the only way to get away from the MANIACs, Kotto and Drake relented.

"What now?" asked Drake as he dusted off his white cloak. "Do we make a run for it?"

Greene chuckled at the thought. "A run for it? Do you actually think that you can outrun an entire platoon of soldiers? Fuck that! They'll be no running from anything."

Kotto heard the comment and moved forward. "Then how are we going to get out of here? Is there someone coming to meet us?"

"No," Greene assured him, "there's no one coming to meet us. Octavian and I are going to take care of the MANIACs all by ourselves."

"You're what?" Kotto turned towards Holmes and was greeted by a simple nod. "How in the world are you going to do that?"

"Oh, *we're* not going to do that. Your house is."

"My house is? What kind of rubbish is that?"

Greene smiled devilishly as he reached into his pocket and pulled out a small detonator. "Not rubbish, *rubble*—because that's what your house is gonna be in a couple of seconds. With a touch of this button, your house and our problems are going bye-bye."

* * *

Payne was relieved when the first wave of MANIACs made it across the moat, but they weren't the men that he was truly worried about. No, the group that concerned Payne was group two, the soldiers who were looking for the secret tunnel. Since they were ordered into the bowels of the basement, Payne knew it would take them much longer for them to evacuate the premises.

He just prayed it wouldn't take *too* long.

"All out," declared Shell, who was the leader of the first team. "Should we secure the periphery as ordered, or lag to assist the others?"

"Your orders still hold." Payne wanted everyone as far away from the house as quickly as possible. "Be advised that six people have been spotted outside the fence. Repeat, six outside the fence. And some of them could be friendly."

"Half dozen on the run: some cowboys, some Indians." Shell waved his men forward before continuing his transmission. "Don't worry, sir. We won't let you down."

Payne nodded as he turned towards Jones for an update. "What can you see, D.J.?"

Jones answered while peering through his night goggles. "The two people on the ground seem to be slaves. Greene just kicked the one on the right."

"Can you make out their faces?"

He shook his head. "Their cloaks prevent it, Jon. But if I were a betting man, I'd say the one getting kicked is a man. He's way too big to be a female."

Payne cursed softly at the information. In his mind, that meant the odds of Ariane being inside the house just doubled. "And what about the other?"

"No idea. It could be Ariane, but I really don't know."

"Keep me posted," he said, rising to his feet. "I'm going forward to help Sanchez's crew."

"You're what?"

"You heard me. I'm going to give them a hand. Hell, I'd

lend them two if I could, but one is all I got."

Before Jones could argue, Payne sprinted full speed towards the moat. He wasn't really sure what he'd be able to do once he got there, but there was no way in hell he was going to sit passively while some of his men were in danger. No way. His men were his responsibility, and he was going to do everything he could to guarantee their safety—even if it meant risking his own life in the process.

Once Payne reached the edge of the moat, he cast his eyes downward and studied the 15' × 12' trench which extended for several hundred feet around the base of the entire mansion. The walls of the pit were made of seamless concrete and had been laid with a steep inverse slope to impede the climb of possible intruders. To discourage unwanted visits even further, Kotto had filled the bottom of the chasm with a fresh water stream and a family of Nile crocodiles that hissed and snapped like a pack of hungry guard dogs anytime humans approached.

"Knock it off," Payne growled, "or I'll make shoes out of your ass."

Captain Sanchez heard the comment as he emerged from the house. "I hope you weren't talking to me, sir."

Payne instinctively raised his weapon, but relaxed when he realized who it was. "Sorry to disappoint you, Juan, but I don't want to do anything with your ass."

Despite the tension of the moment, Sanchez smiled as he traversed the narrow plank with the ease of a tightrope walker. He'd risked his life way too many times to be worried about heights or a bunch of hungry reptiles. Finally, after reaching Payne's side, he said, "I don't want to sound disrespectful, sir, but what are you doing up here? You should be back by the fence where it's safe."

"And let you play with the crocs all by yourself? Not a chance. Besides, you know how I am. I'd rather do jumping jacks in a mine field than sit around, waiting."

"But, sir, aren't you just waiting up here, too?"

Payne was tempted to lecture him on the basic concept of leadership—never put anyone in a situation that you're not willing to be in yourself—but before he could, a second MANIAC exited the house.

The soldier immediately said, "Four more behind me, sir, but I don't know where."

Payne nodded as he got on his radio to find out. "Team two status check, team two status check. What's your locale?"

"I'm comin' out now," answered one of the men, and a moment later he stepped outside.

"Making my way up the stairs," replied another. "About fifteen seconds 'til daylight."

Payne waited until the soldier arrived before he went back to the radio. "Team two status check. . . . What are your positions?"

Unfortunately, the two remaining men didn't reply.

Confused by their silence, Payne asked Chen, the soldier who'd just emerged from the house, if he knew anything about their whereabouts.

"It's tough to say, sir. That basement is a labyrinth of empty jail cells and twisting corridors. There's no telling where they are or if they can even hear you down there. The walls are pretty darn thick."

"Damn," Payne growled. He knew if he didn't get his men out of the house soon, they were going to die. It was as simple as that. So out of sheer desperation, Payne used their real names over the airwaves. "Kokoska? Haney? Do you read me? Speak if you guys can hear me."

But the only noise that followed was the deadly sound of silence.

Chapter Fifty-Four

The squawking of Payne's radio disrupted the silence of the Nigerian night, but the message didn't come from either of the missing MANIACs. It came from Jones, and his words were rather ominous.

"The Posse's taking cover. Prepare for detonation."

Without a second thought, Payne ordered his men from the area while he dropped to his knees to secure the wooden plank with his good arm. After locking it in place, he yelled to the soldier on the other side of the moat. "There's no time for crawling, Chen. Run for it!"

The young MANIAC did as he was told and stepped onto the temporary bridge with a quick yet controlled stride. Unfortunately, as he neared the halfway point of the board, the first explosion erupted and its shockwave knocked him forward with the force of a bulldozer. He instinctively tried to catch his balance using his arms as counterweights, but the jolt was way too powerful to overcome.

As Chen fell from the board, Payne was tempted to lunge for him, but he knew it wouldn't do either of them any good. Even if he'd managed to latch on, there was no way he would've been able to maintain his own balance. So, instead of doing something unfeasible, Payne used his energy to yank the board off the far side of the moat while holding onto his end. Agony gripped its sharp claws into his injured biceps as the plank slammed into the water below, but he didn't have time to notice. He knew if he didn't get to the bottom of the chasm immediately, Chen was going to be the only human in a reptilian battle royal.

After making the sign of the cross, Payne grabbed his Glock and sat on the smooth plank, which rested at a 45-degree angle, then started his descent on the kiddie slide from hell. He got a third of the way down the slope when he spotted Chen, who was injured and struggling to get out of the shallow water by the far bank, and the twelve-foot crocodile that was chasing him.

With the confidence of a big-game hunter, Payne aimed his weapon at the croc's head and fired. The bullet struck his target directly below its eye, causing the reptile to roar in agony and thrash its tail like a flag in a violent storm, but that wasn't good enough for Payne. He realized that wounded animals were the most dangerous kind, so the instant his feet touched liquid he finished the job by depositing two more rounds into the angry beast.

"Holy shit!" Chen gasped from the nearby shore. "That was unbelievable."

"Not really," he insisted. "I practice that move in my swimming pool all the time."

"No, sir, *seriously*. Thank you."

But Payne shrugged off the compliment, feeling it was completely unnecessary. After all, Chen was there to do him a favor. "Are you hurt? Can you make it back up the plank?"

"Doubtful, sir. I messed up my knee pretty bad when I landed."

Payne nodded as he scouted the waist-deep water for more crocs. Thankfully, the others huddled lazily on the opposite shore. "But you'll live, won't you? I mean, I shouldn't just leave you here as an entrée, right?"

Chen smiled through his pain. "No, sir. I don't think I'd like that."

"Good, then let's figure a way to get you out of here."

"Sir? Can't you just get someone to lower down a rope and tie it around my waist?"

Payne shook his head as he crawled onto the bank next to Chen. "I wish we could, but—"

Before he finished his statement, a second explosion ripped through the house, one that lit the surrounding sky with a massive ball of flame and hurled chunks of wood and metal high into the air. To escape the falling debris, Payne shoved Chen under the lip of the concrete ledge and sheltered him with his own body while waiting for things to calm down.

"Does that answer your question?" he yelled into the soldier's ear. "I get the feeling that we might be on our own for a little while."

*   *   *

Jones covered his head as the blast shook the earth but refused to take his eyes off the Posse. They had settled behind a large rock formation near the escape tunnel, and he figured they'd stay there as long as there were more charges to detonate. At least he hoped that was the case, for while they sat on their asses watching the fireworks, his team was moving in to finish them off.

"Can . . . read . . ?" trickled a static-filled message over Jones' radio, but he was unable to make out the voice. ". . . you . . ."

"You're breaking up," Jones shouted into his mouthpiece. "Please repeat."

There was a slight delay before he heard the voice again. "D.J., this is Payne. Can . . . me? Over."

"Jon?" He cupped his hand over his earpiece so he could hear better. "Is that you?"

"Of course . . . me! I can't . . . you've already forgotten . . . fuckin' voice!"

Jones was thrilled that Payne was bitching him out, for that was his way of saying that he was all right. "Where are you? I was told you got caught up in the pyrotechnics."

"I did. Thankfully, Chen and . . . were . . . the moat during . . . big blast. The concrete shielded . . . getting hurt."

Jones did his best to make out the words, but the tumult and the static made it difficult to understand. "Are you hurt? Do you need me to send someone to get you out?"

". . . banged up, but I'm . . ." Dead air filled the line for a few seconds before Payne's voice could be heard again. ". . . word on Ariane?"

"We're still not sure where she is, Jon. Shell called in a moment ago and claimed he saw a female with the Posse, but that report is unconfirmed. Repeat, that is unconfirmed."

". . . about . . . oska . . . Haney?"

"No, there's been no word from Kokoska or Haney. We aren't giving up hope, though. Those two have been through worse."

Several more seconds passed before Jones could hear him again, and when he could, Payne was in the middle of a long message. ". . . is a hole up . . . it might be . . . way into . . . I'm going to . . . Chen . . . it out."

"Jon," he shouted, "you're breaking up. I can't understand you. Please repeat."

". . . hole . . . moat . . . a way into the . . ."

Unfortunately, nothing but static filled their lines from that point on.

* * *

Payne wasn't sure if his message had gotten through, but he realized he couldn't waste any more time on the radio trying to find out. He and Chen were currently sitting ducks, and he knew if they stayed put, it was just a matter of time before something—an explosion, a crocodile, or possibly an enemy soldier—took them out.

"I know you're kind of banged up, but how does a nice long walk sound to you?"

Chen looked at Payne in the flickering firelight and grimaced. "You tell me, sir. How does a long walk sound?"

"Like just what the doctor ordered." Payne slipped his good arm around the soldier's waist and helped him to his feet. "And don't get any wrong ideas, Chen. This isn't going to be a romantic stroll. That last blast opened a fissure in the wall up ahead, and I'm hoping it'll lead to somewhere safe."

The duo trudged through the waist-deep stream for several yards while keeping a constant eye out for crocs. Luckily, the giant reptiles were just as uninterested in a skirmish as the MANIACs were.

"OK," Payne said once they'd arrived at the crevice. "Let me check things out before we try to get you in there. Will you be all right for a few minutes on your own?"

Chen nodded as he slumped to the ground, exhausted.

"Just holler if something starts to eat you."

"Don't worry. I think that's probably the natural reaction."

Payne grinned as he checked his weapon for readiness, then leaned inside the cave-like opening that extended from water level to nearly three feet above his head. Unfortunately, the darkness of the interior prevented him from seeing much, so he was forced to use one of the chemical torches that he carried in his belt. After breaking the cylinder's inner seal, he gave the two liquids a quick shake, and the phosphorescent mixture suddenly filled the manmade grotto with enough light to read a newspaper.

"I'll be right back," he told Chen. "Don't go anywhere."

By using the green glow of the hi-tech lantern, Payne was able to figure out what he had stumbled upon: It was the tunnel that the Posse had used to escape. The cylindrical shaft started somewhere to his right, deep within the bowels of Kotto's basement, and continued to his left, ending somewhere outside the fence on the western flank of the estate. Or at least it used to. Because of all the recent explosions, Payne had no idea if the route was still passable. He hoped it was since he and Chen were looking for a way out of the moat, but he realized he wouldn't know for sure until he explored the mysteries that waited further ahead.

Chapter Fifty-Five

Holmes and Greene laughed with child-like enthusiasm as the first few explosions tore through the house, for in their minds every blast meant a few less soldiers that they'd have to deal with. Plus, they realized if the second part of their plan was going to be successful, they had to keep the number of MANIACs to an absolute minimum.

"Are you bloody sure that this is going to work?" Drake wondered from his position on the ground. "I mean, if these troops are as skilled as you claim, will they really be fooled by something so foolish?"

The comment knocked the smile off Holmes' face. He'd known Edwin Drake for less than a few hours, but in that small amount of time, he'd learned to despise the man. "I'll tell you what, Eddie. If you don't want to participate in phase two of my plan, you can take off your cloak and start walking. It won't make a damn bit a difference to me."

"I didn't mean to offend you," he insisted. "But—"

"But what? You call my plan 'foolish,' then claim you didn't mean to offend me? Fuck that, and fuck you! If you keep it up, I'll put a bullet in your English-muffin ass myself."

The smile on Greene's face got even wider, for he disliked Drake as much as Holmes did. "So what's it gonna be, Eddie? Are you in or out? We gotta know now."

Drake glanced at Kotto for some moral support, but none was forthcoming. Kotto had just watched his house detonated for the sake of the plan, so he wasn't about to give up on Holmes and Greene's idea anytime soon.

"Fine," Drake relented. "What would you like me to do?"

"Just lie there quietly until Levon and I change our clothes," Holmes growled. "When it's time to do something else, we'll let you know."

* * *

Payne helped Chen inside the tunnel and made him as comfortable as possible before he headed west in hopes of finding an exit. Yet what he found was much more exciting.

He traveled less than twenty yards down the concrete shaft when he noticed the artificial light of his lantern start to burn brighter than it had just seconds before. Much brighter. At first he figured the chemical compound in his torch was simply heating up, but after a few more steps, he realized that the added radiance wasn't actually coming from him. The extra burst of light was shining from somewhere up ahead.

Concerned by the possibilities, Payne hid his light in his pocket, then inched silently towards the source of the phantom glow. With weapon in hand, he crept along the smooth edge of the wall until he came to an anomalous bend in the tunnel. For some reason the passageway turned sharply to the left, then seemed to snake back to the right almost instantly—perhaps to avoid a geological pitfall of some kind—but whatever the purpose, Payne concluded that the epicenter of the foreign light was somewhere in that curve.

After pausing to collect his thoughts, Payne reached into the leather sheath that hung at his side and pulled out a 12-inch hunting blade that had once belonged to his grandfather. Even though it was nearly fifty years old, the single-edged bowie knife was sharp enough to cut through a tree and sturdy enough to be used in hand-to-hand combat, something that Payne had proven on more than one occasion. In this case, though, it possessed a less obvious attribute that he hoped to take advantage of: its mirror-like finish.

By extending the weapon forward, Payne hoped to see what was lurking around the corner without actually exposing himself to gunfire. Sure, he knew he wouldn't be able to see much in a simple reflection, but he figured if he was able to get a glimpse of what was waiting for him, he'd be better prepared to face it.

"Show me something good," he whispered to the knife.

And surprisingly, it did.

Payne couldn't tell how many people were gathered up ahead—they were huddled too close together for him to get an accurate count—but it didn't take a Master's degree in criminology to figure out who they were: They were escaped slaves, part of the *original* Plantation shipment that had been sent to Nigeria several weeks before Ariane had even been abducted. People that . . .

Wait a second, he suddenly thought. If these were actually escaped slaves, what were they doing sitting in this tunnel? If they'd somehow gotten free from Kotto's house, why weren't they running down this passageway towards the outside world? Common sense told him that's what they should be doing. And what was keeping them so damn quiet? Were they afraid to speak, or was there an outside factor that was keeping them silent? Something, perhaps, like an armed guard? That would explain a lot, he reasoned. Plus it would also clarify the presence of their light. Payne figured if the slaves were hiding, trying to avoid capture by the Posse, then they certainly wouldn't be dumb enough to use a lantern. That would be an obvious giveaway in this deadly game of hide-and-seek.

No, he eventually decided, the slaves' silence coupled with their ill-advised use of a light suggested one thing and one thing only: This was a trap. Someone was trying to get these people noticed, hoping that someone would rush forward to secure them, and when they did, ZZZZTT! They'd get fried like a mosquito in a bug zapper.

Thankfully, Payne was way too intelligent to fall for such an obvious ploy—especially since he'd taught the maneuver to many of his men during their initial training. And since he'd taught the tactic, Payne knew exactly how to beat it.

"Yoo-hoo," he yelled. "Come out, come out, wherever you are."

Several seconds passed before Payne heard the reply he was expecting.

"Captain Payne?" shouted Haney, one of the missing MANIACs. "Is that you?"

"It sure is, princess. I've come to rescue you from the evil dungeon. Are you alone?"

"No, Kokoska's with me, but he's unconscious. He took a bump on the head during the first blast and has been fading in and out ever since."

Despite Haney's assurances, Payne moved forward cautiously, just in case he was overlooking a foot snare or something even more diabolical. "And the prisoners? Where'd you find them?"

"In a basement cage. Can you believe that shit? They'd be buried under tons of rubble right now if we hadn't gotten to them in time. The assholes were just planning on leaving 'em in there with tiny bombs strapped to their legs."

"Tiny bombs? Were they silver?"

"Yeah." Haney finally showed his face and held up one of the devices to prove his point. "How'd you know their color, sir?"

Payne grabbed the explosive with disgust. "They used the same thing on the Plantation."

After taking a few seconds to examine the mechanism, Payne turned towards the hostages and offered them a smile, trying to reassure them that they'd somehow survived this ordeal and their lives were about to return to normalcy. None of them smiled back, though—which, of course, wasn't surprising. As a group, they'd been through so much in such a short amount of time Payne knew it would take more than a smile for any of them to start trusting the world again. He realized it would take love and friendship and a shitload of therapy to get them back on track, but he prayed that they'd all be able to get over this eventually.

"Sir?" Haney blurted. "What's the status topside? Did everyone make it out OK?"

Payne shook his head as he snapped back to reality. "Chen's resting in the tunnel behind me. He took a nasty fall into the moat, but he'll live."

"And Ariane? What about her? Did she get out all right?"

Payne took a deep breath. "That still remains to be seen."

"Sir?" he asked, slightly confused.

"Don't get me wrong, Haney. She made it out before the blast. I'm sure of that. But if my guess is correct, there's still some loose ends that need to be taken care of before she'll be free." Payne looked down at his knife and studied the austere killer that glanced back at him from the gleaming metal. "Thankfully, loose ends are my specialty."

* * *

Jones tried to reestablish contact with Payne but met with little success. Finally, with no more time to spare, Jones decided to change his priorities and forge ahead without him—something he'd actually done on dozens of missions in the past. The truth was that Payne had a history of flying solo, doing his 'Batman thing' as the squad liked to put it. He never knew why they called it that until D.J. pointed out that Jon Payne sounded similar to Bruce Wayne, and the joke kind of blossomed from there. Whatever the reason, the truth was that Jones was used to stepping in and providing leadership when the squad required it.

"Team one," Jones muttered into his headset, "what's your status?"

Shell answered, "We've got the Indians surrounded. We can move in on your word."

"Good. And what's the risk to the cowboys?"

"Higher than it was a moment ago, sir. Much higher."

The comment bothered Jones, who'd lost visuals on Holmes and Greene a few minutes before. "Please explain."

"The Indians have put on cowboy hats, sir. Repeat, the Indians now look like cowboys."

That meant Posse members were now wearing the same clothes as the others—which in this case meant long white cloaks and hoods that covered their faces.

"Give me the numbers, Lieutenant. How risky are the odds?"

"Let's just say I wouldn't bet my dog on 'em, sir." Shell paused to speak to one of his men before he continued his transmission. "By our count, we're looking at three chocolate and three vanilla, and one of the vanillas is definitely a woman. Furthermore, two of the chocolates have been super-sized, if you catch my meaning."

"The big ones are probably Holmes and Greene. They're the ones we want the most."

"I know that, sir, but here's the problem: Their size doesn't stand out anymore."

"What? How's that possible?"

"The six have gathered in a fairly tight cluster, so it's tough to tell where one person ends and the next begins."

"In a cluster? How badly do they blend, Lieutenant?"

"It's kind of like looking at a giant marshmallow, sir."

Jones cursed to himself before he got back on the line. "So what are you telling me? No go on the snipers?"

"That's affirmative, sir—unless, of course, you can put out that goddamn fire. It's messing up our ability to see."

"It's what? How so, Lieutenant?"

"The frontal glare prevents our night goggles from working properly, and without 'em, our snipers just don't have enough light to shoot."

Jones couldn't believe what he was hearing. Each man was equipped with enough optical equipment to see a lightning bug fart from a half-mile away, but they couldn't see a 275-pound man in the light of a raging inferno. "Let me get this straight: You're telling me it's too bright and too dark for you at the *exact same time*?"

Shell nodded at the paradox and grinned. "Ain't it a fucked-up world we live in, sir?"

*　　*　　*

When he reached the end of the passageway, Payne gazed through the wall of vines that obscured the tunnel's presence from the outside world and studied the scene before him. The six people who'd escaped through the corridor were now dressed identically and standing in a compact huddle—their arms around each other's shoulders and their heads tilted forward in order to obscure each other's height.

"Damn," he growled. Even from point-blank range, there was no way he could risk a shot.

"D.J.," he whispered into his radio, "where are we positioned?"

Jones smiled at the sound of Payne's voice. He knew his best friend would pop up eventually. It was just a matter of when. "We're in a semi-circle with a radius of twenty yards. We'd surround them completely, but the fence cuts off their route to the east so there's no need."

"Have they attempted to make contact?"

"No, which is kind of puzzling. They obviously know we're out here, but they haven't come forward with any demands."

"Yeah," Payne admitted, "that's kind of strange. Almost as strange as their formation. I've never seen anything like it before."

"Me, neither. . . . So, just out of curiosity, where are you right now?"

"Me? I'm about ten feet to their rear, watching them from the door to the escape tunnel."

"Did you say you're *in* the tunnel?" Jones shook his head in amazement, stunned at Payne's ability to turn up in the damnedest of places. "How in the world did you pull that off?"

"Long story. Oh, and just for the record, I stumbled upon our missing brethren. They're a little banged up, but still very much alive."

"Thank god! I was worried about them. Any need for emergency evac?"

"Nah, they'll be fine until this crap is over. By the way, how are *you* planning on ending it?"

Jones laughed at Payne's choice of words. Both of them knew who was going to end things, and it certainly wasn't going to be Jones. "Thankfully, that's not my decision, Jon. Now that you're back as team leader, I can sit back, relax, and watch you work your magic."

"It's funny you should mention magic because that's exactly what I had in mind. With a little help from you, I think we can make the Posse disappear."

Chapter Fifty-Six

Jones waited for Payne's go-ahead before he left the safety of his hiding place and walked towards the enemy. After scaling Kotto's fence with the agility of a cat burglar, Jones continued his approach while doing absolutely nothing to conceal himself. In fact, he so desperately wanted to be seen by Holmes and Greene that he fired his weapon several times into the air just to get their undivided attention.

"You know," he exclaimed, "you guys are pretty damn bad at taking hostages. For this type of tactic to work, you're supposed to issue a crazy list of demands. Well, I've been waiting for several minutes now, and I haven't heard a peep out of any of you. Why the hell is that?"

Greene's bass-filled voice suddenly emerged from the center of the huddle. "That's 'cause we've been waiting for you, my nigga. Now that you're here, I guess we can start this shit."

"Oh, goody," Jones mocked. "But before we begin, I think it'd only be fair if I introduced you to the rest of my negotiating team. Fellas, why don't you come on out and say hello?"

Like battle-hungry warships emerging from a sea of fog, the MANIACs simply materialized out of nothingness. One second they weren't visible to the naked eye, and the next they were, standing with weapons raised like bloodthirsty gladiators welcoming an approaching horde.

"As you can see, we outnumber you by a very large margin."

"What, is that supposed to scare us?" Holmes screamed, his head bobbing ever so slightly as he did. "Shit! You might outnumber us, but there's no way you can shoot us without endangering one of the hostages. And trust me, if you guys come any closer, I'll kill one of 'em myself."

Jones smiled at the threat and took another step forward. "See, I don't believe that for a second. Why? Because if you hurt anyone, you'll be killed. I know it, and you know it. Hell, everyone here knows it. So why even bother to threaten us? It's just so clichéd."

"Maybe so, but it's the truth. I wonder how Payne would feel if I sliced up that tasty bitch of his? How do you think he'd like that?"

"That's a pretty good question. Why don't you ask him yourself?"

"I would, if he showed his punk-ass face. Where's that pussy hiding anyway?"

Payne answered the question by tapping Holmes on the shoulder with his bowie knife. "Right behind you, stud."

Like a well-orchestrated magic trick, Payne had used his assistant to lure everyone's attention forward while the key maneuvering—his silent approach—was actually being done in the background.

Of course now that the deception was over, Payne needed to finish the performance in grand style, and he did so by sliding his blade across his enemy's throat in assassin-like perfection.

Crimson instantly gushed from Holmes' carotid arteries, staining the front of his lily-white cloak like a wounded deer dying in a snow bank, but that wasn't good enough for Payne. He immediately tossed Holmes over his shoulder with the dexterity of a judo champion, then finished him off by falling backwards and slamming his elbow into the bridge of his nose, a maneuver that drove Holmes' nasal bone into his brain with the brutal efficiency of an ice pick.

Death was instantaneous.

With one rival vanquished, Payne sprang to his feet with an arching back flip and searched the huddle for his next target. Unfortunately, he was too slow for Greene who'd latched onto Ariane's throat while shoving a .45-caliber pistol against the side of her head.

"Stay back," Greene demanded as he dragged her towards the tunnel. "I swear to god if you bastards come any closer, I'll kill her."

"Calm down," Payne pleaded. "Don't do anything stupid. Just relax."

But Payne knew that would be tough since he was having a difficult time doing it himself. A *real* difficult time.

Surprisingly, Payne had been a rock—totally poised and relaxed—when he crept up on Holmes, but all of his composure seemed to vanish when he got his first real glimpse of Ariane since this ordeal had started. God, one look was all it took, leaving him more flustered than he'd been the first time they'd met—and back then he was a gibbering tub of goo. She meant so much to him and had become such an integral part of his happiness that he simply couldn't imagine his life without her. And now that her life was in his hands, he was hardly able to handle it.

But Payne knew he had to try, for their sake.

After taking a deep breath, he managed to ask the most important question that he could think of. "Are you all right?"

"Been better. And you?"

"Pretty damn good," he lied. "I've been trying to get ahold of you, though. You're a difficult girl to track down."

"Sorry about that. I've been doing some traveling."

"Traveling?" Payne took a step closer, looking for the smallest of openings to exploit, but he decided it wasn't worth the risk. "Come on, why don't you just admit it? You'll do anything to get out of a butt-kicking on the golf course."

"Darn, you finally figured me out. All of this has just been one big setup."

"You know, I had a feeling—"

"Will you shut the fuck up?" Greene finally yelled. "Your lovesick banter is driving me crazy." To prove his point, he tightened his grip on Ariane's neck, nearly cutting off her airway in the process. "This is my time to talk, not yours. Do you got that, Payne? My time."

"OK, OK, I'm sorry. Go ahead and talk. I'm listening. I swear."

Greene took a deep breath. "First of all, tell your men to get back. When I get anxious, my muscles start to contract, and if that happens, I'm liable to break her fuckin' neck."

"Not a problem, Levon. I'll tell 'em. But first you gotta ease up just a little bit. Let her breathe, my man. Just let her breathe."

"I'm serious, Jon. Get them back now."

"I will, I promise, but only if you stop hurting her." Payne took another step forward, trying to get as close to Greene as he possibly could. "Come on, Levon, why don't you just put down your gun and walk away? I promise, if you do that, we won't kill you."

"Great! So what are you going to do instead? Cart me back to the U.S. where I'll be viewed like Charles Manson? Screw that! I get out of this free, or I get slaughtered right here, right now. There's no quit in me, Payne. None! You should know that. I don't quit."

Another step forward. "It's not quitting, Levon. It's simply the smart thing to do."

"Stay where you are, or I'll kill her. I mean it!"

Payne finally threw his hands up in acceptance. "I won't move from here, OK? I just want to talk to you, I swear. Don't do anything stupid. I just want to discuss things."

"Then get your men to back off!" The tension in his voice proved that he was dangerously close to losing it. "What difference does it make if they back up? They'll still be close enough to kill me if I make a move, right? So get them to back up."

Payne looked at Jones and reluctantly nodded. "Not too far, D.J., but ease the grip slightly."

"You heard the captain. Give them ten more feet of breathing space. But if Greene even looks like he's going to sneeze, take him out."

Like a giant game of Simon Says, the men followed orders, dropping back several steps but never taking their aim off of Greene's head. When they finally reached their magical mark, Jones shouted for them to stop.

"Is that better?" Payne asked. "I did like you wanted as a sign of good faith. I didn't have to, but I did. Now why don't you do the same for me? Why don't you give me something back?"

"Like what? The only thing you want is this girl right here, and you know what? I can see why she means so much to you. I had a chance to check her out in the shower, and let me tell you, mmm, mmm, mmm. She's one tasty piece of ass."

Normally, Payne would've gone after somebody who made a comment like that, but in this case he all but welcomed it because he saw it as a unique opportunity.

"Jeez," he said to Ariane, "you should consider yourself lucky. You've always wanted to hook up with an NFL player, and he sounds interested. This might be your big chance."

Calmly, as if she wasn't in a life-or-death struggle, Ariane turned her attention to Greene. She wasn't sure why, but she knew that she was supposed to distract him with conversation. "You played in the NFL? Oh my god, that is so cool. What's your name?"

But before Greene could speak, Payne answered for him. "That's Levon Greene. The Buffalo Soldier. I told you about him, remember? He's the linebacker I met while playing basketball. You know, the one with the bad left knee."

"You have a bad knee?" she groaned. "How horrible! That's one thing I always hated about sports. Not only the injuries, but also the strategy that goes along with them. The moment a player gets hurt, their opponents always try to take advantage of it. Always."

And then she proved her point.

By bending her leg forward, Ariane was able to raise her left foot until it was directly in front of Greene's damaged joint. Then, after a short pause, she thrust it backwards with as much strength as she could generate, ramming it into his kneecap at a perfect angle. The pain from the blow caused Greene to howl in immediate agony, but more importantly it caused him to loosen his grip on Ariane's neck.

The instant she hit the ground Payne raised his weapon like a quick-draw artist from the Old West and fired. Jones did the same from farther back, and the two of them filled Greene with enough bullets to take down a grizzly. Shot after shot entered his chest and neck, which caused his body to dance to the rhythm of gunfire, until both of them had emptied their entire clips into the man that they had once considered a friend.

When the firing finally stopped, the MANIACs charged forward to deal with Kotto and Drake and the slaves that remained in the tunnel, but Payne wasn't worried about any of them. His only concern was Ariane, and he ran to her side to see if she was all right.

"Oh my god, I'm so happy to see you."

"I love you so much," she insisted, crying tears of joy on Payne's shoulder. "I really do. I can't believe that you found me." She sobbed for an entire minute, clinging to him like a favorite stuffed animal. "But what took you so long? I thought you were supposed to be good at this."

Payne laughed loudly, thanking god for a girl who was able to keep her sense of humor despite all that she'd been through. "You said you were looking forward to a long weekend, so I figured I should take my time in getting here."

"A long weekend is one thing, Jonathon, but an entire week is quite another."

He chuckled, wiping away his tears with her cloak. "Look on the bright side. It's already Friday, so by the time we get back to America, it'll actually be the weekend again."

Ariane sighed as she pulled his muscular body against her chest. She never wanted to let go of him. Ever.

Jones was hesitant to break up the tender moment, but he needed Payne to decide what they were going to do with Kotto and Drake. "If you don't mind," he said, "I'd like to borrow Jon for a minute before you two start shagging on the damn ground."

Ariane glanced at Jones and tried to give him a warm smile, but her sore jaw made it tough. She knew that he'd risked his life for hers on several occasions during the past week and wanted him to realize how much she appreciated it.

"He's all yours, D.J. There'll be no shaggin' until I get cleaned up." She let go of Payne, but gave him a quick wink as she moved to her knees. "Besides, I wanted to check on someone anyways."

Payne raised his eyebrows in surprise. "Did you make a new friend in prison? Ah, how cute."

She tried to smile again. "I think his name's Nathan, but that's all I really know." With Jones' assistance she climbed to her feet, and then gave him a quick peck on his cheek for the trouble. "He doesn't like to talk much, but I'm trying to change that."

Payne clambered to his feet as well, but opted not to kiss Jones. "Big guy, lots of scars? Yeah, he was in the Devil's Box right before me. That bastard Hakeem said he'd left him in there for several weeks. Unfortunately, I have no idea who he is, though."

"I do," interjected Sanchez, who'd been listening to their reunion from afar. "I'm from San Diego, so I should know who he is."

All three turned towards him, looking for information.

"His name's Nate Barker, and he plays for the Chargers. According to ESPN, he's been missing for a few months now, simply disappeared from mini-camp one night."

"Are you sure?" Payne asked. It seemed kind of risky for the Posse to kidnap someone that was semi-famous. "Why in the world would they grab a high-profile guy like that?"

Sanchez offered an explanation. "If I remember correctly, he's the player that originally hurt Levon's knee. Snapped it like a twig up in Buffalo."

Payne glanced back and studied Barker's haggard appearance. He certainly had the height to be a football player, even though it was painfully obvious that he'd lost a lot of weight during the past several weeks. "So, this was all done for revenge? My god, what a sick bastard Levon turned out to be. I would've never guessed it before all of this shit started to—"

"Sirs!" Shell shouted. He was on his knees near Greene's body, and the look on his face suggested that something was seriously wrong. "Get over here, sirs!"

Payne, Jones, and Sanchez dashed forward.

"It's Greene," Shell said. "The bastard was wearing a vest under his cloak, so he's still alive."

"What?" Payne sank to the ground next to Shell and looked into Greene's eyes. Surprisingly, they were open and fairly active for his current condition. "Levon, can you hear me?"

Greene nodded his head ever so slightly, as blood gushed from the wounds in his neck and shoulders. "You got me, Payne. You got me good."

"I didn't get you, Levon. You got yourself. I can't believe you did all this for revenge. I can't believe you threw your whole life away for such petty bullshit."

Greene closed his eyes to escape the agony, but managed to turn his lips into a smile. "No regrets," he groaned. "I got no regrets."

Payne was ready to lecture him further when he suddenly sensed a large presence hovering behind him. Looking up, he was surprised to see the battered body of Nate Barker.

"Levon," the lineman croaked. His throat was dry and

cracked from severe dehydration.

Greene reopened his eyes and stared into the face of his sworn enemy.

Barker leaned closer, letting Greene see his face. "That play where you got hurt? I didn't try to hurt you. I swear, I didn't."

But Greene wouldn't accept it. He quickly closed his eyes and shook his head in denial.

It wasn't something that he'd ever believe.

"Honestly," Barker continued. "I've never hurt anyone on purpose in my entire life. I swear to god, I haven't." Then suddenly, without warning, he placed his foot on Greene's left femur and anchored it under his substantial weight. "That is, until now."

With all of his remaining strength, Barker grabbed Greene's lower leg and pulled it upwards, tugging and yanking on the limb until the weakened joint literally exploded from the excess stress. The loud popping of tendons and cartilage was quickly accented by Greene's screams of pain, which sent shivers down the spines of everyone in the area.

But Barker was far from done. With a devious grin on his face, he lifted his foot off of Greene's leg and slammed it into the middle of Greene's throat. He'd been put through so much over the past several weeks there was no way he was going to stop.

No fuckin' way.

Not until *his* revenge was complete.

Not until *he* felt vindicated for *his* pain.

And no one in the area had any desire to stop him.

Epilogue

Saturday, July 17th
Tulane University Hospital
New Orleans, Louisiana

The door was closed and the room was dark, but that didn't stop Payne and Jones from entering. Hell, they'd broken so many laws in the past few weeks they weren't about to let visiting hours—or the heavyset nurse at the front desk—stand in their way.

Not with something as important as this to take care of.

"So," Payne growled as he approached the bed. "Did you actually think we were going to forget about your role in this? Huh? Did you?"

The injured man didn't know what to say, so he simply shrugged his shoulders.

"Jesus," Jones cried. "You can't be that stupid. What, are you a buckwheat or something?"

The comment brought a smile to Bennie Blount's heavily bandaged face. "I didn't know what to think," he whispered. "I haven't seen you guys since my accident."

Payne placed his hand on Blount's elbow and gave it a squeeze. "We're sorry about that, Bennie. We would've been here much sooner, but we've been tied up in red tape. Of course, that tends to happen when you sneak into a foreign country and kill a bunch of people."

Jones shook his head in mock disgust. "The Pentagon and all its stupid policies. Please!"

Blount laughed despite the pain it caused in his cheeks.

"So," Payne continued, "I understand the swelling around your spinal cord has gone down considerably. How's your movement been?"

"Pretty good. I'm still a little wobbly when I walk, but the doctors think I'll be fine."

"That's great news, Bennie. I've been worried sick about you."

"Me, too," added Jones.

"Of course my big concern now is my face. That crazy dog did a lot of damage."

Payne gave Blount's elbow another squeeze. "Well, stop worrying about it. I'm flying in the world's best plastic surgeons to treat you, so trust me, they'll have you back to your old self in no time."

Jones nodded. "Unless, of course, your old self isn't good enough. They could make you look like Denzel, or Will Smith, *or* give you a nice set of D-cups. Whatever you want."

Payne frowned. "Do you think his frame could support D-cups? I'd say no more than a C."

"Really? I think he'd look good with—"

"Forget the implants," Blount laughed. "My old self will be fine, just fine. But . . ."

"But what?" Payne demanded. "If you're worried about the money, don't be. All of your hospital bills have already been taken care of."

"What?" he asked, stunned. "That's not necessary, Jon."

"Of course it is. After all you've sacrificed, I wouldn't have it any other way."

"Listen to him, Bennie. Even with a truckload of insurance, you'd still have tons of out-of-pocket expenses."

"Yeah, but . . ."

"But, nothing," Payne insisted. "Furthermore, you'll never see another tuition bill for the rest of your life. As soon as you're feeling up to it, you can head back to school and finish your degree, compliments of the Payne Scholarship Fund. We'll take care of everything—including a monthly stipend for beer and hookers."

Blount's eyes doubled in size. "Jon, I couldn't. Seriously."

"Hey," Jones added, "he's not the only one bearing gifts. I have something for you, too." He pulled out a small box and handed it to Blount. "Now I might not be as wealthy as Daddy Warbucks over there, but as soon as I saw this, I knew I had to get it for you. And it's a limited edition, so there are only three others like it in the entire world."

"What is it?" Blount wondered as he rattled the package next to his bandaged ear.

"Well, why don't you open it and find out?"

"Go on," encouraged Payne. "It won't bite you."

Jones covered his mouth and tried not to smile, but the inside joke was just too damn funny. Soon, Payne joined him in loud laughter.

"Am I missing something here?" asked a bemused Blount.

"No," Jones howled, "but Tornado is."

Perplexed, Blount looked at the box, then glanced at Payne, then looked back down at the box. "Oh god," he groaned as things started to sink in, "you didn't."

"Hey," Jones argued while trying to keep a straight face. "It's not as sick as you think. Thousands of people own rabbit's feet for good luck, so I figured, What the hell? A dog, a rabbit. What's the difference?"

"What's the difference?" Blount chuckled, despite his mixed feelings on the subject. "I'll tell you the difference. If I'd been attacked by a rabbit, I don't think I'd be sitting here waiting to see an entire team of plastic surgeons."

"That's true," Jones admitted. "On the other hand, think of all the ladies you'll be able to attract with that thing. God, if you play your cards right, beautiful women will be fighting to be by your side for the rest of your life. You're a hero, Bennie, and that will be your proof."

Blount considered Jones' words for several seconds before he finally spoke. "I don't know about that, D.J. I really doubt women are going to want to meet me because I have this paw."

"That's where you're wrong," Payne said as he strolled back towards the door. "I've got a feeling that trinket has some magical powers that's bound to attract the loveliest of ladies. In fact, let me prove it to you. . . ."

Then, with his typical flash of showmanship, Payne threw the door aside to reveal the most attractive woman that Blount had ever seen.

Dark brown hair. Dark brown eyes. Unbelievable figure. Simply dazzling.

She stood there for several seconds, speechless, unsure of what to do next. Finally, with her composure regained, she grabbed Payne's arm and glided across the room to meet the family member she never even knew she had.

"Bennie," Payne said with a lump in his throat. "I'd like to introduce you to someone who's very special to me. This is your cousin, and my future wife, Ariane."

Author's Note

While conducting my research for this novel, I read hundreds of journal entries that detailed the ungodly horrors that occurred on many 19th-century plantations. But *not* just the accounts of ex-slaves. In order to keep my research as balanced as possible, I studied just as many narratives from slave owners as I did from the slaves themselves, figuring there's always two sides to a story—even to something as clear-cut as slavery.

Actually, I'm glad I did because it wasn't until I read the firsthand accounts of these brutal men that I started to understand how malicious and sadistic some of them really were. Sure, it was unsettling to read about the sting of a bullwhip from a slave's point-of-view, but not nearly as disturbing as the words of one overseer who described the process of whipping his workers in near-orgasmic terms. "The delicious crack of leather on flesh fills my hand with delight and sends my body a shiver."

Chilling, indeed.

And it was those types of quotes that convinced me to write the graphic sequences that I did, scenes that are so full of brutality (the Devil's Box, the Listening Post, etc.) that some readers have actually complained to me about nightmares. Well, I'm sorry about the loss of sleep. But in my mind I know if I didn't stress the gore and bloodshed of plantation life, then I would have been the one losing sleep, for I would've known that my story was something less than accurate.

If you liked THE PLANTATION,
then you'll love the next
Jonathon Payne novel:

SIGN OF THE CROSS